B*loom* *books*

Dear Reader,

Maya Angelou once said that there is no greater agony than bearing an untold story inside of you, and I tend to agree. Ambrose and Calla have been with me for longer than I can remember.

I'd always wanted to write a truly, unapologetically socially awkward heroine. Someone who always says the wrong thing at the wrong time, but is full of good intentions.

As for Row, he is a cinnamon roll with a twist of something bitter. A golden retriever who is not afraid to show his teeth.

I came into this story wanting to write a crazy rom-com, an angsty, gut-wrenching romance, and a women's fiction story, all balled into one. It took me six months, but I did. I truly did.

This was a fun, wild, excruciating, deliriously satisfying ride.

This series has me in a choke hold, and I cannot wait for you to see what I have in store for you with it.

Thank you so much for taking a chance on it.

With love,

ALSO BY L.J. SHEN

Sinners of Saint
Vicious
Ruckus
Scandalous
Bane

All Saints
Pretty Reckless
Broken Knight
Angry God
Damaged Goods

Forbidden Love
Truly, Madly, Deeply

TRULY MADLY DEEPLY

L.J. SHEN

Bloom books

Published by Bloom Books, an imprint of Sourcebooks
P.O. Box 4410, Naperville, Illinois 60567-4410
(630) 961-3900
sourcebooks.com

Cataloging-in-Publication data is on file with the Library of Congress.

Printed and bound in the United States of America.
SKY 10 9 8 7 6 5 4 3 2 1

Dedicated to all the girls who know Prince Charming is nice but the villain really knows how to use all that pent-up rage between the sheets.

Here's to choosing a guy who can be both.

"Everyone wants to shine bright like a diamond, but no one wants to get cut."

—Eric Thomas

TRIGGER WARNING

This book contains subject matter and topics some readers may find triggering or offensive. Your mental health matters. For a full list of the trigger warnings, kindly visit:

shor.by/Xqee

PLAYLIST

"Truly Madly Deeply"—Savage Garden

"The Final Countdown"—Europe

"Creep"—Radiohead

"End of the Road"—Boyz II Men

"I'd Do Anything for Love (But I Won't Do That)"
        —Meat Loaf

"Torn"—Natalie Imbruglia

"Basket Case"—Green Day

"Why Can't We Be Friends?"—Smash Mouth

"Crush"—Jennifer Paige

"There She Goes"—Sixpence None the Richer

"Alive"—Pearl Jam

"Gonna Make You Sweat (Everybody Dance
        Now)"—C+C Music Factory

"Baby Can I Hold You"—Tracy Chapman

"I Will Always Love You"—Whitney Houston

"Human Nature"—Madonna

"All I Want for Christmas Is You"—Mariah Carey

"Lovefool"—The Cardigans

"Doll Parts"—Hole

"Friday I'm in Love"—The Cure

"Never Ever"—All Saints

"I Try"—Macy Gray

"Everybody Hurts"—R.E.M.

"You Get What You Give"—New Radicals

"Back for Good"—Take That

"Gold Soundz"—Pavement

"Whatever"—En Vogue

"What's Up?"—4 Non Blondes

"Desert Rose"—Sting

"All That She Wants"—Ace of Base

"Ordinary World"—Duran Duran

"The River of Dreams"—Billy Joel

"Closing Time"—Semisonic

"Doo Wop"—Lauryn Hill

"Emotions"—Mariah Carey

PROLOGUE
CAL

"Creep"—Radiohead

AGE EIGHTEEN

If someone told me an hour ago that I would be pinned beneath Row Casablancas, partially naked and writhing against the hood of his black Mustang, I would have guessed he'd gotten himself into some kind of trouble and had resorted to drugging me and harvesting my organs to make a quick buck.

Row didn't hate me. He didn't love me either. I would guesstimate his feelings toward me were somewhere on the spectrum between *Look at this adorable little moron* and *Shit, I forgot she existed.*

I was his baby sister's best friend. The awkward klutz who suffered from bouts of verbal diarrhea and extremely questionable fashion sense.

Fine. I didn't *suffer* from the questionable fashion sense. I *owned* it. Sue me for celebrating my individuality.

I always figured he liked me in the same way people liked puppies—because they were cute, dumb, and adored the ground you walk on even if you were a terrible human who peeled clementines in public places. *But I digress.*

Harboring a small, totally manageable crush on your best friend's brother was a cliché. However, I was obsessed with the nineties, an era that celebrated true and tested formulas. Ergo, pining after him fit me like a tattoo choker.

In my defense, Row made it impossible for my adolescent self not to lust after him on account of him: 1) being six foot four inches of lithe, corded muscles, floppy onyx hair, and a jawline stronger than my lifetime of New Year's resolutions combined, and 2) having the entire bad-boy vibe down to a T—including a sports car, athletic genes, witty one-liners, a dimpled smirk, and unlaced combat boots with tight-fitting jeans stacked upon them.

To sum it up, he was a morally gray hunk who was a total red flag—my age group's favorite color scheme. So, yes. *Of course* I, too, wanted to be ruined by Dylan Casablancas's older brother. Who didn't? Our entire high school worshipped at his altar. Fenna McGee once even made a sticker that said, *I'm not saying that Row Casablancas and God are the same person—but have you ever seen them in the same room?*

Point was, Row's tongue was currently shoved so far down my throat, we were playing tonsil hockey. His ballistic missile–sized erection pressed against the buttons of my yellow plaid skirt, threatening to snap them and send them past the Milky Way. And all I could think about was how I was doing Dylan dirty.

Bile coated the back of my throat. Dylan hated it when her friends fell at her brother's feet. She'd make gagging sounds every time someone we knew flirted with him, which made what was happening right now completely inexcusable. But I was semidrunk, exceptionally raw, and uncharacteristically reckless. Plus…Dylan was so used to seeing Row ruining her friends like it was an Olympic sport, what was adding one more into the mix?

I was also a people pleaser, and I *really* wanted to please Row. So I made complimentary moaning sounds I'd learned from the Pornhub University of Fake Orgasms. This included head lolling, enthusiastic panting, and girlie gasps.

Row took this as an invitation to move to second base, coiling his calloused fingers around the front of my throat and flattening me against the hood of his car. The hood still exuded heat from the engine, and I wondered if I'd sport second-degree burns tomorrow morning. My butt cheeks were squeezed together to accommodate his lean waist between my thighs, my heartbeat thrashing against my eyelids like an angry woodpecker.

We were parked on a rocky cliff overlooking the glacial-tipped Maine mountains. The ocean stretched like a tight black sheet across the horizon. The briny scent floated into my nostrils, and goose bumps coated my arms.

It felt so good and yet so wrong, I didn't know whether to burst into giggles, tears, or flames.

Stop this right now, Cal. Dylan is going to strangle you.

Actually, my BFF was more the type to steal my clothes and go on a killing spree. Dylan Casablancas was creative, innovative, and delightfully hilarious. I loved her so much. She deserved better than this.

Row's hand snuck under my beige turtleneck and my yellow plaid vest, cupping my left boob as his mouth trailed along my jaw, leaving wet, hot kisses in its wake, making my spine tingle. His lips were sinful, his tousled hair as soft as silk between my greedy fingers.

Dammit, I'm only human.

We were grinding against each other, and I was in awe of how different his body was from mine. Hard to my soft. Tall to my short. Tan to my pale. He was doing everything right. The way he swirled his tongue over my sensitive spots, drawing happy whimpers from me. The way his thumb rubbed the tip of my hard nipple, making it tingly and sensitive and desperate for more, felt like some kind of dark magic.

"*Fuck*, you're beautiful."

What a terribly un-asshole-y thing to say. Then again, Row never directed his infinite wrath at me. Probably because I was like a sister to Dylan.

There was a bonfire happening in the moorlands below the cliff where we were parked. A farewell bash for us seniors before we all scattered away to our respective colleges. Row had dropped by to pick Dylan up—he was in town for a couple weeks, visiting from his fancy culinary school in Paris—but Dylan had wanted to stick around a little longer. Meanwhile, I'd wanted to go home, eat pickled eggs, and binge-watch *Riverdale*.

Yet we'd ended up on the notorious Make-out Mountain, where couples went to lose their virginity, and sometimes lacy thongs, without being interrupted.

Row and I were friendly. He was always protective of me. I'd asked him to drive up to the cliff so I could take one last look at the ocean before I moved to New York. I definitely hadn't planned on attacking his mouth with mine like a rabid raccoon when we'd both stared at the yolky sun crawling up the sky.

Yet…it had *happened*. It had happened, and now I was in his arms, the cold recipient of his kisses and licks and roaming hands. I froze, yet again feeling guilty about Dylan. She'd forgive me, surely. It wasn't like he was her boyfriend.

Row ripped his mouth from my skin, staring me down through a disapproving scowl. "Are you still alive?"

"Hmm-mm."

"Should I stop?" His fingers immediately loosened around my waist and back, and I suddenly remembered what had made me want to have sex with him in the first place.

"No!" I wrenched him closer and pressed my lips to his, doubling down on that rabid-wildlife conduct. "You…you can't stop." *But maybe he should?* My mind and my body were definitely not in sync.

"Sure I can." His mouth moved over mine again, his voice velvet and smoke. "Consent is a real thing. Google it." I was blushing so furiously, it was a medical miracle my head didn't explode. His mouth grinned against mine, teeth grazing my bottom lip. "Fuck. You're so sweet. So innocent. I want to eat you out."

"I want to eat you out too." *Wait, what?* That didn't sound right. I had social anxiety and literally zero filters when I was nervous.

"Do you, now?" I could hear the smirk in his smartass tone.

Dammit, Cal. "Not, in, like, a cannibalistic way—"

"Show me, then. Use plenty of examples. I'm a slow learner." He growled, deepening our kiss. Our teeth brushed together, and a wave of pleasure rolled along my spine. My skin was cold, but my insides were ablaze. I pushed my palm against his groin over his black jeans. I couldn't believe I was touching him, *really* touching the guy who literally made women melt into a pool of hormones just by glancing at them.

He ripped his mouth from mine, eyeballing me hard. We stared at each other, panting. I had no idea what I was doing. I kept my hand on his penis and rubbed a little, like I did when my cat, Semus, asked for a head rub.

His dick twitched, pushing against my palm appreciatively. Row dropped his forehead to mine, letting loose a low grumble that reverberated inside my chest. "Fuck, Dot. Your goddamn existence turns me on. Your mere breathing makes my balls tingle."

Whoa. Men said crazy things to get laid. Did women know about this? We could've collectively prevented wars. Gone on reckless shopping sprees at Target.

There was something about the fact he called me Dot that sent pleasurable shivers up and down my back. Dylan had come up with the nickname because when we were little, four or five, she couldn't remember the word *freckle*, so she'd named me after the galaxy of star-shaped dots peppered across my nose. The nickname had stuck.

I unglued my hand from his groin, wrapping my fingers along the lapels of his leather jacket, pulling him to me. He smelled delicious. Of cedar, worn leather, and spices. Of an entire foreign land full of Michelin-starred restaurants, romantic chansons, glass chandeliers, and thick, dusty French books. And yet, strangely, also…like *home.*

"Row?"

"Yeah?"

"As you know, I have…uhm…" *Social anxiety from hell.*

"A healthy aversion to strangers," he mumbled into my skin, biting the side of my jaw softly. "Understandable, I'm not a fan of humans myself." He rubbed the sensitive spot behind my ear with his thumb. "If you want to stop—"

"No!" I cried out. This was the first time I was actually having fun being with a guy. Well, it was kind of the *only* time I'd been with a guy since…*since*. "I want you to take my virginity," I choked out, my lips latching onto his. I was shaking with panic, adrenaline, and the morning chill. "Be my first." This wasn't planned in any way. I'd never dreamt of seducing Dylan's brother. But now that it was just the two of us, I couldn't think of anyone else I wanted to do it with.

"Dot." His fingers were buried in my hair as he ravaged me with his expert mouth. Without finesse, without game, without the untouchable coolness he normally carried himself with. "Don't say shit you don't mean."

I'd never seen Row so authentic, so final, so…*out of control.* He was usually unruffled and composed; I felt so drunk with power, my head spun.

"Please," I croaked. "I know what I want."

"And what is it that you want?"

"*You.*"

He tore his mouth from mine, his hooded golden eyes of a ravening tiger studying me. "From one to ten, how sure are you? Ten is without-a-doubt confident, and one is *forget what I said and take me home*?"

"Twelve." I blinked excessively, maybe seven or eight times in a row. It happened when I was anxious. A nervous tic I'd developed when I was four and never gotten rid of. Contrary to general belief, this didn't fall into Tourette's category. It was a chronic tic disorder. My way to wear my heart on my sleeve and show people how nervous I was.

"Are you sure you want me to take your V-card?" His eyes narrowed.

"Yeah, Row, I'm sure. Who else would I give it to? Some trust-fund baby from SUNY? Someone with a broccoli haircut? A guy who doesn't even care about me and would make me sit in his dorm room and listen to his experimental techno music?" Technically, Row didn't care either. But I knew he'd never ridicule or tease me. He had a history of making me feel safe, and feeling safe wasn't something I was used to.

His mouth slacked, and I could tell he wanted to refuse my request. He probably thought I was odd. Just like everyone else in this small town.

"Why?" His thick eyebrows nose-dived. I decided to give him the truth. He deserved it, after all.

"Because I have…" *Severe androphobia.* "Trust issues, and I know I'd never regret *you*. You're the only guy I know who is fuckable and not a fuckup. Make sense?"

"I'm a major fuckup." He ran his fingers over my side bangs, tucking the hair behind my ear. "But too fucking selfish not to fuck you. It's going to hurt, you know." He gave me a cool once-over. "The first time, anyway. It'll get better the more times—"

"There won't be more times," I interrupted him. I appreciated him pretending it wasn't a one-night stand, but that wasn't necessary. "You don't have to say that to make me feel better."

His desire-drunk expression melted into a frown. "I'm not saying that to make you feel better. I'm saying that because fucking you is probably *all* I'll want to do once we start."

"Row, this has to be a one-time thing. Dylan can't know. Please." I placed my palms over his chest. I was a coward and a cheat, and in that moment, I hated myself more than Dylan could if she ever found out. And still, he was my one shot at not dying a virgin.

He must've understood the gravity of the situation because he nodded. "Okay."

"I'm ready, Row. Let's do this." I shoved my tongue into his mouth before he could use it to change his mind. I'd already made a colossal mistake by making out with him. Might as well lose my pesky virginity before I went off to college.

It was the right thing to do.

First of all, because according to the rumors, he knew his way around a woman's body. Second, because his Adonis face was attached to some history, context, and nostalgia. He was comfort, familiarity, and ease, not some sordid mistake. And third, because I knew that despite his reputation, he wouldn't hurt me.

And that last part? It was *huge*.

Row was my security blanket in many ways, even though he didn't know it. When we were kids, he'd throw Dylan and me into the public pool as many times as we asked. He'd taught us how to do cartwheels, drive a car, cheat in poker, pick a lock. He'd given us money for vinyl records even though we never paid him back. Driven us places. Bought us ice cream when we were PMSing. Dislocated a nose or two when someone catcalled us.

Row made sense. I didn't have cold sweats with him. I didn't go into hiding. Whenever I had extreme nervous verbal diarrhea in front of him, he didn't look at me like I was a freak. And I was confident enough in his presence to sass back.

Our bodies fused into one another as he kissed his way down my throat, proceeding south, his head disappearing between my thighs.

"No," I gasped, desperately trying to yank him up to his feet. "We don't have time." But the truth was, I was deathly afraid he wouldn't like the taste of me. "Just…do it." Great, now I sounded like a Nike commercial. "And hurry up."

"You sure know how to set the mood." Row stood up swiftly, returning his lips to mine, refusing to cheapen this experience for me. His strong fingers slowly snaked down my waist, flipping my skirt up. More grinding ensued. His cock slid up and down my slit through my panties and his jeans. I could feel heat rushing between my legs. He made sure I was hot and ready for him before he rolled on a condom, and then he was inside me, sealing my pained moan with an apologetic kiss. Tears seared my eyes, and I held my breath at the sharp sting.

"Okay to move?" he grunted, lodged squarely inside me.

"I strongly prefer that you didn't."

"We can—"

"Stop. I know. Please just fuck me." Didn't I literally tell him not to? My head was a mess. So was the rest of me.

"I don't want to hurt you."

"I know. That's precisely why we should continue."

He pulled out slowly, then thrusted inside. Soon, I was clawing at his shoulders, staring at the sun slithering behind his messy dark hair as he drove into me, my white Mary Janes thumping against his car hood every time he pressed home. I held my breath the entire time.

Clank. Clank. Clank.

Steadfast and determined, he screwed me like I was a hood ornament he was trying to drill back into place. He was kissing and nibbling, exploring and admiring. Didn't he know that on some level, all women lost their virginity alone? It was kissing your innocence goodbye. This was the point it stopped being great and started being taxing. I wasn't so turned on anymore.

Truth was, it hurt. It burned. It *sucked.*

All throughout, Row whispered sweet nothings into my ear. Things I knew there was no way he truly believed. Things like, *Jesus, Dot, I could live inside that tight pussy if you'd let me,* and *You're the most beautiful girl in the whole fucking universe, no close seconds,* and *Watching my dick inside you is more breathtaking than Paris at night.*

It lasted way more than the average time my friends reported their boyfriends had sexed them. I was expecting five minutes— ten, if I wasn't lucky. But no. Row seemed to carry on *forever.* I was planning my 401(k) while he was in there, mercilessly stabbing my poor hymen with what appeared to be his eleven-inch dick.

He had tricks too. With his tongue, his thumbs, his teeth. Tricks I could've admired had my mind not been stuck on how to explain to Dylan what had happened if she ever found out, then groveling into the next century in hopes she'd forgive me.

Dylan was staying here, in Staindrop. She'd decided the student debt wasn't worth a liberal arts degree that would gain her zero opportunities.

"*And anyway,*" she'd chuckled the last time I'd broached the subject, "*it's not like I'm even good at anything. I'd be wasting money on a degree I'd probably never use.*"

We'd promised to visit one another every other month, but I knew Dylan was worried I'd ditch her for new, shiny urban friends.

Finally—praise Jesus—Row grumbled, "Fuck, I'm coming."

"Yeah. Totally. Me too." I lifted my hand from behind his shoulder and bit into my fist to suppress a yelp of agony. I was worried my internal organs had gotten tangled around his penis. What if he pulled out and took my intestines with him? That thing between his legs was a health hazard.

Row was coming inside me when I heard the squeak of car wheels stopping abruptly to my right, followed by gravel crunching. Another couple coming to Make-out Mountain to get some action. A car door slammed behind my back.

Then I heard the unmistakable voice of my best friend.

"Somebody better hold my earrings." Dylan's tenor was like a pair of scissors cutting my heart into a Judas-shaped paper. "Because I'm about to murder a bitch."

"Shit." Row lurched away from me like I was fire. His condomed penis materialized from my body one inch at a time, wet and entirely too big to be nestled inside anything that wasn't a lifeboat. He yanked off the condom, tying it and zipping himself up.

"Please tell me I'm suffering from a brain hemorrhage and not really seeing what I'm seeing." Dylan tramped her way to us, her neon pink ankle boots chomping the pebbles beneath her. She wore a red leather skirt she'd borrowed from me, knee-length plaid socks, and a black sweater. She looked *adorable*. Also, pissed off. *Mostly pissed off*. Way more pissed off than I'd anticipated, to be honest.

Row tossed his leather jacket over my torso, and that was when I remembered he'd removed my shirt and bra sometime during our sexcapade.

Also—why wasn't I moving? Talking? *Breathing?* Oh. That's right. Because my go-to during fight-or-flight situations was the third option—*freeze*. I'd simply turn to stone and play dead.

"Cal!" Dylan stopped in front of me, her dark, upturned eyes glittering with tears. "What the…what the *shit*, dude?!" She tossed her arms in the air like they were boneless noodles before pointing at Row. "That's my brother. What do you think you're doing?"

That was a very fair question. To which I had no good answer.

Dylan's face was devastating. Her full lower lip trembled, and her apple cheeks were stained pink. I had completely miscalculated how much she'd care about this. I peered behind her shoulder. I noticed Tucker, the beefy bully we both hated, sitting in the driver's seat of the car that had driven her here, pretending to read his insurance papers. Probably scared Row would make a punching bag out of him if he realized he was here.

What was Dylan doing with this douche canoe? Was she planning to make out with him here?

Now was decidedly not a great time to interrogate her.

"Dammit, Dot, say something!" Dylan grabbed me by the arms and shook me hard, desperate and panicked. The leather jacket fell from my chest. I was now topless. And anxious. So anxious I couldn't breathe. The flashbacks poured out.

Naked.

Defenseless.

Attacked.

"That's enough, Dylan." Row's voice was pure gravel.

For the first time in my life, I witnessed my best friend ignoring her older brother. Usually, she treated him with godlike respect. Which was maybe why she was so pissed right now? There was no other way to explain it, since she looked ready to murder someone. Ideally me.

Still, I was incapable of producing any sound, let alone words of apology. I was shell-shocked, caught red-handed doing something I shouldn't have. Namely, my best friend's older brother. I sifted through my mind for a plausible reason for what had just happened.

He was my one chance to lose my virginity. I'm broken.

I've actually had a crush on him for ages. I never told you because I care so deeply about our friendship.

*I didn't even plan to do it. It just…*happened.

But they all sounded dumb, even in my head. I had messed up. And I needed to pay for it.

"Stop this right now." Row stepped between us, bunching Dylan's wrists behind her back and pulling her away from me. "You can't kill her," he said dryly.

"Give me one good reason!" She kicked the air manically, trying to break free and throw punches my way.

"For one thing, we can't afford the legal fees."

"We can always hide her body," she spat out, wiggling ferally in his arms. She had no idea how much her words triggered me. A scream clogged my throat.

"You can't even hide your birth control from Mom." Row rolled his eyes.

"You're on birth control?" I gasped. "You never told me that."

"Chill. It's to regulate my hormones. You know I haven't even gone past second bas—" Dylan frowned, catching herself. "Hold on a minute, why am I explaining myself to *you*? We're not even friends anymore."

What?

Tears sprung into my eyes. Blistering white panic gave way to realization: I had slept with my best friend's older brother and she'd caught me. Maybe I didn't think it was a big deal, but what did I know? I had no siblings, so I'd never had to deal with anything like this.

Row was leaving for Paris next week, I was leaving for New York *tomorrow*, and I had just thrown away fourteen years of friendship for the dubious pleasure of being railed by a man with a rolling pin instead of a penis.

"It was my idea." Row's voice sounded disinterested and aloof. I didn't know why he said that. It absolutely hadn't been.

"Don't protect her!" Dylan finally broke free from Row's grasp, pushing at her big brother's chest. Her tears flew sideways. He didn't even budge. Dude was built like a Marvel superhero. "She's a selfish, mean, heartless bitch who betrayed me!"

"I'm a selfish, mean, heartless asshole who did the same." His lips barely moved, but a muscle in his chiseled jaw jumped. "Yet I don't see you plotting my murder."

"Well, *you* I have to put up with." She tossed her hands up exasperatedly. "You're blood. But she? She is...piss!"

Holy hell. I'd never heard Dylan speak to me that way. Not even close. I really was dead to her.

"Watch your mouth," he snarled, his face turning frosty, impassive.

Whoa. Why was he defending me?

"She should watch her legs!" Dylan flipped him off. "While she's at it, she should probably get dressed before she gives Tuck a lap dance."

"Dylan." He pinned her with a look that made me shrivel into myself in fear. Dylan stared him down, and it looked like an entire conversation passed between them wordlessly.

With a slow shake of her head, she let her shoulders sag, exhaling. "God, you're pathetic."

Row? Pathetic? I doubted he could even spell the word. Row

was magnificent. Spectacular. Self-assured, talented, and formidably hot. He'd always been bigger than life. Even as a kid, he had known he was destined to be a great chef. When he was ten, he'd used test tubes and droppers to measure ingredient quantities to come up with new recipes. When *I* was ten, I had taught myself how to laminate my eyebrows using a glue stick and an eraser.

Finally, the words that were bunched in my throat rushed out like a river.

"Dylan, I'm so, so sorry." I crouched down, hastily picking up my discarded bra and turtleneck. I'd been wearing Cher from *Clueless*'s iconic yellow outfit, which I'd sewn for myself. My white knee-length socks were muddied.

"Actually, sorry doesn't even begin to cover how I'm feeling. What I did was deplorable! It was all a huge mistake. I'm sick to my stomach. Horrified, disgusted, revolted—"

"Stop. I'll fucking blush." Row rolled his tongue over his inner cheek, propping his unlaced army boot against the hood of his car. I ignored him. He wasn't really offended. Sarcasm was his native tongue.

"…revolted, no, *repulsed* by my own actions," I continued.

"Did you swallow a whole-ass dictionary?" Row's whiskey-tinted eyes slanted into furious slits. "Also, you can say it felt like shit until you're blue in the face, but your body told me a different story when you dripped all over the hood of my car."

"*Argh!* Blasphemy." Dylan pressed her palms to her ears, squeezing her eyes shut. "The mental image is now burned into my retinas, and I have no other choice but to murder both of you."

"I swear I didn't mean to! I was drunk," I continued, lying through my teeth. I had always been a liar. My white lies were like makeup. Small, harmless concealers designed to fix up the blemishes of my life. To ensure my loved ones' minds were at ease. Lying was second nature to me. If I thought someone I cared about wasn't going to like my answer, I made up another one especially for them.

I shoved my arms into my sleeves, covering up, my eyes clinging to Dylan's beautiful, distressed face. "It was a huge mistake. A
one-off."

I couldn't lose her. Couldn't lose my best friend. She was there
when, in kindergarten, kids had made fun of me for wearing a socks-
and-sandals combo. She had started wearing them to school too, as
a fashion statement. A middle finger to the bullies. Dylan always
marched to the beat of her own drum. She *always* did the right
thing, even if that thing was scary. The opposite of me, she never
lied. She wore the truth like a badge of honor, even if it was ugly.

She had been there when my babushka had passed away, braiding my hair and listening to me for hours. There for the laughs, for
the tears. For the college rejection letters, for fights with my parents,
and when we'd veg out on the couch in our pj's, watching *Teen Mom*
and polishing off my entire fridge.

"All I hear is *me, me, me.*" Dylan's tear-rimmed eyes rolled in
their sockets, and she tipped her head back, chuckling humorlessly.
"It's all about you, isn't it? *You* were drunk. *You* made a mistake. *You*
feel disgusted. *You* have anxiety. What about *me*? Did you ever stop
to think how much I hate it when my friends hit on my brother?
How everyone wants to befriend Dylan Casablancas because her
brother is hot?"

She thought I'd used our proximity to hook up with Row? That
was ridiculous. My crush on Ambrose Casablancas was akin to my
crush on Chris Pine. Just because it was there, didn't mean I ever had
any plans to act on it. He was the least attainable person on planet
Earth, with his mood, hair, and allure all darker than the pit of his
own soul.

Plus, it wasn't like I'd planned to date him. I didn't do boyfriends.
And I *definitely* didn't do relationships. Relationships were for other
humans who could "people" normally and not topple over like a
fainting goat at the slightest social interaction.

"Dylan!" I rushed the four steps between us, erasing them

completely as I fell down to my knees at her boots. The little stones dug into my shins with gusto. Blood oozed from my scraped flesh. "It meant nothing. I swear. I never looked at Row twice before today." *Liar, liar, pants on fire.* "You *know* I always thought he was freakishly tall and a little frightening—"

"And the compliments just keep on coming." A wry sneer rolled off Row's tongue above my head. He was leaning against the hood of his car, arms folded, not a care in his world. "Is your secret talent pissing people off, Cal?" I hated him so much in that moment.

"Worst-kept secret, as you can see." I flashed him a glare, gesturing toward his sister.

"Don't you dare answer my brother like that." Dylan shoved her finger in my face. "He's way out of your league and the height of your love life."

I was in complete agreement with her. Row was the entire deal. Hot, smart, and talented as hell. Not only was he not in my league, we weren't even playing the same sport. He was football and I was... *cheese rolling.* Or something equally as eccentric.

"All I'm saying is I never meant for it to happen. It was a small lapse of judgment." I pressed my palms together, still begging her on the ground, my clothes filthy and askew. For a reason unbeknownst to me, I had underestimated how important it was to Dylan that I wouldn't mess around with her brother. Probably because literally every other girl at our school had. Or had tried to, at some point.

"*Small?*" Row inquired behind me.

"Huge," I corrected, my head so hot I felt like it was going to explode. "Thick too. Better?" I shot him a dirty look.

"Infinitely." He fished in his front pocket for a cigarette, producing a pack of Gitanes. Of course he smoked French cigarettes now.

"Wow. Okay." Dylan scrubbed her forehead, shaking her head. "Guess I'm about to vomit the three slices of pizza I just ate."

"Please forgive me, Dylan. *Please*," I said desperately.

Row shook his head, trudging to the driver's seat. He slipped inside and started the engine.

Dylan stared at me like a queen deciding whether to spare a lowly subject from execution. Her lips curled, arms folded over her chest archly.

"You know, Cal, I've always looked up to you. You're gorgeous, funny, smart, a kaleidoscope of colors and facts about the nineties; I mean, damn, you're a walking Wikipedia about serial killers and ghost stories, and still have the most sunshine personality I've ever known. It's tempting to stick around, to let those Calla Litvin sunrays kiss your skin. But when you strip it all off…the playlists, the outfits, the good times…when you look inside and examine what kind of friend she is…she sucks." Dylan shook her head, her arms dropping to the sides of her body. "Grow up, Dot. And do it far away from me because I never want to see your face again."

She strutted back to Tuck's red truck, slid inside, and barked at him to drive. Shockingly, the guy who had spent the last four years stuffing cigarette ash and condoms into our lockers did as he was told.

I stayed on my knees, in the freezing cold, mulling over her words. My fingertips numbed at the edges. Chill draped across my shoulders like an oversized cloak. I tilted my head sideways, at Row's headlights. He flicked them on and off, his silent way of telling me to get inside before he changed his mind about not leaving me to walk home and catch pneumonia. He was stone-faced. The same standoffish version of himself he gave anyone who wasn't Dylan and his mom. And, sometimes, me.

Cocky.

Calculated.

Corrupt to the bone.

Humiliated, I pushed my palms against the ground, staggering up to my feet. I began limping toward his car, icy mud falling off my knees in clumps. Behind the windshield, Row's expression was flippant.

I tried to see myself through his eyes. This pitiful, crumpled creature. Mangled and stained, like a discarded supermarket list at the bottom of a cart. *A beautiful girl,* the townsfolk all agreed behind my back, *but so very odd, just like her father.*

Tucking myself in the passenger seat, I shut the door and hung my head low and fingered the friendship bracelet Dylan had given me. At least I still had it. My finger caught in the elastic string, and as if on cue, it snapped and broke, the beads raining down my seat and onto the floor. I hastily tried scooping them, but I couldn't feel my fingers.

"That went well." He flicked the bottom of a Gitanes with his finger. Another cigarette popped from the pack, and he clasped his teeth around it, lighting it like a movie star.

"I'm such an idiot." I flicked mud from my knees, banging the back of my head against my seat. I didn't let my tears loose, even though it was near impossible. "I traded my best friend for a fling."

"For all she knows, this could be the romance of the century." He rolled his window down, a cloud of smoke drifting past his lips.

I shook my head. "Dylan knows the score. She knows I can't fall in love. That I'm..." The rest of the sentence perished in my mouth.

"A narcissist?" He bowed a brow.

"Broken." I frowned. "But thanks."

"You're not broken, Dot." He stuck the cigarette in his mouth, patting my thigh offhandedly. "A little cut, sure. All diamonds are."

Not me, I thought. *Underneath my sunshine personality, all you'll find is darkness.*

"So." He swiped his tongue across his upper lip, eyes hard on the road ahead. "I need to tell you something."

He was going to warn me off bothering Dylan. He was so protective of her and knew how much she hated me right now. But I couldn't bear it, the idea of her not being in my life anymore.

"Please don't say anything," I begged. "My night is hideous as it is."

"It's not about Dylan." Of course it wasn't. It was about how awful I was. Sleeping with my best friend's older brother. I was wrong about Row. He was going to hurt me after all.

"Row, *please*. There's nothing to talk about. Trust me, I'm as horrified about you and me as you are. Probably more."

He punched his steering wheel, muttering something under his breath. "Would you get out of your own fucking head for *one* second and listen?" he seethed.

"No thank you. My head is a terrible place. It's exactly where I deserve to be right now."

I wanted to apologize for the way I'd treated him. To try to beg him to reason with Dylan. But I also wanted to hold on to whatever little pride I had left in me.

We zipped past lush New England trees, English lampposts, and the local library, all cloaked by a bluish-orange dawn. The lighthouse gleamed behind a curtain of my unshed tears. With piercing pain, I realized that home wasn't Staindrop, Maine. It was the Casablancas siblings. And I was forever banished.

"I really am sorry, you know," I murmured when he stopped in front of my house, the engine still running. His stare was glued to the windshield, his jaw so tight it looked painful. "You guys are like my family. And I…I…" *Like you so much. You are the two people I always felt truly myself with.* But I didn't have the guts to say these words. I swallowed. "And I hope everything works out for you."

Row's eyes, blank and hollow as a Greek statue's, were still trained on the road ahead. "Good luck at Columbia."

"Good luck in Paris."

"Don't need luck; got talent."

He drove off without sparing me a glance. I stared at my clapboard stilt house, the color of strawberry ice cream, with the wraparound porch, pastel-potted plants, and knitted sweaters Mom wrapped the tree trunks in. Kooky, like its occupants. And I knew it would be a long time before I saw it again.

I never wanted to set foot back in Staindrop.

Not if my life depended on it.

CHAPTER ONE
CAL

"End of the Road"—Boyz II Men

FIVE YEARS LATER

As it turned out, it was death that brought me back to Staindrop.

My father's death to be exact.

"So, where did y'all bury Artem?" Melinda Fitch, our middle-aged neighbor, clutched her pearls in my parents' living room, rearranging them across her heavy cleavage.

"Mom's favorite vase." I gestured in the direction of the mantel above our fireplace. The urn was a beautiful piece, a nineteenth-century silver and enamel samovar my babushka had brought to the U.S. when the Soviet Union collapsed.

Melinda barked out a high-pitched laugh. When she realized I wasn't joking, she paled, pressing her lipsticked mouth to her cup of tea. "Wait, he got *cremated*?" She whispered the last word, like it was a swear word.

"No, we just pushed him in there. It's really not that difficult when you squeeze someone one limb at a time," I deadpanned.

Verbal diarrhea—one.

My flimsy reputation—minus thirty.

Melinda looked ready to bolt through our wall like a cartoon character. Her eyes were the size of derby hats. Most people weren't accustomed to my zero-filter train of thoughts. Over the years, my coworkers and peers had learned how to ignore my foot-in-mouth, nervous blabbering. Mostly, anyway.

Melinda brought another biscuit to her lips, nibbling on its edges demurely. "May I ask…um, why you chose cremation?"

"He was an atheist. He didn't believe in God, religious rituals, or the afterlife." A sharp stab of emptiness impaled my stomach when I spoke about him. "He told us cremation was less burdensome on the ecosystem." I could tell my words flew right over Melinda's hair-sprayed do. She probably thought ecosystem was our AC brand.

My dad had stood out in the quaint small town of Staindrop, Maine, like a dildo in a church. He had taught physics at the local high school until the last month of his life and enjoyed chess, mental math, and volunteering twice a week at the local reservoir, collecting litter. He was ruthlessly pragmatic yet an oddly optimistic creature. His stage four cancer had bitten at his existence a chunk at a time but hadn't stopped him from making every moment count.

Dad had been alive—not just living—until his very last breath in hospice. Only three days ago, we were still hunched over a game of chess, bickering over which hospice food was the most depressing (the porridge, hands down, no matter how much he loathed the Jell-O).

Now my living room was full of people I once knew offering their condolences. Everybody had brought a beet-based dish, Dad's favorite root vegetable (and yes, he ranked them). Casseroles, cakes, au gratin beets, all in different shades of purple.

I went through the motions. Hugging people, answering mind-numbing questions. "How is New York?" *Cold and pricey.* "What are you doing there?" *Waiting tables and mustering the courage to launch my own true crime podcast.* "When are you planning on moving back?" *Never seems like a good timeframe.*

What shocked me the most was how easily I slipped back into

the familiarity of this house I hadn't set foot in for years. How it wrapped around me like an old dress. How drenched these walls were with timeless memories.

The only difference was that now, Dad wouldn't materialize from the kitchen, a newspaper tucked under his armpit and a cup of honeyed tea in his hand, saying, *"Tell me something good, Callichka."*

Spotting Mom on the other side of the living room, I cut through the mass of black-sheathed shoulders and rested a hand over her arm. She was squinting at a dessert tray, pretending to give it great thought.

"Hanging in there, Mom?" I brushed a wayward lock of hair from her eye. She nodded, pressing her lips together. I was her mini-me. Same almond-brown hair piled up in tight curls atop our heads, giant azure eyes, and petite frames.

"It's just…" She shook her head, waving a frantic hand at her face to keep her tears at bay.

"What?" I rubbed her shoulder. "Tell me."

She sliced a piece of sponge cake with her fork. "I feel…*lighter.* Like I can breathe again. Is that terrible?"

"Mom, *no.* Dad was sick for sixteen months, and he suffered every second of it. His relief is your relief. It's hard watching someone you love hating their own existence."

Dad had been sick of being sick. I had been in the room when he passed away. I had held his hand, stroked the thick blue veins running up and down the back of his palm. I'd sung his favorite song, "California Dreamin'" by the Mamas and the Papas.

I had sung it, fighting the tears and the lump in my throat. I'd envisioned him as a small boy, tucked in his cot in Leningrad, dreaming about golden beaches and tall palm trees. He must have imagined it too, because he'd smiled. Smiled as his systems began shutting down. Smiled as a lifetime of educating kids, uncoiling my mother's yarn in precise increments when she knitted mittens, and stealing tea cakes from the cookie jar above the fridge when no one was looking had flashed before his eyes. Dad had smiled through it all. Because he knew that his happiness was my favorite view.

His hand had still been warm when he'd flatlined. The nurse had come in and squeezed my shoulder. "*I'm so sorry for your loss,*" she'd said. But I had gained so much over the years. Love, resilience, and endless memories.

Mom rubbed her forehead, frowning. "Maybe I'm just in denial. It's all going to dawn on me once you go back to New York and I stay here by myself. That's when reality always kicks in, isn't it?" She pressed a fist to her lips. "When everyone leaves and grief is your only companion."

I clutched her in a hug, desperate to comfort her but not really sure how.

"You know, it's going to be weird, the first time I sleep here by myself." She glanced around the room, her throat bobbing with a swallow. "Even when Dad was at the hospice, I always had a friend stay over. I married him when I was twenty-one. I'm not even sure I know how to be alone."

Mom needed someone next to her. The accusations Dylan had hurled in my face the night our friendship had perished crashed over me like a tsunami. About me being a shitty friend. Maybe I was a shitty daughter too. After all, I had managed to successfully avoid Staindrop for four years. I'd seen my parents plenty—we'd met in Portland, New York, and some places in between. But I never made the journey here.

Then I thought about being a parent. The act of sacrificing—your time, your sleep, your money, your attention, your concern, your love. All for…what? So that one day, your kid would give you half a hug and tell you that everything will be okay, then run off to New York, leaving a trail of half-assed apologies?

Mamushka always told me that when you became a mother, you expanded. Found ways to provide more of you to meet your child's needs. Maybe it was time I expanded as a daughter too. Rose to the occasion.

"I'll…I'll stay here for a while," I heard myself say. No permission was given by my brain for my mouth to utter these words. And yet, here they were. Out in the wild. Entering my mother's ears before I could stop them.

"You'd do that for me?" Her head snapped up, eyes flaring with hope.

This woman changed your diapers. Band-Aided your boo-boos. Paid for your utterly useless degree. You are not going to bail on her just because you are frightened of Dylan Casablancas.

And that was what it boiled down to: Dylan. Row was long gone now. He became a world-famous bad-boy chef: restauranteur, reality TV judge, and Michelin-starred prince. Over the years, he had graced my television screen in frightening quantities. Smiling his dimpled smirk during morning shows before Thanksgiving to teach viewers how to make the perfect, moist stuffed turkey. Opening a new restaurant in a trendy European location on *E! News*, a Victoria's Secret model draped on his arm, or as a grumpy judge on a low-stakes Netflix reality TV show, scowling at fancy dishes and barking obscenities at hopeful chefs. An entertainment columnist had once written, *Ambrose Casablancas is what happens when Gordon Ramsay and James Dean have a secret child.* I felt the entire sentence in my bones.

"Yup, I'm here for you." I wrapped an arm around Mom's scrawny shoulders. "We'll make comfort food, watch movies, catch up. I'll stay until January first, how does that sound?"

Let me tell you how that sounded to me—*terrible.* January first was eight weeks from now. That meant I'd bump into Dylan at some point. Into other people I wanted to see even less.

"Oh, Cal." Mom patted her nose with a crumpling piece of tissue, mustering a grateful smile. "If it isn't too much trouble."

"Not at all. I missed you. I want to spend time together."

If my bank account could speak, I was sure it'd tell me I was high. I couldn't simply take time off. I still needed to work in order to pay for my Williamsburg apartment. And by *apartment*, I meant *shoebox*. A terribly expensive shoebox. I had to figure out a way to make money in Staindrop, and God knew the answer wasn't going to be through my pipe dream, my unrecorded true crime podcast, *Hot Girl Bummer.*

"Only if you're sure." Mom clutched my arm. "I don't want you to stop your life for me."

"Don't worry, there's literally no life for me to stop." I pulled her into another all-consuming hug, pressing a kiss to her cheek. "We're going to have a blast, Mamushka. Just like the old days. You'll see."

"Really?" Hope painted her face.

"Really. Nothing will ruin this for us."

As I said that, the door flung open and in walked Ambrose Casablancas.

And a *very* pregnant Dylan.

CHAPTER TWO
CAL

"I'd Do Anything for Love (But I Won't Do That)"—Meat Loaf

Dylan was pregnant.

Eighteen months pregnant by the look of it.

With triplets.

Holy shit, her belly was *huge*. Who was the father, Hodor? When had she gotten married? How come no one had told me?

"Mom," I whisper-shouted, tugging on her sleeve, feeling the full weight of the entire continent pressing against my sternum. "Why didn't you tell me Dylan got *married*?"

Terror laced through my veins. I was entirely unequipped to face the Casablancas siblings. Especially Dylan, who had ripped my heart out of my chest the last time we'd spoken and stomped on it until it had dispersed into dust. And what was Row doing here, anyway? Didn't he have a reality TV contestant to yell at about their stew tasting like a diarrhea puddle? Because that had *actually* happened. I remembered watching that episode in horror and thinking, *I had this man's salami stuck in my canal.*

Mom dazedly stirred her gaze from her sponge cake to the door, where people clamored around a ridiculously glowing Dylan.

"Married?" She frowned, her mouth clamping around an airy piece of buttery cake. "No, Callichka. Dylan didn't get married."

"She's pregnant." I gestured to my ex–best friend, as though this fact couldn't be detected from Neptune. I knew I sounded judgmental. Plenty of people had children out of wedlock. This wasn't the forties. But Dylan had always wanted a grand wedding. With a golden carriage and unicorns and white doves and five different dresses. She'd had ripped-out *Vogue* pages folded neatly inside her underwear drawer with flower decoration inspiration, like Pinterest didn't exist.

"That's right, Callichka. But the wedding ceremony isn't how babies are made. I thought you knew that?" She frowned, cocking her head. "We never discussed the birds and the bees, did we?"

"Whose baby?" I looked around us frantically.

She stared at me like I was insane. "Why, Tucker Reid's, of course. Who else?"

Who else? Good question. Maybe anyone *who* didn't *threaten to wedgie us all throughout high school.*

Were they together now? When had it started? The night she'd caught me and Row? And how had Row even agreed to this? He was very trigger-happy when it came to guys he deemed unworthy of his sister. Which was every human alive, by the way. I was pretty sure Tucker's nose and Row's fist were intimately acquainted.

Also—*Dylan had sex with Tucker Reid?* He was a shithead but… kind of hot? I wanted to dissect that piece of juicy information immediately and at length. Problem was, it was Dylan I wanted to discuss it with.

Tucker. Freaking. Reid. I couldn't get over the revelation.

He was our bully. Well, I guess now, technically, he was only *my* bully. Evidence suggested he no longer unpinned the *Goosebumps* pin-back buttons from Dylan's JanSport and "accidentally" sneezed into the food on her tray at the cafeteria.

As if sensing our presence, Row and Dylan turned their heads in unison, catching sight of me and Mom.

Forever a responsible, sensible adult, I decided now was a good time to swivel toward the person behind me and launch into an avalanche of incoherent words to appear busy and unaffected. I didn't want either of them to know how terrified I was of a showdown with them.

My poor victim was Lyle Cooper, a tiny carpenter in his seventies who used to have fish and chips with Dad every Sunday over beer.

"Lyle. Wow. Haven't seen you in a long time. Let's catch up!"

I was acutely aware of Row and Dylan as they sliced through the throng, ambling to my corner of the room. More accurately, Row was ambling and Dylan was wobbling. They stopped to talk to Mom, who stood right beside me, and I tried to simultaneously converse with Lyle and eavesdrop on their conversation.

"…sorry for your loss, Mrs. Litvin. Mom sends her regards…" *Dylan.*

"…pain can only be dulled by time, and you know we're always here for you…" *Also Dylan.*

"…Artem was the first person to truly believe in me," I heard Row say in his bottomless baritone that licked at my skin like fire. "He saw my potential, made me work for things; they say every kid needs one grown-up to love them and one to believe in them. My mother loved me. But Artem? He believed in me."

My mouth kept on moving, and it occurred to me that I was talking to Lyle and that he was listening, though not with great enthusiasm. A troubled frown engraved his crumpled forehead, and he kept sloping his head back and forth. Was I even speaking in English?

"…all I'm saying is Meat Loaf shouldn't have called it 'I'd Do Anything for Love (But I Won't Do That)' because what's even the point?" I rambled. *Oh God. Someone shut me up. Immediately.* "Well, Mr. Meat Loaf, clearly, you *won't* do anything for love. There's no exception to the word *anything*. Everything is kind of baked into the cake, you know? The song should've been called 'I Would Do *Most*

Things for Love.' But I guess that would have been less catchy. It's all about the marketing."

In my periphery, I caught Row pressing his knuckles to his mouth, enjoying my first-degree murder of whatever coolness I had left.

"Ya know, I was never a big Meat Loaf fan." Lyle took a pull of his Coors, his eyes searching for an escape route from the conversation. "The dish? Sure. Not so much the artist. Springsteen fan, myself."

His eyes crinkled with affection, like I was a six-year-old trying to spell a new word. "Don't worry, Calla." He patted my arm, and I forced myself not to wince and jerk away. "You don't need to be smart. You're mighty pretty, just like your ma."

Dylan chose that moment to unzip her colorful, wet windbreaker and shake it in my general direction. Raindrops caught my dress and peppered my eyes.

"*Oops*. Clumsy me," Dylan singsonged, no trace of regret in her airy tone. "It's been raining like a *bitch* today, huh?"

So much for giving me a break because I'm newly fatherless.

I turned around, coming face-to-face with my former best friend.

Her face alone made me want to cry again. She was so... *Dylan*. Her skin smooth to the point she looked like an AI figure. Every feature perfectly proportioned and Apollo-like. With a wide, dimpled Julia Roberts smile and the long, spidery legs of a runway model. She had that Eva Mendes glow that made her look sexy doing anything, including staring me down like I had just battered a baby panda with its own bamboo stick.

My gut pretzeled into itself a hundred times over.

I missed her.

I missed her, and I still wanted her forgiveness. Her love, acceptance, and quirky jokes.

"Not a problem. Mistakes happen." My eyes twitched four, five, six times. Not even ten seconds had passed, and I already had a tic. I extended a hand for her to shake. "Thank you for coming."

Row was standing next to her, but I had yet to muster up the courage to look directly at him. Dylan rolled her eyes, not taking my hand. *"Ugh."* She looked disgusted with herself for even looking at me. "Come here, you annoying…piece…of…Cal."

Using my outstretched hand, she tugged me forward. I crashed against her belly. She gave me a crush-your-bones hug full of reassurance. It felt like she'd put an oxygen mask to my face, breathing life into me.

"I'm still mad, but I'm also in pieces for you," she mumbled into my hair, stroking it softly, the touch achingly familiar and comforting. "Artem was our bestie. Remember when he let us practice our makeup skills on him?"

"Yes," I choked out, the memories flooding me like a river. "We weren't even that young anymore. Thirteen, right? Totally past the cute stage."

"The man could rock a winged blue eyeliner like nobody's business."

"So true." My chin wobbled. "It really made his eyes pop."

The waterworks officially began. I'm talking Bellagio fountain show. My eyeballs were leaking as she rubbed circles on my back. She smelled like old Dylan: Libre by YSL, bubble gum, and that scent that always lingered at the Casablancas' household, of hearty Italian food.

"Dylan," I gasped, melting into her hug, breaking into a million pieces and knowing somehow she'd hold me together. "It hurts so bad."

"I know." She kissed my ear, wet with salty tears. "I lost my dad three years ago."

Doug Casablancas had died? And I hadn't been there to comfort her?

I pulled away, wiping my face quickly. "What? I'm so sorry. I had no idea. Mom and Dad…no one said a thing to me. I would've dropped everythin—"

"It's me." She stepped back, and it seemed like we both sobered up from that hug. "I asked them not to. It fell on your second semester finals."

"Who cares?" I asked, horrified. "I'd have dropped everything to be there for you. No questions asked."

"*I* cared. One of us had to do something productive with her life. Even though…" Her eyes swept over me. "Looks like neither of us did. What happened to your fancy degree?"

Ouch. I chewed my inner cheek. "Working on a game plan right now."

"You always needed a little push in the right direction." A small smile tugged at the corners of her lips. "Admit it, Dot, my pep talks were your fuel."

"Yeah, well, I was short on those in the past four years." My nose twitched. There was an awkward pause. My mother drifted to a nearby group of people to give us some privacy.

"Whatever, you know?" Dylan blew out air. "I mean, you were a shitbag for screwing my brother. But…maybe the timing was convenient for me too."

"How do you mean?" I frowned.

"It was a great excuse to cut ties with you before you cut ties with *me*." Dylan stared down at her Adidas Superstars, biting hard on her lower lip. "Once you realized the big city was full of supercool people you could hang out with. I didn't want to deal with the rejection. Didn't want to feel like I wasn't good enough for you anymore."

She was crazy if she thought anyone I'd met in NYC could rival the awesomeness of her, but I could tell she didn't want to talk about us. I grabbed her hands. They were limp against my own. It was time to change the subject.

"You're pregnant!" I announced.

She looked up, her face awash with mockery. "*Whoa.* What gave it away?"

I chewed on the side of my lip. "Tucker's?"

She nodded sheepishly before awarding me with her signature eye roll. "It's lobster season, so he's away on the boat for three to four weeks. Depending on the catch."

"Tucker is a fisherman?" My eyebrows jumped to my hairline. I was so far out of the loop.

"Well, NASA reached out for the aerospace surgeon position, but he said the Texas weather didn't agree with him." She waved her hand to her face, fighting her pregnancy sweat. Dammit, I'd missed her sense of humor. "I mean, he's a hunk, but not the brightest bulb in the chandelier. I'm pretty sure half the lobsters he catches are smarter than him."

"I'm sorry," I blurted out.

"Don't be." She ran a hand over her belly. "Remember we did those exams in ninth grade? My IQ is above average, so I think the baby will be fine."

"I meant I'm sorry he is out in the ocean, risking his life."

"*Oh*. I'm not," she answered airily. "All he does when he's around is watch football, drink beer, and complain I don't fulfill my 'womanly' duties. Team Ocean all the way."

There was a beat of silence as we both stared at each other. Finally, I couldn't take it anymore. I mouthed, *You had sex with Tucker Reid, Dylan. Ohmigod.*

That made her snort out a laugh. She slapped a hand over her mouth, frowning sternly. "Shut up. I'm still mad at you. I'm not here to make amends."

"Not even if I beg really hard?" I wiggled my brows.

"Ask again after I eat. I'm hangry." She glanced around the room, taking inventory of the people and dishes. "Now, if you'll excuse me, I'm going to make myself a pregnant lady plate and devour it while listening to a complete stranger reciting birthing horror stories to me. Last time I socialized, Melissa told me about her two inductions, steroids shots, and emergency C-section. Hard to top that, but I have faith."

She sauntered away, leaving me with my heart in my throat and a pathetic determination to make things right between us. I had let her down once, but I wasn't gonna do it again. A Dylan-less life was unthinkable now that I had another taste of her presence in my universe.

"Dot." A husky voice drifted straight into my bloodstream, and I knew exactly who it belonged to. "My sincere condolences."

Reluctantly, I sloped my head all the way up, extending my neck to stare Row in the eye. He was nearly a foot taller than me. Nausea twisted my stomach upside down.

He was so gorgeous. I was so screwed.

Row Casablancas had always been a showstopper, but *this*? This was the face of my feminism leaving my body permanently, buying a one-way ticket to Bora Bora.

The chiseled planes of his jawline, the dent in the center of his lower lip, the crinkles fanning his heavily lashed eyes. What business did he have being so attractive?

His lips moved, and that was when I realized he was talking to me while I was imagining myself riding that mouth like the future of the nation depended on it.

"Can you say that again?" I cleared my throat, thunderstruck by his features.

"Sorry about Artem," he drawled in a tone normally used to announce first-degree murder verdicts. "My aversion to his daughter aside, he was truly one of a kind."

We were definitely not on the same page. I wanted to climb this man like a tree. And he wanted me to fall from one and break my spine. It was obvious he wanted to be polite and move on. His body was already half-tilted to give me his back and walk off. My eyes ticked.

"Yeah." I slipped my hair behind my ear. "I mean…I, uhm, agree."

That's not even a sentence, Cal. Just a collection of filler words.

He turned around, about to walk off and leave me there. Something compelled me not to leave it at that. Guilt, maybe?

"Do you remember much about him?" I blurted out.

Everyone who graduated from Staindrop High knew Dad. He was *that* teacher. With the checked shirts, nine pens in its breast pocket, and a fanny pack he'd gotten for free from his insurance company. But Dad had never discussed his relationships with other students with me. He'd cared about their privacy just as much as he had about his own.

"All the good parts." His eyes crinkled. "Physics and chemistry were my favorite subjects in high school."

"I didn't…know…that." This was awful. Looking at his face and trying to English properly at the same time. On second thought, it was time to wrap it up. "Well! Thanks for coming, I better—"

"I visited him the day before he passed."

He had? I hadn't even known he was in town. How had Mom failed to mention that?

Well, she didn't know he took your virginity and whatever was left of your soul the night before you moved to NYC.

I stared at him, too shocked to pick up my jaw from the floor. "You did?"

"He asked if I was going to attend his 'real fun.'" Row quoted with his fingers. That was what Dad had called his impending funeral. *Real fun*. Because he'd wanted people to be happy that he'd lived, not sad that he'd died. "Said to remind you that he isn't in pain anymore. That he is probably in heaven right now, playing chess with Leonid Stein and Abe Turner and eating beluga caviar."

I blinked at him, registering his words. That was the most Dad thing I'd ever heard. "He didn't believe in heaven."

"He said you'd say that. And to tell you that he was wrong. The first and last time that happened." Row half shrugged.

Tears stung my eyes, but I was smiling. "What else did he say?"

"He asked you not to call it a celebration of life because that always feels like rubbing it in to the dead person."

I felt my chin wobbling. "And you remembered his exact words?"

"Well, it *is* three sentences," Row said coolly, glowering. "And I'm not a fucking idiot."

"Is there anything else? Something more he wanted to tell me?"

"That's all she wrote."

I started laughing and crying simultaneously. Somewhere between touched and moved and completely shattered. Row said nothing. Just stared at me dispassionately with his liquid gold eyes. I wiped my face quickly. I hated that every encounter with this man involved me looking and acting like a hot mess. He twisted again, about to walk off and leave me. Man, he couldn't stand me. I was going to keep him here and talk to him just to piss him off. How dare he? He took my virginity *and* it was my dad's funeral. He was going to be nice to me if it was the last thing he did in his life.

"So how's Paris?" I sniffled, wiping at my eyes.

He stopped midstep. Growled in dissatisfaction. Turned to look at me. "Don't know. Ask someone who lives there." He spun to pluck a clean plate from a stack on the table, piling it with food. He was downright arctic. Whatever grace he might've given me as a teenager did not extend to my adulthood.

"I asked you." I tried peering into his face, dread blooming in the pit of my stomach. "Because you live there. Wikipedia says so. So it must be right. It's right, *right*?"

"Great, another stalker." He scowled, stabbing a piece of prosciutto with a plastic fork, loading it onto his plate.

Another? How many were there?

"You're famous and I grew up with you. Of course I jealousy-googled you. It's not like I stole your sperm. And hey, I actually had the chance." I really needed to shut up. The sooner, the better. Twenty minutes ago would've been ideal.

"I live in Staindrop now" came the reluctant answer. "Though *live* is an exaggeration. This place doesn't even have a fucking Whole Foods."

We were going to be neighbors? Lovely. Things just kept getting worse for me. And I'd spent this morning picking up my father's ashes from a crematorium. Sliding over a clean plate, I joined him, pretending to examine the options I myself had arranged there only an hour ago.

I wanted to make amends with Dylan. I'd just lost an important person in my life and craved balancing it out by returning a special someone to it. The way to Dylan's heart passed through her brother's approval. So maybe him and me occupying the same town wasn't such a bad idea.

"Why'd you move back?" I piped out.

"Opened a restaurant here about a year ago." He grabbed a piece of cherry pie, shoving it into his mouth without tasting it. "Descartes."

His French accent was on point. So were my nipples, which apparently approved of his grasp of the French language. "Really? I hadn't heard."

"The Michelin people did. Gave it three stars. The first restaurant in the state of Maine to receive the honor. Just won the James Beard Award for it, actually. Guess that levels things out."

Sarcasm was a good look on him. Hell, a trash bag probably would be too.

Also, why did he have to be good at everything he touched? It was completely exasperating to someone like me, whose life was a string of failures, interspersed by bodega runs and late-night trips to the laundromat.

"Why the name Descartes?" I munched on the corner of my mouth.

"Taco Bell was taken." He rubbed his thumb over his lower lip, and my nether region clenched in response.

"No, what I mean is, why him of all philosophers?" Descartes was known for the connection he had made between geometry and algebra. My father had been fascinated by him and had spoken of him often.

"Are you always so full of questions?" he seethed.

"Are you always so full of attitude?" I sassed back.

"Yes," he said simply. "Made an entire career based on it. Asshole is my entire personality."

"You weren't always like that," I pointed out, my gaze holding his. "Once upon a time, you were the best part of my day some days."

My confession frightened me. It was too honest, too raw. Row's face remained blank and unimpressed. Not one muscle twitched. "What a crappy adolescence you must've had to put so much stock in someone who didn't give a shit. Go back to torturing Lyle with your VH1 trivia."

"You know, I think I'd rather torture you. You're closer, and unlike Lyle, I don't like you. So I guess you're stuck with me." I didn't care about his scary reputation or the fact that I was usually a ball of anxious sunshine just trying to get along with everyone—I couldn't let him get away with this kind of behavior.

Row's eyes flicked over my frame briefly. He pushed another piece of unidentified food into his mouth. "You changed your hair color."

"Just the tips." I felt myself blushing and was surprised that I did. Yes, I'd had a crush on him when I was a teenager, but I was over him. I'd only thought about him whenever he popped up on my TV screen or in glossy magazine covers. "Indigo. It represents sadness and mourning."

"Didn't ask."

"Didn't care," I fired back. "You won't offend me with your offhanded attitude. I'm not one of your TV protégés."

"If I stop answering you, will you go away?" He scrubbed his jaw with a frown.

I pressed a hand to my chest. "You wound me, Ambrose. I thought we could catch up."

He said nothing, piling more food onto his already overflowing plate. Over the years, Row had opened and helmed upscale restaurants across Europe that were booked six months in advance, but that didn't make him a food snob. He still liked mac-and-cheese casseroles and his momma's famous lasagna.

Me? I chose my meals like I chose my paths in life—badly. Junk seemed to be the recurring theme in both of those fields, and I always ended up feeling like crap.

"I pick the color by my mood," I heard myself drone on, even though Row certainly wasn't keen for me to elaborate. "So, before Dad died, the tips were yellow. I was feeling kind of confident. Brave about the week ahead. I thought I had a few more days with him."

He *harrumphed* to show me that he had heard me but offered no words of consolation. Wetting my lower lip, I said, "You know, I *will* be in town for a while..."

"Not interested," he quipped, tone wry.

"Cocky much? I was going to say I'd really like to reconnect with Dylan."

"You do? Huh, the feeling doesn't seem to be mutual." He brought a piece of Walmart pie to his lips, chewing slowly. If he found the flavor lacking, he didn't show it. He stared at me indifferently. "She despises you."

All thanks to you, slimeball.

Fine, that wasn't fair. I took full responsibility for what happened. I'd played that night hundreds of times in my head over the past few years, and the only excuse I could come up with was a moment of sheer madness. It was like gambling away your entire life savings at the casino.

"She might forgive me." I slammed a bread roll onto my plate.

"I might become a space cowboy."

"No, you won't."

"My chances are better than yours, though," he replied flippantly, popping a piece of cheese between his lips. "If Dylan's forgiveness is what you're after."

"You seem to be taking a lot of pleasure in my misery over my fallout with your sister." I squinted at him.

"A lot? No. A very modest amount? Sure, I'll stand behind that."

Lyle and Randy—the owner of the local food mart—whooshed past us in the cluttered living room, cutting the line to the quiches. Randy sent Row a fuming glare that concentrated enough hostility to fuel a nuclear bomb, baring his teeth at him.

"Hey, Casablancas. Come to ruin another fine piece of this small town?" he all but spat at Row's feet as we stood on the buffet-style line along a table.

Whoa. What the hell? Row was royalty in this place. Staindrop's golden boy. He had been handled with adoration and respect *before* he'd gone on to become the American Alain Ducasse. His shitty attitude added to his mysterious aura and bad-boy persona.

"I think I'm going to spare her." Row dunked a sponge cake in an unidentifiable syrup, sniffing it before tossing it into his mouth. "Not my type and talks a mile a minute."

Too stunned to be properly offended, all I could do was stare at him, jaw on the floor.

"I wasn't talkin' about Calla. I was talking about this house." Randy balled his free fist, taking a step in Row's direction.

"Talk all you want about either. As always, no one's listening." Row smirked defiantly.

Randy shoved his plate in Lyle's chest, stepping into Row's vicinity with his fist raised above his shoulder. "You got somethin' to say to me, *Chef?*"

"Yeah, actually." Row ate the rest of the distance between them, dropping his plate at the table with a loud clank. "*Eat. Shit.*"

Gasps erupted from every corner of the room. Whispers and loud shrieks ensued. And poor Lyle, who still looked only half-recovered from our Meat Loaf conversation, pushed Randy to the other side of the room, shoving at his chest like he was breaking up a bar fight.

"Knock it off and show some respect to Artem. Now's not the time to discuss such things." Lyle hushed his friend, and the two were immediately swallowed by a human flock of gossipers. Everybody's eyes hung on Row's face, and nobody came to his defense.

"What things?" I turned to look at Row, awestruck. "What did you do to make Lyle and Randy, two of the sweetest people on planet Earth, mad?"

He turned to glower at me. "Why don't you ask them?"

Wasn't it obvious? "Because I'm incapable of starting a conversation without turning it into a love fest for everything nineties related, and I will probably give both of them a ten-minute lecture about the origin of 'Kiss from a Rose' by Seal, which, by the way, *is* one of the greatest songs of all time. Ask anyone with ears."

"You can't help yourself, can you?" He gave me an exasperated look, shaking his head. "Well, I think I'm gonna let you brew in the unknown a little longer."

"What an ass."

"You know, I had the same thought when I walked into this place and you had your back to me."

"Are you flirting with me or ridiculing me?" I stomped. Actually *stomped*. The man was insufferable.

"Neither." He picked up his plate and resumed his feast. "Just fact-stating, is all."

Tapping my finger over my mouth, I asked, "How come you didn't kick Tuck's butt for getting together with Dylan?"

"Who says I didn't? Relocated his nose the first time they got together. Then closed the trunk door on his fingers, breaking four out of five, after their post–pregnancy test breakup." Pause. "*Accidentally*, of course."

"No, you didn't."

A somber nod. "He'll never be able to jerk off again. His fingers look like deep-fried Cheetos."

"Also—no, *he* didn't." I cupped my mouth, realizing Tucker

had tried to weasel his way out of taking responsibility for that pregnancy.

"Tried to."

"*Whoa.*" My eyes nearly bulged out of their sockets. "Ballsy."

"That was the next item on my list of bodily organs to destroy if he didn't man up."

"Are they together now?" I was thirsty for tidbits about Dylan's life.

"Why don't you ask Dylan...? *Oh*, that's right." He snapped his fingers, nodding. "Because she hates your guts."

That was it. I'd had enough of his behavior.

"That she hates my guts, I understand completely, considering the circumstances." I tossed my plate into the trash can under the tableclothed table in fury. It wasn't like I had an appetite anyway. "But why do you loathe me? What did I ever do to *you*? I gave you the greatest gift of all."

"Pretty sure you moved away because of college, not as a gesture of good faith." He popped an olive into his mouth.

"I'm talking about my virginity, you swine."

"That was a gift?" He squinted at a piece of Muenster cheese dangling on a toothpick with the utmost concentration. "What's the return policy on that?"

Absentmindedly tidying up the table to do something with my hands, I continued, "I was wrong to do that to Dylan, but I didn't hurt you in any way. Yet you're the one who can't stand me. Why?"

"I can stand you fine."

"Is that why you're being sarcastic with me?"

"I'm being sarcastic with everyone, Dot. Ain't nothing special 'bout you."

"You weren't sarcastic with me back when I was a kid."

"Spared you then." He turned to tap my nose, his grin unbearably patronizing. "New rules now. You're a commoner like everyone else."

"What? Why?" Did he just Meghan Markle me?

"You really wanna know?"

"Yes!"

His jaw locked, and he appeared to be grinding his molars to dust. Still, through the tension, I detected some pensiveness too. Like he was contemplating giving me a real, nonsarcastic answer.

I held my breath. I was in dire need of some truth bombs. I was back in a small close-knit town, unfamiliar and unfriendly, and didn't want to make any more mistakes.

Row opened his mouth to say something. As soon as he did, my mother announced loud enough to wake the dead, "All right, I'm tired and my favorite K-drama is about to start. Everyone can leave now." Pregnant silence. "Other than Calla, I suppose."

It completely ruined my moment of truth with Row. He clamped his mouth shut, turning around and striding in her direction.

I chased him, refusing to admit defeat. "Hey, wait. What were you going to say?"

"Doesn't matter."

"Does to me!"

The human ocean of grievers parted for Row, but the looks the townsfolk gave him no longer oozed awe and admiration. Everyone seemed put off and wary by his presence. This made no sense. Did they not see what I saw? A disgustingly accomplished businessman? An artist? A sex icon? The celebrity who put Staindrop on the map?

"Marina." Row planted a hand on Mom's shoulder, kissing her cheek earnestly. "I'll be around. Let me know if there's anything I can do for you."

"There's something you can do for *me*." I tapped his back persistently. "Answer my damn question."

Mom melted under Row's touch, patting his hand on her shoulder. "Oh, Ambrose, you sweet boy. Tell your mother I send her my regards."

"Sorry she couldn't make it. Still down with the flu."

"That's all right. I know Zeta always means well."

He shook me off his shoulder and disappeared. People began swarming around Mom and me, offering hugs and words of encouragement before taking off to their griefless lives. I thanked them, my eyes frantically searching for Dylan in the room. She was nowhere to be found. Nor was her colorful windbreaker. She had probably taken off with Row. Did she still live at her parents' old house? Surely Mom would know.

Once our living room emptied out, Mom closed the door, pressing her forehead to the wood with a shaky exhale. "I'm going to dash upstairs, change into something more comfortable, and watch *Crash Landing on You* before we start cleaning this place up. I need to decompress."

"Decompress away, Mamushka. I'll do the dishes in the meantime." I nodded, sashaying to our kitchen. I opened the door. Our kitchen was a charming thing, with slim shaker cabinets, copper pot rails, geometric blue wallpaper, and a farmhouse sink. It was quaint, lovely, and cozy.

If you didn't include the beastly man that stood inside it, filling up the entire room.

"Please tell me you are an unfortunate hallucination caused by my lack of sleep." I stepped into the kitchen in a daze. Row was there, washing the dishes at the sink like he wasn't a famous, stunning human with pictures of him in a tux available for download on Getty Images.

Suds of soap coated his sun-kissed, veiny forearms. The black sleeves of his dress shirt bunched around his elbows, straining against his thick arms. He had tattoos. Two full sleeves of delicious ink. All culinary inspired. Knives, herb roots, and a human-looking pig in a chef apron butchering a piece of human flesh.

"You're not hallucinating." He frowned at a pan, trying to scrub a dry piece of potato and cheese from it. "*This time*, anyway."

"What are you doing?" I glowered.

"The dishes. I thought it was self-explanatory."

"Do you always do the dishes in people's houses without asking?" I parked my hands on my waist, committed to being his bitter enemy. I wished we could be friendly. I really did. But Row had chosen war.

"It's a fetish" came his lazy drawl. "Don't tell Sheriff Menchin. He let me off on a warning last time."

I fished my phone out of my dress's pocket—yes, it was awesome and *had* pockets—pretending to punch in a call. "Hello? Nine-one-one? My emergency is an unwelcome guest who won't leave."

He ignored me, scrubbing dirty dishes with gusto.

"Seriously. I can take it from here. Kindly evacuate my premises."

"Not your premises." Row slid a sparkling roasting pan into the rack by the sink.

"Excuse me? Yes, they are."

"Is that what the deed says?" He picked up a dirty plate from the water-filled sink, leisurely scrubbing.

"It's what my mouth says."

"Your mouth just spent forty minutes talking about Meat Loaf." He scowled at the bubble-coated plate he was cleaning. "It's obviously only good for one thing, and that thing ain't an appropriate topic for conversation."

"You're unbelievable!" I screeched.

"You're *incoherent*," he slapped back.

"I don't know why I gave you my virginity."

"If it makes you feel any better, I think I deserved it even less than that Grammy."

Right. I almost forgot. Row had managed to win a *Grammy* for rapping for five seconds in a song by a famous artist. Screw him and his rock-star lifestyle. The most glamorous place I'd ever been to was the first-class lavatory on a plane to Dallas, and even that was because I'd had to bypass the angry flight attendant to projectile vomit.

Leaning against the wall, I folded my arms over my chest. "I see Staindrop has caught up with your personality finally."

He grunted in response, too busy wrestling a lasagna stain from the plate to pay attention to me.

"What did you do?" I demanded.

"You'll catch up."

"Catch me up."

He shot me a disinterested look, before sliding the plate onto the rack. "Nah. That would require speaking to you, which is low on my to-do list."

I was livid. Livid because we were both about to occupy the same town. Because my stomach still felt funny around him, and my stomach *never* felt funny. Unless I had kidney beans. Which I knew better than to eat (other than that airplane incident). But mostly because being next to him made my eye tic less prominent for some reason.

I stood there, watching him being sexy and helpful and sarcastic, and just couldn't take it. He had no right being all those things under my roof. In *my* house. It was time to assert power and control over the situation. "Please leave," I said one more time.

"Please shut up." He picked up another plate to clean.

I jumped on his back, lacing both my legs over his waist from behind, seizing his neck in a chokehold.

That, at least, was the plan. But I had miscalculated it gravely. Because his huge muscular shoulders got in the way of choking him.

Embarrassingly, even as I was wrapped around him, he continued doing the dishes, like a fly had just landed on his back, as opposed to an entire human. His whole body was stone-hard, warm, and delicious. "Go away!" I screeched into his ear. "You're unwelcome here."

"Anyone ever told you that you sound like the ignorant, angry townsfolk in a Disney movie?"

"Don't patronize me." I squeezed my fingers around his neck—which was the width of an ancient oak tree—grunting from the physical effort. "Leave," I commanded.

When my pleas didn't achieve the desired effect, I began poking at his eyes with my fingers.

Now *that* made him stop. Probably because I got his eyeball once or twice.

"Cut it out." He turned off the tap and shoved the clean plate into the rack, trying to swat my hands away from his face. Soap bubbles landed on the tips of our noses and eyes. "What are you, two?"

"Twenty-two." And he was twenty-six. Birthday was May sixteenth. I remembered because he had total Taurus vibes. He clasped my wrists, prying me away as he staggered back from the kitchen sink. *Ha.* Being a stage-five clinger had its advantages. He couldn't get rid of me.

Row reversed all the way to the wall, where he plastered my back against it, prying my arms off. I clung tighter, octopusing around his body.

"Don't wanna hurt you," he warned solemnly.

"Newsflash, you already did." I knotted my legs over his torso from behind. "When we had sex."

"You *asked* me to have sex with you." He slid us both down to the floor, where he leaned his back onto my body, then flipped himself over, so we were missionary style, him on top of me. "*You* came onto *me.*"

"I was drunk!" I lied, swinging my fists toward his face.

He dodged me effortlessly, hemming me in between those Thor arms and the floor. "No, you weren't." His lips thinned, and he looked genuinely pissed off now. "You didn't have more than one drink in you that night. I know you drunk. I know you sober. I know you in every fucking state. Besides, I thought you didn't want—what was it again?" He looked up, squinting as he tried to remember that night. "*A broccoli-haired trust-fund baby who makes experimental techno music to take your V-card.*"

"I was young and impressionable." I writhed beneath him,

twisting and thrusting, our bodies touching everywhere. My heart hammered and not from fear for a change. "Why'd you listen to me?"

"Because you were a willing woman of legal age, and I was twenty-two with a pulse."

I wormed to the right, attempting to roll under him, but he was quicker. He pinned me to the wooden planks by thrusting his nether region to trap my legs against the floor, and just like that, I came sex-to-sex with his massive erection. He bracketed me between his thighs and nailed my wrists together above my head. My nipples brushed his chest each time I panted.

My eyes narrowed. "Let me go."

His gaze dropped to my lips. "Been trying to do that all afternoon, and you keep coming back."

"Sounds about right," I bit back. "It's the only way I come with you."

"Baby." He released a slow, taunting smirk that made me melt into a puddle, constricting his grip on my wrists a smidge. "Just say the word and I'll destroy your pussy and your chance of ever coming with any other man."

Joke's on you. No one other than my Magic Wand has ever made me come.

"I'm serious, Row. If you don't let me go right now, I'm going to do something really awful."

"Like what?" A spark of interest ignited in his eyes.

Ugh. Good question.

"Bite you?" I twisted my mouth uncertainly.

"Don't threaten me with a good time, Litvin."

"I'll sing! You've never known pain until you hear me belt out 'Hello' by Adele. I try to hit all those high and low notes. I also do the echoes, for full effect."

He was fighting a grin, and satisfaction filled my chest because I had almost made him smile and *nothing* made this man genuinely smile. Not even the supermodels he was flaunting all over the globe.

"Say the magic word, Dot, and I'll set you free."

"Plea—"

"Nah. *Our* magic word. The one we came up with together."

Oh *shit*. He was doing that whole routine we'd used to do growing up. Whenever Dylan was busy and I was bored, I would wander into his room and rummage through his stuff. If he caught me—which he rarely did, because he was always out doing big lovely Row things—we would grapple until he would inevitably press me against his bed or the floor and have me beg him for mercy. Only I hadn't used the word *please*. I had used another word that used to make him laugh.

What the hell was the word? Think, Cal, think!

"Asshole?" I let loose a snarky smile. I knew what would happen if I didn't say the word.

He exhaled somberly, like a disappointed teacher. "Not the first hole I have in mind, but I'll take it. Two more shots."

"Banana?" I remembered it was some type of fruit. Or maybe a vegetable? It was definitely food related.

He shook his head again. "Nope, but I see where your mind is going, and I'm not mad about it." His dick twitched between my legs. Okay. Yeah. This was definitely one hell of a welcome back.

Also—I wasn't half as freaked out about what was happening right now as I should have been.

"Give me a clue," I demanded, wriggling. "Is it a fruit or a vegetable?"

"Fruit," he said stoically.

Pear? Passionfruit? Guava?

"Give me another clue." The weight of him was delicious. To the point my mouth watered, my nipples puckered, and I was ninety-nine percent sure I was on the verge of a mini-orgasm.

"Nice try. You didn't deserve the first one."

Fair point. Too bad we were chafing everywhere and an insistent, tingly pressure mounted in my core. Something that horrifyingly resembled the big O. And I'm not talking about Queen Oprah.

"One more chance to get it right, Dot. What's our magic word?"

"Mango!" I tossed the word in his face, flustered.

"Wrong answer." His voice was calm, flat, and resolute. "The word you were looking for was *tomato*."

"You said it was a fruit!"

"Tomato *is* a fruit."

"How can it be a fruit if you put it in salads? Fruits are *fun*."

"So is payback," Row deadpanned. "Enjoy."

He used his free hand to tickle my armpits and neck, feathery fingers skimming all my delicate areas, and my writhing became violent, frantic thrashing. I was the most ticklish person on planet Earth. It was a medical condition. I could pee myself. I swung upward, trying to bite him in retaliation. "Let go of me!"

I was squirming, laughing, and begging, tears prickling my eyes as I tried to escape his fingers, but they were *everywhere*. My ribs, my neck, and behind my ears. I was horrified and delighted that the grumpiest human alive had managed to put a smile on my face on the saddest day of my life.

I was dangerously close to peeing my pants *and* coming, and needed Mom to come down right now before I did something I would never recover from. Desperate, I sent a silent prayer to the universe.

Dear God,

I know I'm not much of a devout Christian. I also know I only gave up something for Lent once, and it was Skittles (and even that was because I'm allergic to Red Dye 40), but I really need a solid right now.

Please make Row stop tickling me. I really can't handle another humiliation, and I have a feeling beginning my stay in

Staindrop with a pee stain the shape of Nebraska on my dress and convulsing with an orgasm while he wrestles me into submission are going to make my time here challenging to say the least.

I promise to be good. To donate what little I have to charity. And to not shut the door in Jehovah's Witnesses' faces when they tell me you want me to do something special with my life.*

*Is starting a true crime podcast special enough? Just being pragmatic here. Your girl has bills to pay and has a scented-candle addiction to subsidize.

Faithfully, Cal

P.S. Please send my regards to Jesus and tell him I'm sorry he died for my sins just so I could sleep with my bestie's brother, then borderline assault him in my mom's kitchen the day of my dad's funeral. He deserved better.

God must've had a slow day because he heard me. Suddenly— *eureka!*—Row's front pocket began vibrating. His phone flashed through his dark pants, and we both stopped, staring at it.

Fine, *I* was staring at his baseball bat–sized hard-on. His zipper looked so strained it was a wonder it didn't dislocate to a parallel universe.

Row leaned backward on his shins, releasing me from his grip as he pulled out his phone and swiped the screen, scowling. "Now what?"

Dude made the Grinch look like Phoebe Buffay.

His jaw clenched, and he straightened his back, running a hand through his floppy, shiny hair. His shirt rode up, offering me a glimpse of his rock-hard, bronzed abs. "You're shitting me," he bit out.

"That explains the smell," I quipped, smoothing my dress down and patting my wild hair into submission. Row ignored me. The person on the other line continued talking. My archenemy rose to his feet, letting out a puff of air as his frown deepened. "I'm going to make a nutcracker out of their bone cartilage." *Oof.* "On my way."

"Hey, where are you going?" I growled. "You didn't even apologi—"

He grabbed his jacket from the back of a dining chair, not even bothering to put it on. The door slammed abruptly, shaking on its hinges. Leaving me to pant on the floor, feeling empty, confused, and with two brand-new pieces of information to digest: 1. Tomato is a fruit, and 2. Row Casablancas was hotter than ever and burning with hatred for me.

CHAPTER THREE
CAL

**EXCERPT FROM ANDROPHOBES
ANONYMOUS FORUM:**

oBITCHuary: Legit gonna hurl myself off a cliff.

McMonster: This better be a figure of speech because I'm about to find your address and have someone bust your door down. My conscience can barely fucking cope as it is.

oBITCHuary: Aww. Who did you kill?

McMonster: Don't change the subject. Are you okay?

oBITCHuary: If you are asking whether I'm suicidal, the answer is no. I just need to vent.

McMonster: Vent away.

oBITCHuary: Do you want the long version or short one?

McMonster: Short.

oBITCHuary: Returned to the small town I grew up in for a personal matter and everything is...off.

McMonster: That's small towns for you.

oBITCHuary: How would you know? You grew up in Philly.

McMonster: Educated guess. How can I make you feel better?

oBITCHuary: Tell me it's okay to take back my promise to my mom and go back to NYC instead of staying here for eight weeks?

McMonster: You know the answer to that question, kiddo.

oBITCHuary: Boo.

oBITCHuary: Well, give me an incentive.

McMonster: Do the right thing so karma doesn't get your ass?

oBITCHuary: Karma is literally still stalking me for a chocolate bar I stole from my grandma when I was six. Too late for that.

oBITCHuary: Let's meet up when I'm back in New York.

McMonster: Aw. Socializing? I thought you were better than that.

oBITCHuary: Come on. We've been talking for three years.

oBITCHuary: And before you say anything, no, I don't care that you work at a fast-food chain and I don't care if you think you look like an ogre. I LIKE you. And I don't like men. Hence why we're here.

McMonster: I'll think abou tit.

oBITCHuary: Okay. Mine are great, BTW.

McMonster: *IT.

oBITCHuary: Sure, Jan.

McMonster: Shouldn't you be scared of men?

oBITCHuary: Well, it's easier to flirt when you have no idea what my real name is or where exactly I live. It's not like you can come over and take me up on my non-offer.

oBITCHuary: Also, my androphobia is not so bad that I can't work around men or talk to them in public settings. I just...don't want to date them. Kiss them.

Be in a relationship with them. I'm not asexual. I am
EXTREMELY sexual. And THANK YOU Harry Styles
for making me discover my sexuality. But I'm scared
if I entered a relationship with a man, he'd hurt me.
Physically. Mentally. Make sense?

McMonster: Perfect sense. So you're not gonna hump
my leg if we meet?

oBITCHuary: I mean, I'd like to keep my options open.

oBITCHuary: Remind me what YOU are doing in an
androphobia forum?

McMonster: Abusive man in my life made me very
fucking wary of my kind.

oBITCHuary: Don't write all men off. They're not all
bad.

McMonster: Yeah?

oBITCHuary: Yeah. There are also people like you.

CHAPTER FOUR
ROW

"What do you mean they resigned by *text*?"

I was standing at the heart of Descartes's dining area, surrounded by rustic décor, stained glass, and useless idiots. I was two idiots short, though. Donny and Heather, my servers, had decided to quit together and hand me a generous twenty minutes' notice, along with a figurative middle finger.

"Let me explain again. I'll refrain from using big scary words this time." Rhyland, my restaurant manager, smoothed his crisp dress shirt with his palm, ignoring the staff milling around us to get the place ready for service. "Now, I'm going to talk extra slowly, since I know your brain short-circuits once you're pissed off. So Donny took out his phone, typed out a text saying he and Heather weren't going to show up for service today, and hit the Send butto—"

"I suggest you get to the point before your balls make it to tonight's entrée specials," I said, cutting him off and glancing at my De Bethune watch. "You have five minutes. Use them wisely."

"First of all? Work on your people skills. You're about as personable as an STD test." Rhyland sucked his teeth, shaking his head. He looked like a fucking Hugo Boss model in a suit. At six foot four with a blond Charlie Hunnam man-bun and a five-workouts-a-week physique, he distracted ninety-nine percent of my employees.

"Second, you're gonna have to tone it down. We live in an era where employees have rights and shit."

"I can guarantee you their rights don't include fucking me over with a ten-foot pole at twenty minutes' notice." I turned my ring on my pinky finger, imagining I was wringing someone's neck.

He scrubbed his face exasperatedly. "See? This kind of language is why three of your ex-staffers filed a complaint against you to OSHA."

"The R&B singer?" I frowned.

"OSHA, not *Usher*." Rhyland pinched the bridge of his nose. "The pro-workers organization?"

"Doesn't ring a bell. Why would Donny and Heather quit together, anyway?" I bit out. I was in a particularly dangerous mood today, having spent the last hour arguing, wrestling, and nearly creaming my pants thanks to Calla fucking Litvin, the bane of my miserable existence.

Rhyland stroked his chin leisurely, his douchebag vibes dripping all over my floor. "Hmm. Let me think. Maybe because they're *engaged*?"

"To each other?" I tried to conjure them into memory, but I was bad with faces. And names. *Fine*, I actually had no fucking clue who Heather and Donny were. I just knew I needed them to open service tonight.

Rhy chuckled. "Shit, Row, do you care about *anything* other than work?"

"Baseball, during seasons the Mets don't suck." I glanced around, throwing blood-chilling looks at my staff to make sure they weren't slacking. "How was I supposed to know they were bumping uglies?"

"Through the power of sight and deduction. They were all over each other like a genital rash after spring break." Rhyland threw charming smiles at servers who smoothed tablecloths and arranged utensils around us. The man could flirt with a fucking Stanley cup and win it over. "You kicked them out of the meat fridge the other day, remember? Told Donny next time you saw his meat in that fridge, you'd make dumpling stuffing out of his intestines."

That *did* sound like something I'd say.

Besides being my restaurant manager, Rhyland Coltridge was also my best friend. He'd been my wingman since I graduated from Le Cordon Bleu and called him up to supervise my restaurant in Paris. Rhyland was a boyfriend for hire by trade—a PC title for what really was de facto a male escort—but I'd convinced him to work with me through a fat paycheck, good food, and a limitless amount of pussy. That last selling point was his favorite. He'd yet to find a hole he didn't want to shove his dick into.

Descartes was our last hurrah together, though. Rhy wanted to be a full-time pretend boyfriend in the Big Apple, after blazing through most of the willing women in Western Europe. The money was excellent, the hours measly in comparison to running a Michelin-starred restaurant, and one of his filthy-rich clients had bought him a condo in Manhattan as a birthday gift. Therefore, three weeks ago, he'd informed me he was done with the customer service field.

"The only customers I want to service are millionaire women who pay me hourly for longingly staring into their eyes during family functions and telling their relatives and jealous ex-husbands how much I love them" had been his exact words.

"You really don't pay attention to anyone other than yourself and your kitchen, huh?" Rhy's green eyes narrowed.

That wasn't completely true. I did notice one person. She had blue-tipped Rachel Green hair, wore overalls unironically, and possessed the ability to be klutzy without looking like a complete moron.

And I wanted to stay as far away from her as humanly possible. This wouldn't be a problem, though. I had the uncanny ability to cut people off, and Calla Litvin had been plucked from my life five years ago, straight from the root. She was squarely on my shit list.

"Let's get to the solution portion of this conversation." I tapped my cigarette pack on my thigh, eager for a smoke. "How are we solving our staff problem?"

It was going to be a bitch to hire and train two new employees *if* I could even find them in this godforsaken town. The citizens of Staindrop weren't exactly fans of mine, and Descartes was booked to the max until its closing date, the day before Christmas.

January first couldn't come soon enough. That was when my one-way ticket to London was scheduled for.

New restaurant. New adventure. Zero baggage.

"Become a tolerable, relatable human being and stop scaring off everyone around you." Rhyland sauntered over to the bar, crouched down to throw the fridge open, and popped open a bottle of Kronenbourg 1664 by banging the cap against the edge of the bar.

"Thanks for the tip." My nostrils flared. "Any other ideas that fit our time constraint?"

"You wanted something immediate?" He took a pull of his drink. "Then your best bet is your sister and your mother."

"The former is on bed rest, and the latter is recovering from the flu. Think harder. That brain of yours is good for more than taking directions from lonely rich women."

"I'm too hot to use my brain. Only average people have to saddle themselves with an actual personality."

"You have a personality," I informed him dryly. "A shitty one, but it's in existence nonetheless."

He pointed at me with the bottle, not even a little offended. "What's *your* idea, Einstein?"

"Find me Donny and Heather, drag them here by the hair, and make them give us the two weeks' notice they owe us."

"Donny's bald." Rhyland took another greedy sip.

"He'll be limbless too, once I'm done with him."

Rhy swished the beer in his mouth, mulling over my words. "Even if I did want to spend my night at the police station awaiting bail for assault and harassment, they've probably already boarded the plane."

Fuck.

Descartes attracted people from all over the East Coast, mainly out-of-towners. The price point and fine-dining aspect of the menu didn't appeal to Staindrop's usual palate, which favored anything that was breaded, deep-fried, oversalted, and swimming in ketchup.

"You must know some servers looking for a job." I began pacing. Service opened in less than thirty minutes, and I had left Taylor, my sous-chef, to handle the kitchen while trying to extinguish this fire.

Rhy gave me a concerned look. "Not anyone desperate enough to work for your grumpy ass. Flip side? You're about to run off to London to open your shiny new restaurant."

Flip side, my ass. He knew me better than that. My perfectionism wouldn't allow this ship to sink, even if it had a hole the size of Antarctica at the bottom. Descartes was still mine, until it closed. I'd die before I failed.

"Hold on a minute." Rhyland held up his finger, brows pinching into a tight V. "Why are you dressed like an Italian mobster who got lost at a Neiman Marcus store?"

I looked down. I wore a black dress shirt and designer slacks, a departure from my signature Henley and ripped black denim uniform.

"Is it a crime to look good?" I really didn't need him riding my ass about Cal right now.

"Hope the fuck not." Rhyland pulled another beer from the fridge, uncapped it, and slid it my way across the bar. "I'd get life without parole, and do you know what they do to people like me in prison?" He gestured toward his face.

"Ten hours of community service and sex addiction rehab?" I asked conversationally. Someone needed to keep his ego from overtaking the continent. I was doing the whole nation a service.

"Oh shit." Rhyland slapped the back of his neck. "Artem Litvin passed away. You went to his funeral today, right?"

Better get it over with. Rhy was going to find out sooner or later that Cal was in town. "He was the one teacher at school I didn't want to set on fire." I shrugged, bringing the bottle to my lips.

"So you saw Cal." Rhyland's eyebrows were floating somewhere above the atmosphere.

"Briefly," I grunted.

"Wanna talk about it?"

"Hard pass. She did enough talking for the entire decade."

"Still adorably weird, I see." He plastered his palms against the designer bar between us. "Well, if you wanna talk about it, we can grab a beer after we close."

Rhy and I never "talked" about things. We bickered and taunted. Sometimes even brawled. Had I really been that pathetic growing up? I remembered being in love with her, but I didn't recall handing her my nuts in a flower bouquet for Valentine's Day.

I banged the empty beer over the bar after one sip, pointing at the thick butcher block between us. "Clean up the condensation before we open. This is not amateur hour."

"Just remember you are not that kid anymore." Rhyland produced a rag from a drawer behind the bar, slapping it over his shoulder. He made his way back to me. "You know, the one who'd have stayed here getting a McJob if it meant she let you in her flowery corduroy pants."

"Shut up."

"Eyes on the prize, Row. You can't afford to veer off plan. You have a new restaurant to open."

"Listen to yourself," I snarled, fingers tightening around the shape of my cigarette pack in my front pocket. "I'm not changing shit for anyone."

"She eats saltine crackers with a fork." He slid the rag over the butcher block, wiping the condensation and ignoring my words. "Anyone deserves better than that. Even your sorry ass."

I still remembered Cal sitting with those saltines at my kitchen table, acting a fool because she didn't like the way the salt clung to her fingers. Rhy was right. The woman was barely civilized. I had no business thinking about her, let alone pining after her. Was she even a woman? She was still acting like a child. She needed a babysitter, not a boyfriend. And I wasn't interested in either position.

"Enough," I barked out. "I'm at no risk of liking Calla Litvin again. Not from afar and definitely not up close. You're wasting your breath talking about her. You have twenty-four hours to find us two new servers." I rapped my knuckles on the bar. "Get your ass in gear."

Rhyland downed the rest of his beer, heaving out a sigh. "Denial ain't just a river in Egypt."

I flipped him the bird, trekking my way to the kitchen. "No fraternizing with the patrons!" I called out, as I did every night.

"No promises," he called back, as he did every night too.

The evening couldn't get worse if a meteor landed directly on my fucking head.

———————

I was wrong.

The evening got worse.

Exponentially so and at a plane-crashing speed. Hot mess would be putting it mildly.

On the outside, it looked normal. Expensive utensils clinked in harmony; chatter rustled through the aromatic air. There was laughter, hushed conversations, and upholstered chairs scraping softly. The kitchen sweltered, the scents of sweet marjoram, thyme, and rosemary clinging to my nostrils. I loved the sensory overload that came with helming a restaurant. The fast-paced culture of it. It drowned out my fucked-up thoughts and forced me to focus on the here and now. And there were *a lot* of fucked-up thoughts, courtesy of my messy childhood.

Our normal ratio was one server for every three tables. This service, it was one server for every six. Considering we had a ten-course prix fixe menu, availability was nonexistent. And the patrons were pissed. Rightly so.

Tables had to wait up to twenty minutes between dishes, and the flustered servers were so overworked, one had spilled red wine on someone's Dior dress and another had stepped all over a customer's casted foot. My chef de partie had decided now was a good time to have a mental breakdown because a customer had insulted his scallop caviar tartare, and the kitchen porter had thrown a tantrum after Rhy had asked her to serve beverages for the night.

Overall, if I could erase this entire day from my memory bank, I would, and pay handsomely for the pleasure.

"Chef!" The maître d' popped her head into my kitchen. A twentysomething Swiftie with blond side bangs and bright red lips.

"No," I said automatically.

She cringed, about to shrivel into her face.

"What is it, Katie?" Taylor, my sous-chef, spun on his heel, giving her his full attention. He was a good-looking kid. Tall, Black, tatted, with hazel eyes that made every female staffer swoon whenever he was nearby.

"There's a VIP customer who wishes to speak to Chef," she said sheepishly.

"No," I reiterated, chopping celery at the speed of light.

"Yes." Rhy zipped into the kitchen, bypassing the maître d'. "People come here to get a glimpse of the famous Chef Casablancas. You need to make an appearance anyway. You do every night."

I put the knife down. We stared each other down. I knew he was right. I hated people, but I loved my career. If parading myself around like a zoo animal meant getting patrons more hyped for my next culinary venture, it was no skin off my back.

"Fine." I slapped the swinging doors of the kitchen open, prowling to the dining area. "Can tonight get any fucking worse?"

"Absolutely," Rhyland said ardently, high on my misery. He joined me as we sliced through the white-clothed tables and candlelit chandeliers. "Wait till you see who wants to have a word with you."

That got me intrigued. It couldn't be Cal. First of all, she wasn't a VIP. Second, she was too broke to afford a glass of water in my establishment, let alone eat an entire meal. Third, even if she had all the funds in the world, she still had the palate of a toddler. Her taste in food—if you could even call it that—was deplorable. She lived on a steady diet of corn dogs, Pop-Tarts, and Sour Patch Kids. She would eat her own foot on national television before willingly tasting an ortolan.

We approached a square table of what seemed to be a couple on a date. The first person appeared harmless enough—blond, leggy, the too-short-to-be-a-model type, in a dress that could moonlight as a sports bra, it was so short. Then my eyes landed on the man sitting in front of her.

Kieran Carmichael.

A privileged piece of shit whose daddy owned the one and only department store in town. The human answer to smegma.

I had suffered through twelve years of school with this prick. We were bitter rivals. Both jocks, both popular, both wanting to piss on each other's territory. Ran in the same circles, dated the same girls.

Kieran's favorite hobby used to be telling me I stank of the fish my fisherman dad sold to his father every day, and I'd enjoyed reminding him he had less personality than a stop sign. Ordinarily speaking, I would put a hole through someone's face if they bothered me and move on with my life, but Kieran was a different breed. His family had power and influence. I had known if I'd messed up his face, my father would have been out of a job, and then there'd be no dinner on the Casablancas table. So I'd sucked it up. Braved twelve years of digs and bullshit.

Now my family no longer depended on his, and it was game on. Two decades' worth of anger seared through my guts, lava bubbling in my veins. "Thought you said a VIP wanted to see me." I eyeballed the maître d' next to me, arching a brow.

"I—I—sir, he is a famous soccer player," Katie stuttered nervously. "For…Ashburn DC?"

"FC." Kieran patted the corners of his mouth with a napkin, a bored smirk mortared on his face. "I have the season off because of an injury."

"Didn't ask."

"Normally they want players to stick around, attend home games while in physical therapy, but my contract bypassed all that red tape. I'm…well, kind of a big deal." Kieran gave us a smile with so much cheese, I got fucking heartburn.

I kept my eyes on his date just to piss him off. "How can I help you?"

"*Ohmigod*, hi!" His date flashed me a megawatt beam, fanning herself with a menu. "Gosh, you're so tall. I've seen you on TV but never realized you were this handsome up close!"

She had a soft Alabama drawl, and I was extremely close to laughing. Kieran was such a fucking cliché, going for the Southern-Belle type.

"Thank you." I bowed my head in faux humility. "How can I be of service?"

"No, really." She squeezed her breasts together, leaning toward me. Subtle as a tank, this one. "We came here because I told Kieran—didn't I tell you, Kiki?—I have to taste everything you make after seeing you on *The Great Chef Down*. And when you tossed pepperoni on that contestant and told him he was a prick pizza—priceless!" She clapped excitedly, laughing.

Was she going to get to the point sometime soon? Because I had a service in crisis and a leftover boner from pinning Cal to her floor this afternoon. My dick still twitched every time I thought about those blue hair tips.

"Annie wanted to let you know the food is delicious." Kieran yawned into his fist, as though admitting I made good food pained him. I hoped it did.

"Already know that." I crossed my arms over my chest.

Kieran glanced at his Rolex, taking a bite of his entrée. "You're welcome for the validation, buddy."

I wasn't his buddy. But I was about to become his undoing if he didn't evacuate himself from my premises. Averting my gaze his way, I said, "Get the fuck out."

"Excuse me?" He tilted one brow, calm and collected. He had ridiculous, shiny light-brown hair and wore a black turtleneck, the international prick uniform. I didn't buy the whole tamed-down version he was selling me.

"I said: *Get. The. Fuck. Out.*"

"We're paying customers," Kieran pointed out unflappably.

"No amount of money is worth you contaminating my restaurant. The lady is welcome to stay." I clasped my hands behind my back, ignoring Rhyland, who shot daggers at me with his eyes. "*Dateless.*"

"She's my cousin."

"Personally, I'm not a fan of incest, but that explains your IQ."

"Oh my goodness." Blondie shielded her face with a manicured hand, ducking her head sideways. "Kiki, you never told me he hates your guts. We should leave."

"I see at least your cousin's parents aren't related. Good idea. I'll show you to the door." I stepped back to give them space to stand up, knowing we were drawing the attention of other diners and still not giving much of a shit. I Loathed this man with a capital *L*. If I could serve him a piece of extra-cold revenge for everything he had put me through, I didn't mind the *Page Six* headline. Nothing kissing a few babies and signing a nice check to an animal shelter couldn't fix.

Kieran stood up unhurriedly, showing no sign of embarrassment, and his cousin followed suit. "Hadn't realized I cut you so deep I carved you into an asshole."

"Don't flatter yourself." I brushed off invisible lint from his designer turtleneck. "You're no more than an anecdote. It just so happens I don't feed bullies—they're already full of shit. Now kindly fuck off."

I ignored Rhyland's stunned face, along with the dozen phones directed at me, agape mouths, and hushed whispers.

"Did you just throw out a customer?" Rhyland jerked his thumb over his shoulder. Diners were shifting uncomfortably in their seats. I wasn't worried. Chefs were known to be douche rockets. Gordon Ramsay's entire career was built upon the ruins of other people's hopes and dreams. "One of the most popular soccer players on earth at that?"

"He's no Messi." I glanced at Kieran's plate, noting it was completely empty.

"No, but you are." Rhy scrubbed his face, probably itching for a joint. "Messy as *fuck*, not to mention reckless."

"Resign."

"Been there, done that," he reminded me. "Can't fucking wait to kiss this job goodbye."

"You can keep the kissing part; I've no interest in your herpes. Now, if you'll excuse me." I stomped my way back toward the kitchen.

A hand reached out to me from one of the tables. Slender, cold fingers laced around my wrist. I turned to look at the person. It was a brunette in her early thirties. Sharply dressed.

"Mr. Casablancas?" She flashed a seductive smile that did nothing for me, the lilt of a French accent ribboning around her words. "My name is Sophie Avent. I'm a reporter for *Cook's Illustrated*."

I never gave interviews. Unless it was a part of my contractual obligation for a TV show promo, in which case I had my people go over the questions in advance with a fine-tooth comb. My past was too tangled, too complicated for me to open my life up for the world's entertainment.

"I was wondering if you would—"

"No," I cut into her words.

"You didn't hear my question yet," she pointed out smartly.

"Unless it ends with *Let me suck your cock*—in which case, the answer would be *No but thank you*—the answer is still no."

"Heyyyyyy there!" Rhyland slid between us, chuckling good-naturedly. Sophie Avent's face looked like I'd just slapped her, and I didn't blame her. There was no excuse for this level of asshole-ness. Normally I reined it in much better. Rhy bowed his head at Sophie, looking genuinely horrified. He was a damn good actor, and an even better liar. "So, first of all—apologies for his crass-ness; easing him into civilization has been a step-by-step process. Clearly, he escaped his cage." Rhyland rearranged the utensils on her table, his heartthrob smile working extra hours. "Second, your dinner is on the house and will be accompanied by a lovely 1998 Chateau Lafite Rothschild and an exclusive ten-minute interview."

That wine was close to seventeen hundred dollars. And my time was *priceless*. Nonetheless, Sophie's expression remained unimpressed. "Did he just…?"

"I wish I could tell you he didn't, but we have an audience, so let's focus on how to remedy the situation and make you happy."

She curved an eyebrow. "You can make me happy, I'm sure." The suggestion had been clear.

"Consider it done, sweetheart. Now!" Rhy patted her shoulder, his *American Psycho* smile still intact. "Please allow me to direct all my wrath—excuse me, *attention*—toward my volatile, genius boss. Be right back to take your order. And number." He winked.

He slapped a hand over my back and led me to the kitchen, his face turning from pleasant to murderous. "What the hell was that?" He punched a wall as soon as we closed the door and were out of sight. The whole building rattled. He pointed at the door. "Every single person in that restaurant was staring at you like you were crazy. Know why?"

I had a feeling I did but waited for him to confirm it.

Rhyland opened his arms wide. "Because you *are* crazy!"

"Kieran made my life hell in high school." I perched against my station, picking up a Georgia peach and halving it with my knife. I tossed it into a pan, along with a spoonful of lemon juice and some sugared rum, tipped the pan down, and let it flame and caramelize. The fire danced in yellows and oranges between me and Rhy, who rested his fists on my counter.

"Yeah, I remember, I had a front-row seat to that horror show. You two had a four-year-long pissing contest, and *everybody* got rained on." Rhyland pushed off my counter, pacing the small space between us as I lowered the flame. "But you're no longer in high school, and he might no longer be a dick."

"It's a free country; I can serve whoever I want." I tilted the pan here and there, letting the peach simmer in its own juices. "And I choose not to serve male genitalia."

What I needed was a cigarette. Didn't give a shit that it was probably giving me cancer. Didn't have much to live for anyway.

"Fine. Kieran is a sore subject for you, so I'll let it slide. That thing with the journalist, though?" He pointed at the door. "That's sexual harassment."

"I said I *don't* want to fuck her." I glowered at him, sliding the peach onto a plate.

"You said she wants to fuck you."

"Where's the lie?" I flicked my gaze over his shoulder to watch through the partition window as a server handed the Sophie chick our best wine. "If I had a drink for every journo who made a pass at me, I'd be Hemingway."

Rhy tucked his iPad under his arm, shaking his head. "Women don't like to be told they aren't desirable. You'd know that if you ever bothered talking to one."

"You're making me sound like a misogynist. It's not like I talk to men either. I'm an equal-adversity person."

"Well, the good news is, *now* tonight can't get any worse." Rhyland stared out the door's window.

"Chef?" Taylor came to a screech in front of me, holding on to my butcher block.

"Yeah?"

"The grill station is on fire."

CHAPTER FIVE
CAL

McMonster: Still alive?

oBITCHuary: Just barely.

McMonster: Reassuring.

oBITCHuary: You sound disappointed. How is my beloved NYC?

McMonster: Same way you left it. That bad?

oBITCHuary: Worse, actually.

McMonster: What happened to take you back there anyway?

oBITCHuary: My father passed away.

oBITCHuary: Sorry I didn't say anything. It just seemed... Well, honestly, I'm really raw right now. Just typing it out and facing this as my new reality is difficult. But it wasn't a surprise. He'd been sick for a while.

McMonster is typing...

McMonster is deleting...

McMonster is typing...

McMonster is deleting...

McMonster: Sorry for your loss.

This was a very weird response from McMonster, who was usually so attuned to my feelings I sometimes suspected I was being catfished by a female therapist. I'd been speaking to him almost every day since I'd signed up to the androphobia forum some years ago. My *actual* therapist had thought it was a good idea for me to talk to people who shared my experience and dread of men, but as it turned out, it was just this specific person I clicked with.

My fears felt intimate, too private to share with strangers. But the thing about McMonster?

He didn't feel like a stranger at all.

CHAPTER SIX
CAL

"Torn"—Natalie Imbruglia

"You should do something with yourself." Mom pressed her frozen foot across my cheek on my sixth day in Staindrop, making me yelp in protest.

We were both strewn over the couch in the living room, eating ice cream and watching a reality TV show about lavish LA realtors who dressed like Barbies. I slapped her foot away, screeching, "I'm trying, Mamushka. Running a true crime podcast is a career, okay?"

So far, I'd been dragging my feet about getting a real job after graduation because the idea of doing my own podcast with the occasional guest appealed to me more than becoming an intern in some marketing agency that refused to pay me enough to subsidize my weekly subway pass. I'd even gone as far as writing a few episodes on my laptop but always ended up canning them for being too long, too graphic, too informative, too quirky, and just…too *me*.

I was currently in the research phase of the operation. Which in practice meant I was occasionally googling *how to start a true crime podcast*. Now all I needed was written episodes, a studio, a producer, a marketing manager, and motivation.

Clearly, I was *this* close to making it happen.

"I'm not talking about your work in New York." Mom shook her head, sticking her spoon in a mountain of pistachio ice cream to flick a lock of hair off my face lovingly. "I'm talking about this place. This town. If you're going to stick around for a while, you need a job."

"Oh. Sure. Right." I stared at her skeptically. "And where am I going to get *that*?"

Staindrop wasn't exactly the Big Apple of opportunities. It was more…the Small Raisin of unemployment. I knew she was right. I *did* need a job. I'd just figured that job was going to be selling my internal organs on the black market or being a phone sex operator for old married men.

"Let me tell you where you're not going to get it—this couch."

"I'll get a job." I waved her off airily, with confidence I definitely did not feel.

"You better because I don't want it on my conscience if you lose your New York apartment. It's rent-controlled."

"Don't worry." I diverted my attention to my cookie dough ice cream to avoid eye contact. "I'll figure something out."

"And you need to start reconnecting with people too." Mom was on a roll, poking me with her elbow. "I know how much you missed Dylan. I'm not sure what happened between you two, honey, but what you had is sure worth fixing."

"I tried." Along the years, I had. I'd sent letters. Text messages. Birthday presents. Telepathic pleas. I'd have tried smoke signals if I didn't know she was borderline asthmatic. She had never replied to any of them.

"Try harder."

"Do you want me to stalk her?" I stabbed the spoon into my ice cream, losing my appetite.

"Aggressively court her," Mom corrected. "Your generation is so touchy about personal space."

"*Mamushka*." I felt my nostrils flare. "I don't think she wants anything to do with me. I'd hate to be a pest." But I wasn't so sure, after Dylan's behavior last I saw her. Then again, it was literally my father's funeral. Maybe she cut me some slack because it was a special occasion.

"A good friend is a treasure, and treasures are hard to come by."

"Then why did *she* give up her treasure?" Though, really, I ought to try one last time. My out of control anxiety aside, Dylan wasn't horrible to me at the funeral.

Mom twitched her mouth back and forth, pondering the question. "I'm thinking maybe you did something that made Dylan think you weren't her treasure anymore. Is it possible you hurt her, so she decided to hurt you back?"

She was right, of course. I was the one who'd betrayed Dylan. I was the one who needed to atone for my sin.

I thought about what Mom said when I went to bed in my childhood bedroom later that night. Darkness clasped me like loving arms. It was like being cocooned in a time machine. My obsession with the nineties was a result of acute longing for a time I hadn't been here to witness. A time without social media. Before the internet took off. It represented anonymity and serenity to me. Two things I cherished more than anything.

And this room? This room almost made me believe I was right there, in the nineties. The faded purple walls. *Beverly Hills, 90210* and Green Day posters. Heavy quilts piled up on my single bed. Polaroid pictures of Dylan and me were pinned onto a detective board, strung together by red string.

Dylan and me roller-skating.

Dylan and me in a snowball fight.

Dylan and me at prom (as each other's dates, *obviously*).

Dylan and me at a Death Cab for Cutie concert.

Dylan and me doing cartwheels in the sun.

Almost every happy memory I had was attached to Dylan

Casablancas. And she was now going to be a *mother*. Mom had a point. Patching things up wasn't just about Dylan being there for me—I wanted to be there for her too.

I stewed in memories and regrets for a few hours, wide-awake and tormented by all the time lost, before flinging my blanket off and padding barefoot to my closet. The clock signaled that it was two thirty in the morning.

"Shut up, clock," I muttered as I tossed my closet doors open and rose on my toes to reach the tallest shelf, where a Dr. Martens shoebox decorated in plastic rhinestones and doodles rested.

The Shoebox of Dreams

The box where Dylan and I threw little Post-it notes with our bucket-list items. Our hopes. Our birthday wishes. Walking back to bed, I sat crisscross on the duvet, flicked on my phone's flashlight, removed the lid, and picked up one of the heart-shaped folded notes.

Bucket list: bungee jump—Cal.

Bucket list: visit all 50 states—Dy.

Birthday wish: the perfect '90s CD, burned especially for me—Cal.

Bucket list: flash a president—Dy.

I tilted my head, frowning. How much weed had we smoked senior year? Too much was the probable answer.

Birthday wish: make me the best dessert ever using only ingredients that start with an M—Dy.

I went through the box the entire night, alternating between giggling and sobbing.

Bucket list: kiss Stephen Henry. And Kyle Cowen. And Ray Mohringer—Cal.

A miserable smile slashed my face. Teenage Cal had pretended to be boy-crazy. I didn't even remember these boys' faces and definitely hadn't wanted to kiss them for real. But I had longed to appear normal, like other girls. Dylan had been privy to all of my made-up crushes during high school. I'd fed her lies—about who I liked, who I wanted to kiss and date; no wonder she hated that I'd hooked up with Row. She thought her brother was just another notch in my belt.

Birthday wish: cake made out of something gross like broccoli or cauliflower so I can force everyone to "celebrate" with me by eating it—Cal.

This last one made my heart stop in my chest. Three years ago, on my birthday, I *had* gotten a special delivery of a gross cake during a shift at the restaurant where I had been working. It had had broccoli, cream cheese, rhubarb, and a few other cake-looking ingredients and had actually been surprisingly decent. It had tasted like a veggie casserole.

I had figured it was a joke my mom had played on me and hadn't worried too much when she'd vehemently denied sending it.

Could Dylan be the one who had sent it?

Was that her way of reaching out to me? Had I missed this crucial sign?

Well, I wasn't missing any more of them. I was going to win Dylan's friendship back.

As soon as the sun pierced through the clouds, I started working.

CHAPTER SEVEN
CAL

oBITCHuary: I think I'm going to make a move.

McMonster: Like...ask a guy out?

oBITCHuary: OMFG NO. I'm going to try to win my old best friend back.

McMonster: Sweet.

McMonster: What made you grow apart?

oBITCHuary: Ugh. I did something stupid.

McMonster: ?

oBITCHuary: Her brother.

McMonster: ??

oBITCHuary: Jk. He is not stupid. Just scary. And hot. And scary. We slept together.

McMonster: Is he why you are afraid of men?

oBITCHuary: Actually, no. In fact, he is the only person I've managed to be intimate with since I got scared off in the first place.

McMonster: Sounds like a nice guy.

oBITCHuary: Nice? No. Good? Yes. There's a difference between the two. He taught me the hard way.

CHAPTER EIGHT
CAL

"Basket Case"—Green Day

It was a humbling experience, standing in the pissing rain on Dylan's doorstep with a baking dish swathed in foil, shivering in my ladybug rainboots as Zeta Casablancas regarded me with the suspicion of a prison guard.

"Calla, *cucciolotta*, I am so sorry for your loss." She sniffled through the tiny crack in the door.

Not sorry enough to let me in, I thought uncharitably.

"Is she waiting for you?" She peered beyond my shoulder, still blocking the entryway.

Mrs. Casablancas was a distrustful woman, though I had a nagging feeling she hadn't always been this way. Zeta was as tall as treetops and as glamorous as the sun. She had given up her career in Milan to move here with Dylan's late father, Doug, after meeting him on a night out in New York. Someone who up and left their entire world to enter someone else's couldn't be a person with trust issues, right? Something had made her the way she was today. I couldn't recall one time I'd seen her happy. Growing up, I'd always assumed she missed her family in Italy.

"Uhm, well, not *exactly*." I shivered, drenched to the bone. Mrs. Casablancas made no move to let me in. It stung, because she used to love me like a daughter. Used to braid my hair and laugh at things I said (most of them weren't jokes, but still).

"Dylan is pregnant. It's not good for her to get too excited," Zeta explained.

"I just want to apologize." I bent my knees, not above begging.

"For what?"

Screwing your son.

"Our…misunderstanding four years ago."

Her gaze lingered on my face, fingernails drumming on the old wood, their sound pleasant but unnerving. She sighed. "I'll go check if she's accepting visitors."

"Thank you."

"If I don't come back in three minutes, leave."

"Yes, ma'am. I promise."

The door slammed in my face. I proceeded to dance in place in an attempt to dodge the rain. Spoiler alert—it did not work. The Casablancases' house was a twenty-minute walk from mine, nestled at the foot of the tree-covered mountains. The place was a far cry from the pastel-colored historic structures of the street my family resided on. This felt more like a cabin in the middle of the forest. A great spot for a murder-mystery plot.

Pacing, I wondered if there was even a point in sticking around. I knew my former best friend. If holding a grudge was an Olympic sport, Dylan's neck would break from all the medals.

A minute passed. Then two. Five minutes melted into seven. The rain fell down harder, in thick sheets. God, what was I doing here, soaked to the bone, pining for a childhood friendship that had collapsed in a spectacular fashion? This was silly. It had been four years. It was time to let go.

Not yet, Callichka, Dad chided in my head. *Have faith.*

Shut up, Dad. You were an atheist.

Seven minutes passed. Then ten. Then twenty.

Twenty. Whole. Minutes.

"Sorry, Dad. She isn't coming out," I murmured. I took one last look at the Casablancases' cottage—dilapidated, the rotten wood wet and sagging, yellowish windows, and a rickety front porch.

I tried, Dylan. I really did.

I put the dish down on the first step, turned around, and walked away. A screeching sound assaulted my ears. An old window cracking open.

"Calla Polina Litvin, you are *such* a quitter." Dylan's head popped through the window in her attic. Her dark locks danced in the wind, thick and glossy. She was waving a white shirt in her fist. *A white flag?* "It's like that time we went to the regional hockey finals and you bailed ten minutes in because there weren't any hot players."

"Hey," I yelled back. "No one on that rink was over a six, and you know it." I stabbed a finger in the air in her direction. I remembered that day. I had left because Dylan was clearly PMSing and needed cake, not eye candy.

"Whatever, Dot. We were fifteen. It's not like you were going to reproduce with one of them."

"Did you stare at me through your window to see how long it'd take me to break?" I squinted, somehow still unable to be mad at her. She mimicked zipping her lips and throwing the key out the window. I pretended to catch the imaginary key and tossed it back to her pointedly. She "unlocked" her lips and sighed in defeat. "Ugh. Fine. Yes. But in my defense, I hardly have any source of entertainment these days. I've watched everything worth consuming on Netflix."

I pressed my lips together, fighting a smile. "May I come in?"

She rolled her eyes. "Guess so. It's high time you say your piece."

"Actually, I *am* pissed. You let me stand in the rain for twenty minutes and *watched?*" My mouth hung open in disbelief.

"Hey, *you* let *me* have sex with Tucker Reid." She pointed at me.

"I would *never.*" I clutched my chest, staggering backward as if she had shot me. "You shunned me from your life, so I couldn't be there to remind you that you are all that and a bag of chips and deserve so much better. You betrayed both of us."

"Not me, my vagina."

"Dylan Maria Casablancas!" her mother roared from downstairs. "Watch it before I wash your mouth out with soap."

"What about *your* betrayal?" Dylan demanded, ignoring her mom. "Which part of your body was in charge the night you—"

"I regret that night every single day of my life." A lie. I didn't regret it, even though I should have. I only regretted getting caught. Row was the only man other than my dad who made me feel safe.

"*Whoa.*" Dylan puffed her cheeks. "Was he really that bad?"

"Not bad! Not at all!" I pretzeled inside my soaked clothes. Great. Now I had offended her beloved brother. "He was great! Wonderful."

She made a gagging sound. "But...?"

"But he is...uhm, *gifted*."

"Like, talented?"

"Like...the length of my height?"

"Dylan! My goodness! I'm coming out there with a broom!" Zeta threatened from inside the house. China crashed noisily in the kitchen, followed by more cursing in Italian. "I spilled all my minestrone. God forgive both of you girls because my ears never will."

Dylan and I stared at each other...before dissolving into deranged laughter.

I grabbed the foiled dish and made a beeline for the door. She opened it before I could knock, and we were face-to-face, flushed, panting, shaking with exhilaration (and me, possibly also with hypothermia).

"Holy crap, you look so pathetic!" Dylan said cheerfully, gathering my cheeks in her hands. "I love me some good groveling."

Inside, the house looked totally different from how I remembered it. Growing up, nobody in this town had a lot of money. But the Casablancas took the blue-collar cake. Doug had been a solo fisherman with a rickety old boat, and Zeta was a homemaker. Some days, especially at the end of each month, the electricity hadn't worked and they'd rationed cans of food. Until Row had started working when he was a teenager and turned things around.

Now I saw that the inside was completely refurbished. The wooden floors were gleaming and brand-new. The lights were bright, the furniture substantial and modern, and there were shutters. Row's doing, no doubt.

As if reading my mind, Dylan tipped her chin up proudly. "Row's building Mom a whole new house, you know. Four thousand square feet. White picket fence, red roof. It's almost done. Just off Main Street and Winchester Road."

"Oh wow," I breathed out. Row was a total pain in the butt, but no one could deny, he loved his family something fierce.

"Yeah." Dylan's face clouded. "He is kind of forcing me to live there too, since… Never mind. Anyway, we're battling it out. I don't need his charity."

I had no interest in talking about the person who had made us fall out right now, so I tried to refocus her. "So I brought you a few things."

"Edible things?" Dylan squinted, rubbing her belly through her yellow satin nightgown.

"Fifty percent of them, yes."

"*Yummy* edible things?" Dylan elevated an eyebrow. "Because Mom and Row are making me eat all kinds of healthy shit full of iron and magnesium and whatnot."

"*Dylan*, you're on bed rest!" Zeta materialized from the kitchen like something that needed to be purged, brandishing a kitchen towel as though it were a weapon, clad in a house robe. "You don't look very restful, and you're definitely not in bed."

"Bring your apology offerings upstairs." Dylan snapped her fingers and tilted her head to the stairway with a flourish. I followed her, my heart in my throat.

On our way up, I asked, "Are you and Tuck still…?"

"Together?"

"Yeah."

"Guess so." She offered a little shrug, throwing the door to her room open. Holy crap. Row really did gut this place and redo it. It looked fantastic. All pastel colors, throws, and decorative pillows. The room Dylan had dreamed about when we were teenagers. The room she *deserved*. "Though I'm not so sure how much of it is Tuck wanting to be with me and how much of it is Tuck not wanting to die at the hands of my cranky brother."

"Your brother *is* frightening," I admitted, looking around in astonishment. "But I don't know anyone who'd agree to spend the rest of their life with someone they don't love just because they're afraid to get punched in the face."

"You haven't met Row's punches. Tucker has, and he is not a fan."

"Still…this must be exciting for you." I mustered a smile. I was excited about her having a baby; I was not excited that she was still with Tucker.

"The new construction is supposed to house Tuck, me, and the baby." Dylan fell to her bed, sighing miserably. "The deed is gonna be in Mom's name, so Tuck won't get any greedy ideas after we get married. Guess Row wanted all of us together somewhere pretty and new so he wouldn't have a guilt trip when he leaves again."

"You're getting married?" I whispered.

Dylan nodded miserably. "Tuck popped the question."

"Aww."

"…after Row almost popped his *knees*."

"Oh. That's…sweet?" I remained standing, waiting for an invitation to sit down.

If Tuck had two brain cells to rub together, he knew Dylan was eons above his league. Unfortunately, I seriously doubted those two cells were in existence.

"I mean, you're engaged! Having a baby! Getting a new house!" I threw one hand up excitedly, hoping my fake enthusiasm was contagious. "My only achievement in the last four years is staying alive, and even that was purely accidental."

"Thing is…I'm not sure I want to share this magnificent new house with him. Or if I want to share *anything* with him at all. Other than the baby, of course, which I don't have choice about. We've been together for four years…" *Four years. Sweet Jesus.* "But he also has a terrible temper, is about as intellectual as an expired bag of trail mix, and we can't agree on anything other than the indisputable fact that the worst LaCroix flavor is cherry blossom." Heavy silence fell between us before she added, "Plus, what if I don't want to live in a big fancy house in Staindrop? What if I want to live in a small cool apartment in Boston? Or go back to being a PA in Greenwich?" I didn't even know that had happened. "I feel like all my decisions were made for me the minute I got pregnant. People who are trying to take care of me are actually suffocating me."

She was making a snow angel over her unmade bed, staring at the ceiling hollowly.

"Is Tucker really that bad?" I whispered.

"Dude, the worst. He has no sense of humor either. Before he went off lobster hunting, we attended a twenty-four-week ultrasound checkup, and when we were in an elevator full of people on our way to the sonographer, I asked him very loudly, 'So when are you going to tell your wife about us?' and you know what he did?"

I pressed my lips together, stifling a laugh. Dylan was so fantastically herself, it sometimes took my breath away. "Peed his pants cackling, as he should?"

"You'd think so, right? But no. He got all mad and started yelling at me that I was immature and too much to handle. What does that even mean?" Her eyes—a shade darker than Row's—sparkled with unshed tears. "Shouldn't the person you love be the perfect amount for you?"

Well, I'm no expert in love, but I think that if someone loves you the way you deserve to be loved, they could never get enough of you.

Rage scorched through my body. Dylan was clearly unhappy, and that made me want to use Tucker's arteries as shoelaces. The jerk.

"Dylan…" I cleared my throat. "You should do what makes you happy."

"I know." She worried her lip, sitting upright. "But Chris Hemsworth is married. And lives in *Australia*. I'm not built for long distance, Dot."

That made both of us laugh somberly.

"Hey! At least you got a baby out of it!" I reached to rub her belly with my free hand, which looked like a prosthetic glued onto a supermodel's body. "You've always wanted a baby, and you gotta admit, this is so much better than stealing one."

"Not if you have to push it out of your body. Plus, if I steal one, I can have my pick." She pouted.

"Hmm." I pinched at my puckered lips. "You have a point. If only kidnapping children weren't illegal and stuff."

"Oh, Cal, what have I done?" Dylan moaned, throwing an arm over her eyes. "Tuck and I are the least compatible people on earth. We both come from families of giants. I'm only thirty-one weeks along and the baby is already, like, five pounds. It's going to come out your size."

"Hey, I've been told I'm pocket-sized." I swatted her knee.

"For an *adult*."

"That's a very big word for what I am." I was torn between being devastated for her and happy for myself that we seemed to be friends again. "So…why *were* you with him? Before the pregnancy, I mean."

"Boredom? Loneliness? Temporary insanity?" She hitched one shoulder up, drawing circles over her nightgown with her fingernail. "Everyone left for college. You all lived your cosmopolitan lives. I stayed behind to take care of Mom. My universe was small and insignificant. I bused tables every day, got back home, ate my frozen dinner in front of Netflix. Slept. Rinsed. Repeated. Tuck was there, making a good buck and easy to boss around. He took me to nice restaurants, weekend getaways, movies; he was a great distraction." She paused. "Oh, and he *really* loves giving oral. Like, I'm talking thirty-minute sessions and multiple orgasms."

"Wow. He really didn't strike me as the giving type."

"I know, right? I've met plastic utensils more charitable." She popped her head up from her pillow, patting an empty space on her bed. "It's probably an ego thing, but at the time I did not complain. But enough about my life. Let's see what you brought over. It better be good."

"Oh, it's the best." I inched toward her with my offerings. First, I put the foil-covered cupcake pan on her nightstand, unpeeling the edge for easy access. "Found our shoebox last night."

"You mean the one that you stole from me?" She gave me the stink eye.

"I didn't steal it; we had joint custody over it, remember? Giving it back was never an option because you were mad at me. Anyway, I started going through our notes. One of your birthday wishes was a dessert made out of *M*-lettered ingredients. I did my best."

I had made her marshmallow cupcakes with milk, M&Ms, and Maltesers. Yeah, I'd had to cheat and use eggs, butter, and flour, but overall, I had brought my M game.

"Lookie here." She removed the foil, bringing one of the cupcakes to her lips and taking a bite. It looked moist and soft on the inside; my heart swelled with pride. "*Damnrm*," she murmured, mouth full. "I don't know if it's amazing or if I'm just not used to eating junk anymore."

"It is amazing." I flipped my hair—black-tipped, for obvious, morbid reasons. "And there's more of them coming—including foot massages and doing your nails if you forgive me and take me back as your BFF."

"A foot massage can get you into premature labor." Dylan's eyes widened in horror. "Hard no to that one."

"Guess I'll have to fan you with a palm leaf and tell you how pretty you are." I stuck my finger into the frosting of one cupcake, popping it into my mouth.

"Well." Dylan licked the frosting off her thumb sulkily. "I *am* very pretty."

I perched my ass on the edge of her bed, careful not to wet it with my clothes. Dylan took another bite, craning her neck to peer at the plastic bag behind me. "What else did you bring me?"

"Siri, play 'Material Girl.'" I slapped her hand away when she tried to snatch the bag from around my body, laughing.

"Siri, play 'My Best Friend Screwed My Older Brother.'" She finished her cupcake in one bite. "Oops. Never mind. No one wrote a song about a betrayal so cutting and deep."

"I'm sure there's a country song about it," I muttered. "It's not like I slept with your boyfriend."

"If you'd have slept with my boyfriend, we wouldn't be having this conversation."

"Why?"

Dylan snorted. "I'm not a medium, silly. I can't speak to the dead."

I was glad I had come here.

"Chop chop." Dylan clapped. "What's my next gift? You can't squeeze any of the Hemsworths into a bag so small, so I already know it's not what I want."

"I sincerely hope you are not on any FBI watch list." I sighed, producing a burned CD from the plastic bag and handing it to her. "I made you a playlist of baby shower songs."

Dylan flipped the CD to its back, where I had slid a piece of paper with a handwritten song list. "This better not have 'Isn't She Lovel—' Oh!" She jutted her lower lip out and nodded, impressed. "'Plug In Baby'?"

"Epic intro," I confirmed.

"'Baby Got Back'?" Her gaze skated my way, eyebrows arched.

"Fun, right?" I beamed.

"'There Goes My Life'?" Dylan gasped, punching my arm. *Hard.*

"Hey, that's what the rumors say!" I rubbed my arm, chuckling. "Whatever happened to no kids before we hit thirty? You broke the pact."

"No, *he* broke the condom. And you're horrible."

"You still love me."

A reluctant moan escaped her lips. "Ugh, I really do. It's such a curse."

I kicked off my boots, crossing my legs over her bed, my heart galloping happily in my throat. I pulled her nightstand drawer open, knowing tiny hairbands were waiting for me in a small tin box, and patted my thigh. Begrudgingly, she rested her head on said thigh, staring up at me, blinking at her ceiling.

"So I have a question," I said.

"No, you cannot be the godmother."

"Shush. Of course I'll be the godmother." I began parting her hair into neat sections, getting ready to Dutch-braid it. "I wanted to ask if you sent me a broccoli cake for my nineteenth birthday."

Her eyebrows shot up. "That's random."

"But true…?" I peered into her face, brushing each piece of her hair with my fingers.

"No. The only thing I wanted to send you over the years was anthrax, and I was too scared to get caught." Dylan shook her head. "Not me. Sorry, Dot."

"I'm asking because you're the only person who knew about my gross cake wish," I explained, even more confused than I was before. If it wasn't Dylan, who was it?

"Oh Christ." She rolled her eyes as I began braiding her satin-soft hair.

"Christ, what?" I frowned.

"Christ, Jesus…?" She pressed her lips together, eyes flaring in her alarm, like she had said something she shouldn't.

"Tell me."

"Shut up." She clamped her mouth shut.

"Come on, Dylan—"

She leaped up, grabbed one of the red and pink cupcakes, and shoved it in my mouth. She missed by a few inches and it landed on my ear and hair. I gasped audibly. This was a declaration of war if I ever saw one.

I picked up a cupcake, hurling it in her face with surprising force. It hit her eye. Dylan's jaw slacked. "No, you didn't."

"Did too." I crossed my arms over my chest.

She picked up the cupcake she'd shoved in my face from my lap, smearing it all over my face. I, in return, shoveled cupcake crumbs and frosting into her mouth. Soon, we were flinging cupcakes at each other while making squeaky sounds. I got her cheek. She got my hair. Dylan's church-bells laughter filled the room. I was laughing too, until I remembered she was on bed rest and wasn't supposed to get too excited. That was when I raised my arms in the air in surrender. I was pinned under her, trying to scoot back and sit up. "Stop! You're on bed rest."

Dylan, who had been about to shove a cupcake down my throat and suffocate me, collapsed backward on the mattress and groaned. "Oh, right. I have to take it easy."

"Why are you on bed rest, anyway?" I straightened up onto my elbows, peering at her frosting-covered face.

"They scheduled me a C-section. They think the baby's gonna come out the size of a Saint Bernard. Like, ten-pounds big. I'm the poster child for safe sex, Dot."

We stared at each other silently. Pieces of cupcake dangled from our hair and lashes. Her face was a red and pink mess, and I guessed mine looked much worse. We both started laughing, toppling over in her bed. I didn't even know why we were laughing. Just that we needed that laugh very much, even if for different reasons.

Me—because I missed Dad, the only man in my life I'd ever loved and because my fear of men stopped me from pursuing my other dreams, like the podcast.

Her—because she was with a man she didn't like, on a journey she hadn't chosen.

We were laughing like there was no tomorrow, a never-ending giggling sound, when the front door slammed downstairs, and I heard the voice of the man who had nearly made me come in my dress on my kitchen floor a few days ago.

"Where's Dylan?"

Oh shit.

CHAPTER NINE
CAL

McMonster: Had a hellish day at work.

oBITCHuary: Hey, at least you have a job, show-off.

McMonster: Didn't you say you worked in the food industry yourself?

McMonster: Oh shit. You're unemployed now, aren't you?

oBITCHuary: Thanks for reminding me.

McMonster: Hey, always happy to be of help.

oBITCHuary: I'm super broke. Might lose my apartment if I don't find something soon.

McMonster: I'm sure something will come up.

oBITCHuary: In the small town of Staindrop? Fat chance.

McMonster: You should have more faith in yourself.

oBITCHuary: Why?

McMonster: Because you're you.

CHAPTER TEN
CAL

"Why Can't We Be Friends?"—Smash Mouth

"Great. Now we'll have to sage the whole fucking house."

Row was glaring at me like I'd just crawled from a sinkhole to suck the soul out of his mouth. Standing next to him was his BFF, Rhyland, who I remembered as sex on legs with a dry sense of humor. Rhy was wearing black cargo pants, designer sneakers, and a white V-neck. Row was wearing a gray Henley, dark jeans, and the expression of a man who'd love nothing more than to attend my funeral.

"That was my initial thought," Dylan said levelly, placing a reassuring hand on mine. "But then she tried bribing her way into my good graces with treats and gifts." Dylan collected her hair into a crusty, cupcake-y bun. "I have no principles and a sweet tooth, so you can guess how that went."

Row and Rhyland had run upstairs when they'd heard our breathless giggling. Row had said we sounded like distressed seals trying to communicate carnage.

"What's on your face and hair?" Row demanded, his eyes swinging between us with a frown. He really ought to look less sexy. He made my hormones go wild. In fact, even though I thought he was a prick, I never feared him like I did most men. He rarely made my eyes tic, either.

"Cupcake," Dylan answered airily. "Dot brought me some sugar bombs."

"Then proceeded to bombard you with them?" Her brother quirked an eyebrow.

"She started it." I coughed into my fist.

"Snitch!" Dylan slapped my thigh with a gasp.

I winced. "Dude, he is big and bad-tempered and already hates me. He won't touch you."

"Yeah." Rhyland's eyes ping-ponged between us. "But he sure as fuck would touch Cal, as history has taught us."

That earned Rhyland a slap on the back from Row.

"*Aw.* Too soon?" Rhy laughed.

"Behave yourself." Row's voice was a lot of things: calm, menacing, and blood-chillingly threatening. Surely, he didn't know I feared men. Even if he did, why would he care?

Rhyland seemed unbothered by the chiding. "When have I ever? Too late to start now."

I scooped pieces of cupcake out of my bra, dropping them into my palm. Rhyland whistled low. "In other news, Cal Litvin is all grown-up and looking delicious, all puns intended."

"Seriously?" Row turned to him again. "Look away before I pluck your eyeballs out with a spoon." Row's gaze flicked along my locks briefly when he realized that I had changed the tips, but he didn't comment on the matter.

Rhyland pressed his lips together, shaking his head. "Goner."

"This time it was done faster than a light laundry cycle," Dylan told Rhy. I had no idea what they were talking about. I just knew that with each sentence, they brought Row closer to obtaining a criminal record.

"Cal, leave," Row barked.

"No, Cal, stay." Dylan knotted her arms over the top of her belly, staring at him pointedly.

Wow. Way to make me feel like a Labrador getting trained to be a service dog.

I looked between the siblings, itching to remove myself from the situation. "Who should I listen to?"

"The person who can toss you out the window without breaking a sweat," Row recommended dryly. "And has every inclination to do so."

"The person whom you'd like to make amends with." Dylan dipped a finger into my bra and sucked some icing into her mouth. "And is also on bed rest and shouldn't become upset."

I firmly planted my ass back on her bed, sending Row an apologetic grimace. "Sorry, buddy. Not gonna make the same mistake twice."

"Speaking of mistakes, how's that baby cookin', Dylan?" Rhyland asked conversationally, leaning his shoulder against the doorframe.

Row shot him a pissed-off look, which, in my humble opinion, was the only look he was capable of. "Hey, shithead, don't you have new staff to find me?"

"You need new staff?" Dylan cocked her head. "How come?"

Actually, I was intrigued too. He owned a bougie restaurant. The tips must be divine. And I was used to working for top-notch eateries in Manhattan. Plus, it would show Dylan that I would keep my hands to myself this time. I was going to be platonic and professional with that mountain man.

Also, did I mention that I needed to pay my New York rent? And utilities? And general existence?

"Two of our waiters ran off to elope and do a coast-to-coast." Rhyland lazily perched against a wall, popping a thick eyebrow up skeptically. His main job seemed to be leaning against sturdy objects and looking sensual. Kind of like Jason Momoa. With better hair product.

"Ugh. *So* romantic." I fanned my eyeballs, feeling teary-eyed. Then I saw the look Row gave me and quickly added, "*And* irresponsible. Totally irresponsible. Especially with the time it takes to learn every ingredient on the menu and correct timings. I would never."

I paused, then clarified, "Leave without at least a month's notice, not...get married. Although, judging by my love life, ain't nobody needs to save up for a wedding gift." My inability to exist without saying or doing something stupid never ceased to amaze me. They said the spotlight can either make you shine or melt. I knew where I was standing. My eyes ticked like crazy.

Rhyland gave me a once-over. "Did you say timings?"

I nodded enthusiastically. Mom was right. Getting out of the house was a great way to find job leads. "Yeah. I looked at Descartes online. You do a prix fixe menu, right?"

Rhy took a step deeper into the room, in my direction, looking enchanted. "Table d'hôte."

"Don't even think about it, Rhy." Row raised his finger to his best friend, and I swear that thing was thicker than an oak trunk. "Don't even *think* about thinking about it."

Too late. My mind was reeling. The money I would make could set me up not only with rent and utilities but also with maybe renting out a little studio to record my podcast. Or perhaps just the equipment to set up in my own apartment.

"Ever worked as a high-end server, Cal?" Rhyland asked. I'd read on the Descartes website that he had a management position there. Growing up, Rhy was to Row what I was to Dylan. But I couldn't imagine him doing something so straitlaced. He was more the type to bull-ride and axe-throw. Run away from a burning castle with a princess tossed over his shoulder. He had always been too charming for his own good.

"Yes!" I exclaimed, ignoring Row's death glare that was currently burning a hole through my temple. "I worked for Avant Garden for two years while I was in college and just finished a two-year contract at Tsukimishi."

"Don't care if she won the Georges Baptiste Cup for best server for seven consecutive years." Row jabbed his thumbs into the belt loops of his jeans. "She isn't hired."

"I was also a chef de partie at Teddy's one summer." I perked up sunnily, flashing Row what I hoped was an adorable smile. "I have three references and a bevy of experience working under pressure. *And* under assholes too!"

Rhyland barked out a laugh, clapping at my little performance. "She's the one, Row."

"Glad you're familiar with assholes." Row checked his phone, tucking it back into his pocket. "Because the only job you'll be getting in this town is scrubbing toilets, and not mine."

"Honestly?" Dylan ignored her brother. "You sound perfect for the job. Doesn't she, Rhy?"

"Chef's kiss." Rhyland touched his fingers to his lips. "And other party favors, if this guy has his way." He wiggled his brows and looked at me just a moment longer than he should.

I stiffened. I didn't like men's eyes on me. Even if I knew Rhyland.

"You're about to be six feet under if you don't knock it off." Row's lips barely moved, and my muscles immediately uncurled and relaxed. One thing hadn't changed—he was still protective of me because I was an extension of Dylan. Growing up, Row was always one phone call away if I needed a ride home, even if he spent the entire drive ignoring me.

"My interest in Cal is purely professional," Rhyland drawled, and he wasn't only good-looking—he was good *everything*. He had that aura that made him look famous somehow. People gravitated toward him, like planets circling the sun. "No offense, but I like 'em with a bit more meat and edge. You look like an infant saint in a medieval painting."

"A cherub," I burst happily. "That's the best compliment."

"It's an insult he'll pay for," Row countered. "And it's not happening."

"Get your head outta your ass, she has *experience*." Rhyland threw a hand in the air, losing patience. "We can't afford to pass that up."

"Besides, she is the only person who would agree to work for you." Dylan laughed evilly. "You're dead to everyone else in this town, and I'm too pregnant to pull doubles like yesteryear."

Why was *Dylan* vouching for me? Did that mean our beef was officially squashed? Or was working for her brother her idea of a cruel punishment for me?

"He isn't dead to people here, but they're sure about to kill him," Rhyland corrected with a smug smile. "This reminds me—Row, you do have life insurance, right?"

Row opened his mouth, no doubt to give him one final warning before he broke his nose, when the door whined open.

"What's going on here? What's the commotion?" Zeta stuck her head in the door, scanning the four of us. Dylan sat dutifully on her bed, looking like a birthday cake had exploded on her. I was by her side, Rhyland was standing next to us, and Row was on the other side of the room, looking fifty shades of pissed off.

"Row is two servers short and Cal just offered to fill in. She has experience." Dylan threw out her hands in a can-you-believe-it gesture. "Talk some sense into your son, Mamma."

"You'd be crazy not to hire her." Zeta tutted, palming her cheek worriedly. "No one else would work for you in this county."

"I think you missed the *R* in country." Rhyland took out a small tin box from his pocket, rolling himself a joint.

Whoa. What had Row done, and why wasn't he in jail for it?

"In less than two months, the restaurant will be permanently closed. Cal is probably looking for long-term." Row's jaw ticked in annoyance.

"Two months from now, I'll be leaving. I'm flying back to New York January first, so actually, this is perfect," I countered.

"Of course you are." He scrubbed his face, muttering, "*Shit.*"

"What now?" I sighed. Was there anything I did that he didn't find appalling?

"I'm flying to London the same day," he explained.

"Why, what a coincidence!" Rhyland looked between us,

amusement adorning his sculpted face. "You can share an Uber to the airport. In the meantime, you only have eight weeks to suffer one another. Doable, right?"

"Wrong," Row said at the same time I exclaimed, "Easy peasy!"

Seriously, what was his deal?

"What happened to your faces and hair, girls?" Zeta took us in for the first time, her grip on the doorknob loosening.

"Cupcake fight." Dylan pretended to flex her biceps, kissing her nonexistent guns. "I won."

Zeta's eyes landed on my face. "I see you played dirty and aimed for the eyes."

Dylan laced her fingers under her chin and blinked innocently. "What can I say? I fight like a girl, which means I *always* win."

Something amazing happened after Dylan said that. Zeta's features softened for the first time since I'd known her.

"You're smiling again." Zeta's eyes glittered, her attention fixed on her daughter. "Look at you. You're…you're…*happy*."

"Don't be ridiculous, Mom." Dylan wiped the smile off her face instantly, shooting me an embarrassed look. "Even if I were, it's not because of Cal."

"Apropos Cal—you're hired as a waitress at Descartes," Rhyland announced dryly, pulling out his phone and tossing it into my hands. He tucked his joint behind his ear. "Program your number and email in and we'll hammer out the small print. Congrats, kiddo."

"Yes!" I jumped up in the air, mustering some courage and offering my open palm for Rhyland to shake.

He stared at it dispassionately, not making a move. "No, thanks, sweetheart. Touching you is not on my agenda. I like my limbs exactly where they are."

Tucking my crusty cupcake hair behind my ear, I said, "I won't let you down. I promise."

"I won't let you *in*." Row marched toward Rhyland, fury rolling off him like vapor. "She isn't hired."

"I'm vetoing this one, Sir Frowns a Lot." Rhyland clapped Row's shoulder. "You need employees, and I need you off my back. Fair trade-off."

"Row, can I speak to you alone, please?" I pretzeled my fingers together. I didn't want this opportunity to go to waste. Plus, we'd been at each other's throats ever since I had gotten here. If I was going to worm my way back into Dylan's life, I needed to patch things up with him regardless of my potential employment.

"No," he said, point-blank.

"Ambrose Rhett Casablancas, where are your manners?" Zeta shrieked.

"The trash?" Dylan guessed.

"Buried twenty feet under, next to radioactive waste?" Rhyland suggested.

"Maybe he left them in the womb before you pushed him out," Dylan theorized, picking frosting from her split ends.

"What happened? You used to be fond of her." Zeta wiped her forehead with her elbow, a smear of spaghetti sauce running across it. "Give the girl the time of your day."

"Last time I gave her the time of my night, she ruined it." He bared his teeth at me.

I turned crimson red thinking about the night he had taken my virginity. "Can't we let bygones be bygones?" I asked hopefully.

"Stop saying *bye* and *gone* without leaving." Row's scowl deepened. "You're giving me false hope here."

"Please be reasonable." My voice was low and steady. I was beyond qualified, and he needed the help. Couldn't he look past his dislike for me?

"On the contrary, I'm very reasonable. I'm reasonably sure you and I are not going to get along as coworkers. Look, it's a small town, and I will probably run into you, but by God, I'm not going to actively let you into my goddamn sphere."

Sensing the urgency of the situation, I flung myself over to his corner of the room, pressing my hands together and bending my knees. My fingertips accidentally brushed his muscular forearm. A shock of electricity shot through my spine at our fleeting touch. "Row, plea—"

He pulled away fast, hissing as though my touch wounded him.

"Jesus Christ, get off me." *Get off him*? I had barely touched him. A look of pure panic must've shown on my face because I flushed hot, and cold shivers ran through me at the same time. Worse still, I felt my eyes stinging with tears. *You're not going to cry, girl.*

Not over a boy, and not over a job.

"*Fuck.*" His fingers caught the back of his hair, and he tugged roughly on the velvety strands. "You're hired." He pulled away from me like I was literal fire, rubbing at the spot where we'd touched like he wanted to clean himself. "Happy? You start tomorrow. Bring comfortable shoes and an entirely different personality. And don't—I repeat, *do not*—get anywhere near me. The kitchen is off-limits, you hear?"

"Ambrose." Zeta put a hand to her heart. The overlapping chatter stopped, and everybody was staring at him as though witnessing something greatly tragic.

"*You.*" Row ignored her, turning to Rhyland. "Send her a contract and our menu to learn. If she fucks up once, she is gone. If she fucks up *real* bad, you pay out of pocket for whatever she breaks. Understand?"

Rhyland saluted at him using only his middle finger.

"I won't let you down." I cleared my throat. But Row didn't hear me, still laser-focused on Rhyland.

"If you come onto her, I will kill you. If you make me regret it, I will resuscitate you, then *re*-kill you. If she screws anything up, I'm killing both of you. I want her out of my sight, out of my mind, and out of my fucking way. *Capisce?*" Row continued.

Rhyland flipped him off with a smile, then curled his middle finger and gave him a thumbs-up. "Clumsy me. Yeah, got it."

He turned to me now. "No verbal diarrhea, no offensive attire, and no arguing. Got it?"

"My attire is not offen—" I started protesting, before thinking better of it. "Right. Right. Sure thing, boss."

"Isn't she a ball of sunshine?" Rhyland all but clapped with delight. He loved seeing Row reining in his primal instinct to throttle me.

"Isn't *he* a bouquet of grumpiness?" Dylan gestured to her brother.

Row raked his fingers along the back of his neck, fisting his hair. "Goddammit." He turned around and stomped out of the room.

"You won't regret it!" I crooned after his descending back as he took the stairs down.

"Already fucking am."

CHAPTER ELEVEN
CAL

"Crush"—Jennifer Paige

FIVE YEARS AGO

It was the first summer Row came back from Paris, and the town was reeling with his presence.

Even though he wasn't yet famous, people lined up to meet him at the Casablancases' door like he was Mick Jagger, hoping some of his stardust rubbed off on them. They kissed the ring, gushed about his success, and begged for recipes they could wow their families and neighbors with. For the first time since Dylan and I were in kindergarten, Row didn't pay me any attention. Didn't tug my braid with a teasing smirk, sneak me the last piece of cherry pie, or give me a piggyback ride upstairs, purposefully banging me against the wall to make me laugh. Every time I visited my best friend and he was there, he'd award me with a silent nod and walk off. I was air, invisible and unnoteworthy.

To make matters worse, my traitorous hormones decided to notice him. I'd always known Row Casablancas was hot in the same way I always knew the sun was—you needed to be a moron not to recognize this simple fact of life. Yet, that summer, he'd returned with a new, foreign glow. An erotism my seventeen-year-old self simply couldn't ignore.

It stunned me that I couldn't take my eyes off Row because I didn't find guys attractive.

Scary? Yes. Untrustworthy? Always. Their physical advantage unnerved me. But not Row. Apparently, Row was in a different category than everyone else.

"Stop looking at my brother like that," Dylan warned me one day when we were lying on towels in her backyard, working on our tans. Row and Rhyland were across the lawn by the edge of the forest, chopping wood for wintertime. They were both shirtless, sweat glazing their skin, Row's golden cross necklace dangling between his sculpted pecs, glinting like the smooth surface of a sunlit lake.

Thump.

"Like what?" I pushed my sunglasses up my nose, feigning innocence.

"Like you're interested in his wood, and not the kind he's chopping." She hiked up onto her elbows, ripping her sunglasses from her eyes to award me with a scowl. "He can't be your next conquest, Cal, okay?"

Her words were ridiculous, but I only had myself to blame for the misconception.

Because I was a lying liar who lied and wanted to make sure everyone around me thought I led a normal, happy life. I was careful to tell Dylan I had crushes on boys, and that I kissed them often. I didn't want her to know that, on top of being the one who blinked all the time and suffered from social anxiety, I also had a violently fearful reaction to men. So I occasionally told her I made out with guys. I was careful to swear her to secrecy so as not to start vicious rumors about other people.

"Dude, I'm only looking at him because he is blocking my view of Rhy." Lie number 3,447,358 slipped past my lips.

"You are a terrible liar." Dylan took a slow sip of her iced tea. "Quit ogling my brother, Dot. Unless, of course, you're catching feelings for him."

Thump.

Wood splinters flew sideways under Row's axe. The scent of pine oil tinged my nostrils sharply. Row's abs contracted with each movement. He looked like an Abercrombie & Fitch Super Bowl ad. I waited for the part where I wanted to run away from him to kick in, but it never did.

"*Feelings?* For Row? Dude, no way." I sat up straight, horrified. Luckily, my complexion hid my intense blushing—I was already purple from trying to get a tan.

Thump.

Dylan scrunched her nose. "Wow. It's not that hard to believe, you know. He's a great guy."

"He is. Nonetheless, I'm not crushing on your brother," I lied. I was. Stalking his Instagram two hundred times a day, even though he was too cool to be on top of his social media. Tormenting myself by imagining all the chic European girls he hooked up with.

Thump, thump, thump.

Row's bronze deltoids and triceps bulged delectably under a thin coat of sweat.

"You better not be." Dylan jerked the straps of her bikini top down her shoulders to allow for an even tan. "He deserves a fairy tale, not some meaningless hookup."

"I don't even do that many hookups," I protested weakly. Zero was the number of hookups I'd had in recent years. Even that was exaggerated.

"Still. You only do crushes, never relationships."

Not in the mood to be reminded how Row was way above my league, I picked up my daisy dukes from the lawn and hopped up, slipping them on. "I better head home. Dad wants to teach me how to pickle eggs."

"Jesus, Cal." Rhyland stuck his axe's blade in the ground, retying his man-bun. "Some of us want to eat in this century."

"Don't slam it before you try it, Rhy." I winked, pretending that he didn't scare me. He did. A little. In a manageable way.

Row had his back to me, still chopping. He was pretty far away, but I could see the new tattoos snaking up and down his skin, swarming with colorful ink. I wanted him to turn around. To award me with his sleek, predatory gaze that turned me inside out.

"Fucking humidity is making it hot enough to scald a lizard." Rhyland grabbed his shirt from the yellowed grass, slipped it on, then began rolling himself a joint. "I'm tapping out. Cal, wanna bum a ride?"

I did, but I also didn't like the idea of being alone with a guy who wasn't Dad or Row. "Thanks, but I—"

"I'll drive her." Row hurled his axe against the tree trunk he'd used to chop the wood, burying the blade inside. He picked up a kitchen towel and wiped off his hands. "Gotta buy some ice anyway."

Can't you just shave some off your heart?

"Oh, I don't want to burden you." I braided my hair over my shoulder awkwardly.

Row threw me a dry look. "You're about a decade late and a dollar short. Get your stuff, Dot. Hopping in the shower, then we're leaving."

"Don't let her proposition you." Dylan cupped her mouth, yelling to him. "She made out with, like, four guys from our grade this year alone. Never know what she's carrying."

I kicked her ribs lightly, a smile on my face. A sharp stab of guilt sliced my chest open. I hated lying to her. "Thanks, Row."

Dylan lingered in the backyard, working on her tan and flipping through a magazine.

"Wait in the living room," Row instructed, shouldering past me on his way up the stairs. I followed him with my eyes, waiting for the faint sound of the shower to hit my ears, accompanied by the whining of the rusty pipes behind the walls. I took the stairs up to his room on my tippy-toes. I wanted to get a glimpse of Row's universe uninterrupted, something I'd never had a chance to do before. I didn't feel too bad about snooping. Row never had given a crap about privacy.

Once I entered the room, I breathed as shallowly as I could without losing consciousness to mask my presence there. I didn't know why I was feeling so self-conscious all of a sudden. It wasn't like I had a chance with him. Dude had fished chicken nuggets and queso from my hair when I'd drunk-vomited into his toilet in the middle of the night two years ago, after Dylan and I had stolen his dad's vodka and gotten shit-faced. He'd once caught Dylan popping a zit the size of Montana on my chin. There was no allure or mystery where I was concerned.

Row was taking his sweet time. The shower was still running, so I treated myself to a small tour of his room. In my defense, it was barely even his room anymore. Zeta had been using it as a makeshift pantry for all the sauces and olive oil she made and sold to the locals. I opened drawers, sifted through dilapidated vintage books, and rummaged through his closet. Most of his stuff was gone—sold or taken to Paris—but there was one drawer in his closet that seemed stuffed, full to the brim. It was jammed, so I had to yank it open using force. As soon as I did, huge stacks of paper greeted me. Documents…books…*pictures?* Yup. There were pictures there too. Funny, he didn't strike me as the sentimental type. I recognized one peeking out from the bottom of the mound, of me and Dylan at a county fair, and plucked it out with a smile. My beam collapsed when I realized he had cut me out of the picture. Scissored a square where my face had been.

What the…?

With trembling hands, I started going through the pictures in his drawer. There were dozens of them. All of them of me and Dylan, or just me. In all of them, my face had been cut out. What the hell? Why would he do this? We weren't friendly anymore, but we weren't enemies either, as far as I could tell. Tears prickled my eyes, but I didn't let them loose. The bedroom door opened with a familiar old-house grunt. I twisted around savagely, my cheeks stinging pink.

He stood there, his six-pack on full display, his hair a damp mess. A towel was wrapped around his slim waist. "What the fuck are you doing here, Dot?"

Hot, liquid anger swirled in my gut, making my entire body hum with fury. "Why?" I raised a stack of ruined pictures in my fist, tilting my chin up daringly. "Why do you hate me? What did I ever do to you?"

There was no other way to explain the sudden change in his behavior. His eyes met mine across the room. Surely, he couldn't break my heart before I gave it to him. He had no permission to do so.

What was I talking about? I had no heart to give. It'd been smashed into powder, ground into dust.

Then why is it pulsing so loudly between my legs now that it's just the two of us?

"It's not what you think," he said woodenly. His voice sounded foreign, detached; my knees buckled. He didn't deny it. God, what excuse could he have for doing something this mean? This *creepy?*

"You don't know what I think." A miserable smile slashed my face. "But tell me how it is anyway."

"Can't." Face expressionless. Eyes dead. Muscles stiff.

"Why?"

"Reasons."

"Reasons?" My neck and face heated further with rage. "That's not even an answer."

"Course it is." He ambled deeper into the room, unfastening his towel. I looked away, squeezing my eyes shut. Why was he a ruthless douchebag all of a sudden? What had I done to deserve this? "I don't owe you jack shit, Dot. You aren't my friend. Just my little sister's annoying sidekick."

By the rustling coming from his direction, I gathered he was getting dressed. "You used to like me," I heard myself say, and hated how childish and whiny I sounded.

"No, I used to *tolerate* you," he amended. "Still do."

My eyelids fluttered open, my pride overriding my fear. Luckily, he was already dressed, in ripped jeans and a worn-out white Henley, the clothes clinging to his defined muscles like they were sewn onto him.

"Cutting my face out of all of Dylan's pictures is actively hating me," I breathed out.

"Maybe you're not as lovable as you think." He tucked a cigarette behind his ear, smirking at me. I stared at him, dumbfounded. I didn't deserve this. Either he was going to tell me what the hell I'd done, or he could take a hike.

"Know what?" I grabbed my backpack from his floor, slinging it over my shoulder. "I'll walk home. Thanks for sending Rhyland off just so you could be a major dick to me."

"Speaking of dick, heard you've been getting lots of those recently."

"Yours is not gonna be one of them, so if that's why you're bitter…" I crouched down to tie my shoelaces. "Hope you stew on that fun fact."

I stormed out of his room, taking the stairs two at a time. My pulse was pounding between my ears. His parents weren't home, and Dylan was still outside, so there was no one to witness whatever shit show this was. I heard his feet pounding on the rotten wood of the Casablancases' stairs, and my heart dropped to the pit of my stomach. His hand caught me by the shoulder, spinning me around. He pinned me against the rails, panting hard, like he was running. We were flush against each other when I noticed his hands caged me from either side, fingers curled over the banisters. Our faces were so close, I could see the individual pieces of stubble on his face. My whole body drew in a breath, my nipples pebbling against my swimsuit, brushing the ragged fabric. Heat pulled beneath my navel, and I swore I could smell my own arousal. Could he too? Crap. I hoped not.

Row's jaw flexed. "Don't do this," he warned.

I waited for the fear to finally arrive. For the terror to kick in at our proximity. For my tics to make an appearance. But all I felt was burning desire and unbearable anger. Those two feelings danced together seamlessly, flooding the space between my thighs with heat. My breaths quickened, pulse pitter-pattering across my skin. "Do what?"

"Jump to conclusions." His throat bobbed, and he looked like he was struggling with something. His eyes dropped to my lips. "I don't hate you."

The alternative, that he *liked* me, had never occurred to me. Because even though Ambrose Casablancas always spared me his wrath, he was also too impossibly dazzling, popular, and gorgeous to notice me. He'd always had the most glamorous girls flung over his arm, and breaking hearts and noses were his official hobbies. There wasn't one woman in this town who wouldn't let him warm her bed.

"Why did you do this, Row?" I licked my lips, swallowing hard. I held his gaze, ignoring the confusion teeming inside me. The liquid honey that uncurled behind my belly button and how empty I felt. How…unsettled.

"Are you really that dumb?" His lips hit my ear; the hair on my arms stood on end.

"Are you really that rude?" I stomped on his foot. "Just answer the damn question."

He took a deep breath, closed his eyes, then opened them again. "Remember the paper ring I gave you?"

I rummaged my memory bank for a paper ring but came up empty-handed. "No?"

Row's jawline was a hard square line of annoyance, and he barely moved his mouth when he spoke. "You were in first grade. Everybody fake-married their classmates. Nobody offered for you, so I made you a paper ring to stop you from crying. You were a mess."

I stared at him, shocked. He had. Now I remembered that he had. But back then, he had just been Row, Dylan's awkward big brother.

"And when you were in ninth grade and forgot your lunch?" There was a desperate, determined zing in his eyes, like he wanted me to read between the lines. "I drove to Wendy's to buy you some, skipping physics."

"What are you trying to say, that you were once nice to me, so now you have a free pass to be a douchebag?" I thundered.

"No." His eyes crinkled with disappointment. Whatever I was supposed to understand, I didn't. "I'm saying I don't hate you and never have. I just don't want to be around you, and you should fucking respect that." His breath smelled of spearmint and cigarettes, and I wanted to kiss him. Wanted to know if he tasted as good as he smelled.

"But…why?"

"Because you're *temptation*." He released the banisters, slamming his fists against them with a loud thud. I jumped a little. "Look at you. With the sun on your skin, freckles everywhere, mouth red as a cherry. My dick swells just from knowing you and I share the same zip code. Whenever you speak, all I can do is stare at your mouth and imagine it wrapped around my cock. You're a shiny apple, and do you know what people do to shiny apples?" His nose glided down mine, and I could almost feel them. His pouty, perfect lips.

"What?" I croaked.

"You *eat* them." We were chest to chest. Heartbeat to heartbeat. "To the core."

Oh fuck. Best blush? *Anything* coming out of Row Casablancas's mouth.

I got it. We couldn't do this to Dylan. Act on this attraction. Throw caution to the wind. Nothing was worth letting her down.

Not even a taste of heaven. And besides, what good would it do me? I'd probably puke in his mouth from fear once he had his hands on me. My whole body felt like he'd set it on fire, tight and sensitive to the touch, and I wondered what would happen if he actually did touch me.

His gaze glided to my lips. I felt like he'd wrapped me in a soft, warm blanket. Like the universe had shrunk around us and we'd become the very center of it. Mostly, I felt safe because even when he was angry, he was my comfort object.

"I just…" My voice was strangled, pained. "I just can't stand the idea that you hate me. I don't know why. I just can't."

"I don't hate you." He couldn't help himself. He raised his hand and picked at the string of my bikini, careful to avoid my skin, rolling the thin material between his thumb and finger. We both watched, transfixed. "I so don't hate you it's not even fucking funny."

I pressed myself against the railings, closed my eyes, and enjoyed his proximity. No touching. No lines being crossed. Just his heat pulsating next to mine, feeding off each other's energy.

"Your little sister's annoying extension, right?" I gulped.

"No, Cal." His nostrils flared. "*Nothing* about how I feel for you is sisterly."

His fingers rolled south—still only touching my bikini string—skimming the area where the cord met the triangle covering my breast. It was so obvious my nipples were hard. I opened my eyes and saw how his stare glided to my breasts. My own gaze slid down, and I found him hard behind his jeans, his dick nearly poking my center. On instinct, I arched my back from the banister, my pussy meeting his cock through our clothes. Neither of us breathed for a second.

This was wrong. We were crossing a line now, and we both knew it.

"Ever wondered what it might feel like?" he surprised me by asking.

"What?" My voice was hoarse, my heart hammering its way out of my chest, cracking the bones embracing it, one beat at a time.

"Kissing each other."

All the time. "No." I shook my head, arching farther, my center meeting his, the imprint of his dick jamming the slit of my pussy through our clothes. *So delicious, so empty.* "Never."

"Fuck, Dot." He gave my bikini string a rough tug, loosening its hold. The right triangle dislodged, falling slightly, exposing the plump mount of my breast and one pink nipple. "You're always pretty, but especially when you lie."

"You think I'm pretty?" I bloomed beneath his gaze like a flower opening its petals to welcome the sun's rays. His eyes were on my breast, and panic swirled through me. The forbiddance of it all turned me on. The idea that Dylan could walk in on us any minute now and catch us. It made me even wetter.

"I think you're a liar too." His tongue traced his lower lip, eyes still on my nipple. "I think you lie all the time, to make people around you feel better. Don't you care about that?"

"No." I struggled to swallow, feeling his dick pulsating, growing even harder and thicker between my thighs. "Because now I think I know why you cut me out of all those pictures."

I was bluffing. Lying again. Because it frightened me that he saw through me. Through my act.

He placed his rough, warm palm on the base of my neck, stepping back to remove his dick from my core, and tilted my head up so our eyes were locked in a war, releasing the most devastating words I'd ever heard in the English language. "I wasn't the one who cut you out, Dot," he said. "Dylan did."

CHAPTER TWELVE
CAL

oBITCHuary: Well, I'm officially employed.

McMonster: Should I pop the champagne?

oBITCHuary: No. Save it. I'll smash it on my new boss's head when I get desperate.

McMonster: Hmm. Promising start.

oBITCHuary: The man legit despises me, Mac.

McMonster: I have a nickname now?

oBITCHuary: FOCUS.

McMonster: Right. Shitty boss. Why does he despise you?

oBITCHuary: I think because I once slept with him and it ended up with a lot of drama and zero orgasms for me. He was my first. And...well, my last. Pathetic, right?

McMonster: IDK. Maybe if he knew all that background he wouldn't hate you?

oBITCHuary: LOL. If he knew all that background he'd make fun of me until the cows came home.

McMonster: What does it mean, that you chose to sleep with him even though men make you anxious?

oBITCHuary: That I have terrible judgment?

McMonster: Or (playing devil's advocate here, bc that's apparently what he is) he doesn't make you feel threatened.

oBITCHuary: Don't take his side, Mac!

McMonster: I'm not taking any sides. I'm just making you look at the big picture.

oBITCHuary: The picture is wonky. And about to make me work my ass off. Ten-hour shifts.

McMonster: Suck it up, buttercup.

CHAPTER THIRTEEN
CAL

"There She Goes"—Sixpence None the Richer

"And then what happened?"

Mom chased her vodka shot with a pickle and some herring to take the bite off the alcohol. We were cocooned in our kitchen. I brought my shot of vodka to my lips and knocked it back with a pained groan. Semus, a.k.a. my sociopathic cat, was sitting in my lap, doing his best rumbling engine impression, purring his life away. He'd been peeing inside my sneakers ever since I'd moved back home, putting the message across that he hadn't appreciated my four-year absence.

"Then he said I was hired." I hiccupped. "Well, actually, he might've said I was *fired*. It was hard to tell, seeing as he looked like he was going to kill me."

"Row was always the dark and moody type." Mom let out a dreamy giggle. "It's part of his charm. They don't make 'em like that anymore."

"What, murder-y?" I squeezed one eye shut, scrunching my nose.

"Alpha-y. It's all about cinnamon rolls and consent these days."

"Yeah. Consent. So gross, right?" I pinned her with a pointed look.

Mom laughed. "Oh, you know what I mean."

I didn't, but I had bigger fish to fry. "Why does everyone hate him around here? What did he do?" I sank my nails into the seam between Semus's tail and back. He lifted his butt, eyeing the herring longingly while I massaged him.

"Oh, that nonsense. He's a scapegoat. I actually think he is trying to be helpful." Mom nibbled on a piece of raw onion. "Small-town folks really know how to blow things out of proportion."

"Blow *what* out of proportion?" Extracting information from my mother was like milking a shark. I moved to rub Semus behind the ear, knowing full well he would try to bite off my finger whenever he decided he was done with my ass. Every pet had its own theme. Cats' trope was enemies to lovers, hands down.

"Cal, gossip is the lowest form of conversation. I don't engage in it." Mom kicked back in her chair, staring up at the kitchen ceiling. "Especially about someone so—"

"Don't you dare say *nice*, Mamushka."

"I was going to say *brilliant*. Nice is such a mediocre thing to be. Row is extraordinary. Your father cared deeply about him."

This was news to me. When I found out that Dad and Row knew each other and cared about one another at the funeral, it gave me an unexplainably fuzzy feeling. Like returning to a home-cooked meal after a shitty day at work.

"Anyway, I'm so happy you got a job." She reached to pat my knee.

Semus slapped her away.

"So am I," I murmured into a bite of my shuba salad. *Happy* wasn't a word I would use to describe my upcoming employment at Descartes, though. *Terrified?* Sure. I could also get behind *worried*, *nervous*, and *vomit-y*. Now that I grew out of my awkward kid phase and was just awkward, period, I was going to get the undiluted version of him. And judging by what I'd seen on TV, I was in for a world of pain.

"But enough about my glamorous career. Mental health

check. How are you feeling, Mamushka?" I reached to pat Mom's knee.

"It comes and goes. One moment I feel fine. Normal, even. The next, I can't breathe." She paused pensively, before adding, "This morning I found a note Dad left me in my nightstand drawer."

Nightstand drawers had been Dad's favorite format of communication. He had left us notes there frequently. He'd liked the surprise element of it.

"What did it say?" I licked the shuba from my fork.

"He asked me for a favor, the cheeky man!" She burst out laughing.

"Are we buying a yacht and cruising the Mediterranean?" I asked hopefully. We could really use a vacation.

"Let me amend—he asked me for something that won't devastate me financially." Mom poured herself a third shot of homemade vodka with garlic. Babushka's recipe. "Something I've been wanting to do for a long time anyway."

"Sell your mittens?" My eyes widened, my fingers finding Semus's chin and neck for a little rub. Mom had made hundreds of pairs of mittens over the years, gifting them to anyone: NICU babies, friends of the family, and anyone else who was willing to take them.

She nodded sheepishly. "People like mittens, right?"

"Mamushka! Of course. What's not to like about mittens? They keep you warm, they're stylish, they rhyme with kittens. Can it get any better? I think not. Mittens are proof that God exists and that we're his children."

She laughed. "All right. I'll think about it. How do I even go about it?"

"You open an Etsy shop and sell them online. Super easy. I can set it up for you."

A beat of silence passed between us. "He might've left you something too," she said.

"Oh, I wouldn't count on it with my luck."

"What are you talking about?" She gasped. "Honey, your luck is fin—"

Halfway through her sentence, Semus bit my finger, drawing blood. I was just bringing a pickle to my mouth and jerked back, the pickle juice squirting into my eye.

"Motherfluffer!" I fell flat on my ass, causing the disloyal cat to jump for safety but not before sinking his claws into my thighs to remind me who was the boss. I rolled on the floor, screaming, "My eyes! My eyes!"

"Never mind. Go rest, Callichka. I'll do the dishes."

CHAPTER FOURTEEN
CAL

"Gold Soundz"—Pavement

Before I went to bed, I glared at my nightstand. It was covered in green leopard print that was peeling and curly. I was afraid to open the drawer.

What if Dad hadn't left me a request? A message? A keepsake to hold on to?

I started making up excuses for him in my head. Why should he have left me a note? It wasn't like I still lived here. He'd had no way of knowing I'd end up staying home for any amount of time. And he had seemed so forgetful, so spacey the months before he'd moved into hospice.

Just open it, Cal, you big stupid baby.

My heart felt like a mangled piece of paper, ready to be torn. *Decisions, decisions.* In the end, hope trumped fear. I pressed my eyes shut, curled my fingers around the knob, and pulled the drawer out inch by inch. I opened my eyes, holding my breath.

There was a small USPS envelope resting inside it, neatly sealed atop a pile of decade-old nail polish. My body wilted with relief. It was so supremely Dad to use a USPS envelope. He liked free stuff. Our ideal dinner used to be Costco samples with their sundae for dessert.

Padding over to my study area, I pulled a small metal ruler from my bleached denim pencil case and used it to rip the letter open. I tugged the single A4 page out along with a postcard, struggling for breath, knowing these were going to be the only new words I'd ever get from him.

My eyes burned at the sight of his familiar handwriting. He had the most distinctive penmanship. Cursive and neat, it looked like it belonged in another century.

Dear Callichka,

If you're reading this, it means that I'm gone. I hope you decided to spend a few weeks with your mother. I think you can both use the time together, and while I'm not sure what kept you away from Staindrop this long, running away from a problem never gets rid of it. Problems are like monsters. Fearing them only feeds them and makes them bigger. Please remember you are stronger than whatever wall is standing in your way. All you need is the right momentum (Newton, laws one, two, three).

My chest filled with warmth. The first thing he'd wanted from me, I'd already pledged to do—I was going to spend some time with Mom.

A little riddle to break the ice:
Question: Why did the scientist take out his doorbell?
Answer: Because he wanted to win the no-bell prize.
(Kindly pretend to laugh at this. If I find it extremely funny, even in my current state, then so should you.)
Now that you're in an agreeable mood, I need you to do a few things for me. Allow me to point out that you are not in a position to turn me down, complain, and/or argue because I'm:
1. Dead, and therefore cannot hear you.

2. Always right.

3. One hundred percent going to haunt you if you fail me. I have a lot of free time right now, Callichka. Do not try me.

I thought long and hard about what it was I wanted from you. Birthdays, if you ask me, are overrated. It is death days on which you are granted all your wishes. And sure, I could've asked you to finally start your podcast, get things moving, take the plunge. But I believe that you cannot rush art and growth. So I'm going to let you take your first steps into your career at your own pace, even if I find it outrageously slow.

I snorted. My dad had been a teenager when he'd moved to America. He'd still had this Soviet air about him. A sternness that had collectively labeled anyone without a steady career, two degrees, and the durability to drink their own body weight an utter, useless slacker.

These are my two requests for you (and remember, you CANNOT say no):

1. Take me somewhere nice and spread my ashes. Let me explain. I'm afraid your mother will use my presence in her living room as an excuse not to move on. She deserves to move on. Deserves to fall in love, to laugh, to enjoy the remainder of her days. Which brings me to my next point: I would really rather not be there, on the mantel, when she and her new partner make out for the first time. Yes, I want her to move on. No, I don't want it happening in front of my face. Or rather, dust. Spread my ashes somewhere beautiful and tranquil. Somewhere with a great view. Somewhere I can be free.

2. Remember how much you loved running? You stopped for the wrong reason. Whatever it was, it wasn't worth it. Pick it up again. You're not truly free until you break the chains of your fears. And you, Callichka, are afraid of running. Once you get rid of that anxiety, you will become invincible. You will record your

podcast. You will push the envelope. You were made for stardom.
So go on. Touch the sky. That's where I'll be waiting for you.
 I've enclosed a little something for you to consider. Just an idea.
 And always remember what I told you: the darkness envies the
moon because it helps the dark shine. Don't let people tell you, you
are anything less than perfect.

 Love you more than a flower loves the sun,
 —Dad

I was crying so hard, it took me ten minutes to manage to read the card Dad had included in his letter. It was a 10K run for a children's hospital in Portland. The run was set to take place here in Staindrop on Christmas Day, less than seven weeks away.

Admittedly, the slogan—*10K for Kiddies*—wasn't the height of sophisticated copywriting. It sounded diabolical, not to mention extremely illegal. But I got why Dad wanted me to do something like this. It would make me commit to running every day, something I hadn't done in years. It would be for a great cause—helping children. And it was also taking place right here, so it would force me to stick around for at least a few weeks.

"Jesus, Dad, you know I don't run." I shoved his letter and the postcard back into the envelope. In truth, I *loved* running. I just couldn't disassociate it from the worst day of my life. "Also, where am I going to release your ashes?" I shook my head.

A knock on my bedroom door startled me. I blew out a breath. "Open!"

"It's me," Mom piped from the other side. For some reason, I wasn't relieved she wasn't Row. She wedged her head between the door and the wall. "Well?"

I picked up the envelope and raised it, smiling with exhaustion.

Mom cupped her mouth, suppressing a gasp. "What did he ask you for?"

"To spread his ashes somewhere nice and make sure you move on and make out with someone on the couch."

"Oh dear." She blinked, digesting my words. "He was heavily medicated the last few weeks."

I snorted. "No, Mom. He loved you enough to want you to be happy, even if it's not with him. That's a good thing."

She struggled to swallow, waving a hand in the air. "Too soon to talk about this."

I decided to change the subject. "He also asked me to take up running again."

She bit down on her lower lip, toeing a circle on the carpet through her silk slippers. Semus materialized from behind her, meowing and looping himself through her legs. He curled his tail around her ankle and gave me a *Bitch's still here?* look.

I picked you up from the shelter, you ass.

"Mamushka, was it really that important to him I run again?" I asked. Though I already knew the answer. *Yes.* The way I'd given up on my passion, and the unknown reason for it, was traumatic for everyone in my household. My parents never quite believed my story of how I got the injuries. I still limped whenever I was excited or exhausted, even though I had gotten the all clear from my doctor years ago.

"You were really good at it," she admitted, wincing apologetically. "It made you happy, and your smile was his favorite view."

"Well, I'm too rusty." I slammed the envelope into my nightstand drawer, banging it shut. "I can barely walk without breaking a sweat," I lied. I was in good shape from years of busing tables and navigating through New York carless.

"There are seventy-year-olds running marathons." She readjusted the belt of her robe. "Besides, you seem in great shape to me."

"It's not that simple," I huffed.

Running wasn't just about running. It was also about other

things. It signified pain, humiliation, and uncertainty for me. Besides, if God wanted us to run, why had he invented Zumba and Pilates? They were so much more fun.

"Simple? No." She rapped her knuckles over my doorframe. "Worth it? Definitely. I don't think he wanted to make your life easy, though."

"No?" I looked at her miserably. "What did he want to make my life, then?"

"*Better*. Good night, Callichka."

"Good night, Mamushka."

CHAPTER FIFTEEN
ROW

oBITCHuary: Do you have a girlfriend?

McMonster: ???

oBITCHuary: I just realized I never asked.

McMonster: What does it matter?

oBITCHuary: Dunno. It just does. Would you answer? It's not a government secret.

oBITCHuary: (It isn't a government secret, right? Because I have the tendency to get myself into all sorts of unideal situations...and let's just say, I cannot take part in a witness protection program. I'd blow my cover before I chose a new name. In fact, how can one choose a new name? It's gonna take me forever. SO many options.)

McMonster: I don't have a girlfriend.

oBITCHuary: Boyfriend?

McMonster: No.

oBITCHuary: ANY kind of sexual/intimate partner?

McMonster: The answer is no.

oBITCHuary: Same for me.

McMonster: I know. We've discussed it.

oBITCHuary: Why are you single? Haven't found the right girl yet?

McMonster: Oh, I found her.

oBITCHuary: Then what is the problem?

McMonster: Only one of us fell.

oBITCHuary: Wow. I cannot imagine not falling for someone like you. Silly girl.

McMonster: That's the worst part, though.

McMonster: She isn't silly at all. She is fucking brilliant.

CHAPTER SIXTEEN
ROW

Well, well, well. If it wasn't the consequences of my fucking actions.

I was breaking out in fucking hives. And why wouldn't I be? I was allergic to Cal Litvin—and about to spend a whole lot of time with her. All because of Rhy, that thundercunt, who'd decided to make a point. If money was what she needed, I could've written her checks to keep her away.

Yet here I was, about to pick Cal up for her first shift at the restaurant because Little Miss Broke Ass didn't have a bike to her name, let alone a car. Her mom did own a car, but she also had errands to run. It always amazed me, the lengths I went to for my sister and mother. They had talked me into this disastrous arrangement.

"Rowy, you smell so good! Is that a new aftershave?" Mom crooned as soon as I walked through her door, the scent of her eggplant parmesan hanging thick in the air.

"No," I grumbled, trying to break loose from her leathery clutch as she pressed a kiss to my cheek. "Same cologne."

Which I haven't worn since I was sixteen.

Not that today was a special occasion or anything. I'd happened to find it in my bathroom cabinet when I was going through old medicine. Completely coincidental.

"Where's Dylan and what's-her-face?" I peered around.

"Upstairs. Making excited, giggly sounds again." Mom couldn't contain her grin as she perched her arm on the stairway handrail, looking up. "I guess Dylan forgave her for whatever she did, huh?"

"Guess so."

I hadn't, though, and my grudge was as big as my cock.

Once upon a time, I was in love with Calla Litvin. She had broken my heart in two. Whether she had done it knowingly or klutzily didn't matter. I wasn't letting her anywhere near that organ again.

The wood plank stairs rattled under my boots as I made my way upstairs to Dylan's room. Squeaking and shrieking filled my ears. Wherever that damn woman went, laughter followed. She was practically a clown. Staying the hell away wasn't going to be hard the second time around.

"Don't you dare!" Dylan crowed behind the door, snort-laughing. "Dot, it *hurts*! What are you doing? This is treason. If you leave a scar, I'll give you an irrational fear of colanders. Cease this fuckery."

A *scar*? What the fuck was she up to now?

"Trust me, okay? I read a manual on the internet. I'm eighty-three percent sure this'll work." Cal sounded breathless, like she was wrestling a bear in there.

"Normally, a certified nurse or a doctor does that, right?" Dylan sounded unconvinced.

"Sure. But I've seen videos. And I'm a pretty fast learner," Cal reassured her. "Other than that time I built an IKEA chair upside down. But I'd had one too many eggnogs and it was four a.m."

What the fuck? I wasn't going to let this woman-child hurt my unborn niece. I banged the door open with my fist without knocking.

"Get the hell away from my sis—"

Both of their heads flew up in unison. They were sitting on the bed. My sister had one breast in Cal's hand—covered by Cal, thank *fuck*—little plastic shot cups scattered everywhere around them.

"Sweet Jesus, Row!" Dylan quickly shimmied her shirt down, protecting her modesty. "I'm not decent!"

"Unfortunately, that's not new." I screwed my fingers into my eye sockets.

"Hey, Row," Cal chirped.

"Hey, pain in the ass."

"You're twenty minutes early." Cal raised one clear shot cup, squinting at it.

So now it was a crime to be punctual?

"Why were you trying to murder my sister's breast?" I glowered at Cal. The tips of her hair were lavender now, which probably meant she was feeling somewhat hopeful.

Don't worry, sweetheart, I'm about to rectify that situation quickly.

Cal perked up in her denim vest and kilt. If the phrase *You are what you wear* were a thing, she would be a color-blind toddler.

At least she wore Blundstones, a good waiting choice.

"I'll have you know I tried to squeeze colostrum for the baby so that when she arrives, she'll have all the nutritious goodness."

"It was horrible." Dylan hung her haunted glare on my face. "Squeezing colostrum is basically bullying your boobs until they cry."

"Too much info." I brought a palm up, shaking my head. "Too little alcohol in the world to erase the mental image. Dot, grab your shit. We're leaving."

"*Argh*, but it's so boring here alone in this stupid bed." Dylan rubbed at her belly, blowing a lock of hair from her face. "How many serial killer documentaries can one consume before becoming one?"

"I'll come back soon." Cal placed a hand on Dylan's shoulder, rubbing it soothingly. "With Sour Patch Kids, tamales, and refried beans."

"And you'll leave my nipples alone?" My sister's lower lip jutted out in a pout.

"No promises. We need to make sure Baby Reid has everything she needs." Cal hopped up to her feet, bending down to pick up her backpack, giving me an eyeful of her ass. I redirected my gaze to the ceiling, fighting a blush.

My sister barked out a laugh. I hated everyone and everything. Fuck my life. I should *not* be affected by this woman's unremarkable ass when I had supermodels throwing themselves at me on the reg.

"So, Cal, do you still find my brother hot?" Dylan tutted.

"No!" Cal's ears pinkened. "God, no! I... We... No."

I wanted to say the feeling was mutual, but unlike her, I wasn't a liar. Even though I despised her, it had to be said—Cal looked like a porcelain doll with those huge glittery sapphire eyes and strawberry mouth. The only things that made her look fully human were those freckles peppered across her nose, like poppy seeds.

Dylan's laugh transformed into a wicked cackle. "Oh God. You two."

"Don't worry. He hates me now." Cal shot me an accusing look. "Right, Row?"

I turned around and started down the stairs.

It was going to be a long-ass seven weeks.

CHAPTER SEVENTEEN
ROW

The drive to Descartes was spent mostly in silence, which was usually my favorite soundtrack. Not so much right now, though, because the person sitting next to me was full of funny tidbits, fascinating opinions, and quirky ideas my adolescent self itched to hear.

Cal tried to strike up conversation, but I cranked up the radio each time she did. Worked well, as there was some kind of Backstreet Boys special, so she was dancing in her seat, pointing at me every time she belted out the lyrics. She was a little ball of sunshine and I was a big gray cloud that wanted to piss acid rain on her parade.

At some point, I lit up a cigarette and rolled the window down. Her giant pair of blues immediately glued to the side of my face. She stared at me like I had just informed her I was kidnapping her to sell to the highest bidder.

"Could you not?" She cleared her throat.

"Could I not what?" She had better not tell me what to do in my own fucking car.

"Give me cancer not even a week after I said goodbye to my father who lost the battle to the illness."

Shit.

With a groan, I tossed the still-lit cigarette out the window.

"You should probably quit," she said.

"You should *definitely* shut up."

"Hey, I'm just looking out for you." She sounded genuine. But if that were the case, she wouldn't have broken my fucking heart all those years ago.

It annoyed the crap out of me that she was now contaminating my new Silverado. I'd had to get rid of the Mustang a couple years back because her white-musk-and-apples stench had been engraved into the seats. Now, here I was, surrounded by her scent again.

I was determined to keep Descartes afloat until we closed down. Showing Rhyland that I didn't feel jack shit for the woman was a side bonus. I never backed out of a challenge.

As soon as we arrived at Descartes, I disposed of Cal with the maître d' and told the latter to make sure she didn't set anything on fire.

"Especially the customers." I raised my index in the menace's direction.

Cal's sapphires flared. "That happened *once*. Who told you, anyway? I thought Rhyland was the one who talked to my references."

Jesus Christ.

Apparently, Cal had been trained in the day since my idiot best friend had hired her. Rhyland claimed she wasn't a complete disaster. But seeing as the klutz had walked into every glass door in town over the years and had once burned Mr. Wallace's toupee while trying to light his birthday cake candles, I had my doubts.

"Anyway, I'd like to begrudgingly admit this place is breathtaking." Cal tugged at her Dutch braids to loosen them. Everything she did was annoyingly sexy. The way she fixed her hair, sipped from her Stanley cup. *Breathed.*

"Shit, I thought you noticed," I said.

"Noticed what?"

"I have eyes and don't need you to state the fucking obvious."

Descartes was a work of art, every damn inch of it. Live ivy crawled up the arched ceiling. Makeshift trees spurted out of the center of each rustic table. The sleek iron bar and hand-painted china made the place a once-in-a-lifetime experience, and that was before they tasted my orgasmic food and heavily curated imported wine.

"You chose callas for flowers." Her eyes smiled right along with her lips. She picked purple and white flowers from one of the vases on a table, bringing the petals to her nose. "Aren't they the most beautiful thing in the world?"

No. Not even close. I swallowed.

"They're devastatingly toxic," I drawled. "Reminds me of someone, actually."

"It's probably going to be sad, saying goodbye to this place." She ignored my snark, looking around.

"Nothing will trump the happiness of not seeing you again," I maintained.

She put the flowers back in the vase carefully, her eyes ticking. "Can you at least pretend not to hate me?"

"Probably." I threw a batch of keys into her hands. "But it's not worth the effort. Go to the back office and get changed into your uniform."

Cal glared at the dozens of keys resting in her palm. "Which one is it?"

"Your guess is as good as mine."

"Row, there are, like, thirty keys here!" Her cheeks stained red. I hated being an asshole to her, but it had to be done. I couldn't let her worm her way back into my heart. Not even my dick. She was danger, and anyway, I was best alone.

"Forty-four. Better get goin'."

The maître d', Katie, winced at her. "Chef is an acquired taste."

"Uh-huh," Cal muttered, scorching my face with a blazing scowl. "Tastes like ass to me."

Katie gasped.

A muscle jumped in my jaw. "Do you want this job or not?"

Her tic returned in full force. *Blink, blink, blink.* She tried to control it by averting her gaze to the ceiling. "I'm starting to rethink it."

"That's a surprise." I just couldn't shut up apparently. "Thinking was never your strong suit."

She took a deep breath, flattened her lips, and tipped her chin up. Finally, she walked off toward my office upstairs. I punched the double swing doors to the back of the house, heading into my lair.

"Chef!" Taylor looked up from his station, dipping a spoon into a simmering sauce and tasting it. "Good afternoon."

"We'll see about that." I slipped into my chef shirt midwalk, buttoning it up. "How much Wagyu beef is in the house?" I parked my ass in front of the sink, scrubbing my hands and arms clean. My kitchen was neater than a hospital. All white uniforms and squeaky quartz tops. It had earned me a reputation as a frightening boss, but whoever survived under my reign for over a year was usually snatched by the competitors or went solo to see great success.

"About twenty pounds, Chef," one of my commis chefs called out.

"*About?*" I snapped my head up, shooting him a death glare. "Did I ask you to fucking guess? You better take your inventory before I step into my kitchen."

I fastened the buttons of my uniform shirt at rapid speed, scowling at everyone in my radius.

"Yes, Chef. What I meant is twenty-two pounds exactly, Chef," choked out the rookie.

"That's better."

"Thank you, Ch—"

"Where's my Wüsthof knife?"

My chef de partie muttered, "The *last* thing I'd give this man is a sharp object."

"Run that mouth again, Chef, and you'll be running to the unemployment center near you next." But I wasn't that much of a dweeb to fire someone for speaking the truth. Especially when that someone worked fourteen-hour shifts five times a week for me. This was a demanding, harsh business. Not for the faint of heart. And I fucking loved it.

Loved that it was stressful, full of tension, hard on the body and the soul. Loved that most people in my position were nursing a fucking cocaine habit to keep them functioning. Running a Michelin-starred kitchen was like waking up and going to war every day. I felt like Napoleon, high on that power. Food wasn't just food. Food was community; it was passion; it was art. It was the stepping stones of the body, nutrition, and science. It was chemistry and facts, and at the same time creative abandon. Food was *everything*.

A knife was handed to me by a brave soul, and I began sifting through my four-hour braised point-cut brisket. I tuned out the world and started working.

I cut, slashed, and scythed expertly, minding the overlapping muscles. My hands flew over the meat. This was my zone. My talent. My *thing*.

Making food was like stitching up a fantasy. Food was an erotic experience.

Cal's voice drifted into my mind.

"I'm starting to rethink it."

Normally, I didn't mind being a dick to people. But with her, I cared. She didn't like men for whatever reason. She might not like me, but at least she wasn't scared of me. Though that was about to change if I continued acting like a dickhead.

I slammed the knife against the tender meat, suppressing a grunt.

"Tastes like ass to me."

She hated me. Why wouldn't she? I had spent every moment since she'd gotten back reminding her I hated *her*. My fingers tripped over the knife, almost dropping it. I cursed softly.

It didn't help that I couldn't look directly at her. That her existence was a stench I couldn't unsmell. She was here now, not only in my territory but deep inside my head. Running circles in her little boots. I was just not used to having her in my vicinity. I'd get over my weird fixation in the next few weeks. Maybe even days.

You've gotten over her. She's the past.

But if that was the truth, why didn't I tell her I was McMonster?

My suspicion Cal was oBITCHuary had been confirmed the day she'd told me she was back in Staindrop. I'd put two and two together. And still, I didn't fess up.

A sharp pain ripped through my forefinger.

Shit.

Blood oozed from my index, a thin river of crimson snaking along the cutting board. A fragment of my skin was nailed to the meat, which would now need to be thrown into the trash. "Shit, boss, are you okay?" Taylor rushed in my direction, tearing a wad of paper towels and pressing them against my finger.

"I'd be better if you'd fuck off," I muttered. I hated being coddled.

It was the first time I had cut myself in the kitchen in over a decade.

And it was a great reminder of what I already knew.

When Cal was around, I bled.

———

My mood got progressively worse as the evening went on. Not because we were short on staff. We weren't. Rhy had managed to hire two qualified temps from Vermont at an outrageous hourly rate. Still, I was distracted, uneasy; I checked on Cal through the window slit between the kitchen and the bar to make sure she wasn't vomiting in anyone's soup or accidentally falling in their lap. Seemed like she wasn't.

Another thing she was not—a fine-dining server.

Her timings seemed acceptable, she properly cleared the tables, was well-groomed, and held a flawless posture. My issue was that she was friendly. *Too* friendly. Her giggle was in my ear all the fucking time. Contagious and joyful, even through the pockets of chatter and utensil noise. She stopped to chat with tables she wasn't in charge of. Often and at length. Leaned down and cooed over photos people showed her on their phones. She even helped one of the patrons with the zipper of her dress.

It was unprofessional. It was tacky. And it was getting on my last nerve.

Looking at her from the outside, you couldn't tell she had anxiety. But I knew better. I knew how she lied, how she bottled it all up to show a perfect front. Knew that deep inside, she was frightened of showing her true colors, her true feelings.

Like right now, Cal was standing in front of an elderly couple that screamed old money and appeared to be playing a game of charades with them. Either that, or I was witnessing her having a stroke. She contracted her face, then did a little dance that had the woman tipping her head back, laughing, and clapping.

Rhy glided into my kitchen armed with his iPad, going over inventory midshift. I grabbed him by the collar and dragged him over to the kitchen window, drawing petrified looks from my employees.

"Rhyland," I seethed.

"Ambrose." He was entirely unaffected by my behavior, even giving me his *I-know-you're-having-a-terrible-time* smirk. "I see you're in a good mood."

"I'll be in a better one once you explain yourself. What the fuck am I looking at?" I pointed at Cal through the partition. She fluttered around the room, a colorful butterfly flapping its wings. She landed at a table with two businessmen who eyed her like she was fucking dessert—and seemed to be in the middle of a fervent conversation with them. One that included whiskers, by the way she wiggled her fingers next to her nose. I did notice she stood as far away from them as possible, like she worried she'd be pounced on.

"The subject of your desire?" Rhyland braced an elbow on the windowsill.

"What. Is. She. Doing?"

"What *you* should be doing." He grabbed a cherry tomato from a nearby bowl, popping it in his mouth. "Working."

"She's making a spectacle of herself. Look at her." One of the businessmen sat back and *clapped*. Like she was a circus monkey. A dark flame kindled in my chest, urging me to dismember him like a lobster.

Rhyland shoved his head in the wide slit of the window, scratching his golden stubble. "I'm seeing a woman so lovable she just got tipped four Benjamins and refused to part ways with them when I explained to her we use a tip pool. Things almost got physical."

"But then you remembered I'd pelt you head to toe, turn you upside down, and stuff your inner organs with wasabi if you so much as lay a finger on her."

His grin widened. "You're so good at not loving her. Highly convincing."

"Shut up."

"I honestly haven't seen acting this bad since Tommy Wiseau." He smirked. "You deserve a Razzie Award."

"I hate you," I grumbled.

My best friend's chest rumbled with laughter. He tapped my back with the intention of breaking a bone or two. "Point is, people respond to her. She is personable, knows the entire menu by heart—cocktails and wine included—and never keeps customers waiting. Don't worry about her. She's doing great."

That's what I was worried about. It would be so much nicer to slip a check into her mailbox every weekend and forget she existed. A charity of sorts.

"These fecal matters are looking down her shirt." A muscle in my jaw twitched.

"The uniform is a turtleneck." Rhyland's brow knitted in confusion.

I ignored him. "Throw them out."

"Row, you can't start beefing with anyone who sniffs around Cal's ass."

What a ridiculous thing to say. Of course I could. I'd been doing that since she was in middle school. That someone had still managed to somehow hurt her along the way, make her find men distrustful, was something I took as a personal failure.

"Thought you said you're over her." He grabbed another cherry tomato, tossing it high in the air and catching it in his mouth.

"I am. Now I'm just paying it forward by making sure she isn't ruining more lives."

"Don't bother, Rhy." Taylor, wiping the residual accents off plates of poached lobster and fennel salad, sighed. "Chef's been like this all evening. Can't rip him away from that window."

"Am I no longer allowed to check on my own restaurant?" I turned to pin Taylor with a glare. "Also, your fennel–cucumber ratio is wrong. Start from scratch."

"There are no mistakes in art," Taylor pointed out.

"There are when it's in my fucking kitchen. Start. From. Scratch."

"Sorry, Taylor, gotta steal your boss for a few seconds." Rhy placed a hand on my back, leading me from the kitchen to the industrial pantry at the back of the restaurant.

"All yours!" Taylor gladly handed me over like a problem child who had shit on his day care cot. "Can you replace his batteries before you bring him back? He's out of focus today."

I watched as Rhyland closed the door to the cool, sprawling room. Five rows of fourteen-foot-high Sub-Zero metal shelves engulfed us. I leaned against the green leaves section, parsley poking into my ear.

Crossing my arms over my chest, I asked, "What do you want?"

Rhy smoothed out his suit, looking at me like I was an abandoned, drenched puppy. "Thought it was gonna be funny, but now I see the error of my ways. I may have stepped out of the Overton window, strong-arming you into hiring Cal. I wanted to make a point, and I made it. Since I now found replacements for Heather and Don—"

"We're not firing her." My nostrils flared.

I didn't want to give Cal more power than she already had. Her existence in my domain didn't throw me *that* off-kilter.

"You can't concentrate for shit," Rhyland said matter-of-factly.

"She demonstrated the 'Macarena' out there at some point." I pinched the bridge of my nose. "She's like a car accident. Hard to look away from but horrifying nonetheless. Just because she's got my attention doesn't mean that it's positive. I'm over her."

"Over her, my ass. Every time she bends over, you look like you need a cigarette. Look, I can give her a backend job. We need someone to do the filing, anyway. You'll never see he—"

"She's a decent server. You said so yourself, right?"

Rhy pursed his lips, his expression uncertain. "She's a highly endearing individual. Like, the human answer to a unicorn. This can't be news to you."

"She's still off-limits," I barked out.

He raised his palms up. "Hey, no problem there. I'm not ready for children yet, and she definitely is one. I'm worried, though."

"Why?"

"You give her too much power over you."

A sarcastic smile found my lips. "Power is never given, you fool. It is taken. And anyway, I'm more pissed off than enamored." I shrugged. "Keep her."

"What about you?" He gave me a skeptical look.

"I'll survive." I had once, hadn't I?

A knock on the door was followed by Taylor sticking his head inside. "Chef?"

"What?"

"Are you getting rid of our new server?"

I clenched and unclenched my fists. Was there anyone in this zip code who didn't want to get into Cal's pants?

"No. Why?"

"Because the entire kitchen loves her. I think she is singing an Adele song to one of the patrons." Taylor beamed. "Using a baguette as a microphone."

CHAPTER EIGHTEEN
ROW

The doors to the Silverado slammed behind us. Cal immediately reached to turn on the radio. I covered the volume knob with my palm before she could touch it. "We need to talk."

"Why?" she moaned. "We get along so much better when we don't."

"We get along best on different continents," I grumbled, ready to be done with the conversation before we'd begun.

She cocked her head, turning her entire body to look at me, the seat belt clasped inside her little hand. She breathed out a tired sigh, letting her head fall backward. "Please don't fire me. I just earned thirteen hundred bucks in tips and I think I might actually be able to afford renting some recording equipment when I get back to New York. I could finally start my business. I've been dreaming of starting a podcast since I wa—"

"Slow your roll, Little Miss Crapshine. One, I'm not gonna fire you. Two, I don't care what you do with the money you earned. Waste it, burn it, donate it to Satanists in need. If we're gonna work together, we need to set up some ground rules, though."

"Oh." She sat back, nibbling on the skin around her nail. "Sure."

The engine roared to life, the vehicle purring as I turned to face her. She was a sexy trainwreck decanted into a cheap uniform. Her light-brown hair was tangled in disarray. Pink tips framed her face.

Her cheeks matched them in color, and she looked so thoroughly fucked all I could think about was laying her down on my truck bed and fucking every single hole in her body until it was the shape of my cock.

Watching her waiting for my words made my dick hard. Come to think about it, watching her *breathe* made my dick hard. She could probably pick her nose and smear it all over my windshield and my dick would still go ramrod straight, awarding her with a standing ovation.

My issue was, there was no one else like Calla Litvin. I'd met plenty of sexy women over the years. Smart ones. Successful ones. Drop-dead gorgeous ones. But their qualities always carried that sameness that bored me. Cal was different. I never knew what was going to come out of her smart mouth. She approached everything she did with the enthusiasm and curiosity of a child…and the body of a *very* grown-up woman. It was time to douse her eagerness with a truth bomb.

"Not sure what you're used to doing down in Manhattan, but in Descartes, you will not be playing charades, dancing to infamous nineties songs, or singing Adele ballads to customers. You've made a fool out of yourself under my roof, and I won't tolerate it."

She blinked rapidly, digesting the words that seemed harsh even to my own ears. There were better ways to drive the point home. I could've had Rhyland put in a word. Unlike me, he had the tendency not to offend entire nations every time he opened his mouth.

"I understand," she said finally.

"You do?" My gaze swept skeptically over her face.

"Mm-hmm." She forced a smile on. I hit the accelerator, scowling at the road ahead. Her eyes clung to my face like they were the glue to keep it from falling.

"Problem?" I growled.

"Several, actually." She nodded. "Where shall I start?"

"How about telling me why I should care?"

"Because you have a conscience, and because, no matter what you say, you're a good-hearted person who historically stands up for what's right. When people's feelings are involved, there's—"

"Spare me the big Disney speech. Just spit it out." I clutched the steering wheel in a death grip. "Use as few words as possible."

"So I finally found out why everyone hates you. Suzanne, who owns the spa down the street, was one of my customers tonight. She filled me in." She puckered her lower lip, pinching at it between her fingers.

Here we go.

"Are you really going to do what they're saying you're going to do?" Cal asked worriedly.

"Yup." I itched to light up a cigarette.

"But…why?"

Descartes was built over an old railroad that was no longer in operation. I'd bought the land—all five acres of it—for a pitiful price and restored the train station building, turning it into a dazzling restaurant. Gutted it and spent most of my savings on it. I had attracted tourists. Revived this shithole. And put Staindrop on the map. Six months ago, when I'd received a jaw-dropping offer from GS Properties, one of America's biggest construction companies, to sell the land and everything on it, I hadn't thought twice. I'd needed a way out and a fat paycheck for my next venture, and they'd needed space to build a luxurious monster mall attached to a hotel close enough to the Canadian border.

I wanted to get out of here, fast. I'd already achieved what I came here to do and saw no need to stick around in Buttfuck Creek. That was why the locals were angry at me. For cashing out and handing the town's keys to a bunch of corporate suits who, in their eyes, were going to kill its quaint charm and small-town legacy and inject it with Botoxed designer stores.

"Why not?" I stroked my jaw. "Descartes was a vanity project. I came, I saw, I conquered. Time to move on. Selling the land is the logical thing to do."

"For you, maybe. But what about the people in this town? The small business owners? The folks who grew up here and stayed because they love the old-fashioned lifestyle?" Her entire body was angled toward me. I had her undivided attention, and suddenly I felt like someone had poured lava down the pit of my stomach.

You're not smitten. You're horny. Which is a form of excitement that can be dealt with using your right hand and some shower gel.

"The local morons couldn't spot a good idea if it hit them in the face with a Sub-Zero fridge," I drawled. "Building a five-star hotel is exactly what this place needs. Employment is nonexistent, opportunities are scarce, and once Descartes shuts down, people won't even make this a pit stop to get gas and take a piss. Whatever family businesses are still open here are struggling and would only benefit from the rush of tourism."

"Even if what you're saying is true, the station is the crown jewel of this town. It is the second oldest train station in America. It's historical. It's a holiday draw—"

"It's dead." I cut her off through gritted teeth. I didn't usually give a crap about criticism, especially not regarding this subject matter, but being seen as the villain in Cal's eyes didn't sit right with me. "You haven't been here in four years. Business is at a standstill, the population is in decline, the median salary is thirty percent lower than the national average. It's mostly elderly people and poor folks forced to stick around who are left. If building a hotel and a mall means cannibalizing one drawcard, I'll take my chances."

"It's not for you to decide though, is it?" She tilted her chin up courageously. "Let them vote. It's a democracy."

"The country is, my wallet isn't," I corrected her. "I'm selling."

"They'll never forgive you if you go ahead with it."

I took a right turn and entered her street, with its manicured trees, white picket fences, and ice cream–colored houses. "Good thing I don't give two shits about what people say, huh?"

"You think you're cool because your hackles are so far up you can't see past them." She shook her head.

"Don't patronize me, Dot." *What the fuck? What are you saying?* "I'm a self-made millionaire and not even twenty-seven. The shit I've achieved, you haven't learned how to spell yet." I needed to shut the fuck up and do it as soon as possible. I didn't like myself around her. The gap between Row and McMonster was insane.

Cal stared at me speechlessly. "Bite me."

"Thought you'd never ask. Just say where."

She looked pissed, but she didn't look scared. And I didn't know why, but it made me very fucking pleased that my sexual innuendos didn't scare her.

I parked in front of her house and unbuckled. "I'll walk you to the door."

She undid her seat belt. "No thanks. It's literally less than ten ste—"

"It was a statement, not an offer."

She massaged her temples, drawing an exasperated breath. "You're the only man I know who manages to be chivalrous and a complete jackass in the same breath. It's a talent."

"One of many—" The rest of the sentence died in my throat when I spotted Kieran fucking Carmichael loitering outside her door. At two in the goddamn morning. What was he doing here?

Was dying this week on his bucket list or something?

I didn't want her to feel targeted by some huge jock. He was obviously going to be a threat to her, which meant I had a great excuse to finally beat him to a pulp.

I tossed my door open, advancing toward him. With each step, the anger inside me simmered hotter. His stupid face was illuminated by the blue light shining from his smartphone. Probably rereading his favorite book—*How to be a Dickface: The Full Guide.*

"What's even the point of walking me to my door when you run ahead of me?" Cal moaned behind my back. Kieran's head snapped up from his screen, and his languid expression melted into wariness. "Casablancas. What are you doing here?"

"Was about to ask the same question. Channeling your inner Richard Ramirez?"

"Heard Cal's in town." Kieran leveled his gaze with mine. "Came to say hi."

"In the middle of the night?" I got into his face, my toes brushing his. He wore a popped-collar polo and futuristic sneakers. All he had left was to tattoo the word *douche* across his forehead.

Cal appeared at my side, wheezing from running after me. She slid between us, blocking me. "Thanks for the ride and the truly riveting conversation. Especially the part where you made me feel like shit. I'll take it from here."

"I'm not leaving before he does." I pointed at that asshole. I wasn't being protective; I was being responsible. I didn't want something happening to an employee of mine on my watch. *Yes, I'll go with that.*

Cal pushed me away with a huff. "Kieran is here because I invited him."

She'd *invited* him? I had no idea these two even knew each other. Kieran had graduated from high school the same year as me. They had no friends or hobbies in common.

You know nothing about her new life, shit face. They might be besties. With matching friendship bracelets and half-heart necklaces. For some reason, the last thought made me want to dip Kieran's head in a bleached toilet full of piranhas.

I had been so comfortable in the knowledge she didn't have a boyfriend, didn't have sex with other people, didn't date, that I forgot to factor in Cal was a liar. She could've lied to me as oBITCHuary. But no. That didn't seem right. She was truthful with McMonster. That was what made it so fucking hard to stop talking with her—the idea that I was somehow saving her, becoming her lifeline.

What if she'd invited Kieran over for a hookup because

McMonster had helped her overcome her fear of men? I was going to kill Kieran fifty times over.

"How do you know him?" I demanded. As if I had the right.

"Not that it's any of your business, but he tutored me for English through middle and high school." But as she said this, she folded her arms, shivering as she looked at him, and not from the cold. Was she uncomfortable? Had he done anything to her?

"Got extra credit for it," Kieran added with a smirk.

This tracked. Even though he was a smug piece of work, Kieran wasn't stupid. And he'd done a shit ton of extracurricular stuff at school to pad his CV.

"You don't need another asshole, Cal. You already have one," I pointed out. "Kieran, leave."

Did you just comment on her rectum? Really? There was no rock bottom when it came to my attitude with Cal. Rhy was right. Maybe we did need to move her to do some filing in the back office.

"Still a charmer, Row." Kieran's lips twisted in a smirk. "The people's prince. You know, Cal, he kicked me out of his restaurant last week."

"His ego couldn't handle a better-looking man sitting there," Cal guessed, stopping a good ten feet away from him. Yeah, she was definitely wary of him, even if she tried to hide it.

"Are you saying I'm handsome?" Kieran smirked.

"I'm saying Row isn't," she quipped back, burrowing deeper into her jacket and taking another step back from him.

Seriously, what had I done in a previous life to deserve this kind of karma? Decapitated puppies and kittens in the town square?

"What's he doing here?" I repeated, my tone cold. "You're an employee, and I'm not leaving until I know you're not in some kind of danger."

Cal's expression turned timid. "I've been having difficulties falling asleep since Dad passed away." She clutched at her arms, hugging herself. The wind swept those cherry-blossom hair strands over her face, and her cheeks turned a similar shade. That sobered me up. She had just lost her *father*. "I need company. Someone to talk to, to keep me away from my own thoughts."

"Could've taken you to Dylan's." I felt my nostrils flare.

"Dylan needs to rest."

"Could've talked to me." *Seriously. No. Rock. Bottom. None.*

"Sometimes I want to talk to someone who doesn't scowl or berate me."

"Specify next time, then. I'm not a fucking mind reader."

"You aren't? Well, then I won't keep you guessing—I want you to go away. *Now.*"

The tips of her small red mouth curved upward, and she brushed invisible lint from my shoulder. The touch was short-lived, but it was enough to make me swallow a hiss of depraved desire.

She. Touched. Me. Willingly. She never touched men. It had taken me a while to figure it out growing up. She'd hidden it with her half-assed lies about hooking up with randoms.

"I'm okay. I swear. Kieran won't hurt me." She dipped her chin, holding my gaze seriously. But her eyes told me another story. Her eyes told me to stay. To fight. That she wasn't feeling very safe at all.

Her eyes, or your delusions? Rhy's voice inquired in my head.

"I can stick arou—"

"Row? *Go.*"

I didn't want to leave her with Kieran. Didn't want to give them the opportunity to reconnect, laugh, talk. But it wasn't like I had a choice. And there was something else that pissed me off. The idiotic hope Kieran would make her feel better somehow.

Inhaling sharply, I turned around, descending her porch without a goodbye.

"Will you pick me up tomorrow?" Cal piped up behind my back.

I kept on moving toward my truck, not looking back. "If you're at Dylan's. Mom's house is on my way."

It wasn't, but I clung on to the last shreds of my self-respect like it was the edge of a cliff on Everest. She'd been here less than a week and already I had hired her and driven her around like a chauffeur. Way to maintain fucking distance.

I swung the driver's door open and started the engine, flicking the wipers on to get rid of a thin, icy crust on the windshield.

"Hey, Casablancas!" Kieran put his fingers in his mouth, whistling loudly before waving his hand. "Safe trip, buddy."

I flipped him off as I drove past her house and into the night. I rounded the curb, then parked in front of an unfamiliar house, choking the steering wheel with my fingers and grunting in frustration as I glued my forehead to the horn, letting loose a long, continuous blare. I then took out my cigarette pack and smoked four cigarettes in a row, until I became dizzy.

Cal was back, and so was my fascination with her.

I was officially, royally, and completely *fucked*.

CHAPTER NINETEEN
ROW

McMonster: You said you work as a server.

oBITCHuary: Yup.

McMonster: How do you handle working with men?

oBITCHuary: I'm mostly scared of men in private settings. Like, when I'm alone with a man in an elevator (which is never, I always leave), or when I'm alone on the street. When it's in a room full of people, I'm pretty certain no one is going to pounce on me. That's why I said we should meet for coffee. If we meet at a Starbucks, I am less likely to run away.

McMonster: LESS likely? Meaning it could still happen?

oBITCHuary: Hey, everything's on the table until you prove to be sane and not a cartel lord.

McMonster: Gotta love a woman with high standards.

McMonster: Are you an extrovert?

oBITCHuary: I think a lot of people would assume I am because I'm happy and upbeat. But...I'm just a people pleaser. There's a difference.

McMonster: What's the difference?

oBITCHuary: I act perky and happy because I want to make others feel better, not necessarily because I feel good. I just give them the oBITCHuary they want.

McMonster: A smart person would want the oBITCHuary you really are. There's no better version of you than your real self.

oBITCHuary: Aww. Did you get that from a fortune cookie?

McMonster: Brat.

McMonster: So.

oBITCHuary: Sooooo? 👀

McMonster: There's something I need to tell you.

oBITCHuary: Oh?

oBITCHuary: Are you a serial killer? Because that's going to be amazing for my podcast and disastrous for our friendship. Plus, you can forget about that coffee meeting I have planned for us when I come back to New York.

McMonster: I'm not a serial killer.

oBITCHuary: Is it going to make me like you less? Whatever it is you're going to tell me?

McMonster: 100%.

oBITCHuary: Then don't.

McMonster: ?

oBITCHuary: Seriously, don't. I like you. I don't like men. I want to continue liking you. Please don't burst my bubble. I feel like you're helping me make progress. I don't want to lose it.

McMonster: I'm not a liar.

oBITCHuary: You're not lying to me. You're omitting information I am disinterested in. There's a difference.

McMonster: No, there isn't.

oBITCHuary: Well, *I'm* a liar. So, you know, meet me in the middle. Jeez.

CHAPTER TWENTY
CAL

McMonster: Good night?

oBITCHuary: Hmm, I don't recall you ever contacting me in the middle of the night before. Has it been a good night for YOU?

McMonster: It's actually been an epic shit show.

oBITCHuary: Anything I can do to help?

McMonster: Yes. Let me tell you what I need to tell you.

oBITCHuary: Other than that. I really want to stay friends. I don't have many. And I'm still on probation with my childhood BFF.

McMonster: My, my, you can be selfish when you want.

oBITCHuary: Only with you.

McMonster: That's all right.

oBITCHuary: Why?

McMonster: Because you're the only person I'm selfless with too.

CHAPTER TWENTY-ONE
CAL

"Alive"—Pearl Jam

My alarm clock notified me that it was 6 a.m. by blaring into my ear in decibels that shook the purple walls of my bedroom. I smacked it off and rolled onto my stomach, moaning into my pillow. Even after a trillion-hour shift at Descartes and crying to Kieran for forty minutes straight about Dad, I still couldn't fall asleep last night. My mind was on overdrive, replaying my interactions with a certain sulky, tattooed chef the size of a prehistoric animal all night.

Row was right. Yesterday, Kieran's presence had caught me by surprise. I had texted him that I was feeling too sad and anxious to sleep, but I'd never expected him to show up at my house. Then again, I'd never expected Row to refuse to evacuate my premises. How did he know I felt uncomfortable around Kieran? How did he know I was scared?

Well, I wasn't scared *per se*, but I had sat on the other side of the wraparound porch of my house, across from Kieran, like a freak. Clutching my phone, 911 already saved on the screen just in case, as we'd talked into the night.

Now I needed to both keep my promise to Dad to pick up running again *and* somehow appear to be a functioning human for work today. My Spidey senses told me there was a lot of caffeine in my near future.

Dragging myself to my closet, I stuffed my legs into neon-green leggings, slipped on a pink Dri-FIT shirt with a matching headband, and grabbed a fanny pack for my keys and scrunchie. I also put on two yellow wristbands for the cuteness factor. I wasn't hoping to bump into Prince Charming. With my luck, I was more likely to bump into Ted Bundy. But Dad had loved this outfit. He'd said it screamed Cal, and it was a homage to him.

Mom was still asleep when I tiptoed my way out of the house. Cool, briny breeze assaulted my nostrils. I did a few torso twists and leg stretches on my front porch as I scanned my surroundings, dread drip-drip-dripping down my belly.

You can do this. There is nothing to be afraid of.

Only there was. Which was why I hadn't run in so many years. My worst memory was attached to running. But I couldn't let my father down. He hadn't known what made me stop running, but he had known that running was important to me. I needed to at least try.

There will be no evil men, no lonely woods, no bad people. Just you and the music. And your maddening urge to pee every time you run, probably.

Squaring my shoulders, I squinted beyond the mountains stretching along the coastline. I decided to take a two-mile route downtown, make a U-turn at the harbor, then jog back home. It was a familiar route—one I'd run with my dad often before my injury—and I knew there would be at least a handful of pedestrians around. After watching a ten-minute TED Talk about motivation on YouTube, I began power walking down the street. At first, I strode fast. This was no issue. I was used to walking—I was a New Yorker now, after all—then gradually, I picked up speed.

See? It's just like riding a bike. Minus the crotch pain and freezing fingers.

Soon, the soles of my shoes pounded the pavement. The first few minutes felt fine. Good, even. Physically, I broke the barrier. I was running again. Fast too. Then I realized…I *was* running. Just like that time when my life had turned upside down. A shock wave of anxiety zipped up my spine, and my whole body turned to ice.

Do it for Dad. Don't quit now.

Fear clogged my throat, cutting my oxygen supply. My heart pulsated violently in my chest, and my hands felt like two pillars of salt, heavy and foreign to the rest of my body. A persistent, dull pain throbbed in my right shin, reminding me of that day all those years ago. I was reliving that moment all over again. The memory crisp, vivid, and in full color.

The woods.

The blood.

The laughter.

"Leave the weirdo to die. It's not like anyone's gonna miss her."

Air. I needed air. I sucked in a breath, but my windpipe was crammed with lint. My vision swam. My eyesight became milky, fogged with terror; my mind screamed at my feet to stop moving, but they continued running of their own accord, going harder, faster; I looked around frantically. I wasn't on Main Street anymore. At some point, I had veered off course. There wasn't a soul on this residential, tree-lined street. No one to help me.

Calm down. Everything is okay. You just need to figure out how to stop moving.

But my brakeless feet wouldn't slow. My body was a broken vehicle, and all I could do was swerve it off the pathway to try to soften the blow.

"She dead yet?"

"Smells dead to me."

"I think it's the cabbage. Dirty Russian whore and her stinky food."

"Quick, let's go before her nerdiac friend finds out and gets us in trouble."

Tears needled my eyes, and I choked on the little air that still swirled in my lungs. Why had Dad asked me to do this? How careless could he have been? How cruel? This was a mistake. I'd have to—

Thwack.

Dirt filled my mouth, cold and crunchy. My face was pancaked over loose construction sand. I spat grit, slowly digesting that I had fallen down. Tripped over a stone and dived right onto my face. My right leg was scorching with pain.

I needed to move, stand up, call for help, but found that I was too paralyzed to do anything at all. The floodgate of memories had been broken, and the trauma I kept at bay was rushing like a river, drowning every positive thought in my head.

"Look at her leg."

"Ugh, gross."

"She's never gonna run again."

"Dot?"

The last voice belonged to the present. It also belonged to someone who absolutely despised me. What was Row doing awake, anyway? Did he ever sleep? Was he a vampire? I mean, he *was* painfully beautiful and permanently sulky. Though he *did* cook with garlic and wasn't destroyed by fire.

"Are you hurt?" His low, husky baritone rumbled over my head. My face was still stuck in the mud, which was currently my preferred location. Now was not a good time to face your former crush turned boss from hell. I shook my head without lifting it up, feeling so thoroughly mortified, I prayed for a deadly heart attack to spare me the conversation.

"Can you move?" he gruffed.

"Are you asking because I'm blocking your path or because you're worried about me?" I moaned.

"Can't afford to be one server short."

"And they say romance is dead." My lips moved around the claylike mud.

"Plus, you're on my property and I can smell an insurance claim from miles away."

Normally, I was the first to appreciate a good sarcastic quip. But I was currently spiraling worse than a Slinky over my pathetic attempt to run two miles, so all I managed was whimpering into the mud. I felt like an injured animal, cornered by a big bad wolf.

"Is it okay if I touch you?" His voice hovered above my head. He sounded like he was standing on a treetop. How tall was this man? "Just wanna make sure nothing is broken."

I am broken, Row. Permanently so. Even if my body is all healed.

"Gently," I croaked, feeling so pathetic I wanted to cry.

"Of course."

Row placed his palm between my shoulder blades. It was warm, heavy, and reassuring. A hint of a tremble danced through his fingertips. It wasn't too cold out, so it gave me pause. Maybe he was an alcoholic. That could also explain his mood swings.

"You gonna stay there for long?" he inquired.

"Maybe enough for a quick power nap," I mumbled into the dirt. "I thought you were going to check my leg isn't broken?"

"It's not your leg I'm worried about."

I hated that he always did that. Seemed to know so much more about me than anyone else. It was ridiculous, but sometimes I felt like he knew me better than Mom. He always knew when I lied and when I needed something I was too chicken to ask for. Like right now? I really needed that big warm, reassuring palm on me.

"How did it happen?" he asked quietly, his hand still on my back. I wanted him to keep it there forever. I also wanted him to go away and never come back.

"I was jogging. My legs kept running when I told them to stop. And then I kind of lost my vision for a moment and my breathing got all weird. I think maybe I'm broken." My voice cracked a little, and I felt like the tiniest, stupidest creature on planet Earth. "Best if you leave me to die here."

"Your broken is still the most whole thing I've seen."

Maybe I was hallucinating, but I could swear I heard McMonster. But of course I hadn't. McMonster was down in New York, and I'd never even heard his voice. Known his name. This was Row. Infuriating, sexy, my best friend's brother, Row.

"What?" I raised my face from the dirt, peeking at him.

"Didn't say anything." Row clasped my shoulders very gently, lifting me up to collapse over his broad chest. He was on his knees in the dirt, right there with me. And I wanted to throw a tantrum like a toddler because now I couldn't even hate him all the way. Underneath his relentlessly cold exterior was a compassionate creature who built the women in his life their dream house and *literally* pulled people from the mud.

God, please don't let me crush on him again. My heart couldn't survive season six of This Is Us; *what makes you think I can withstand him?*

I wanted love. I wanted sex. I wanted all the things other people had and I didn't. But I wanted them with someone I could trust. And that someone was McMonster. Not Row.

"Just leave," I moaned into his neck. He smelled like himself again, not the cologne I'd smelled yesterday when he'd come to pick me up. Of winter and leather, warm spices and Ambrose Casablancas. My skin hummed with pleasure.

"Dot, I'd never leave you like this." There was a two-second pause. "You're a construction hazard. Someone could trip all over you."

That made me snort out a laugh, which resulted in snot shooting out of my nostrils. In the absence of a tissue, I balled my shirt over my fist and quickly wiped my nose with my sleeve. "You didn't see that," I mumbled.

"See what?" He tugged me up to my feet, tucked me under his arm, then ushered me in the direction of the construction site I'd decided to fall in. I guessed it was Dylan's gift house. The place looked almost ready to move into.

"My wiping my nos—*ohhh*, I see what you did there." I sniffled, burying my face into his pecs to avoid eye contact. "Sorry about the, *erm*, nervous breakdown."

"That's all right. No one wears nervous breakdowns better than you." He gave my shoulder a squeeze.

Being in his arms felt good. No, not just good, *divine*. I could see myself getting addicted after that first hit. I felt like nothing could hurt me as long as he had his arm wrapped around me. Which was dumb because Row was the very thing that could rip me into shreds.

He shoved one fist into his front pocket. "So what do you think?" He jerked his chin to the property in front of us. "Tell me while I take you inside and break in that first-aid kit."

I blinked the dirt out of my eyes. "Oh. Wow."

This pretty much summed up my feelings toward the mansion. It was huge. One of those modern, avant-garde architecture thingies that looked like an origami piece. A low, wide white block of concrete. A wraparound pool engulfed the property, and bare cement steps led to the heavy front doors, which we ascended together. It looked futuristic and clinical. One of those homes you saw in reality TV shows and wondered how people actually lived in them.

"C'mon, Dot. You used more words than that to describe a tissue yesterday." He pushed the doors open.

"Hey, that was a supersoft tissue. My nose was very grateful. Was it the Costco brand?"

"Answer the question," he chided softly, and I knew what he was doing—taking my mind off my obvious panic attack. Keeping me engaged.

"Am I interrupting anything?" I looked around. My echo bounced across the walls and ceiling.

"No, I made a pit stop here before heading to the restaurant for an inventory count."

"You visit the restaurant *before* you pick me up?"

"Yeah. I get there at around ten, help with prep and inventory, staff meeting, marketing, then go back home for a quick shower before picking you up." Then he stayed until we closed shop, at around midnight.

"Do you have a life?" I blurted out.

"A *what*?" He feigned confusion, walking over to a beige luxury kitchen and popping open an exotic quartzite drawer. He produced a first-aid kit. "You hate the house, don't you?"

"*Hate* is such a strong word. I only hate political grifters and frosted tips as a hair trend. Even David Beckham couldn't pull it off."

"Are you going to tell me what you think about this house anytime in the next century?" He grabbed me by the waist and hoisted me onto one of the two kitchen islands facing each other. Like a lightning strike, every hair on my body stood on end. To make matters worse, he didn't let go of my waist while he pulled a wad of antiseptic wipes from a container. I wondered if he felt it too. Like he was brought to life by a simple touch.

Calm down, girlie. He doesn't like you. Just wants to make sure you don't die on his property.

"Should I check you for a concussion?" He scowled. "You haven't said anything in over a minute. I'm starting to get worried here."

"The house is…modern." I cleared my throat.

"And you don't like modern?" He propped my right leg up, straightening and holding it by the back of my ankle. Pulling my legging up, he exposed a nasty-looking scrape. It looked worse than it felt, oozing blood and dirt. "Gonna sting a bit. Pinch me if it gets to be too much." He slung one of my hands over his rock-hard shoulder.

Swoon.

"Modern is great." I swung my gaze upward, toward the ceiling, refusing to be turned on by this innocent, tender moment.

"Liar. You think it has all the charm of a Walmart warehouse."

"It's not what I'd choose for myself," I admitted.

He wiped my scraped shin with the antiseptic wipe, and I dug my fingernails into his shoulder with a wince. It burned worse than acetone on a paper cut. "Right. You'd go for something Victorian. Lots of arches, iron railings, church-like steeply pitched rooftop."

That was freakishly accurate. "Are you able to read people's minds? Like that Mel Gibson rom-com? Is that, like, a medical condition?"

"Absolutely not." He patted my shin clean of blood and dirt with the tenderness of a loving parent, and I dug my nails deeper into those jacked-up deltoids, this time not because it hurt but because I hadn't touched a man in years and was extremely deprived. "I make it a point not to read anything. Reading might lead to opening my horizons. I like 'em narrow and flat."

"You're not as bad as people think you are," I admitted begrudgingly. "More than anything, I think you're misunderstood."

"You sound like every woman who's ever tried to fix me."

"Don't worry, I won't try to do that. I don't have superpowers." I decided to change the subject. "So where do *you* live?"

"The Half Mile Inn, up on Main Street." He dumped the used antiseptic wipes into a nearby trash can and ripped open a gauze wrapper with his teeth, pressing it against my wound.

"You live in an *inn*?" My eyes bulged out.

"Yup." He draped a bandage around the gauze, securing it to my shin, still laser-focused on his task. "Have been since I moved back here."

"Why?"

He shrugged. "Don't wanna get comfortable somewhere I don't plan on staying. I purchased an apartment in Chelsea, though. I plan to stick around in London for at least eight years."

My heart deflated like a balloon, floating aimlessly before crashing in the pit of my stomach. I couldn't tell if it was because it meant the next goodbye would be morbidly final, or because I was jealous he was in a position to buy a whole-ass apartment when I couldn't even afford to rent a bike in New York. Either way, the pang of sadness unsettled me.

"That's…awesome!" I hopped off the marbled counter, all bandaged and good as new. "Uhm, thanks for wrapping me up. And for the distraction."

"You're welcome." He leaned against the opposite island, arms idly crossed across his chest, making his biceps bulge.

More staring. Zero words. I didn't move, and neither did he. In fact, we were both frozen in place, waiting for something, *anything*, to happen. It was just that…it was the first time since he'd taken my virginity that we weren't enemies, and I liked it. I *missed* it.

Too bad he has better things to do with his time than engage in a stare-off with you.

"I should leave," I blurted out again at the same time he said, "Wanna see the rest of the house?"

"Yes!" I shrieked. I didn't want to go. Didn't want to be alone with my thoughts.

He shook his head and chuckled, the international *you're-cute-but-ridiculous* male gesture, and it felt like my face had been licked by a group of squishy puppies. "Start with the living rooms." He cleared his throat, tilting his head sideways.

I followed his back, inwardly patting myself on the shoulder for my cunningness. Now I could ogle his butt and triceps to my heart's content, make impressed sounds, and he'd think it was the house I was admiring.

Row weaved through the two living rooms, giant pantry, dining room, kitchen, two downstairs bathrooms, and the adjoined cabana that spilled onto the backyard portion of the pool. There was a *lot* of house. I sincerely hoped Tucker's sense of direction was better than his grades in high school, otherwise the man was bound to get lost here frequently.

"Why'd you decide to take up running again?" Row asked when we were going up the stairs to the second floor (his butt was twelve out of ten, by the way).

"My dad bullied me into it. Made it his last wish. Can you

believe it?" I grumbled. "Guilt-tripping me beyond the grave. That's some next-level helicopter parent shit."

Row made a *hmm* sound. He didn't know what had happened to me that day. Even Dylan wasn't privy to the entire story. "What's so terrible about running?"

"I kind of have PTSD."

We ambled along the colossal hallway of the second floor, where he showed me the nursery, the guest room, and the laundry room. "From doing something healthy?" he taunted.

"From running."

"Why?"

"It reminds me of a very nasty injury...and a situation I never want to be in again."

"You won't be," he said decisively, stopping by the double doors of the master bedroom. "Know what you are?"

"What am I?" I had a feeling whatever he was going to say was going to change my life, so I had to listen carefully.

"Beef Wellington."

Okay, maybe not.

"I'm not following." I batted my eyelashes. What business did I have batting my lashes, anyway? Why was I flirting with this man, whom I found out yesterday wanted to *destroy* my childhood town? The place my beloved mom still lived in. Literally erase its identity and replace it with plastic, mass-market, easily digestible junk.

"You're a beef Wellington, Dot. All soft puff pastry on the outside, but once you take a bite, you realize the inside is almost always too raw."

"I'm not ra—"

"You do the happy-go-lucky schtick, and that's why you're stuck. Because you don't dare. Your father's right. Running again should be a priority for you. Otherwise, you're gonna be stuck in the same place forever."

"Thanks for the quick psychoanalysis." I picked up my pace,

which he matched easily. I was irrationally annoyed now. "But you know nothing about my life."

"I know enough. Yesterday you said you want to start a podcast. What's stopping you?" His expression was calm, his tone deadly.

"Hmm, life? I work a full-time job at a restaurant!" I tossed my hands in the air.

"Five days a week." He knotted his arms over his chest. "Two spare days to do whatever the fuck you want."

"Actually, I pulled some doubles in the last few months." To help pay Dad's hospital bills, but he didn't have to know that. "Anyway, I need money to rent recording equip—"

"The top-notch stuff, yeah. But some people start their podcasts recording themselves on their phones," he said, cutting me off. "What's your next excuse?"

I clamped my mouth shut, then opened it again. "I need to think very carefully about my first episode. If it's not good enough—"

"Then you make another badass episode. Record it from scratch. Send all the demos to your friends and get better after they give you feedback. I burned my first three omelets. The second one, I almost set fire to my entire house with. Didn't make me quit."

"Your medal's on the way."

He suppressed a smile, folding his arms and making me turn cherry red. "Next?"

"Stop, just stop." I poked his chest, partly because he was pissing me off but mostly because I wanted to see if it was as hard as it looked. Suspicion confirmed. "Nobody asked you for a pep talk."

"Well, I'm giving you one on the house." He stepped out of my way so I'd stop jabbing his chest. "You need to start running or you're never gonna get anywhere worth visiting."

"You saw my panic attack out there." I pointed at the door. "I can't."

"Of course you can. It will be hard, uncomfortable, but worth it." He leaned forward, popping the doors to the master bedroom open. "And if running alone scares you so much, ask your mom to run with you."

That made me snort out loud. "Mamushka's only cardio involves unscrewing the ice cream tub's lid every evening after dinner. And Dylan is pregnant with an entire day care." My shoulders slumped with a sigh. "Maybe I'll take Kieran."

He paused, his back to me, before pushing the doors open. "Good idea, if you need some deadweight. Fox Sports said his leg is busted."

Yesterday, Kieran had mentioned that he and Row weren't each other's greatest fans. He hadn't gotten into what had caused the rift but alluded to it being his fault. That he had been a dumb, power-drunk teenager and that he regretted the way he'd treated Row. This made me feel guilty about mentioning Kieran at all. Especially because Row's instincts last night had been right—I *hadn't* wanted to stay alone with Kieran. He had sort of ambushed me, and I'd felt like a caged animal throughout the entire duration of his visit.

Row continued, "And this is the maste—"

A blood-chilling shriek left my mouth, drowning out his last word.

"*Shit.*" Row backed out of the room, plastering his palm over my eyes to shield me from the image in front of us. Too late. It was already permanently seared into my brain.

"Is it *dead?*" I slapped his hand away, peering behind his massive shoulder. Violent nausea slammed into the back of my throat.

There was a coyote lying right in the middle of the empty room. It looked like roadkill, its eyes open, dead, and empty. Its guts spilled onto the floor. My eyes watered at the smell, and I palmed my mouth to keep myself from heaving.

"Unless the tire marks on its body are a fashion statement, I'm pretty sure it's dead." Row tugged me by the arm out of the room, turning me in the other direction and forcing me to march out into the hallway.

"This is sick."

"Agreed." But Row seemed more pissed off than surprised. Which begged the question—had he been the target of something similar before?

"Who could've done this?" I glanced over my shoulder at his face. Row advanced toward the hallway window in a daze, his scowl deepening, trying to see if someone was lurking nearby.

"Anyone of the nine hundred and twenty-eight people living in this town. Every single one of them is a suspect, seeing as they all hate my guts."

"This happened before?"

"I've had people pranking me, but this is some next-level shit. Vandalizing my property is a step too far." He squared his shoulders. "I'm going to break some skulls."

Well, this was terrible news to me.

Because just as he said that, I keeled over, emptying my stomach onto his brand-new lush carpets.

CHAPTER TWENTY-TWO
ROW

Row: You okay?

Cal: I was a second ago. Now a stranger is texting me and I'm a little freaked out. Who is this?

Row: Row.

Cal: Oh. Hi, boss. What do you want?

Row: To see if you're okay. Hence my above question. Program me in.

Cal: Aww. Casablancas. Are we having a moment?

Row: Of regret. You're my employee. I wanted to know whether you are good for service tonight. Get over yourself.

Cal: Boo.

Row: ARE YOU OKAY OR ARE YOU NOT OKAY? HOW HARD IS IT TO ANSWER A YES OR NO QUESTION?

Cal: I'm okay.

Row: Good.

Cal: Are you okay?

Row: Now that I'm about to finish this conversation? Very.

CHAPTER TWENTY-THREE
ROW

There were countless things I disliked in this world. A never-ending list of shit that ground my gears. To name a few: overcooked seafood, foreign films that won Oscars, *any* music made after 2015, the vast majority of humans, and porn that had more than three minutes of plot.

But the thing I loathed more than anything else, hands down, was getting visitors while I was working. Especially when I had to leave early for some bullshit town hall meeting.

Which was why I was currently every shade of pissed off under the sun.

"No visitors," I maintained to Rhy, charring an octopus at my sous-chef's station. Had I or had I not said I hated overcooked seafood?

Rhy wedged his shoulder between the metal shelves, which were laden with containers full of produce. The kitchen was approximately the temperature of the sun. "Listen, man, I get the frustration, but you gotta hear her out."

"No, I don't." I slid the perfectly browned octopus onto a plate with a poached egg, blackberry jam, and a mandarin salad. "Being accommodating is your trait. Being an asshole is mine."

"She's your ex-girlfriend." He puffed out his cheeks.

"*Ex* is the operative word here." But she had never been a

girlfriend either. Allison Murray and I had seen each other a handful of times when I'd first moved back. It had lasted barely a couple weeks. She was like a Range Rover. Pure status symbol and unreasonably high maintenance. Her entire allure was that Cal seemed to hate her, and Cal didn't hate anyone.

"Right." Rhy blew out an irritated exhale. "How about you need to see her because she's the mayor of the town you live in?"

I tossed another octopus into a buttered pan, sprinkling it with herbs. "Not for long."

"It's probably about GS Properties." Rhy unscrewed a bottle of S.Pellegrino, taking a long sip. "She might have info she doesn't want you to be ambushed with later today."

That got my attention. I grabbed a dishcloth from my station and wiped my hands, dumping it onto the butcher block. "Give me five. I'll meet her in the upstairs office."

I made a Rose Kennedy, double the vodka—her favorite—before trudging my way upstairs. Allison and I had never meshed well. She was the wrong type of go-getter, the kind that ran people over on her way places. She had tried too hard to impress me, to keep me, to seduce me, which resulted in me breaking things off before I'd even had a chance to take her for a spin.

When I pushed open the door to my office, Allison was already there. Perched on the edge of my L-shaped desk, legs crossed in a tight gray pencil skirt and a white blouse, the first three buttons undone.

She had scarlet hair and matching lipstick, and red-soled heels higher than Willie Nelson. At twenty-six, she was the youngest mayor in the United States. Impressive, even if Staindrop had fewer citizens than some sheds.

"Ambie." She looked up from her phone, setting it down and uncrossing her legs à la Sharon Stone in *Basic Instinct*. "I see you brought me my favorite." Her ruby lips parted alluringly.

"Pardon my shitty manners." I placed the cocktail on the desk and stepped back, resting a shoulder against the wall. "But what brings you in, Al? I gotta wrap things up before the town hall meeting tonight."

"Actually, the meeting is the reason I stopped by." She took a demure sip of her cocktail through the tiny black straws, blinking at me through synthetic lashes.

Allison always checked the pulse to see if I might be interested in taking her out for dinner—and having her as my dessert. It always flatlined. Monogamy wasn't my thing. I didn't want a family. Didn't want kids. Didn't want any dependents. The less responsibility I had, the fewer chances I had to fuck something up. Artem's voice chuckled in my head, *Simple math never lies.*

What's more, I had no idea why she was interested in me. She had seemed just as bored as I was the couple times we had gone on dates.

"Anything I need to know ahead of the meeting?" I pulled a cigarette from behind my ear, lighting it up. No Cal around to chide me for killing myself, thank God.

"Yes, there is." She glided from the desk, smoothing her hand over her skirt and trotting her way toward me. She slid one hand up my chest, her fingernails toying with the collar of my shirt, scraping the skin beneath it. The nails were red, like the rest of her.

Anger flared through me. Yesterday, I'd been hoping the hot, desire-soaked need to plow into Cal and fuck her until she was boneless was the result of being abstinent for too long. But no. Carrying a muddy, disheveled, panicked Cal to safety apparently made me harder than having a willing woman in a full sexy librarian outfit try to undress me in my back office. Clearly, there weren't enough years in my life for the amount of therapy I needed.

"Spit it out." I clasped her wrist, removing her hand from my chest. "And don't start with the regulatory bullshit. I spoke to the developers. They said the zoning falls just outside of the historical landmark's limit."

"It is. Well, technically, I guess." Her manicured fingernail trailed down the seam of my chef jacket again. "Still, I would feel soooo much more comfortable if you withdrew from the deal altogether."

"I'm not compression socks." My jaw clenched. "I'm not here to make you feel comfortable."

"*Ugh.* Ambie, be realistic here." She balled her fists, pounding them on my chest before letting out a brattish snarl. "This town has been historically maintained for the hundred and ten years of its existence. I cannot have it all go down the drain on *my* shift. You know how much money Daddy spent to make this happen?" She motioned toward herself. "I didn't come this far only to come this far."

Ah, the famous Tom Brady quote. Only Allison and Tom both had it wrong—sometimes, you needed to know when to quit.

It was no secret Mr. Murray had dropped serious bucks to make his little darling the most important person in this zip code. He wanted Allison in Congress and had the means to make it happen. I knew Staindrop was just a pit stop on her way to DC.

I slanted my head sideways. "I think what you mean to say is this place has been at a standstill for decades longer than it should have been. People are fleeing it by the dozens. Your population's been shrinking for nine years straight."

"Those who stay here like it the way it is." She curled her fingers with a pout, checking her pointy fingernails. "They're going to blame *me* for letting it happen."

"What do they expect you to do, murder me?" I arched an eyebrow.

"If that's what it takes." She screwed her lips into a scowl. "I contemplated this, but the odds weren't in my favor. With your size? I'd be lucky to give you a paper cut. Anyway, people are blaming me for what you're doing, and that's disastrous for my career trajectory."

"It's not ideal," I agreed.

"See?" She perked up. "Totally not ideal. It's not too late to—"

"But it is also not my fucking problem."

"Ugh, come on!" She threw herself at me, and now we were chest-to-chest, face-to-face, groin-to-groin, and my anger morphed into fury. This woman was all over me, and my dick was softer than a bath sponge. Yesterday, up to—fine, and *including*—the time I'd found a *dead fucking coyote* on my property, my erection could have been detected from Mars. In fact, that Cal hadn't noticed I was sporting a stiffy the size of the Empire State Building while showing her around attested to how out of it she had been.

I wasn't horny. I was just horny for Cal. Problem was, if I scratched that itch, I'd shed my flesh until I hit bone. I also didn't want her to do McMonster dirty. Which was fucking deranged.

Because I *was* McMonster.

"Do you really want to go down in the history books as the person who let the powerful boot of capitalism crush the romantic town of Staindrop?" Allison penetrated my thoughts.

I looked around the room, scratching my neck. "Don't flatter this shithole. No one is going to write a book about it."

"Ambie, I'm serious."

"Me too. Not even a leaflet. I doubt we're even on the map."

"If it's money that you nee—"

"Respectfully, Al? Fuck off." I was no charity case. If there was one thing I hated, it was people waving money in my face like I was a problem in need of fixing.

"You can't sell the land. It's historic. It's special. It's…it's…haunted!" She threw her arms out desperately. "That's a well-known fact."

I advanced toward the door. "Look, I appreciate the last-ditch effort to try to save your career, this town, or whatever it is you're fighting for, but it ain't happening. It's a good deal, and I'm taking it. I just built a house for Dylan and my mother and bought my own apartment in London. The cash flow will help, and I actually think the plan's good." I did. Not that it mattered to anyone. People couldn't see past their anger once you moved their cheese.

"You bought an apartment there?" Her throat bobbed, and she had that look in her eyes of a kitten that had been kicked to the curb.

I strangled the doorframe on a sigh. "Told you I'm leaving for good."

"I thought…" She rubbed at her temple, frowning. "I thought you meant in a few more years. Not…like, now."

"Seven weeks." *And not a moment too soon.*

"So you're basically killing this town, then bailing on it?" Her expression hardened, and she was pretty, but she wasn't Cal-pretty. Her skin glowed but wasn't punctuated by freckles. Her eyes were blue, but they didn't sparkle. And when she smiled, the world didn't stop spinning.

"Sadly, I'm bailing before." I bowed my head sarcastically. "The developer said they aren't going to break ground until next year. Blueprints are ready, though."

"And what is it that I'm hearing, that Calla Litvin is working for you now?" Allison changed the subject sharply, her eyes roaming my face wildly. "She's the poster child for useless. Are you doing your sister a favor? I thought Dylan finally ditched her all those years ago."

"Are we done here?" I folded my arms over my chest.

Allison shook her head. "She's a weirdo."

"Yeah?" My hand grabbed the doorknob. "Well, normal people are boring, and ordinary and average are fucking synonyms. Who wants to be that?"

"Wait, Ambie, come back here! We're not done talking."

She started chasing after me. My answer came in the form of the door being slammed in her face.

CHAPTER TWENTY-FOUR
ROW

oBITCHuary: Can you send me a picture of your ear?

oBITCHuary: Any ear would be fine (but left is best).

McMonster: Have you been day drinking?

McMonster: WHY?

oBITCHuary: I find ears attractive. Like, when I look at a man (in pictures, I'm mostly too horrified to check them out IRL) I always look at the ears. I'm trying to see if we could be a good match.

McMonster: I thought you only wanted to be friends.

oBITCHuary: Ugh. You are a master negotiator. Trade-off?

McMonster: I don't mean to sound rude, but I really couldn't give two craps about your ears, Bitchy.

oBITCHuary: Well, Mac, I was thinking more...like...a picture of my lips?

McMonster: Which pair?

oBITCHuary: Sheeeesh.

<oBITCHuary sent an attachment>

McMonster: Very kissable.

<McMonster sent an attachment>

McMonster: Verdict?

oBITCHuary: Also very kissable.

McMonster: You're weird.

oBITCHuary: But you love it.

McMonster: But I love it.

CHAPTER TWENTY-FIVE
ROW

Staindrop's library was a two-story redbrick colonial building with bottle-green shutters and a sage roof to match. Both the American and Maine flags danced in the wind on either side of the arched white entryway. By the number of cars parked along Main Street, I gathered every single asshole in the town was in attendance.

I slammed the Silverado's door and trudged my way in, muttering profanity all throughout. I went past security, guessing such a measure had been taken precisely to prevent someone from putting a hole through my head. *Thank you, Allison.* An unfamiliar guard patted me down with inappropriate gusto. Swore he copped a feel when he reached my nether region.

It was nice to see an unfamiliar face, though. Then he started talking and ruined everything.

"Where are you workin' out? You're buff, nice definition." He tried to make small talk while running his fingers over my biceps and maintaining eye contact. "Just moved up here with the wife from Alabama and lookin' for a good gym. Not into the CrossFit nonsense and all that jazz. Just need an old-school place."

"I work out at running a kitchen for sixteen hours a day," I provided dryly.

He laughed. I didn't. His smile vanished. "I see what it's like. Good day, sir."

"That ship's sailed." I shouldered past him, going through the double doors of the conference room, which could easily moonlight as a high school theater. It was stuffy and windowless, with old creaking floorboards and a stage that had seen better days. Probably during World War II.

Allison was already sitting onstage behind two classroom desks pushed together, her lips pressed against a microphone, wearing a sensible blazer and too much makeup. She looked flustered. Contrary to general belief, I didn't enjoy seeing people suffer. I just didn't care much unless they were blood related.

Next to her were her assistant, Lucinda, the council members' spokesperson, Melinda Finch, and a clerk recording the meeting—old Robbie Smith.

The room was crammed with wooden library chairs, which were occupied by townsfolk who stared at me like I'd just stirred their soup with my dick.

Allison acknowledged my presence by letting out a prissy huff and giving Lucinda a pointed look, jerking her head in my direction.

"Ten minutes late, but at least he made it, ladies and gents." A sugary grin stretched across the mayor's face.

"Wouldn't miss it for the world." I proceeded inside. If I was going down, might as well do it in a fashion. People booed from the crowd. I ambled nonchalantly past them.

"Mr. Casablancas, please join us on the podium to answer questions regarding the impending deal with GS Properties."

"I'm still not sure where the recording button is…" Robbie, beside her, stabbed his laptop keyboard, recoiling quickly, as if it were going to bite him. He had cotton candy–white hair floating over his head like a halo, suspenders, and thick-framed glasses.

"Go, Rowy! We love you!" My sister pumped her fist in the air from the ocean of wooden chairs, letting loose a loud whistle. "Woot woot."

I kept my pace even, my posture straight as I shot her a glare.

"What're you doing here? You're supposed to be on bed rest." Her beaming face nestled among a hundred scowls in the crowd.

"You're my beloved big bro. If you're to be publicly crucified, you know I'll always be there."

"To support him?" Mom smiled.

"To livestream the entire thing."

My mother began huffing and making dissatisfied faces, while Dylan waved me off. "But seriously, don't worry about me. Mom is here to keep me safe. Dot too. She's my bitch now!"

Sure enough, I spotted Cal, with her black overalls and white turtleneck and that face that was equally fascinating and painful to look at. My own personal sun, shining too bright and too hot.

She gave me an awkward wave, and I almost tripped, it threw me off so badly.

Then I noticed Kieran. He was sitting next to Cal, wearing a designer peacoat with the collar popped straight like a *Succession* character. Was he vying for the Douchebag World Championship? If so, he could count on my vote.

Also—why wasn't Cal at work? Guess it was her day off. I'd made a point of not checking the schedule to prove to myself I didn't care.

Great job, assface. Very convincing.

I took my place onstage between Robbie and Allison. The old man was still wrestling with his laptop, physically grabbing and shaking it into submission. He whipped his head in my direction. "Got any idea how to record on this thing?"

Scooting my chair closer to his, I peered at the screen and double-clicked the recording software. "Is it connected to the camera on that tripod?"

"Should it be?" The man's bushy white eyebrows flew to his forehead. "I'm filling in for Helene. Don't have the greenest clue how to operate this thing."

It took me eight more minutes to connect the camera to the

computer so that my public crucifixion could be documented in full-color HD. When I retook my seat, Allison announced that she would moderate the town hall meeting, in which the topic at hand would be me signing the GS deal and what it meant for the future of Staindrop.

"Also, just to address the elephant in the room, even though Ambie—I mean, Mr. Casablancas—and I used to be partners, I assure you I will be treating this with the utmost professionalism this town deserves."

We had never been partners. This shit had gone too far. I turned to look at Cal despite my better judgment. Her face was blank, caged up. What did I expect? To see her bawling into her ridiculous Lego-shaped purse? She'd never wanted me. Even when I had been balls-deep inside her, she'd been doing it so she could fuck off to college hymen free.

"Thank you, Miss Murray, for being less discreet than a ten-foot dildo," I drawled, perching back lazily in my seat. People gasped.

"Excuse his unpalatable sense of humor." Allison sent me a flirtatious smile from across the panel, even though I knew she wanted to kill me for that last comment. "Now, please raise your hand if you have any specific questions regarding the contract with GS or what it might entail."

A group of elderly women shot up from their seats in the front row.

The Righteous Gang.

I knew them well. They were town hall staples. There to yell when the first Starbucks had opened in town (then closed three months later), when I'd transformed the old train station into Descartes, or when a kid had ridden their bike on the street between two and four in the afternoon. Everything, from the width of the crosswalks to the fucking weather, offended them.

"We made a song of protest." Agnes, the one with the orange-green sweater and hat made out of *leaves*, rose to her feet.

"Of course you did." I slouched back in my chair, folding my arms over my chest.

"What's that supposed to mean?" Mildred, clad in a bandana and a peace sign necklace, thundered. "What happened to the lovely boy who used to mow my lawn?"

She referred to me, but that didn't stop me from answering, "He probably moved down south, where the minimum wage is at least five bucks an hour more. This is why you should want me to sell. You need more jobs in this shithole."

A collective gasp filled the air. I ignored it. I spoke the truth and let everyone squirm and deal with the consequences.

"Perhaps this isn't the best time for a song." Allison's crisp, impatient smile reeked of fury. "Any questions? Concerns? Input?"

"I don't think this thing is recording." Robbie squinted at his screen.

"We're singing our song," Gertrude, the founding member of the Righteous Gang, declared solemnly, shaking her walking cane in our direction. "Our voices will be heard."

"Would you mind?" Allison glanced at me, uncertain. "I want to get this thing going."

Channeling my inner Simon Cowell, I nodded. "Floor's yours, ladies."

The three lifted their faces upward and belted out their song in a cadence they one hundred percent had ripped off from Eminem's "Stan."

Dear Row, we wrote to you, but you didn't answer
We also left messages in your voicemail, texts, and
whatnot—are you even listenin'?
This town ain't just yours; it's also mine.
You know what ruining it would be? Yeah, you
guessed it—a crime.
Especially as you haven't even been around in so long

There's a word for how you treated all them people on
TV—it's called wrong.
Anyway, hey, you know the thing about Maiden
Cliff's old train station?
It's been there since before your parents were born—it's
one of the founding railways of our nation.
We used to be your biggest fans, that's the saddest part.
We even screened your Thanksgiving cooking special in
the museum of art.
Now you're nothing to be proud of, just a villain in
Staindrop's story.
Mark our words, you'll be the last one to say you're
sorry.

Gertie dropped an invisible mic to the floor, folding her arms over her chest and doing a peace sign with her fingers. Mildred slipped on her shades casually. The entire room stood up and clapped, cheering and whistling. I had to hand it to them—that was pretty neat. I'd have given them my Grammy if I didn't think they'd use it to maim me.

"Well?" Agnes probed. "What do you say, Mr. Casablancas?"

"While I enjoyed your little stunt—wasted talent, by the way—I like the sound of getting eight million dollars richer next month even better. That's when I'll be signing the contract, by the way."

That caused a little more commotion. And when I say *a little*, I mean *a fuck ton*. There was screaming involved. "Bad apple," "patronizing prick," and "Satan's spawn" were all hurled my way, as well as some personal items and one orthopedic shoe.

Randy, forever the overachiever, threw a chair toward the stage but missed by at least three feet. Chaos erupted, with everyone's wrath focused on me. I just sat there, cool as a cucumber, wondering what to make myself for dinner.

Allison shot up from her seat. "Everybody needs to calm down.

There is no need to get physical. This is not the Staindrop way to settle things!"

"Ah, zip it. If it wasn't for Daddy buying you this job, you'd be glazing donuts at Dahlia's Diner down the street," Lyle rumbled into his thermos from my right side.

"I would never have her!" Dahlia proclaimed from the depths of the auditorium. "She'd probably lick them à la Ariana Grande."

"This is going to change the entire makeup of the town. Business owners are gonna go hungry," another woman piped up.

"Who's gonna pay my kid's college fees? My utility bills once money stops rollin' in?" Randy barked from the end of the room, ripping his baseball cap from his head and dumping it on the floor. "I run a goddamn food mart. They're bringin' in a Hannaford!"

"What about my inn?" Gertie patted her nose with a crumpled tissue. "The one *you're* staying in, young man."

"A mall would stand out here like a sore thumb." Melinda Fitch sniffed from the other side of the table we were occupying. "I would hate for big modern eyesores to stain our unique landscape. People come here from all over to admire the quaint view."

"Too bad they don't stick around to buy a cup of coffee, pump their gas, and get a souvenir," I shot back. "You're running this place into the ground, and just because you don't like change, doesn't mean you don't need it. If you'd see the blueprints—"

"Absolutely not!" Allison shook her head vehemently. "They'll be overwhelmed and even more upset if you show them what kind of monster you want to build here."

It wasn't that I didn't understand where the townsfolk were coming from. It was that I: (A) thought the pros outweighed the cons in opening up the town and (B) didn't give a shit either way. I had come here for vengeance and gotten it. It was time to move on.

Letting out a provocative yawn, I explained, "Folks, I do apologize, but I don't have time for songs and dances. If you've got a specific question, I'll answer it. I've read the plan, studied the blueprints, and know the vision for the hotel and mall they're planning here. Otherwise, let me go back to the only business in Staindrop that's currently not losing money." I spun the ring on my pinky finger. "And while I've got your attention—I would refrain from pranking my ass with roadkill and hate mail. In case you haven't noticed, I don't play so well with others, and when I hit back, it's much, *much* harder."

Randy snorted from the end of the room. "Not as hard as the punch I've got saved for you, boy."

My eyes slowly lifted to his. "I smell a fucking challenge, Randy. Let's go outside and test it out."

"No!" Allison yelped. "Stop this nonsense. No one is punching anyone. I don't need this headline attached to my name."

The town hall meeting lasted for another forty minutes, during which I got grilled about the details in my as-yet-unsigned contract with GS Properties. I answered questions honestly and to the point, reminding people every now and then that I was volunteering information they had no business asking me for.

By the time the meeting was over, so was my will to live. I had a migraine that threatened to split my head in half and was in no mood to return to Descartes. I waited for the room to empty and helped Robbie with his laptop while people filed out. Mom, Dylan, Cal, and Fuckface loitered near the stage, with the latter helping stack chairs into a tall pile, one on top of the other.

"Man, that was brutal." Captain Obvious, a.k.a. Kieran, wiped invisible sweat from his forehead after pushing a stack of chairs to the far corner of the room. "You okay, bro?"

"Not your bro." I hopped off the stage. "And not your business. Dylan." I spun on my heel, facing my sister. "You shouldn't be on your feet. Let's go."

"Is it just me, or does Allison have more plastic on her face than the Container Store?" Dylan chatted happily, ignoring the tension hanging thickly in the air as she rubbed the small of her back. "Did she have a mini facelift? And like, why? She's younger than some of the cans Mom has in the pantry."

"Honey, you handled it *so* well." Mom laced her arm through mine, smiling sympathetically.

I peered at Cal, but she seemed busy reading something on her phone, determined not to give me the time of the day.

Was she pissed about Allison? If so, good.

"He held back on the snark," Kieran agreed. Why was Fuckface being nice to me? He had nothing to gain from this. Maybe he wasn't a world-class prick anymore (though I highly doubted it), but there was still no need to suck up to me. Unless he wanted to show Cal he was a good guy. The thought made me want to kill him violently, creatively, and slowly. "He only offended eighty percent of the people in the room, if that."

"Honestly? Who cares about that train station?" Dylan puffed, rubbing at her belly as she wobbled toward the exit. "Before Row bought it and made it a restaurant, it was straight-up deserted. It smelled of piss, weed, and garbage."

"People are afraid of change, *signorina*," Mom said quietly, a shudder only I noticed moving through her. "That's why we keep making the same mistakes."

Only Cal remained curiously silent. Ironically, it was her words I craved more than anyone else's. I nudged her with my elbow. "Earth to Dot. Now's your turn to lay into me. Your five minutes start now."

"Pass." She took a sip of her coffee. Probably some offensive pumpkin latte bullshit. "What they did to you was brutal, and I believe everyone deserves a bit of grace. Even, and especially, those who don't give it to others. I will, however, give you a generous piece of my mind tomorrow, when you pick me up for work." She tried to smile, but I didn't see any teeth. "That gives me a full twelve minutes, not five."

"Are you timing our rides together?"

She hitched one dainty shoulder up. "The arctic gusts of wind

from your scowls give me chills. Pumpkin spice latte?" She aimed
the coffee at me.

"Thanks, I'd rather use Tabasco as eyedrops."

"Hmm. I'm enjoying that mental image." She wiped a thin foam
mustache off her upper lip, and I wanted to trail the same path with the
tip of my tongue before sealing her mouth with mine. "Anyway, I tallied
every time you used profanity on my phone." She raised her ancient
iPhone in the air between us. "You should donate a dollar to the local
elementary school's baseball team for every cuss word you used."

"I'll go bankrupt."

"A fitting punishment for your sins." She smiled happily. "Want
to know how many times you cursed?"

"Not really."

"Forty-four. That's an average of more than one a minute."

"That's bullshit."

She flipped an invisible notepad open and pretended to cross
something off with an imaginary pencil. "Make that forty-five. I see
you're eager to buy Staindrop Elementary another field."

"Someone is being mouthy these days." Not that I had any
complaints. I'd come for seconds and thirds of that attitude.

"Oh, did you mistake my anxiety for weakness?" Her eyes flared.
"Rookie mistake. My tongue is more lethal than any man's fist."

I bet so, sweetheart.

I was waiting for her to give me shit about Allison. But she
didn't. Instead, Cal swung her gaze to the ceiling and chewed on her
lip, looking thoughtful. "I may or may not have also recorded 'The
Protest Song' on my phone and put 'Stan' in the background."

"Liar." I pursed my lips. Dylan, Mom, and Fuckface trailed
behind us, though really, they might as well have been on another
planet.

"Their beat was something fierce." She stopped dead in her
tracks and swiped her phone screen. The Righteous Gang's version
of "Stan" filled the air.

I couldn't help it. I let out a chuckle and shook my head. "You're a nut."

"When I checked the BPM, I realized Gertie is a straight-up musical genius." She rose on her tiptoes and plastered the phone closer to my ear. "My favorite part is when they call you a villain. I could listen to it until my ears fall off."

I was smiling. Why was I smiling? This was ridiculous. *She* was ridiculous. Besides, I never smiled. Smiling was reserved for other people, who were capable of being happy. The height of positivity I could reach, emotionally, was being not pissed off.

Dylan pushed between us, flinging an arm over each of us. "Aw. Look at you two not even trying to scoop each other's eyes out."

"It's good progress from the time Cal brought you cupcakes." Mom caught up with our pace, nodding in approval.

"Having everyone home is so much fun." Dylan sighed.

"Tucker isn't home, though." Cal frowned.

"I said what I said." Dylan rolled her eyes.

Fuckface turned to me, changing the subject. "Hey, didn't know that you and Allison used to knock boots. I took her to prom, you know."

"Had no idea she was contaminated. I'll scrub extra hard today in the shower," I drawled.

"Be sure to use bleach too. We were drunk that night and some funky things went down." Kieran tipped an imaginary hat, making my mom choke on her take-out coffee. "Thing is...she doesn't seem like your type."

"What's my type?" I humored him.

Kieran stroked his chin. "Someone who isn't completely dead inside. Someone cheerful to level out your darkness. You need a yin to your yang." He gave me a once-over. "Your yang is kind of terrible."

Glancing quickly at Cal, I noticed not only did she not have any opinion about my short affair with Allison but she didn't look too bothered by the revelation either. Why did it drive me up the fucking wall that she wasn't jealous?

Because you still care, and she is still not interested.

I wanted to yell at her, *I'm McMonster. I'm your fucking fantasy. Me. The same guy who has always been there, in your periphery, waiting to save the goddamn day and not take any credit for it.*

I taught you how to drive. I made your birthday presents up until your sophomore year. I fucking took your virginity because you asked not so nicely, even though I knew it was going to undo me.

I pushed the exit door open and held it for everyone other than Fuckface—he could hold his own damn door. When I stepped outside into the frosty winter evening, I bumped into my mother's back. She was standing frozen to the sidewalk, staring at the street. So were Dylan and Cal.

"Mom?" I peered down at her face to find it was pale as a sheet.

"Honey..." Her jaw nearly hit the floor.

I followed her line of sight. My Silverado, which was parked across the street, had all four tires slashed to ribbons. They were so badly ripped, the barrel was completely naked from the tire. A rush of heat climbed up my neck.

"Motherfucker." I stomped my way to the truck, bending down to take a better look at the prankster's handiwork. My blood simmered to a dangerous temperature. The dead coyote had been uncalled for. I had let it slide, filing it as a last-ditch effort by some punk before the town hall meeting. There was the mysterious hate mail too, but getting trashed was no news to me. I was used to it from being (A) a celebrity and (B) a major asshole.

Now this? This was personal. Not to mention inconvenient. I couldn't go anywhere without my truck. Someone was following me around and making my life hell, and I was going to get to the bottom of it.

I looked around the street for cameras, tugging hard at my overgrown hair.

"Don't even bother." Dylan appeared by my side, clutching her lower back with a pout. "None of the cameras work. I tried getting the city to pull out some footage last week because this dumbass gave me a parking ticket for taking a quick nap by the fire hydrant in my car."

"You're shitting me." I gritted my teeth. What kind of Main Street didn't have *one* working camera?

"I know, right?" Dylan bristled. "Taking a catnap is a basic human right when you're in your third trimester. We should normalize that everywhere."

Fuckface popped into my periphery, staring at the wheels and scratching the side of his neck. "Shit, man. Those tires are done."

"Do you ever say things that aren't fucking obvious?" I ground out.

Kieran shrugged, unmoved by my attitude toward him. "Not usually. I'm fuck-hot and on the brink of becoming a billionaire. I can be as dumb as a rock and people will still be interested."

"That's not true. You're very bright. I'm sure you can tell him something he doesn't know," Dylan encouraged with a dreamy grin. "Try it."

"Before Alex Ferguson took over Man United, Aston Villa was the more successful club. Bet you didn't know that."

"I didn't!" Dylan chirped. "Did you, Cal?"

"Nope." Cal perked up. "Did you know there was another pilot with Amelia Earhart when she disappeared? His name was Fred Noonan."

"I knew that!" Dylan snapped her fingers. "He was hot."

This vandalism bullshit didn't fly with me. No matter how angry people were.

Who could have done this? *Randy.* Randy could and would. He was my most outspoken adversary in town with plenty to lose if the deal went through.

"You keep talking about boring shit." I turned around and marched straight down Main Street. "Be right back."

"Hey, where are you going?" Dylan called out.

"I have a sucker punch with Randy's name on it." He'd be at Dahlia's Diner, eating his sad discounted senior meal. Randy and Lyle had a Thursday routine.

"Row, no!" Dylan yelped. "What are you doing? He's like a thousand years old!"

"You don't even know that it's him," my mother pointed out, her voice becoming fainter as I put some distance between us.

I didn't care at this point. Someone was targeting me, and I needed my pound of flesh. Once upon a very long time ago, I had been someone's punching bag.

Never again. Lesson learned. These days, I always hit back, and twice as hard.

They hollered my name as I zipped down the street, past the food mart Randy owned, the auto shop, and the gift shop not one soul had stepped into since 1998. Dahlia's Diner appeared before me in all its modesty. Neon-red roof, glass bricks, and red door with an *open* sign nailed into it. Christmas lights adorned its roof, flicking on and off. I spotted Randy through the window, sitting in the corner, digging into his biscuits and gravy. I was about to slap the door open and rearrange the organs in his face when I heard a voice behind me.

"Don't you dare open that door, Ambrose Rhett Casablancas."

Cal.

My steps faltered, my hand already on the handle. I didn't turn around to face her. "Go back to your date," I hissed out, remembering that she was here with Fuckface.

"You don't know that it's Randy. Even if it *is* him, he's an elderly gentleman who is dead afraid of losing his family's only source of income. Have you no conscience?"

I didn't grace the question with an answer.

She sighed. "All right. What about a beating heart, got one of those?"

Yes, and you need to stay the hell away from it.

Her words washed through me, going in one ear and out the other. But the touch of her fingertips as they fluttered between my shoulder blades did not go unnoticed. There was a jacket and a Henley between us, and still, where we touched, my skin tingled, coming alive. It was a weird sensation. Like being awakened from a long bout of sleep.

I inhaled sharply, clinging desperately to my anger. She thawed me where I wanted to stay iced. The last thing I needed was another complication in my life. And Cal made me feel…she made me *feel*. That was the main problem.

"I won't be bullied again." I ground out the words.

I had always pretended to be untouchable. Athletic, popular, successful, talented. I had been a great student, on the rowing team—letterman jacket, a sports car, and a harem of fangirls. I never showed weakness and didn't plan on starting now.

"Again?" She tilted her head to the side.

Nice going, asshole. One touch, and you start spilling secrets.

"The coyote," I mumbled, then scowled, twisting my head to glance at her. "And why do you smell like the apocalypse?" She didn't smell like her usual green apples and white musk.

"Semus has been peeing in my shoes to make a point ever since I got back." She sighed, not even a little self-conscious.

"Semus is your cat?" I clarified. *Please let it be the fucking cat. If it's a stalker, I'll get a life sentence.*

"If he were a human, would I be so calm about it?" She pinned me with a look. I stifled a smile, just barely. She made not smiling impossible. "Anyway, can you give me two minutes to talk you out of making a ginormous mistake?"

"No."

"Then I quit, and I'm taking my expertise and ten-ton bucket of charm with me." She was blinking hard, a tic that told me she was nervous. I didn't have the fucking heart to deny her.

I groaned. "You're going to be the death of me."

"Here's hoping." She crossed her fingers. "How would you like me to kill you?"

A chain of three hundred orgasms while buried inside you.

"Let me smoke however much I want and shut up about it."

"No can do. You mean the world to Dylan, and she means the world to me. So can I have two minutes?"

"You can have one. Make it quick." We were both looking at an oblivious Randy and Lyle through the diner window. Cal's profile was a vision. Cute, pert nose. Bee-stung lips. A dusting of freckles on her nose and cheeks. Even the curve of her eyebrow held grace.

"Look, I get it. They don't understand you." Her shoulder brushed mine, and for one second, I forgot how to fucking breathe. "You're a mythical creature, Casablancas. Too big for this world. I spent my entire childhood watching you, and I still don't think I've figured you out." Her voice sounded like it came from the bottom of her soul. "It's aggravating, seeing someone treat this world like it's their personal oyster. And it's frightening when that someone takes something you know so well and decides to turn it into something else entirely. Give them time to adjust. They're not bad people."

"Are you fucking Fuckface?" I blurted out. *Jesus.* Had I caught her verbal diarrhea virus? I knew the answer to that question. But I still needed the reassurance.

She whipped her head toward me. "Excuse me?"

"You heard me. It's a yes or no question."

"He's my friend."

So? I'd had plenty of "friends" who could recognize my dick in a thirty-cock lineup. "That wasn't what I was asking."

"Well, that's the answer you're getting, so deal with it."

"I don't want you anywhere near him. He's a bad influence." I recognized that was rich coming from me, a man whose entire existence was deplorable.

"And Allison?" Her eyebrows shot up. "What kind of influence is she?"

It was pathetic, how pleased I was she had fallen into the trap I'd set up for her.

"You knew I disliked her." Cal's throat rolled with a swallow. "Yet you still went and dated her."

"That was a feature, not a bug," I admitted, my voice coming out harsh and hot.

I had wanted to hurt Cal. Dig under her skin. Team up with her enemy. So long as she hadn't known it, as long as it was all in my messed-up head, it had felt good. But now that she *did* know, I couldn't bear being the one to make her feel bad.

I turned around and walked back to my truck. She trailed behind me.

"Holy shit, did I just manage to talk you out of beating an elderly person?" She giggled, a bounce in her step as she chased me. "Does it mean that I earned my place in heaven?"

"Hope so for your sake. If we're neighbors in hell, I'm stealing your trash can."

"I'll egg your house," she retorted, catching up with my step.

"I'll butter your floor."

"I'll send embarrassing deliveries to your doorstep. You'll be a social pariah." She evil laughed before her smile dropped. "Fine, maybe not. You'd probably like that."

"How come you're so comfortable around me?" I asked. I always found her no-filter prattling adorable. "You barely have tics. And you don't mind us standing close together."

"It's less prominent when I'm around someone I know," Cal explained. "When I'm around someone…" She trailed off. "I, uhm, trust."

"You trust me?" I asked. My heart picked up speed. Probably a minor heart attack. Nothing to worry about.

"Not to kill me, I guess."

We were headed toward Mom, Dylan, and Kieran, who were still loitering by the Silverado, pointing at faulty street cameras and making some calls. Bystanders were bracketing them, gasping and taking pictures. Great. More humans. Wasn't I lucky?

"Have you started running again?" I asked.

"Next question."

I pierced her with a look. She reddened, picking up an orange leaf from the street and twisting it between her fingers by the stem. "Ugh. It's hard, okay?"

"Anything worth doing is." I stopped by my truck, fighting the urge to kick it in frustration. I also wanted a cigarette, but I didn't want another lecture. Cal shoved the leaf into her hair, like it was a feather in a cap.

"So…" Kieran clucked his tongue, looking between us. Uh-huh. What was he going to do next? Tell us that the night was dark? Winter was cold? Cats were superior to dogs? "My car's parked right here, in case you need a ride." He motioned toward a gunmetal Maybach.

"My feet thank you, good sir." Dylan patted his back, already strutting toward his car. Mom followed her, and Kieran unlocked the car so they could slide in and wait in the warmth.

"Thank you, Kieran. How lovely of you to offer." Mom rearranged the thick, silky scarf on her neck as she slid in.

Cal looked between me and him, and for a moment I had the idiotic hope she was going to choose to stay here with me and figure out my truck shit.

"Row, are you coming?" Cal asked.

"No," I said stiffly. "You go."

She tilted her chin up, squinting at the sky. "Gonna rain soon."

"I ain't made out of sugar."

"Don't I know it." A tired smile twisted her pink lips. "Cyanide, maybe. Don't be so stubborn. Come."

"I'm good."

She shook her head, throwing me a frustrated look. "I swear, your ego is the most giant thing I've seen."

"That's not true, and we both know it."

That made her blush down to her toes. Her face was so pink, she looked sunburned.

"See you at work tomorrow?" She bit at the side of her thumb.

"Unfortunately." Fuck. No more rides together. I should not feel as disappointed as I did. I hated our rides together. Spent the majority of them lecturing her.

"Okay. So…bye?" she squeaked.

"Bye."

I kept my back to Kieran's Maybach as I called my insurance. Maybe the bastard was reformed after all, but it didn't matter either way.

Nice guys didn't always finish last.

But if this specific one wasn't careful, he'd end up in my trunk.

CHAPTER TWENTY-SIX
ROW

oBITCHuary: Okay, I have a confession to make.

McMonster: If it can end up with a criminal charge, I'd rather not know.

oBITCHuary: I'm starting to have feelings.

McMonster: What kind of feelings?

oBITCHuary: Horny ones.

McMonster is typing...

McMonster is deleting...

McMonster is typing...

McMonster is deleting...

oBITCHuary: Are you okay?

oBITCHuary: It's been twenty minutes and I can see that you're online.

McMonster: Sorry, had to go scream into a pillow.

McMonster: Anyone specific that makes you horny, or is it just general horniness?

oBITCHuary: My not-so-nice dick of a boss.

oBITCHuary: Who also happens to have a VERY nice dick.

McMonster: The plot thickens.

oBITCHuary: Not just the plot.

oBITCHuary: Sorry, I'll stop. No straight guy wants to hear about some other dude's penis.

McMonster: So what are you planning to do about it?

oBITCHuary: Nothing! He's my best friend's brother and pretty horrific most of the time.

oBITCHuary: Plus, I really like you.

McMonster: I really like you too.

McMonster: I should really tell you that something.

oBITCHuary: Tomorrow, okay? Promise. I'm pooped. Good night, Mac.

McMonster: Good night, Bitchy.

CHAPTER TWENTY-SEVEN
ROW

"*Ugh*, this is so good my mouth just orgasmed." Dylan threw her head back, closing her eyes. "What did you put in this?"

"Peas, salmon, risotto, my entire fucking soul." I sat across from her in my mother's kitchen, sorting out a Rubik's Cube.

"Your *soul*? I can't eat anything raw, dude. What the fuck?" Her plate of asparagus risotto in pea sauce and honey-glazed salmon was balanced over her huge stomach, which served as a table. She was midbite, the green sauce dripping down her chin. "Your soul is perpetually bleeding. I can't have that."

I didn't look up from the cube, an unlit cigarette tucked in the corner of my mouth. "You're extremely funny. Pissing my pants here."

"Moooooooooom." Dylan cupped her mouth. "Row said a bad word."

"Row, give your sister fifty bucks," Mom called from her bedroom.

I pinned Dylan with a glare. "It used to be a dollar."

Dylan shrugged. "Inflation, baby. Besides, you can afford it."

"How's Tuck doing?" I changed the subject. Dylan didn't want to accept my gift in the form of a house I'd built for her. She thought it was too much and didn't want to be a charity case. Truth was, she wasn't. It was a way to calm my raging guilt for leaving her and Mom behind.

"Not sure. He stopped calling since I never pick up." She dragged her finger along the sauce on the plate, sucking it. "And I never pick up because he's a jerk."

"Why the shit are you marrying the man, then?" I tossed the sorted cube on the table. It never took me more than a minute to solve.

She stood up, carrying her plate to the sink to wash it. I made a move to help her, but she shook her head. "Absolutely not. If you don't let me do something around here, I'll go mad. I think I'm halfway there already."

She squirted enough soap to bathe a baby whale and began washing the plate. "You and I both know why I'm marrying him: *Mom.* I'm already a huge disappointment—no, don't give me that look, I know I am. No college, no prospects, a baby out of wedlock. The least I can do for my child is marry her father."

"The least you can do for your child is do what's right for you and give her an example of an independent, fearless woman choosing her own path in life," I countered. "You hate Tuck, and I don't blame you." I still had no idea what had inspired her to waste so many years with that tool bag. "What kind of—"

"Look." She raised a wet palm up to stop me, grabbing a rag from the counter and wiping her hands with it. "I don't want to talk about Tuck. How are you feeling about Cal being here?"

"Indifferent." I raised an eyebrow.

She rolled her eyes, walking my way and patting my knee. "Oh, Rowy."

"It was a childhood crush." My cheekbones stung. "I don't have any feelings for her anymore."

"Well, just so you know, if you want to jam the clam, I no longer care." She dropped onto the seat next to me.

"Why would I want to *jam a clam?*" I stared at her, vaguely disturbed. "Is this a fucking TikTok challenge or something?"

"You know." Her eyes flared for emphasis. "If you want to sour the kraut, so to speak."

I glowered, still not getting it. "Kraut is not soured, it is fermented. It's actually easy, all you have to do is salt the—"

"Oh my God, what I mean is you guys can screw each other for all I care. I won't stand in your way or throw a big fit." Dylan tossed her hands in the air. This caught me by surprise, considering her epic meltdown four years ago.

I squinted at her. "Why the change of heart?"

She flipped her dark hair to one shoulder, looking for fuzzy individual hairs she wanted to pluck with a careless shrug. "I didn't want you two to hook up because I was afraid your feelings were going to get hurt. I love Dot to death, but she's never been in a serious relationship with a guy. I mean, she claimed to have hooked up with a bunch of people, but I mostly saw her actively running away from them when we were growing up. Especially after freshman year of high school. It's like something in her switched and she became this distrustful person. I was the only human, outside of her parents, she could open up to." Dylan wet her lips. "I guess, deep down, I was always afraid Cal wasn't capable of love. Or at least, not the kind of love you deserve. I guarded your feelings. But since you obviously loathe her right now, I no longer care. You are both adults. You can do whatever you want."

"Not that I'm actually considering this." I rubbed the bridge of my nose. Greatest fucking lie to ever be recorded on earth, by the way. "But are you saying that if Cal and I hooked up tomorrow, you wouldn't care?"

"Not in the least."

"Because I don't have feelings for her?" My eyes narrowed.

"Because you hate her and will never fall in love with her again," she corrected.

I studied her intently. Why did I want to call bullshit on her? Maybe because Dylan knew me like the back of her hand and knew I hated Cal like Hemingway hated a good drink. She was planning something. I'd ask her what it was, but I had just gotten a free ticket to do what I wanted—my baby sister's best friend—and the less I read into that, the better.

"As I said, I have no interest in Cal." I sat back, toying with the cigarette between my fingers.

"*Of course* you don't, you sweet summer child." There was a pregnant pause, in which she dragged her teeth against her lip. "Can I have a treat now?" She knew she wasn't supposed to have sugar.

"One cookie," I allowed.

"Yay." She pumped her fists in the air.

"It's sugar- and gluten-free, by the way."

"Nay." Her two thumbs dove to the floor with a pout.

"But I personally made it, so it doesn't taste funny."

"Thanks. I promise I won't tell Mom."

CHAPTER TWENTY-EIGHT
CAL

oBITCHuary: What was it that you wanted to tell me yesterday?

oBITCHuary: Mac? Hello?

oBITCHuary: Super ready for your big secret over here.

oBITCHuary: Rude. I hate it when men with perfect ears think they're too good for this world just because they have superior lugholes.

oBITCHuary: Yes, I just used the word lugholes.

oBITCHuary: Mac?

oBITCHuary: 🙁

CHAPTER TWENTY-NINE
CAL

"Gonna Make You Sweat (Everybody Dance Now)"—C+C Music
Factory

Everybody dance now!

The unreasonable demand blared directly into my eardrums, jarring me into action. It was way too early and I was still in my bed, blinking at the ceiling after another sleepless night.

Was I hallucinating now? Hoped not. I really couldn't afford therapy.

My head whipped to the alarm clock. Six twenty in the morning.

The singer urged me to take a chance, to come and dance. For guys to grab a girl, not to wait, to make her twirl.

The music shook my flimsy walls, but I had no idea where it was coming from. It was probably Semus, my nemesis, who had decided to up his warfare from sneaker-peeing and messed with the stereo. Was *he* the one who'd slashed Row's tires? He certainly had the bravado.

I checked my phone on my nightstand. The music app wasn't on. I scrambled to my feet in my oversized sweatshirt and dug for my Walkman in my backpack, but it was turned off. *Ugh.* If I didn't find the source of the song soon, it was going to wake Mom up.

Everybody dance now!

I raced to my window, flinging it open and slapping my hands over the sill, poking half my body out. What I saw underneath made my heart fall apart like alphabet letters on a fridge, scattering into pieces at the bottom of my stomach.

It was Row, clad in sweatpants with a teal jazz design, a yellow headband on his forehead, and a colorful windbreaker three sizes too small he must've borrowed from Dylan. His phone was hooked up to a speaker, jamming out one of my favorite nineties songs.

I rubbed my eyes, blinking the cobwebs off. Nope. He was still there. Looking like he had gotten tangled in every item in Nicki Minaj's closet.

He appeared to be a list of things: hot, ridiculous, charming, adorable, and completely out of place. My eyes stung and I couldn't breathe. All the jealousy and soul-numbing pain I had bottled up last night when I'd found out he'd dated Allison Murray dissipated into mist, leaving my body.

"Well?" Row glared at me in his Richard Simmons gear, running in place as the song continued playing. He looked supremely unhappy about the situation, tossing a still-lit cigarette butt on the ground in a huff. I bit down a laugh. "You gonna come down here and run, or what, Dot?"

He had done this for me?

He had come here at six twenty in the morning to drag me out for a run?

"Row, what are you doing?" I balanced my ass on my windowsill, shaking my head in fascination. The smile on my face was so big and wide, it threatened to split my cheeks.

"What does it look like I'm doing?" His frown deepened. "Being fucking delightful and helping you overcome your fear."

"Why?"

"Got my reasons. Come down."

Running had *not* been on my agenda today. Or…you know, *ever*, after the horrific incident on his property the other day.

"Rain check." I clutched a hand to my heart, just to make sure it didn't beat out of my rib cage. "Too anxious."

"Gonna be right here with you."

"Might get another panic attack."

"Brought an inhaler right here with me." He patted his pocket.

"I'm out of shape."

"False. Your shape is fucking delicious. It's the rest of you I have a problem with. Next."

"What if I fall again?" I choked out.

"You won't," he barked out impatiently.

"How do you know?"

"Because I'll always catch you." He threw his hands out, exasperated, as if the mere idea revolted him. "When have I ever let you take the hit for something, Dot?"

Now that I thought about the question…*never*. Grumpiness aside, I could always count on Row. To give me a job, drive me around, fix my problems…

Still, this wasn't a problem. This was straight-up PTSD. He couldn't get into my brain and rewire it.

"Row, I'm…I…" I covered my face, heaving and feeling like an idiot. "I just *can't*."

He turned off the music and set the speaker on the ground, shoving it sideways with the tip of his sneakers.

"Who told you that? Not only can you, but you *do*. You've done your own thing ever since you were eighteen. You're talented, smart, independent, and a badass; most importantly, you're your father's daughter, and you know this was his last wish. That's the reason you can't fall asleep." He pointed at me with his long, thick finger. "Because you're not keeping your promise to him, and it's killing you. So get your ass down here, and let's keep some promises."

"*Argh.*" I hung my head between my shoulders, white-knuckling the windowsill. "Stop making sense and go back to offending people. It's so much easier to shut you down that way."

"I fully intend to offend you throughout this whole ordeal. *Also*"—he readjusted the headband on his forehead, slapping it against his skin—"you know you want the entire town to see me running around looking like John Fonda."

"John Fonda?"

"*You know.* The male Jane Fonda."

Laughter fizzed in my chest, bubbling up my throat. "Baby, you wish you had her thighs."

"She wishes she had *my* thighs," he countered.

Our eyes met. He was smirking. That lopsided smile hit me like a rusty dagger straight into the heart.

"You've got ten minutes to get ready." He pushed his sleeves up, lighting himself another French cigarette. "Coffee's on you when we reach Main Street."

"I hate you." I bumped the back of my head against the window frame.

"Right back at ya. And, Dot?" He tipped his head up to look at me, and for the first time since we'd both moved away, I felt like I saw *him*, really him. No masks. No bravado. No quips. Just old Row.

"What?"

He winked. "You can do this."

CHAPTER THIRTY
CAL

"I can't do this," I wailed barely fifteen minutes later, slugging behind Row as we jogged on a tree-lined street. My arms dangled by my side like two strings of overcooked pasta. "I quit."

"Quitting is for quitters."

"Quitters are *my* people." I pounded my chest with my fist. "I'm so much of a quitter, I didn't even *start*. Never recorded that podcast, remember?"

Row slowed to match my pace, and I noticed the bastard didn't even break a sweat. Rain peppered our faces. It was a drizzle, the kind you barely noticed.

"Are you tired or triggered?" The rain accented his delicious scent, and I had to remind myself it was creepy to lean into him. Then again, it wasn't my fault he was tall, dark, handsome, and so inked he looked like a desk at detention.

"I'm triggered," I bit out unnecessarily harshly. "Do you really think I'm that out of shape?"

"Tell me why you're triggered."

"I keep remembering what made me stop running, having flash-backs of that day."

The way they fisted dirt from the ground. Dumped it on me, burying me alive.

A tremor rolled down my backbone. I stuck my tongue out to catch some rain, like I used to do when I was a kid. No dice. I normally needed my coffee to kick in before reality did. But this morning, I'd had none. Row knew better than to dig into whatever had triggered me.

"You need to focus on the now," he said decisively. "Look around you. Tell me what you see."

"I see it's raining. Let's head back."

"Nice try. I want you to pay attention to your surroundings." He grabbed my shoulders, anchoring me in place. "Try it."

A paperboy leisurely rode his bike hands-free, tossing newspapers at doors. The steep road was decorated with green streetlamps and clouds of orange-leafed sweetgums and maples. The roar of waves crashing against rocks nearby reminded my bladder I hadn't peed before I left the house.

Noticing Row's unusual outfit, the paperboy followed us with his gaze, bumping into a trash can with his bike and flying onto a soft pillow of leaves.

I winced. "You okay there, bud?"

"Yup. Great. Never better!" he called out, sticking a hand out of the pile of leaves and waving it at us. "Hi, Mr. Casablancas."

"Hi, nosy little shit."

"Name's Bert."

"Okay, nosy little shit."

"Hey, you're the one who chose to look like a Eurovision participant, so don't be testy." I poked an elbow into Row's ribs, mainly to have an excuse to touch him. We slowly returned to jogging. "*Speaking* of Eurovision, are we ever going to address the fact that Australia partakes in the competition? I mean, it's a Commonwealth country, but so are Singapore and Trinidad. Where do we draw the line?"

He listened to me talk about Eurovision for a few minutes—I was a big fan—but didn't have much to contribute to the conversation.

Soon, we fell into silence, still jogging, and my mind drifted back to that moment in the woods, washing away all other thoughts like a current.

Smug faces framing the sky as they peered from above me.

Sneakers digging into my ribs, kicking me.

"I want to stop." My voice shattered inside my throat like broken glass, and my eyes burned. "I appreciate you trying to help, but—"

"Why green?" he snapped, desperate to keep the conversation going. To keep me moving.

"Huh?" I sniffled, frowning at him as we continued jogging down the road.

"Why did you change your hair tips to green? What does the color represent?"

Jealousy. Because you dated Allison.

"Peace," I heard myself say. "I want peace, I want tranquility—I *really* want to get some damn sleep—so I colored it green to manifest that kind of energy in my life. Now tell me why you want me to run."

We were at the bottom of the road and took a right toward Main Street, which was farther than I'd run last time.

"Dylan," he said, picking up speed, desperate to keep me jogging.

I pushed myself to keep up. "What about her?"

"You asked why I was helping you. I'm doing it because of Dylan. She missed you. Bed rest has been brutal on her. You know she can't stay still. Used to pull doubles at Descartes, then go partying into the night in Portland before the pregnancy. Ever since you came back, she's been smiling more. It's like a part of her that died has been resurrected."

"I missed her a lot too." I pressed my lips together. "Is that the only reason you're helping me?"

"Isn't it enough?"

"It is. I'm just wondering if there's something else."

"No," he harrumphed. "Wait, yes. Now I remember—I also want to fuck you again."

I tripped over my own feet, about to dive into the ground. He caught me by the hem of my shirt, jerking me upright.

I'll always catch you. When have I ever let you take the hit for something, Dot?

"You did *not* just say that." I slapped branches out of my way as I regained my balance.

"Did too. Fair warning—I want much more than fucking this time around. I want dates. I want laughs. I want you to be honest with me. All the stuff that freaks you out for some reason. No strings attached. No commitment. Just fun. A perfect do-over."

"Why do you need a do-over?"

"So my last memory of us won't be you almost vomiting because we had sex."

"I almost vomited because your sister *caught* us!" I shrieked. "Which is exactly why this won't happen again. You're high if you think I'm betraying her trust a second time around."

"Thought you'd say that. I have great news for you."

"What?"

"She no longer gives a fuck."

"That's not tru—"

"It is. Ask her yourself."

The confidence with which he'd said that made my heart twist like Play-Doh. What had changed between then and now? Why was she okay with us hooking up all of a sudden?

"Why wouldn't she care?" I asked in a panic.

"Because it no longer matters."

"How c—"

"Come on, Bitchy. Put two and two together."

Bitchy.

He'd called me Bitchy.

The rain intensified, knocking on our faces. I skidded to an abrupt stop. A wave of memories crashed into me all at once, nearly knocking me down on my ass. Everything became crystal-clear in one swift moment.

Row defending me when Dylan caught us having sex.

Row teaching me how to slow dance in his room before my very first prom because I knew I would be too terrified to ever dance with anyone else and didn't want to miss out.

Row and I sitting on the hood of his car, in front of an endless ocean, the moon, and the stars. Me saying, "Isn't it beautiful?" and him answering, "Yes, you are."

Row being essentially in love with me.

I couldn't even touch the other revelation right now. It was too much to process.

Bitchy. Bitchy. Bitchy.

McMonster. Selfless, sweet McMonster. Who seemed to know me inside out. Who could read me like an open book. Could it be?

But it couldn't be.

No. It couldn't.

Not him.

Not the shiniest boy in Staindrop.

"No more running." I planted my feet on the pavement, clutching my knees, panting. Tears prickled the back of my eyeballs. Row looked on high alert. Neither of us seemed ready to acknowledge the fact that he was McMonster and I was Bitchy.

For the first time since I'd known him, he looked like a boy. Not a heartthrob, not a world-famous chef, not a formidable boss—just a boy. My head swam with so many questions. I had to comb through them, to wait before I launched on the elephant in the room.

"I'm going to go back to the Bitchy confession in one moment. I just have to..." I held my head with both hands like it was about to explode, pacing the small corner of the street. "Why doesn't Dylan care about us anymore?" I straightened. "Give me the truth."

Raindrops framed his face, his hair clinging in coal strands over his forehead. He stole my breath, and I had a feeling he was about to steal a few other things if I let my guard down.

His chest fell and rose. His lips parted, condensation rolling out of them. "She moved on."

"You're lying." My tears were falling freely now, mixing with the raindrops.

"I am," he admitted. "She wasn't the one who moved on. I did. *I* moved on. That's why it doesn't matter anymore."

"I'm so stupid. So stuck inside my own head I didn't see the signs. All the little tidbits. The romantic moments. The sweet gestures. The compliments you never seemed to pay anyone else but me. Tell me I'm crazy, that I'm hallucinating, sleep deprived." I grabbed the back of my head, folding over and letting out a yelp. "But I think, once upon a time, you wanted me. As a *girlfriend.* You had feelings for me. You…you…" *Say it, don't be scared. He is safe. You know he'd never hurt you.* "You liked me."

My epiphany was sharp and painful, like a blade twisting into my stomach. There was not enough air in this world to keep my lungs from burning.

"Let's not get carried away over here." He walked backward, away from me.

"She was feral when she caught us, Row. And Dylan is normally chill." I was chasing him now, on the verge of running. I tried to snatch the soaked sleeve of his windbreaker. "She didn't want us to hook up because she thought I'd hurt you."

He said nothing, just stared at me, looking slightly alarmed.

"I'm sorry it took me this long to figure it out." I jogged after him, picking up speed. He kept walking backward, staring at me like I had stripped him of his clothes at gunpoint.

"You had feelings for me." That whole time I had felt unworthy, the shiniest boy in the world had thought differently. "That was why Dylan was so mad at me when she found us. That was why you stayed that night to give me a ride home, even though I was horrible to you and completely blew it with the way I handled everything."

"That is enough." His jaw was so tense, it looked like it was about to snap out of his skin.

"It's why you taught me how to dance in tenth grade." I ignored him, stumbling toward him blindly, happily, excitedly. "Why you were never grumpy with me"—I was in a trance, my tongue as loose and unhinged as my thoughts—"and when we bumped into each other under the mistletoe when I was in eleventh grade, you pressed a Hershey chocolate to my lips and smiled. You said, *Same place next year?*"

"Actually, that time I was turning you down politely." He was swatting me off like I was a fly that had slipped into his shirt.

"You made me a paper ring." Jesus, how long had he had feelings for me? "You had an Oh Henry! in your drawer for me to steal every time I came over, because I once told you they were my favorite. You always had one ready. Every single time." I stopped running, wheezing. "They don't even make them anymore. How the hell did you find them?"

"How did I fin…? Does it matter?" He shook his head, raindrops flying from his hair everywhere. "What mattered was that your skinny, anemic ass ate them. You were severely malnourished as a teen. Lived off chicken nuggets and chips."

I stopped running. He came to a halt too. Everything was drowned out. The world stopped moving.

Row flung his hands in the air, turning to me fully.

"Bitchy," I said simply. "I'm Bitchy. And you are—"

"Mac." He completed the sentence, a mocking sneer finding his lips. "Feel cheated?"

I shook my head. No, I didn't. I couldn't explain it without sounding deranged, but I had always known, on some level, I was talking to Row all these years. "How did you find me in this forum?"

"I didn't." His jaw jumped again. "One night I searched *andro-phobia* because I was curious about…something." He rubbed his cheek with his knuckles. "I was in between shifts working for this asshole chef in Paris. I stumbled upon this forum. You had to sign up to be able to read the threads. You started talking to me."

I had. I'd liked his name. I'd liked that he'd liked all my comments without ever contributing to the conversation. It had made me feel like there was someone on my side. Row looked everywhere but at me, avoiding eye contact.

"Wait, why did *you* search androphobia?" I narrowed my eyes. "You're not afraid of men."

"I was afraid of *a* man." His jawline turned stony. "Everyone is fighting their own demons, Dot."

"So…we just happen to have the same problem?" I scratched my head, confused. "That seems highly unlikely."

"Believe it or not, I had no idea that it was you until you came to Staindrop. I mean, I had my suspicions, but I never confirmed it."

"You lied about your life," I noted. He'd said he lived in New York and was a measly sous-chef. That he was originally from Philadelphia. That he lived with roommates.

"What was my alternative, telling you that I was a millionaire, famous chef who made it to *People*'s 'Hottest Thirty under Thirty'?" He arched an eyebrow.

Touché.

"Well, you could've told me the second you found out."

"I *tried*." He wrenched a cigarette from his pocket, took one look at my face, and tossed it on the ground, stomping on it in annoyance. "Repeatedly. You kept telling me not to."

McMonster was Row.

Row was McMonster.

The man I'd thought I might fall in love with was the same man who hated me so much these days he couldn't even look at me. I didn't know what to do with this information. I couldn't even unpack it. Something occurred to me then.

"How did you know I'm, you know, not comfortable with men?"

"How did I…?" He squinted, like I was ant-sized and he had

to look carefully to see me. "Maybe because I notice every fucking thing about you?"

I blinked. One, two, five hundred times. He did?

Row tilted his head upward, letting the rain pound on his face, a dark, humorless chuckle escaping him. "Fine. Want the truth? Here's the truth: no, I didn't 'have feelings' for you." He air quoted the words with a sneer. "I was in love with you. Honest to fucking God, full-blown, snatch-my-heart-out-and-let-you-use-it-as-a-stress-ball in love with you." He looked disgusted with himself for uttering each word. "And you didn't give half a shit about me."

That wasn't true. I had been busy weeding through my adolescent trauma and distracting myself with nineties memorabilia. Reimagining my life without Instagram, and Snapchat, and WhatsApp. I had been drowning while simultaneously pretending everything was going swimmingly. I had felt so broken, so unworthy, the prospect of precious Ambrose Casablancas hadn't even occurred to me.

Row had seemed as bright and far as a star. Ethereal, out of this world. Whichever galaxy he belonged in, I wasn't welcome there.

"Y-you fell in love with me?" I stepped forward, my eye tic out of control. I didn't care. I never cared when Row and Dylan were privy to them.

"I didn't fall." He omitted a sharp, irritated huff. "You fucking *tripped* me."

"I…I thought you pitied me for being, I don't know…weird and eccentric and awkward," I whispered, torn between glee and grief. "That you saw me as your little sister's annoying best friend."

"I did." Row ran his hand over his wet hair, tipping his head back again and closing his eyes. "Until I didn't. It was stupid. We would've never worked out." His prominent Adam's apple bobbed with a visible swallow. "Which was why it fucking killed me. It killed me that all I had to settle for was a quick fuck on the hood of my car. And that all you had to say about it was that it was a mistake and meant nothing to you. So Dylan was doubly pissed off. Both about your betrayal and about shitting all over my heart."

Tears ran down my cheeks, warm in contrast with the rain. We were standing in the middle of the street, drawing curious glances from the few people who ran for shelter, holding their umbrellas and coats over their heads.

"I'm so sorry, Row." I wiped my face with my sleeve. "I thought I was an oddity to you. The ugly duckling who loitered outside your room, hunting for scraps of attention. When I asked you to be my first, it was because I trusted you, and as you're well aware, I'm skittish around men. Humans scare me. That's why I'm obsessed with true crime. So I figured…" My throat constricted around my next confession. "I figured you could never love me, could never want something more, and wouldn't hurt me. A good deal for everyone involved. I was getting rid of my virginity, and you got some no-strings-attached action."

He scrubbed his face, ignoring the rain that kept on pouring. "Doesn't matter now. It's done. Over. I have no feelings for you anymore other than mild annoyance."

"I know." I swallowed, but the lump in my throat only grew larger. "I can see you…"

You.

I can see you.

Your pain. Your struggle. Your heartbreak.

You're wrong. I cared.

Before you were famous. Before you were rich. Before you got into People's *"Sexiest Men Alive" list. Which, by the way, should* not *have put George Clooney before you. I always cared. You were always so dear to me. Not as a friend. Not as a lover. As* Row. *The most magnificent man to ever walk the earth.*

"Your lips are blue. Let's get inside." Row jerked his chin toward the Christmas-decorated door. "It's Friday. I need all hands on deck at Descartes today. Can't afford you getting sick."

"Liar." I sniffled, finding glee in my avalanche of emotions. "You just want that free coffee I owe you."

"You read me like an open book," he sighed. "In German."

We jogged inside. The place was full to the brim with locals who sent us judgmental looks behind the rims of their coffee cups. Ignoring them, Row collapsed into the only red vinyl booth available. I slid into the seat opposite to him. We were both soaked to the bone.

"Stop looking so happy. You're ruining my day. *And* my appetite." He craned his neck, trying to catch the attention of one of the servers floating between curved booths.

"Can't help myself." I squished my cheeks, grinning. "This is not an ego stroke. This is an ego...*masturbation*. You were kind of my Brain Boyfriend."

"Brain Boyfriend?" He tilted a thick eyebrow, instinctively wiping the table clean, like it was his restaurant. "As opposed to... Ass Boyfriend? Because that sounds like more my speed."

"A Brain Boyfriend is the guy that you make movies about in your head. You play-staged dates and vacations and romantic getaways. Like, daydreaming. Before I went to bed, I would play our meet-cute in my head and fall asleep imagining what it would be like."

It had been a very safe way for me to imagine what a relationship would be like without actually participating in one. I wasn't asexual. I liked dicks. With my entire heart and my whole vagina. I was just wary of the people attached to them.

"Meet-cute?" He frowned. "But we'd already met."

"In my dreams, I was someone else. Someone new."

"Ah, the irony." He sat back, folding his arms. "In *my* dreams, you were you. Did Dream Row at least get some NC-17 action?"

"There were a few notable moments." I coyly collected my wet hair into a high bun. "One of them on a washing machine, even."

"Were they as traumatic as the real thing?"

"I mean, in one of them I put a red shirt in a cycle full of whites." I flicked a balled-up straw wrapper his way. "What do you think?"

His lips twitched, fighting a smile, but it broke loose anyway. Oh my. A smiling Ambrose Casablancas could light up the world better than the rising sun. "What other brainy dreams did you make up to avoid the real thing, Dot?"

"Oh...too many to count." I absentmindedly flipped through the song list of the little jukebox. "Dream job, ultimate kiss, apartment...I can pretty much imagine anything if I put my mind to it." I tapped my temple. "This baby is all free, and inside it, I'm living my best life."

"It also doesn't require you to lift a finger, fail, get burned. You're missing out on all the real things."

"Reality is never as good as the dream." I shrugged. "Why try?"

"Reality is better," he argued. "It's gritty and three-dimensional. What's your dream kiss scenario?"

"It keeps changing. But there are a few ingredients that stay the same. Moonlight, music, and a chin tilt." I paused. "Shouldn't you be writing this down?" I needed to stop flirting with him, but I was too excited about this new discovery, and I'd just found the perfect distraction to take my mind off the misery of losing Dad.

"No need. My memory has never failed me." He brushed his thumb over his lower lip, awarding me with an arousal-induced brain aneurysm.

I laughed awkwardly. "Well, I think we had our run. Hey, wait a minute." I straightened my back, my eyes widening. "Row, I ran."

"You did." His lips twitched again. "Bitched about it the entire time, but you did four miles and some change."

"No. You don't understand. I *ran*." I stood up, pounding my hands on the table between us, making customers jolt with surprise.

Row folded his arms over his chest, leaning back in his booth smugly. "Told you you're pretty great."

"I am, aren't I?"

"Now you can do it every morning."

"Are you crazy?" I fell back onto the vinyl, my smile collapsing with me. "You distracted me with a *love declaration*. I can't do it without you."

"Are *you* crazy?" He unzipped his windbreaker, revealing a tight, short-sleeved white Henley and muscle definition that would make Channing Tatum weep with envy. "I'm not running with you every morning. I just wanted to prove to you that you can."

"But I want to run the 10K for Kiddies," I cried out.

"Sounds like a *you* problem, Dot."

"We are all one according to Buddhism. So technically, your problem too."

"Grew up Catholic. So technically, I can tell you to fuck off, then confess I was an ass and say my Hail Marys and still go to heaven. What's taking them so long to serve us?" He looked around. He was right. It had been ten minutes and we still didn't even have menus.

"Maybe it's your BO." I threw another balled-up straw wrapper at him.

"Maybe it's your BS," he retorted, tugging a napkin over, squishing it, and tossing it in my face. "Stay here; gonna inform Dahlia her staff is slacking off."

"Please don't be…" I trailed off, wincing. *Rude? Disgusting? Overbearing?* He stared at me expectedly. "*You*," I finished, gulping.

"Gotcha. I'll try to be Kieran. If you see my tongue trapped in someone's rectum, send help." He gave me a once-over. "Unless it's yours. That's intentional."

Oh. My. God.

Row slipped out of the booth before I had the chance to combust into a trillion pieces. He headed toward the red-checked Formica counter, where Dahlia was chewing gum in decibels more fit for a Taylor Swift concert and banging an order into the computer with her mile-long nails. I perched my chin on my knuckles and drummed my fingers on the table. My mind was still reeling from the revelation that Row had once loved me. That he was McMonster. I couldn't wait to get home and reread our entire conversation thread starting three years ago.

Calm your tits, Cal, and while you're at it, tell the rest of you to chill. It wasn't like we could ever be something *now.* And for plenty of reasons:

1. He was a famous multimillionaire with 1.7 million Instagram followers, a Netflix deal, and Michelin-starred restaurants, and I was so broke I couldn't afford to feed the rats that were squatting in my apartment.

2. He was moving to London and I was returning to New York.

3. Regardless of what Row had said, Dylan still might not be on board with us knocking boots, and I definitely wasn't pushing my luck a second time.

4. Just because I wasn't scared of Row physically, didn't mean I wasn't scared of forming a relationship with him.

Through the heavy fog of my overthinking, I heard "These Boots Are Made for Walkin'" by Nancy Sinatra jamming through a nearby jukebox.

I whipped my head to see what was taking Row so long and found him by the register, still talking to Dahlia, a bombshell of a woman in her fifties, with a strong Louisiana accent, big bleached hair, a slim waist, and enough makeup to cover the state of Idaho. Dahlia was all about Elvis, Jesus, and horses. Her only fear was God. Even he, I suspected, couldn't comment on her business and get out of it in one piece. One of her faux-lashed eyes was twitching—a telltale sign she was angry—while Row appeared completely blasé, save for the red tips of his ears. Ropes of dread tightened around my stomach. This didn't seem like a conversation as much as it did a standoff.

Row turned away from her, approaching me with his head held high. "Rain check on that coffee, Dot."

"Why?" My voice trembled, but I stayed put in the booth.

From behind Row's back, Dahlia peered at me apologetically.

"Let's just go," Row grumbled.

"Are they refusing to serve us?" I scanned the hostile looks daggered at our booth, blush creeping up my neck.

"No." His nostrils flared. "They're refusing to serve *me*. Now can we fucking leave?"

That was why they'd chosen this song on the jukebox. *Unbelievable.* My inner kindergarten teacher came out swinging, ready to put the whole town of Staindrop in some serious time-out.

"Not before I give her a piece of my mind." I shot up to my feet, ambling over to Dahlia at the counter. She flinched when I stopped in front of her. Row trailed behind me like a mortified teenager whose mother had decided to go full-blown Karen on kids from his school.

Maybe it was because of his love declaration earlier. Hell, maybe it was because I knew Row needed a break, even if he didn't show it, but I couldn't sit there and watch others treat him like dirt.

"Cal, honey!" Dahlia popped her gum in greeting, snatching my hands and squeezing them over the bar. "You look beautiful. Heard 'bout your old man. So sorr—"

"What is this bull crap about you not serving us?" I pulled my hands away, planting them on my waist. My eyes twitched nervously, but I pushed through the tic. Surprised by my directness, Dahlia choked on her bubblegum, slapping her coffin nails to her rib cage with a cough.

"Honey, you're *always* welcome in this establishment. There's a uniform with your name on it if you ever need to make an extra buck. Although you do look like you might need a size up." Her eyes quickly zipped over my body. "But see, Ambrose here's another story. The way he's been doin' this town dirty—"

"He *saved* this town." My palm landed on the counter with a smack, rattling the utensils and coffee cups on it. "Brought at least thirty jobs into Staindrop when he opened Descartes, and he is

building the only new construction here in a *decade*! And, and, and…"
I looked around me, registering the agape mouths of every patron at
the diner. The Righteous Gang was there too. Agnes, Mildred, and
Gertie were huddled around their pioneer breakfast. "He talks about
Staindrop in interviews. All the time. He told *The Atlantic* that it has
the best views in America and that everyone should come to see it at
least once. To *The New York Times*, he said that Dahlia's Diner was
the first place he'd ever tasted poached eggs. This man is a regional
treasure. How can you treat him like an enemy?"

Okay, so I *might've* googled him one or three thousand times
since he'd reentered my life. Sue me for being thorough. Serial killers
came in every shape and form. You can never be too careful.

Melinda and Pete were seated in the far corner of the room,
murmuring intensely between themselves. A few other locals I
recognized from the town hall meeting were following my unfold-
ing public meltdown.

"Sorry, honey." Dahlia scrunched her nose. "Ambrose Casablancas
isn't our own anymore. Mayor Murray told us all about what he has
in store for us. He's ruinin' this town, and in Staindrop, we don't
forget."

"Let me tell you something, Dahl." I pointed at her with a
squint. "If he's not welcome here, then neither am I. People are treating this man like he is subhuman. Vandalizing his new construction.
Slashing his tires. Sending him hate mail—"

"All right, little spitfire. Time to leave." Row's fingers curled
around my bicep. Desire twirled around my limbs like ivy, sending
shivers down my spine. Crap. Keeping him out of my corduroy
flared jeans was going to be a struggle. "I'd rather pass a kidney stone
than sip the shitty coffee here anyway." Row pinned Dahlia with a
provocative look.

"Excuse me?" Dahlia, whose face was now the color of a crime
scene, straightened her back. She flung an accusing finger his way. "You
didn't seem to have any issues with my cuppa joe while growin' up."

"I have since developed this thing called *taste*," he answered, deadpan, eyes raking her. "Judging by what you did with the place, I trust it doesn't ring a bell." He eyed the turquoise walls with distaste.

It was going to be hard to make Grumpy McGrumpson here win people over.

"He didn't mean it." I smiled politely.

"Yes, I did." Row stood his ground, his hand *still* on my bicep. The fog of desire made it hard for me to breathe.

"Take that back." Dahlia's nostrils flared.

"Nah." He flashed a half-moon smirk. "And your skillet dish? Drier than fucking Lent month in Italy."

"That's it." She pointed at our booth. "Sit your ass back down, and I'll serve you the best damn coffee your mouth's ever tasted."

"Dahlia!" Melinda gasped, a forkful of maple-drenched pancake midway to her mouth. "We had an arrangement."

"I hereby unarrange it." Dahlia's lips thinned into a snarl, and she seemed determined to prove Row wrong. She rounded the counter, grabbing two menus and the lobe of his ear. "He called my eggs dry and my coffee shitty."

"So is your customer service." Row doubled down, head tilted to one side. Laughter bubbled in my chest. Row remained Row, even famous and rich.

"Your mother won't be happy to hear from me about your manners, young man. I'll be exchanging some words with her later today," Dahlia threatened.

"Words are fine, as long as you don't exchange recipes. My sister won't survive your cooking."

I touched his arm briefly, trailing behind him. "Not helping our cause of winning hearts and minds, Casablancas."

"That's your dream, Cal. Not mine." He wormed out of Dahlia's hold, throwing me a mischievous smirk. "I'd rather be hated for who I am than loved for who I'm not." Of course he was a Kurt Cobain fan. He had the same grungy, don't-give-a-fuck air about him.

"Thanks, Dahlia. For serving us that coffee." I shoved Row back into our booth. "We'll take it with two eggs sunny side up, hash browns, sausage, and a side of fruit. No cantaloupe."

"Don't wanna stay where I'm not welcome," Row grumbled. At this point, I was just pushing him as an excuse to touch him more. "And I *definitely* don't want the heart attack that comes with whatever she calls breakfast."

"Well, we're staying here as a matter of principle. I don't like the way these people are treating you. We are not letting them win." We sat back down.

"Even if we lose?" He scowled at me.

"Even if we lose." I nodded, aggressively unwrapping my utensils. "We're going to eat every bite, drink every ounce of coffee, and by God, we are going to pretend to enjoy it."

CHAPTER THIRTY-ONE
ROW

oBITCHuary: Hello.

McMonster: Hi.

oBITCHuary: So...

oBITCHuary: I went back and read through our chats. I totally admitted to you that I'm attracted to my shitty boss, didn't I?

McMonster: Yup.

oBITCHuary: Enjoying the ego stroke?

McMonster: I'd enjoy it more if you aim south. And, you know, use your tongue.

oBITCHuary: I'm never going to be able to look you in the eye.

McMonster: May I suggest other organs that will welcome your attention, then?

oBITCHuary: I'm so terrified I'm going to yield to temptation.

McMonster: Don't worry, I'm sure I'll fuck it up before we get to it.

oBITCHuary: WHY are you even interested? You could have any woman in the world.

McMonster: And you're that woman. Where's the mystery?

oBITCHuary: I'm completely normal.

McMonster: Respectfully, Cal, you're not.

oBITCHuary: LOL. I meant average.

McMonster: You're not that either.

oBITCHuary: What am I, then?

McMonster: If I have a say about it? Mine.

CHAPTER THIRTY-TWO
ROW

Space.

I needed it. All of it.

Three oceans between me and Calla Litvin would be ideal. Though I didn't rule out helping Elon Musk populate Mars and relocating altogether. Why the fuck not? People would have to eat there too. And I was no stranger to shitholes. I had grown up in Staindrop, for Christ's sake.

What had I been thinking, showing up outside her window like a lovesick puppy in a goddamn nineties outfit? I hadn't been, of course. It was my dick that had come up with the plan. All puns intended.

I remembered vaguely feeding myself some bullshit excuse about doing this in honor of Artem—the man *had* help me turn my love for physics and numbers into becoming a Michelin-starred chef by dragging me into the communal teacher's kitchen and cooking with me—and something about Dylan being happy.

Point of the matter was, I had done something selfless for someone who wasn't an immediate family member.

And that was…unsettling.

I'd done good deeds before, but I had never gone out of my way to make them happen. Giving a shit was dangerous. It led to all kinds of issues. And I had a history of giving Cal whatever she wanted without asking for anything in return.

Then there was my retroactive love declaration. What the fuck was that all about? I wasn't in love with her anymore, but it was still embarrassing to admit.

Maybe because the attraction was still there, despite everything.

I mentally wrote it down on a blackboard a thousand fucking times, à la Bart Simpson.

You don't like her.

You don't like her.

You don't like her.

But I did. Both Cal and Bitchy. A lot.

It was the middle of service, and Descartes was so packed, you couldn't squeeze a needle inside. Ninety-nine percent of the patrons were out-of-towners, and the one person who wasn't had a birthday, and her family—from Massachusetts—didn't know this place was Satan's favorite section in hell, so they'd booked a table here.

I didn't mind being the most loathed man in Staindrop. What I *did* mind was not having a goddamn truck. I had gone to get a rental from the next town over yesterday, and all they'd had left was a pink Jeep Wrangler. I had opted to stay carless until my Silverado returned from the shop and now had to walk everywhere. Descartes was down the street from the Half Mile Inn, so that wasn't an issue. But I had to get a taxi to visit Mom and Dylan, and fuck knew who had given Cal a ride here today.

Even if it's Kieran, you can't say shit about it. You're not her boyfriend. Not even her friend.

"Chef, can I ask you a question?" Taylor caught up to my steps, smoothing a hand over his jacket nervously. I was doing the rounds between stations, making sure everything was operating smoothly.

"Is it food related?" I grumbled.

"No."

"Same answer, then."

The entire kitchen looked up. One of my sous-chefs accidentally dropped a bowl. The dishwasher burst into tears.

Taylor grimaced but soldiered on. "You're extra prickly today. What happened?"

I'd made a conscious decision not to sneak a peek at the enchanting two-left-footed professional oversharer during her shift tonight. That was what had happened. And of course, I was pissed off about it. Not because I couldn't see her, obviously. But because I needed to check on my patrons and staff.

Really, what a dumb decision to make. I should head over to the partition window right now and take a look.

"Nothing happened. What do you want?" I made a pit stop at our chef pâtissier's station to let her know the raspberries looked older than an IHOP early-bird customer. Taylor was glued to my side.

"What's gonna happen to all of us when this place closes down?" he demanded.

Everyone stopped working and stared. My mother had once told me I was like a newborn. I only seemed to acknowledge a person's existence when they were right in front of me. I had never stopped to think of the lives I'd be leaving behind when I moved to London.

My real answer—*How the fuck should I know? I'm no fortune-teller*—was on the tip of my tongue. But Taylor didn't deserve my real answer, and neither did anyone else here. Some of the people working for me had to drive an hour each way to get here. They chose to work at this restaurant because it was important for them to get the experience, to nail this thing called upscale, gourmet dining.

I leaned a hip on Taylor's counter. "GS Properties is planning to build a mall. Last I checked the blueprint, the food court alone is going to contain twenty restaurants. Most will be high street, but chain companies offer insurance, 401(k), all the frills of a steady job. I tied it into the deal that all of my staff would get employed in the establishment of their choice once they start operating." They were also going to get a contract comparable to the one they currently had with Descartes.

"I don't want a steady job; I want to make art." Taylor's eyes zinged with determination.

I moved through to the seafood station, snatching a head of garlic from the chef's hand. "Garlic goes in the pan last. Pay attention or hang your apron." I crushed the garlic over a butcher block with the base of my palm, glancing at Taylor. "Employers will be clamoring for you, considering your experience. Then there's the hotel's restaurant. The investors said they want it to be fine dining to the highest degree. Seasonally updated menu, nine courses, European executive chef. I'm talking a Bib Gourmand awarded eatery, at the very least."

"Yours has three." Taylor folded his arms, curving a brow.

I shrugged. "Genius is hard to come by and impossible to keep."

"Will you write us letters of recommendation?" Melanie peeped up, one of my chefs de partie. "In case, you know, some of us decide to move away and try our luck in a big city?"

I stopped to lift the lid of the saucepan she was working on, sniffing. "I'll sign whatever you print out."

She nodded briskly, drawing a breath. "Thank you."

"What about the existing small businesses? Do you think they'll survive the change?" Dustin, the busboy, rubbed the back of his neck fidgetily. His dad had a mom-and-pop shop down the street.

"Most of them," I replied honestly. "I dug into GS Properties' proposal, and they seem to focus on the swanky shopping experience. They're not gonna open a Walmart here."

Dustin's shoulders sagged in relief. "Sweet. Thanks for letting me know."

"What about your new restaurant?" Taylor ran his tongue over his inner cheek, contemplative. "The one in London. Are you bringing in any…local enforcement?"

"Rhy's done with my ass." I shook my head. "He's moving to Manhattan."

"I meant anyone you think is a good fit."

The penny dropped. Poor kid wanted to come with me. Problem

was, I didn't do baggage. I'd only ever had Rhyland tag along because I knew he wasn't deadweight. Even during our heyday working together in France, Italy, and Monaco, Rhyland and I had always done our own thing. Different apartments, different social circles, schedules, hobbies, women. He was allergic to routine, and I was allergic to…humans, I guess.

Speak of the devil, my best friend rushed into the kitchen, his face whiter than the *Brady Bunch* cast. He grabbed my shoulder. "Row."

I turned around, sending him a leveled look. "What's up?"

"We've got an injured staffer." Rhy pushed his sleeves up his massive arms. "Cut forehead."

What was he telling me this for? I only knew one way to treat people—like crap.

"Do they need medical attention?" I spooned a handful of sauce from a pan, bringing it to my lips. "Too much rosemary," I chided my chef de partie.

"Unsure." Rhy scratched his neck. "Wanna come see?"

"Do I look like a doctor? Ask them," I said slowly. "Or better yet, call an ambulance. We don't need another Usher lawsuit."

"First of all—OSHA. Second, I wanted you to know because—"

"Unless they bled into someone's plate and a health inspector just walked in to witness it, I really don't see—"

"It's Cal," he cut into my words, face thunderous. "Cal is injured."

All the blood drained from my face. It rushed straight to my feet, which started moving. Running. I pushed Rhyland out of the way. He collapsed against metal shelves laden with bowls and whisks. The contents spilled over the floor with noisy clanks. I stormed the dining area, whipping my head, looking for her through the white-hot panic clouding my eyesight.

How had she cut her forehead? What the hell had she done now? Bang her head against a steak knife as a party trick? Had someone hurt her? A man?

Where the hell is she?

"I took her to the upstairs office to avoid a commotion." Rhy appeared by my side, rubbing the back of his head with an accusatory glare. "Zeta is taking care of her. She dropped by with some lasagna for your dinner."

Only my mother could pop into a three-Michelin-starred restaurant to deliver her chef son a meal he probably had to microwave.

I took the stairs three at a time, Rhy at my heels.

"How is she doing?" I was foaming at the mouth. Now was a good time to admit to myself that I *did* give a shit. Lots of shits, if I was being honest. An entire fucking sewer.

"Your mom or Calla?"

I shot him a glare behind my shoulder. He grinned. "Pretty good." He redid his man-bun as he took the steps. "The cut looks kinda nasty, though."

"Your face looks nasty."

"Supremely mature. Also a bit rich, coming from you right now. I could fill up an entire Olympic pool with your sweat. Chill the fuck out."

"It's hot in the kitchen." Had we always had five thousand stairs?

"You're used to the kitchen heat. It's the Cal heat that throws you off-balance. Shit," he snorted out. "You're worried, aren't you? I've never seen you this way before."

I slapped the door open so hard the handle made a dent as it slammed into the wall. I didn't know what I was expecting to see, but it wasn't Cal, resting on the upholstered brown leather couch next to my desk with her head propped against the armrest, my mother sitting on a chair next to her, pressing napkins to her forehead. The napkins were red as fine wine. Naturally, it didn't stop Cal from making a long, pointless speech.

"...all I'm saying is that objections at weddings exist solely to make the lives of overworked scriptwriters easier. Like, when did anyone ever oppose a wedding in real life? Also, the legalities of a marriage are established when you apply for a wedding license. Look, don't get me wrong, the *While You Were Sleeping* objection scene was *epic*, no complaints here, but when you think about it—"

"You're bleeding." I rushed to her side and fell onto my knees by the couch, fingering the batch of sticky napkins on her forehead. She looked sleepy and beautiful and *fuck*, that was another reason I didn't do relationships. Imagine caring for someone, then letting them wander the world, exposed to all kinds of shit? This girl was prone to dying from her klutziness. That she had lived this long was a miracle.

Cal's enormous, cloudless-sky eyes peered back at me, soot-lashed and innocent.

"Duh. I was there when it happened." I didn't know whether to laugh or berate her. "Wow. You're really pretty." She touched my cheek dazedly. "I mean, you're always pretty, but today you are extra pretty. Extraprettinery."

Shit. I hoped she didn't have a concussion.

"Does it hurt?" I croaked. Since when was I croaking? I was a grunter, a groaner, a bellower, sometimes. *Not* a croaker.

"Not really. But I think I'm getting a little woozy."

"You're anemic." *Oops.* Was not supposed to know that.

"I am!" she said brightly. "Oh, that reminds me, I need to refill my iron prescription. I haven't done that"—she scrunched her forehead, and the bleeding started again—"in three years or so. How'd you know anyway?"

She had mentioned it once during a sleepover at Dylan's when she was fifteen. That was why I'd kept all those Oh Henry! bars everywhere. She was bound to faint if she didn't take care of herself.

"Row…" Mom put a hand on my shoulder, and that was when I realized I was cradling Cal's head in my hands like she was dying in my arms. Her forehead probably needed stitches. There was a shit ton of blood. "She got hurt; she isn't dying."

"Are you a doctor?" I bit out.

Mom blinked, surprised by my harsh tone. "Well, no…"

"Then spare me your medical assessments." I twisted my head toward Rhyland. "Take Mom downstairs and call a doctor."

"I can just drive her to urgent care." Rhy ran his knuckles over his stubble. Right. Like I'd put her in the same car with a man who wasn't me.

"No. Call a doctor. I don't want her sitting around in a clinic the entire night." After realizing how it sounded, I added, "She still needs to finish her shift."

"Ambrose Rhett Casablancas," Mom gasped. "You force this poor girl to work tonight, and you'll be needing stitches too after I'm done with you."

Cal cackled. "I could marry you right now, Mrs. Casablancas!"

"Thank you, sweetie. The constitution of marriage disappointed me once. Not interested in trying again." That was the most she'd said about her marriage to my father in thirty years.

"Come on, Zeta, follow me. Row stocked up on the rosé you like." Rhyland approached Mom, resting a casual hand on her arm. She flinched at his touch, scooting away. I had to work my jaw back and forth to avoid cursing.

Rhy faltered, his face pinking. "Sorry about that."

"Don't be ridiculous." Mom mustered a weak giggle, rising up and sliding her purse over her shoulder. "Got an electric shock, that is all. Calla, you feel all better soon, okay, *cucciolotta*?" She tapped Cal's arm.

"Doubtful, with your son around." Cal grinned.

Mom let out a laugh, reaching to tuck a lock of hair behind Cal's ear. "I see you are handling him just fine."

I swatted Mom's hand away. "She's injured. You could hurt her."

Mamma ruffled my hair. "You're my favorite son."

"I'm your *only* son."

"Same difference."

Cal blinked at me as the door clicked shut behind them. "What's *cucciolotta*? She's been calling me that for years."

"Little puppy."

"She picked up on my golden retriever energy." A smile teased her mouth.

"Don't smile. Any movement you make might reopen the wound," I chided her.

She sighed. "Can you please stop treating me like I've been run over by a semitrailer?"

"Now that's an image for my spank bank." I tucked her flyaways behind her ear softly. "Can I take a look?"

She flinched. "Will you be gentle?"

"When have I not been?" I growled.

Her eyebrows shot to her hairline in response. "That time you threw me and Dylan into the pool when we were in fourth grade and I accidentally bumped my head. And in grade nine when you stepped on my toe and broke it when I asked you to teach me how to slow dance before prom. Oh! And there was also that ti—"

"It was a rhetorical question. Yes, I'll be gentle." I scowled. At least now I knew it wasn't a concussion. I slowly peeled the damp napkins from her forehead, holding my breath. "How did you manage to hurt yourself?"

"You know, easily, as per usual." She focused on a point on the ceiling to brave the burn that came from the dry blood gluing her skin and the cloth together. "I was running to get one of the patrons the wine menu—"

"You were running?" I snarled.

She gave me a pointed look. "I thought you encouraged me to run."

"In open spaces. Away from sharp objects. With a fucking helmet, preferably."

Way to charm her pants off, Casablancas, Rhyland's voice chortled in my head. *I'm sure she's seconds away from printing out your wedding invitations.*

"It's not even how I fell, okay?" She tapered her eyes. "I was trying to show Katie I can do a straddle split."

I didn't know whether to laugh or bash my own head against the wall. *Fuck.* Why was she so unapologetically, wonderfully herself?

"What made you think you could do a straddle split?"

"The fact that I was an athlete in high school and that I'm awesome?" She blinked at me seriously. "I'm extremely flexible."

"Would love to test that theory."

I shed the napkins from her forehead, dumping them on the floor. The cut stared right back at me. It didn't seem too deep, but there was a small chunk of skin missing, and I knew it would leave a scar.

"How do I look?" She gulped. Her head was still nestled in my arm.

"Beautiful," I admitted dispassionately. I was an asshole, not a liar.

"I meant the wound." She chewed on the edge of her thumb. "Is it hideous? Ghastly? Frightening?"

"It's small. Crescent shaped." I licked the pad of my thumb and rubbed away some dried blood around it to take a better look. *Don't say it. Don't.* "And it's perfect because it's on you."

Her lips quirked into a tired smile, and she pressed her cheek into my palm. "Hello, McMonster. Nice to have you back."

"You never lost me."

"You're only saying that because you're hopelessly in love with me."

"Don't make me kill you."

"Why not?" The corner of her lip moved along my rough palm. "It would make for a perfect excuse to procrastinate. 'Sorry, can't come tomorrow. I'll be dead.'"

"Nice try, but you are showing up to the shift tomorrow, even if it's in a coffin."

"I actually want to be cremated."

"Not gonna work. You're already too hot."

"Is that a pickup line?" Her eyes flared.

"That depends on whether it's working or not."

"Well, it's cheesier than a deep-dish pizza." She tried hard not to laugh. "I think I finally found something you're bad at. You're terrible at flirting."

"That's because I've never had to work very hard to get women to fall into my bed," I said, not an ounce of cockiness in my voice. "You're ruining my stats."

"Don't be so touchy. I *like* cheese. I would do heinous things for fried halloumi. This is a no-judgment zone." She laced her fingers through mine on her cheek.

For the first time in years, I experienced a moment of true happiness. It revolted and alarmed me. I pulled away, resting her head on the armrest. "You're bleeding again."

"Oh shit." She raised her hand to touch her wound before thinking the better of it. Her eyes widened in horror. "That couple never got the wine menu. I need to…" She tried standing up, but I shoved her back down to the couch.

"Who cares about their wine?"

"Hmm, *you*, Mr. Stickler." She poked my chest. "Ugh, I'm getting lightheaded again."

I stood up and walked over to my desk, opening the left-hand drawer. I ambled back toward her, unwrapping an Oh Henry! and thrusting it into her hand. "Sit up," I ordered.

She did, leaning against the headrest and snatching the candy, staring at me intently as she tore a bite off the chewy bar. The corners of her mouth lifted. "Hmm. Tastes like heaven. Wonder why you kept one in your drawer."

"You're not the only one who likes Oh Henry!" I seethed.

"We both know I am," she said around a huge chunk of chocolate, her smile widening. "Which is why I can't find these puppies anywhere. Where are you getting them? The black market? A time machine that's taking you to the nineties? Come on, share the wealth."

A thin river of blood snaked from her forehead down her cheek. Where was that damn doctor?

There was a knock on the door. Rhyland walked in. "Kitchen needs you."

"Kitchen can go fu—" I stopped, realizing Rhy's lips were a breath away from forming a shit-eating grin. "I'm busy right now," I corrected myself.

"Busy doing what?" He propped an elbow against the doorframe.

"Are you blind?"

"Are *you*? Cal's forehead seems under control." Rhy took one look at her, and even that was enough to jack up my blood temperature. "And Taylor's having a moment. Someone sent their steak tartare back. They want it cooked."

"Tartare means *raw*. Fixing stupid is above my pay grade."

"Respectfully, your pay grade is too generous for anything short of curing cancer." Rhy sauntered in, grabbing a stress ball from my desk and giving it a squeeze. "Anyway, he wants to know what to do."

"If Taylor wants a shot at wiping tables at La Vie en Rogue, not to mention joining me in the kitchen, he needs to pull himself together and rise to the occasion. We don't serve well-done steak. They can go to Applebee's for that."

"You need to go to the kitchen," Rhy reiterated, setting the ball back down.

"Row..." Cal said tentatively.

"No," I barked, still staring at Rhyland. "Final answer. Now leave."

Cal glanced between us sheepishly, slowly rising to her feet.

"Not you." I whipped my head in her direction. *"Him."*

"I don't wanna cause any trouble." Cal shook her head. "I can wait here by myself. I mean, I'm stuck on this *Best Fiends* level, anyway."

A knock sounded from the door.

"What now?" I stood up, ready to murder someone. Kieran, ideally.

"I'm sorry he is a sociopath," Rhy told Cal.

"It's okay." She gave him two thumbs-up. "Totally not your fault."

A man in an old-school leather jacket and a checked accountant button-down shirt walked in, pushing his glasses up his nose. "Hello, I'm Dr. O'Hara."

"Thank goodness you're here!" Cal slapped a hand to her chest dramatically. "Chef over here needs you to remove the stick from his ass. Oh, and while you're here, mind stitching my forehead?"

CHAPTER THIRTY-THREE
CAL

oBITCHuary: Favorite movie?

McMonster: The Wrestler.

oBITCHuary: RUDE. Ask me what's mine.

McMonster: I already know.

oBITCHuary: Well?

McMonster: Little Miss Sunshine.

oBITCHuary: WRONG.

McMonster: RIGHT. Stop lying.

oBITCHuary: FINE. It's a masterpiece and I stand behind my decision. Steve Carell's best work to date.

McMonster: Gotta have a good memory when you lie all the time. You need to keep track.

oBITCHuary: Exactly. Keeping my brain active. That's smart thinking. Favorite color? DON'T SAY BLACK.

McMonster: Purple. Yours is orange.

oBITCHuary: HOW DO YOU KNOW ALL THIS?

McMonster: I pay attention. Favorite word?

oBITCHuary: uyedin'éniye

oBITCHuary: It's Russian. It is the state of being alone without being lonely. Yours?

McMonster: Well, now I can't tell you mine because it's not half as good as yours.

oBITCHuary: There are no right or wrong answers.

McMonster: Titties.

oBITCHuary: Okay. I take it back. That is the wrong answer.

McMonster: I like the sound, I like the organs, I like the meaning. The prospects. Everything. It's a great word.

oBITCHuary: This is bad.

McMonster: Hey. You asked.

oBITCHuary: Not the word. THIS. You and me.

McMonster: Why?

oBITCHuary: Because we're utterly inevitable.

CHAPTER THIRTY-FOUR
CAL

"Baby Can I Hold You"—Tracy Chapman

After my forehead got stitched and bandaged, Row insisted on walking me home. An ordinarily chivalrous offer, unless you took into account the fact that I had an actual ride home in the form of Kieran Carmichael and his comfy Maybach. Apparently, Zeta had told Dylan about my injury. Dylan had called Kieran and demanded he save the day.

"I'll walk you," Row declared when I grabbed my backpack and coat from the break room. "You're not getting into that moron's car."

"Pretty sure I am." I collected my hair into a high ponytail. I was exhausted from lack of sleep, my head injury, and his constant bull crap. I also didn't know what to make of Row's behavior toward me. One second he told me I looked perfect while bleeding; the next he seemed annoyed by my existence.

Row removed his chef jacket, revealing a tight-fitting olive-green Henley. "It's not safe."

"How is bumming a ride with Kieran unsafe?"

"He looks like a substance abuser." Row slipped on his flight jacket.

Laughter spluttered from my mouth. "No, he doesn't. As a professional soccer player, he gets tested for drugs all the time."

"Those panels don't check for mushrooms."

"You're reaching."

"Yeah, the end of my fucking patience. You don't like being with men in a private setting, remember?"

"Yes," I huffed, not liking that he brought up things I'd told him as oBITCHuary. "I also remember trying to get over myself. Having Kieran take me home is a great step forward."

"Grab your umbrella, Dot. We're outta here." He ignored what I said.

He was dropping everything midservice to walk me home, and I wasn't sure what to make of it. As if reading my mind, Row jammed his beanie over his head angrily. "It's the second time you've been injured on my property. Just making sure you're up and standing. Don't get any ideas."

"I didn't say anything."

"You looked happy again."

"Is it a crime?" I suppressed a laugh. He was ridiculous.

"It should be."

We said goodbye to our colleagues and exited through the back door. Chill grazed our faces as we stepped into the crisp winter. Staindrop looked like a tipped-over snow globe, the dandruff of snow feathering the ground. I stuck my tongue out in delight and caught a few flakes.

"First snow of the season!" I twirled, opening my arms. I had on Mom's kick-ass mittens. "Dad loved the snow."

My father and I would wake up on winter mornings to a white-covered world. We'd run outside and make *Minecraft*-inspired snowmen. We'd hold their twig hands days later, as they melted, and say our teary goodbyes. They'd all had names, backstories, and motivations. Dad had said not to be sad because the snow melted into everything we touched and the same could be said about losing a loved one. The person who left us was still there—soaked into memories, objects, and other people. We all left a mark on this world.

It was only now that I understood Dad's greatest gift to me wasn't the bike I'd gotten for Christmas or even the Barbie house he'd gotten me when I was six. He had taught me creativity and imagination. And they were my safe place.

I turned around to check if Row was still there. He was. And he was staring at me in a way that made me feel naked yet somehow all fuzzy and warm inside.

"Let's go, Dot."

Descartes was a twenty-minute walk from my house. But it was a steep hill down toward the harbor. The street was lined with small shops adorned with pine wreaths, naked trees tangled in Christmas lights, and fluffy pillows of snow decorating rooftops.

The first few minutes were spent in silence. I tried to keep my mouth shut. We both needed a second to wrap our heads around what had just happened today.

Do not start a conversation.

Do not. *No matter how much you want his words.*

And his smiles.

And…fine, even his frowns.

"So why did you and Allison Murray break up?" my mouth inquired.

Damnit, mouth. You're grounded.

"What happened the day you broke your ankle?" He ran his tongue over his teeth, and I didn't know if he'd speculated the connection between the two subjects, but my heart skipped a beat.

"That's…personal." I grimaced.

"Same answer." Silence. Then, "Jesus, look at you. You're shivering." He dumped his bag on the ground, slid his jacket off his shoulders, and wrapped it around me, even though I already had on a big puffy coat. His jacket oozed warmth that seeped right into my bones.

"You can't do that. You only have a shirt on," I protested, only to have him rip the beanie from his head and slam it over mine, rolling it down.

"Here, that's better." He said that because my face was covered all the way. Bastard.

"You'll be cold." I pushed the beanie up, blinking at him.

"Don't worry about me."

"Someone needs to."

"Yeah, well, no one did, and I turned out just fine."

It was ridiculous, but I knew arguing would bring us nowhere—he was a *Taurus*, for crying out loud—so I quickened my pace. He shoved his hands into his front pockets. He had a leather messenger bag slung across his shoulder. Pink stained his high cheekbones. He looked like fan art of a fantasy villain.

I dug my teeth into my lower lip, dying to know what had made snooty, bitchy Allison worthy of being his ex-girlfriend—other than the banal stuff, like how she was a knockout, smart, ambitious, and had a killer wardrobe and, oh, an actual career.

"Those brain wheels of yours are a little rusty," Row muttered, still staring ahead. "I can hear them turning all the way from here."

"Let's trade info," I bargained. "I'll tell you about my injury, and you'll tell me about your relationship with Allison."

"*That* desperate for gossip, huh?" He chuckled humorlessly, but I could tell he wanted to hear my story.

"You never had a girlfriend growing up." I shrugged defensively. "I'm interested to know what made her different."

"At the price of telling me something you haven't shared with anyone?"

I swallowed. "Secrets are burdensome. Maybe I want you to carry some of my baggage." *Maybe I've been wanting to tell McMonster for a while now.*

"Will you carry some of mine?"

I nodded, not breaking eye contact. I didn't know why, but I really, *really* wanted to carry some of his baggage. Even if it meant showing him the most embarrassing, scarred part of me in return. Maybe if he knew what I'd gone through, he would understand why I didn't do relationships.

"So what do you say?" I held my breath for his answer.

He halted his steps, turning his head toward the other side of the residential street. "Hey, wasn't that your hangout spot?"

I swiveled to follow his line of sight and saw we were on the edge of Staindrop's community park. A lousy excuse for a playground. Two slides, two swings, one seesaw, and monkey bars. In high school, Dylan and I had come here in the summers to drink and gossip.

"A slice of heaven," I said breathlessly, my cheeks stinging with a smile. I twisted my head to face him. "Detour? For old times' sake?"

I couldn't read his face in the dark, but I thought I heard him smile. "Heaven better buckle up." He treaded in that direction, giving me his back. "Because the devil's about to drop in for a visit."

CHAPTER THIRTY-FIVE
CAL

"What's Up?"—4 Non Blondes

I discarded my backpack on the ground, rushing toward the swings. I grabbed the frosty chains and planted one foot over the rubber seat, hoisting myself up, finding my balance, then started rocking my body, creating momentum. "Now all that's missing is a stolen bottle of your dad's Tito's!" I howled into the night, a cloud of condensation rolling through my lips.

Row sighed like a wary parent, producing a bottle of vodka from his messenger bag and raising it between us. I wasn't sure whether he'd planned this or if it was just another item to add to my evidence file that he was an alcoholic. First shaking hands, now this.

"Ambrose Rhett Casablancas!" I shrieked, beaming in delight. "You knew our darkest secret?"

"That was a *secret?*" He scowled. "I've met thongs more discreet than you two."

Row trudged toward me, holding the vodka bottle by its neck. He perched on the swing next to mine and cracked the bottle open, taking a swig and passing it to me. I sat down and took a gulp, kicking my feet to sway back and forth.

I squinted at the mountains draped by the night. Suddenly, I had the distinct feeling I was in exactly the right place, at the right time, with the right person. A tiny part of a trillion-piece puzzle that neatly fit into this universe.

"So." Row received the bottle from me, unscrewed the vodka cap, sipped, then handed it back to me. "Start from the beginning. What happened that made you stop running and swear off humans?" He swished the clear liquid in his mouth. "Who did this to you?"

"Sure you want to find out?"

"How else would I know who to kill?"

His face told me he wasn't kidding.

My heart told me he was a safe person to open up to.

"I was bullied at school." The words rolled off my tongue without prior consent from my brain. Like Row's heartbeat next to mine was enough to squeeze the truth out of me. "Actually, it started in preschool. That's when kids realized not only was I an odd bird but I also came from an eccentric nest. My parents would send me out with socked feet and sandals in the summers. I looked ridiculous, and ridiculous makes five-year-olds laugh." It was silly for my throat to clog up about something that had happened almost two decades ago. "But what my peers found amusing in kindergarten, they found worthy of antagonizing meabout in elementary school. I dressed odd, I spoke odd, I *lived* odd. I had my eye tic every time I was nervous, which made me shy away from all the plays, parties, and major school events. To rub salt on a corroding wound, my parents were thrifty, so instead of eating at the school cafeteria, they sent me with cold meat sandwiches. They'd buy liver sausages and pork tongue at a deli and tuck them in my sandwiches. My lunches smelled from miles away and I'd be teased for it mercilessly."

"Why didn't you tell your folks sandals and socks don't go together? That you prefer jelly and sunflower butter on your sandwich?" Row's thick eyebrows slammed together angrily.

I pressed my lips together. "Because what people saw as quirks were actually my parents' upbringing. They grew up in Russia. It was the makeup of their DNA. The way they'd been brought up. I didn't want them to think they weren't doing a good job or that I was ashamed of what we are, of *who* we are..." My nose stung, and I held back tears. It was all so silly. Water under the bridge. Then why did thinking about it make me feel like I was drowning? "I think...I think being an immigrant can go two different ways. You either preserve, or you hide. My parents chose to wear their heritage like a badge of honor, and so, their legacy became mine. Every day I was taunted, I kept reminding myself of how lucky I was. I had two languages. Two cultures. Two worlds to enjoy. I could read Tolstoy in his native tongue. How lucky was I?"

Row's sunset eyes were glowing embers in the dark. He stared at me wordlessly, and in that moment, it *did* feel like I was unloading my baggage onto his broad shoulders. "You chose to get hurt so your parents wouldn't. I get it."

The bullies were gone now, but the scars they'd left lingered. "Anyway," I sniffed. "Kids didn't like me. Other than Dylan."

Dylan had had total main-character energy from the get-go. She had been there to shoo the bullies away. To snitch on those who'd pulled the chair from under my butt. She had chosen to sit with me at lunch unfailingly, and one day was even brave enough to try my tea sandwich with the liver, even though it had smelled like a whey protein fart. She stood up for what she believed in, and she believed in kindness.

Row nodded in my periphery. "How many people are we talking about?"

"Like, sixty percent of my grade?" I let out a snort. "It made it worse that I didn't *want* to fit in. I didn't try to dress, look, and talk like everyone else. I had the audacity to like my baked milk cookies and pork stew lard and Hypnotic Poison." I still wore the latter.

"People always tell you to be your true self, but when you're unapologetically you, it pisses them off," Row grumbled.

"It's the chicken-and-the-egg situation," I sighed. "I'm not sure what came first—me having social anxiety and being bullied for it, or being bullied to the point I developed a fear of interacting with humans."

"You don't fear interacting with humans. You interact with them all the time—you moved to New York, got a degree, work in hospitality. It's the fact you don't bend to boring social norms that makes you stand out." Row elevated an eyebrow. "I'm here to tell you, don't ever change."

"Why?"

"Because your quirkiness is one of your best fucking features."

A delicious sensation of pride and warmth washed over my entire body.

He rubbed his palms over his legs to gather heat. "Anyway, back to your story."

"In high school, the bullying got worse. Before, I was weird but meaningless enough not to warrant any special attention. But now, I'd started taking up space. Boys began noticing me. I joined the track team. I was an award-winning mathlete. A lot of people decided to overlook my weirdness and befriend me. They all wanted something from me, but I was so hungry for positive attention, I was happy to give it to them. That's when the lying began. When I realized I could mold myself to be whatever people wanted me to be, and that made them stay, at least for a while. For the first time in my life, I actually had friends who weren't Dylan. My stock went up, and that's when shit went down."

"They were jealous." His eyes darkened to two black holes, threatening to suck me in whole, and his mouth latched on to the vodka bottle angrily.

"Jealous?" I kicked the ground, throwing my body backward on the swing. "Doubt it. I don't think these girls wanted to swap places with me. They just didn't like me in their sphere. The track team was the worst." I squeezed my eyes shut. "I was really good. Competed for first place in my freshman year with this girl who was desperate to get a scholarship through track. She was a senior, and neck and neck with me. She always had a nasty remark at hand when I passed her. I called her Queen Bitch." In my head, anyway. I was incapable of being rude, even to the most awful people.

Row passed me the vodka. When I grabbed it, it seemed much lighter. We were both whimsically drunk. In that existential spot where the world made more sense because you'd stepped out of your point of view for a minute.

The clear liquid scorched a path down my throat. Finally, I got to the part I'd never shared with anyone. The part that had carved me into who I was today with a rusty Swiss knife. A girl who'd sworn off men forever. "Worse than potentially taking the first spot from Queen Bitch as the fastest female runner at school, she found out one day that the boy she liked, Franco, was my secret boyfriend. He was eighteen. I was fourteen. We did...*stuff*." Almost went all the way. Stupidest thing I'd ever done to be liked. "It was wrong. I knew it was wrong. I still did it. He was the captain of the hockey team. Made me feel seen. Grown-up and beautiful. He said we were his favorite secret. I agreed to lie for him, not even telling Dylan about us."

Franco had been using my body and my pariah status to get his rocks off. I'd always known that in the back of my head. But fourteen-year-old me had been desperate to make a friend in the popular hockey hero.

Row hummed with hot, furious energy. I could practically feel his fury trickling into my system, hiking up the temperature in the park by ten degrees. He glided his tongue along his upper teeth, stifling a curse. "Continue."

"It all came to a head when Queen Bitch caught us in the locker room...well, *me*, giving Franco...uhm." *Head.* I couldn't say it. But I didn't have to. Row's nostrils flared and he closed his eyes, bracing himself for the knockout confession. "Franco could've gotten in insane trouble for messing around with me, but he thought himself so untouchable, it didn't even cross his mind."

My heart was about to spill out of my chest like a broken egg, I felt so raw talking about it.

"You were abused." Row's lips curled over one another like burned paper. "You should've never gone through this alone."

"When she caught us, Franco just…laughed. I wasn't sure how I was expecting him to react, but I knew it wasn't that. He told her I was a groupie, a stupid little whore. He pushed me off him so carelessly, and when I hit the back of my head on the grimy floor, he let out a snort. She tried to laugh it off too, I think. To show that she didn't care. But I think it was just too much for her. I was the weirdo freshman. I wasn't supposed to take her scholarship *and* the guy. I don't even know why she wanted the scholarship so bad. It's not like she didn't have money. So during one of our morning five-mile rounds around the woods, she went after me." An icy shiver licked over my skin. "Along with everyone else on the team. They all looked up to her. Bigwig dad, money, looks, reputation. Everyone on the team wanted to please her."

"What was her name?" His voice was low, husky, deadly.

But I was in a trance, transported back into the moment. "What started as a routine practice ended up as a bloodthirsty chase. They'd had enough. I was drawing too much attention, making too much noise. Coach wasn't there that morning. It was just us girls. Queen Bitch, the ringleader, said, 'Time's up, Litvin. You didn't really think you were going to get away with it, right? Being normal and popular and shit.'"

I still remembered every word like it was yesterday because each had left a scar on my heart.

"The woods stretch out for hundreds of acres from either side of this town." I kept my eyes on the ink-black sky, avoiding his pitying look. "I knew I stood no chance against all of them. It was just me and them and their hate."

Row's fingers were screwed tightly into his eyes. "Dot…" His voice was gruff. "That time you broke your ankle…you didn't fall, did you?"

Everyone had thought my injury was a freak accident. After all, I *was* a klutz. I closed my eyes. "They chased me."

"Let's see how fast you run now, you little shit."

"Said they'd skin me alive when they got to me. It took them twenty minutes to catch me."

"The irony wasn't lost on me. Turns out I really was the fastest. But then my teammates were everywhere. Snaking between trees, lurking behind bushes. Queen Bitch was the one who ended up snatching the hem of my hoodie. 'Well, well. If it isn't Franco's little hussy girlfriend. You know he only dates you because you're a Russian whore, right?' She dragged me by my feet toward the river. I kicked and screamed, clawing at the wet ground. Two of my fingernails snapped out of my skin. I begged for help."

"Aw, she's a feisty one. Franco said your tics go crazy when you go down on him. Is that true?"

It was. And I had been nauseous with humiliation because he'd shared the most intimate, shameful part of me with my enemy.

"You know he told me he put pictures of you naked on porn sites? Your face is all over the internet with you cupping your tits. What kinda freshman whore even sends a senior naked pictures? Jesus."

The revelation had poured hot, renewed rage into me. I'd managed to kick her in the face. She had stumbled back, bracketing her nose, blood gushing between her fingers.

"Catch her, Becky!" Queen Bitch had called out to Rebecca Stanton, who'd stood limply on a tree trunk, watching with horror.

"She's so fast, though!" Rebecca had whined.

"Just do it!"

Disoriented, Rebecca had pounced on me. She'd grabbed my foot and tugged it sideways sharply. The cracking sound it had made bounced with an echo over the treetops. A shriek had pierced the air. The pain had been so sharp, I couldn't breathe.

I sometimes wondered why I was so afraid of men when girls were the ones to physically abuse me. I once touched that subject with a therapist, though, and she said something that resonated with me. After the abuse, it was women who picked me up and saved me. It was Dylan. It was Mom. It was the therapist herself. They were my safe haven.

"Everybody freaked out." I blinked furiously, my eyes matching the drum of my heart. "Queen Bitch said they should mercy-kill me, because my legs were my best asset, and now that I couldn't open them to seniors or run, I was truly useless."

"We could get away with it. No one will be looking for her for hours."

"Queen Bitch decided burying me alive was the ultimate solution to her problems. At first, everyone was so shocked they just went along with it. The power of herd mentality, I guess. They flung dirt on my face and body as I cried and screeched and begged her to rethink it. They knew I wouldn't snitch on them. Knew I would never go against the powerful teammate who led this thing against me. Clout in small schools is everything." My entire body rocked back and forth as I came face-to-face with the memory. "They were screaming and arguing by the time I couldn't breathe. I had so much mud on me. I could barely hear them, their voices muffled. I don't know who convinced them to stop or how, but they did. Queen Bitch wanted to kill me for real, but…the others were too scared, I guess. Two girls dug me out of the shallow grave and yanked me up. They ran away before I could ask for water, for help." I tried to swallow the bitter lump in my throat. Failed. "I had to crawl my way back to town with a broken ankle."

I let the vodka bottle slip from between my fingers. The liquid sloshed on the sand. The silence around us was a big loud wall. I wanted to scream to penetrate it.

"The worst part"—I heard my voice floating between us, and I knew that my lips were moving but wasn't sure what was going to come out of my mouth—"is that when I finally reached the edge of the woods, where the forest kissed the residential street, the thought crossed my mind to make a U-turn and die. I didn't want to face my life post this incident. Post the attack. Post Franco."

I had already made up my mind not to tell my parents what happened. It would have crushed them. I'd just had to keep on lying. Spinning the untruths like cotton candy on a stick. Fluffy, sugary, and inviting.

Franco hadn't lied. He had put my pictures on some small porn sites. Probably to appease Queen Bitch and show her that I had meant nothing to him. I'd go on these sites years after the fact to punish myself for trusting. For believing a guy like Franco could love a girl like me. I felt violated. Ripped to shreds and robbed of my consent.

"And Franco?" There was a slight tremor in Row's voice. A wave of queasiness washed through me.

"He visited me at the hospital, but only to tell me he was now dating Queen Bitch and not to interfere. He said he'd ruin my life if I said one word about what had happened. That he'd kill me with his own hands if I took away everything he built, because he'd have nothing to lose. I was fourteen and scared shitless. Crushed from the rejection, injury, and betrayal. Bottling up everything, feeding my parents lies so they wouldn't be worried—lies like *I had an accident, I fell, I was actually close with my teammates.*

"It turned out not only were Franco and I nothing but that he actively hated me for 'putting everyone in a bad spot.'" I air-quoted Franco. "He ended up dropping out of college a year or so later. In and out of jail for selling drugs. You know, I thought it'd make me feel better, how bad his life turned out to be. It didn't, though. His misery didn't erase mine. His failure didn't diminish the fact that he took away from me the ability to trust a man. He made me see every strange man on the street as the enemy, as the villain."

"He's dead now," Row said, his voice devoid of emotion. I wasn't surprised or moved in any way. Didn't feel anger, joy, or relief. "A mutual friend told me a few months ago. Overdose. Shame."

"Shame?" I raised an eyebrow.

"I'd have loved to kill him myself."

"That's a nice sentiment, but I would never want you to screw your life over for someone so meaningless. Queen Bitch is still around." I stared at my feet, flinging them in the air to keep me warm. "All the other girls are here too, as far as I know."

"I need a name." There was something in his tone this time that indicated he would shatter the earth to dust if I ignored him. "I need to know who did this to you."

"Allison." My eyes met his across the swings. "Queen Bitch is Allison Murray."

Even though I'd kept my mouth shut about that day, my dislike for her had been public knowledge. Dylan had even made a voodoo doll of her for my entertainment for one of my birthdays. We'd never used pins on it, but I'd once given it a nasty haircut.

The silence engulfed us like thick smoke, trickling into our lungs, suffocating us. I couldn't look at him, but from the corner of my eye, I saw the shift. Row was normally pure power. Greater than life and self-assured. Now, he fished his cigarette pack from his front pocket and flipped it open with his thumb, pulling a cigarette using his teeth and lighting it up. His hand tremored in the dark. *"Fuck."*

He smoked half the cigarette in complete silence, staring into nothing and trying to calm himself down. Finally, he flicked the cigarette out to the sand.

"Dot, I—"

But I interrupted him, quickly wiping my tears away. "Whatever. You know what they say. What doesn't kill you makes you acutely emotionally damaged to the point of having dysfunctional relationships with everyone around you. Thing is, no matter how much time passes, I will always be that girl who was running away from her problems, from her bullies. I will always live with the consequences of not telling on a bunch of people who wanted to *kill* me. They should've been punished."

"They should've," he agreed, bracing his elbows on his knees, drawing closer. "But that girl who ran away? She grew up to be a strong fucking woman with zero outside help. You shouldn't be so hard on her. She did her best."

I wished it were that simple.

I couldn't bear how raw and self-conscious I felt, so I changed the subject quickly. "Tell me how you got to romancing my nemesis. Spare no detail. Unless she's a better kisser than me. I really don't want to know that."

He snapped his mouth shut, closed his eyes, and took a deep breath. "She was a mistake."

I snorted out a laugh. "Are you saying that because of what I told you right now?"

"I'm saying this because she was like putting a Band-Aid on a decapitated fucking head. I'm saying this because…because…" He spluttered, running his fingers through his moussed hair, looking adorably, uncharacteristically boyish. His edges smoothed and his claws withdrawn. "I didn't even touch her, okay?"

"What?" I blinked, confused.

"I. Didn't. Even. Touch. Her," he said, slowly now, his eyes glittering in the dark, boring into mine. "We went on a few dates, mainly in hopes you'd find out and see that I've moved on from your ass. I don't remember where. I don't remember what she wore. What we talked about. I only remember how she made me feel."

"How?"

"Bored to fucking tears."

"She wasn't what you were looking for?" I licked my lips, feeling guilty about drawing so much pleasure from hearing this.

"She wasn't *you*."

My jaw fell open. "I… We…" I wasn't completely unaware. I knew Row was attracted to me. That he wanted us to be *something*, at least for the duration of our time in Staindrop. "I hadn't realized your feelings ran that deep."

"Unfortunately, I'm not as good a liar as you. I can't stop think-ing about you, and it's killing me. Killing me that I somehow ended up wanting the only woman I could not have. That someone came along and ruined you before I had the chance to even show you how great it could be. That this someone was fucking Franco. It's killing me that I now need to spend the rest of my life trying *not* to kill Allison Murray, despite her being highly murderable. It's killing me that we could've been there for each other, but we weren't. That we could've healed each other, but instead, we just cracked deeper and harder. Most of all, it's fucking killing me that I only feel alive when you're around."

This was his moment. His moment to kiss me. We were inches from one another. Drunk. Vulnerable. Sad. Full of so many emotions and cloaked by a silky sheet of starlit night.

But he didn't kiss me. Instead, he pulled away, releasing his hold from the swing and ruffling the back of his hair, staring down at his feet.

"He noticed," he croaked.

"Huh?" I sniffled, still stuck on the fact that he liked me.

"My dad. You were wrong. He noticed when you and Dylan stole his vodka."

My stomach tightened. "How come he never said anything?"

Row licked his lips, squinting hard at the houses across the street, gracefully stacked together, like in Monopoly. "I took the fall."

"Row, why—"

"Doesn't matter."

"Don't tell me that! We could've apologi—"

"Wouldn't have worked."

"But wh—"

"Because." The roar ripped from his mouth. "He would've hurt you, and I'd have killed him if he did that."

Stunned, I watched as he yanked his phone out of his pocket, tapped the flashlight, and tossed it into my hands. He stood up from the swing and turned his back to me, slowly raising his shirt. I aimed the flashlight at his back.

My chest caved inward. Scars ran like a busy road map across his triangular back under the elaborate ink. Long, jagged, faded, roaring poems of pain. Some pink, some white. Some shallow, some deep. All told the story of unbearable pain, years of abuse, and unforgivable trauma.

My fingers quaked around his phone. Violent nausea washed through me.

His back was still to me when he spoke. "My father was a raging alcoholic. He drank himself to near death at least twice a year. Whenever he wasn't catching fish, he was getting hammered and causing all kinds of trouble. Most times he went fishing in the middle of the night, I lay in my bed praying the boat would flip over and he'd drown. Never come back. You didn't know because Mom and I wheeled him away from view, tucking him in their bedroom whenever Dylan had company. We tried to make her life as normal as possible. Or at least not as screwed up as ours."

It had worked. I'd had no idea. I mean, yeah, Mr. Casablancas hadn't been the nicest person in the world...but I'd never thought he had an alcohol problem. I'd just thought he was naturally grumpy. Like Row.

"I wish you'd have told me." I rose on unsteady legs. His back was still to me, and I had a feeling he preferred it this way. "Or Dylan. *Someone.* We wouldn't have stolen his bottles. We thought no one noticed. I can't believe I caused this."

His shoulders trembled with bitter laughter, and he slid his Henley back down, spinning in my direction. Molten amber eyes met mine.

"*You* didn't cause shit. You were just teenagers doing teenager stuff. He'd have found something else to get pissy about and hit me. I mostly managed to keep him away from Mom and Dylan—not always from Mom. She had to tolerate some abuse."

"And Dylan?" My voice was brittle, crisp, a crunchy autumn leaf under a boot.

He shook his head. "I don't think she knows. We did a great job, and he worked long hours, disappearing days at a time when he was in the midst of his binges."

I thought back to the flippant comment Dylan had made about her father passing when she had come to Dad's funeral and didn't know if Row was right in his assessment. Knowing Dylan, she *did* know but figured Zeta and Row took comfort in her obliviousness.

Taking a step toward him, I said, "That's why your mom flinched when Rhyland touched her."

The column in his throat rolled. "He'd drag her around the house by the hair when Dylan was at school. Kick her ribs. One day he—" He stopped.

I put my hand on his chest. His heart was beating wildly. Our scents, heat, and breath swirled together, and I felt closer to him than I'd ever been before. Even when we'd had sex. "You can tell me," I whispered softly. "I want to be your safe space too."

"One day, Dylan was sleeping over at your house. You stole his Tito's. It was his last one, and he was too broke to buy another. I told him it was me. I was afraid he'd drive to your house and fight you for it or something. He'd cracked my rib only two weeks earlier. So this time, Mom tried to protect me. He hurled her against the stove while it was on. Gave her a second-degree burn. Her entire arm was pressed into it, the skin melted onto it."

Was that why Zeta always wore long sleeves? Even in the summer?

"Then, when she was sobbing on the floor, clutching her arm, he took his dick out and pissed on her. 'There, honey. That'll put out the fire.'"

"Row." My fingers curled around the fabric of his Henley, clutching him tight, breathing him in, putting him back together.

Row.

Row.

Row.

I'd always felt this kinship between us. Like our souls were a two-part friendship necklace. Now I knew why. Because we'd both tasted darkness. Looked evil in the eye and survived. We were always destined to connect. Mac and Bitchy. Row and Cal.

Row's eyes dimmed. "When I saw him do this to her, something snapped in me. I couldn't take it anymore, living in this never-ending nightmare, losing sleep over the idea he'd hurt Mom, or Dylan, or… or *you*." There was a tense pause. "I beat the shit out of him. So bad I punctured his lung and broke his jaw." I could imagine the entire scene in my head. Row taking back his power, finally controlling the narrative. "Mom was hysterical. More about me landing in jail than anything else. The only reason I didn't finish the job was because he wasn't worth shitting all over my future."

"I'm glad you didn't. Your conscience wouldn't have survived it. You are too good…incorruptible." I shook my head, tears flying off my cheeks. "What happened next?"

"He came back home after a week and a half. No one went to visit him. We told Dylan he had a stroke and that he didn't want her to see him like that. She never questioned it. I made it clear to him he wasn't welcome in the house unless he sobered up. So…he did."

"Just like that?" I squinted.

"No, I'm giving you the bullet-point version." A rueful smile touched his lips. "There were tears, arguments, and meltdowns. Furniture and promises broken." He scrubbed his jaw. "We couldn't afford rehab, so I had to lock him in my room. He climbed the walls. He begged and bargained. Tried to assert power over us again. But in the end, I tired him out. He kicked the habit."

A ragged breath passed between us. It felt like we were sharing oxygen. Row continued, "But it was no victory. There was no happy ending. The trust was gone. Mom was scared and resentful, and Doug became a shadow. Moving around, casting darkness every-where he went."

"How did he die?" I rasped.

"Liver failure. The damage was too much, even after he quit. Can't say it was a sad day for me. I never forgave him."

"Unpopular opinion…" I trailed a finger up his chest. "It's okay not to forgive people who destroy our lives."

Row clasped my hand over his heart. He leaned into my palm, and it felt like the universe was giving me the rarest gift, tying us together in a red satin bow. I wondered how drunk we were. If we were going to regret our confessions tomorrow morning. Or if it would finally break the corroded wall we'd built between us all those years ago.

"Opening Descartes was my fuck-you moment to him." A broody chuckle escaped him, and he was especially gorgeous now, bare and vulnerable, swimming in the dusk like a mythical creature. "He'd always wanted to open a restaurant. It was his dream. He went to culinary school when he was young. Had to drop out when Mom got knocked up with me." A sharp exhale. "I was a mistake, and Mom's Catholic parents didn't like out-of-wedlock mistakes. So, in a way, I stole his dream twice. Once when he quit school, and a second time when I got accepted to one."

"You never asked to be conceived." I rubbed the edge of his neck with my finger distractedly. His erection was pressed against my belly, but now wasn't the time to concentrate on it.

"He wanted to show the world he was more than a blue-collar drunkard." Row sucked in his teeth. "But the truth was…he wasn't."

"You opened an entire restaurant to spite a dead man." I shook my head, chuckling at the madness of it all. "That is so…unlike you."

"Why?" he asked.

"You normally don't care."

"Oh, I care." He looked away, turning his head as if the truth had slapped him. "I care too fucking much, that's the problem."

A snowflake landed on my nose. Row scooped it with the pad of his thumb, slowly popping it into his mouth. I grinned.

"What?" His forehead creased. "I wanted to see why you always taste the weather."

"Verdict?"

"Tasteless."

Our mouths were less than an inch away. A rush of warmth and adrenaline coursed through my veins. My lips gravitated toward his. Row pulled away slightly. I groaned in frustration. He flattened his hand on my stomach, walking me backward, toward the swings. "Anyway. I learned from a very young age that hope was the cruelest form of punishment. You offer me hope, Cal. It's a tempting deal, but I'd be a fool to take it, knowing who you are and who I am."

He was still backing me toward the swings, while I watched his face, mesmerized. "Who am I?" I whispered.

"A person who can't fall in love, doesn't want to fall in love, and has deep trust issues with men. Flaky and unreliable." He continued walking me backward, and I continued stumbling in his desired direction.

"And who are you?" I gulped.

"A man who can't fucking resist you." He dragged his fingers through his mane. "But I'll be doing both of us a disservice if I don't state this outright—I don't care about the consequences. I want you. And what I want, I get."

"Row, I…" But I didn't really know what I wanted to say. That maybe I could fall in love? That I was afraid if we started something, I would be left destroyed?

He removed his hand from my tummy, plastering a finger over my mouth to shut me up. The backs of my thighs crashed against the swing's seat.

"Don't, Dot. Don't try to convince me you're unlikable. I want you. You're funny, authentic, sassy, and have the best ass I've ever seen. And I'm not being hyperbolic." Pause. "We're going to have a brief, no-strings-attached hookup while we're both in this shithole, and then we're gonna go back to our respective lives. Whatever state I've gotten myself into after this thing is my business and my business alone. If I can't have the heart, I'll take the pussy."

I could do this. I could do casual. With him, my body could open up. It was my heart I was worried about.

"We're two passing ships." He cupped my cheek.

His hand was warm and inviting, and I wanted to press into it, to get lost in him. Did he say this to assure me or himself?

"Now that we've established we're both messed up." He threaded his fingers in my hair, tugging it slowly to extend my neck and tilt my head up to meet his gaze. "How about we make tonight interesting?"

"Was this evening not eventful enough for you?" I spluttered.

He chuckled, rubbing the spot next to my bandaged forehead soothingly. "Remember you and Dylan had a game? You called it swingers."

"Is that what we called it?" I snorted. "Clearly, we did not think it through."

"You stood up on the swings and whoever fell first lost."

I remembered that. Amazingly, I should add, considering the amount of concussions I'd suffered as a result.

"What are we betting on?" I probed, feeling beautiful and alluring and worthy under his gaze. Every girl needed a Row Casablancas to make her feel seen.

"If you fall first…" He bracketed his arms on either side of me, gripping the swing chains and trapping me in place, his vodka breath skating down my face.

"If I fall first?" I whispered, wondering if we were still talking about the swings.

"You let me kiss you."

His words soaked into my skin. Goose bumps rolled over every inch of my flesh.

"And if I win," I said slowly, watching him as his eyes traced my lips hungrily. "You make me and Mamushka a three-course picnic lunch. We're going to spread Dad's ashes and I want to make a day of it."

"Done," he said without missing a beat.

I pressed my finger to his chest. "And *I* would be the one in charge of the menu."

"You'd choose cheese sticks and corn dogs." He looked disgusted.

"Hey, I have a little more class than that."

"Lies." He studied me skeptically. "What are you thinking?"

"Pop-Tarts, curly fries, and soy burgers."

"Soy?" He gagged, glancing around, making sure we didn't have an audience. He lifted a finger between us. "Nobody, and I mean *nobody*, can know I made those…"

"Dishes?" I smiled brightly.

"Culinary crimes."

"Shouldn't have told me that. Now I'm fully prepared to blackmail you with this piece of information when the day comes."

"It's not gonna come, since you're not gonna win." He worked his jaw back and forth. "Fine. Deal."

We were up on those swings in seconds. Me, standing straight and clutching the chains in a death grip, and him, crouching down so his head wouldn't bump against the metal frame.

We ready, set, go-ed, then started swinging. I cheated a little, barely moving back and forth, then gained more speed and force when I realized Row was moving with so much momentum, the entire frame shook. He almost tipped me off with every move of his body.

"Can you tone it down?" I grumbled. "I might need more stitches after this game."

"Here to win, not make friends." He swung himself faster and harder.

Dread filtered into my system. I didn't want him getting hurt. In fact, the idea of Row feeling any kind of pain made me want to scream. Especially after what he'd told me about Doug tonight. *"Row.* You'll hurt yourself."

"Used to the pain."

"Are you serious?"

He shrugged, swinging harder, looking like a boy determined to slay an imaginary dragon, the unoiled cylinders of the swing frame squeaking under our weight. "Why do you think I have so many tattoos? Pain is the only thing that reminds me that I'm alive."

I want you to remember you're alive for all the right reasons. Through smiling. And laughing. And kissing. Everywhere. Anywhere on your body.

Without thinking about what a colossal mistake I was making, I hurled myself off the swing, landing face-first on the cool, snow-sprinkled sand. My face was pressed against the ground. The cold felt good on my forehead wound.

I heard the rusty chains of Row's swing screech, followed by the heavy thump of his body landing next to mine. "Shit, Dot. You okay?"

He rolled me over to my back and covered me with his entire body, lying flat on me, pressing himself against me. His bulging muscles warmed me, his erection nestled between my thighs. Desire shot up my belly like an arrow straight from my center, making my breasts swell, nipples stand on point, and mouth pool with saliva.

"Your heart." I curled my fingers against his chest, in awe of how warm he was. "It's going wild."

His Adam's apple moved with a swallow. He brushed a finger along a constellation of my freckles. "Yours too."

"I lost the bet." I gazed up at him. My lips stung with expectation. My heart was a hummingbird, flapping its wings against my rib cage, desperate to escape.

"I noticed." His eyes dropped to my mouth. Silvery snowflakes fell from the sky, framing his gorgeous face. "On purpose."

Gulping, I tried to change the subject. "Speaking of hearts, you know what I don't get? How anyone ever thought 'My Heart Will Go On' is a fitting theme song for *Titanic*. I mean…how on the nose is that? After Jack *literally* saved Rose while slowly dying of hypothermia in front of her very eyes—and yes, there *was* enough space on that door for both of them—they have the audacity to use a song with lyrics that say she will go on, *move* on, to live her best, rich bitch lif—"

"Dot?"

"Hmm?"

"Shut up."

I opened my mouth. Closed it. Opened it again. "Make me."

"Baby, thought you'd never ask."

There was no hesitation in his next move. His lips came crashing down on mine hungrily, sucking my oxygen and ripping my mouth open savagely, his tongue claiming mine in a kiss that made me whimper. I became lightheaded as our tongues entwined. He cradled my head in his rough palms to keep me contained, but I still thrust and thrashed, catching his lips whenever he pulled away for breath, biting and groaning, begging for more. The bandage on my forehead rustled, unfurling between us as we devoured one another. The kiss was impatient, demanding, feral, like he was already rooted deep inside me. Like this was the main dish, and not an appetizer, not an item to cross off a checklist and then move on to something else.

I scooped his lower lip between my teeth, sucking it into my mouth, tracing it with my tongue. I snaked my hand between us and shoved my palm into his pants and boxers, cupping his dick and squeezing hard. The fat tip of his cock dripped warm precum into my palm. He let out a hiss of pleasure, pressing into my hand, and liquid warmth spread inside my chest.

"Shit, fuck," he hissed into my mouth. In a frenzy, I circled my fingers around his shaft from the base, my thumb struggling to meet my index he was so thick. The kiss became wetter, sloppier when I began pumping his dick, stroking while massaging his balls with my pinky each time I hit the root. A feral growl of pleasure left his mouth. He grabbed my ass with quivering fingers, grinding against my hand with punishing force, releasing one of my ass cheeks only to slip his hand under the layers of jackets and shirts I was wearing, finding my bra and twisting one of my nipples through it. A shot of pleasure arrowed through me, and I moaned loudly, my center exploding with heat.

My phone began ringing somewhere from the depths of my bag. I recognized the ringtone. "Friends" by BTS. *Crap.*

"Dylan…" I groaned into our kiss.

"Wrong sibling," he grumbled huskily, sucking and licking, exploring my mouth like it was ancient ruins in Greece. He rubbed my nipple with his thumb, pinching and teasing it, making the rush of heat between my legs unbearable and uncomfortable. I needed release. "But fuck, you can call me Stalin and I'd still stay for the pussy right now."

"No, Row, *Dylan* is going to kill us." I flattened a hand on his chest, ripping my mouth from his as I tried to sober up. I jerked my hand from his crotch, blindly patting the snow for my bag as the ringtone kept on singing.

Row reluctantly unglued his mouth from mine, breathless and off-kilter. His hair was a delicious mess. I tugged the phone from my backpack, but he grabbed it before I could answer and tossed it a foot from us. "She knows."

"Hmm, what?" I must've misheard him. A side effect of all my blood moving to my clit.

"I told her." Row bracketed my ears with his elbows, thumbing away my flyaways, staring deep into my eyes.

"Told her *what?*"

"That I was going to fuck you in every position. On every surface in this town. In every hole in your fucking body." He was dead serious, looking me straight in the eye. "She said she's okay with it. Oh, and that you're prone to ear infections."

I was. And I appreciated the fact my best friend didn't want me going deaf because of one horny, ill-advised decision.

"You told her you want to…screw me?" I blinked.

"No, Dot. I spared her every obscene thing I want to do to you. Like how I want to watch my cum dripping from between your lips. Fuck you against windows and doors and national goddamn symbols." He was still staring, and our genitals were still pressed together, waiting for the okay to pounce on each other. "So instead, I just mentioned I wanted to pursueyou. Scratch that itch, to put it diplomatically."

I wanted him to scratch the itch. Hell, I wanted him to peel me sheet by sheet until I was completely raw. And it scared me, that I wanted all those things with him. That I wanted anything at all with a man after what Franco had put me through.

"Cal, are you crying?" He frowned, looking concerned. "That's... not something that happens too frequently when I get together with a woman."

Oops. My face felt extra cold and wet. "A little." I rushed to wipe off my tears. "I'm just moved that Dylan's forgiven me, is all." Technically, *not* a lie. "I won't do anything until I ask for her permission, though. Just to be on the safe side this time."

He gave me an exasperated look. "Fine. My dick's about to fall off from the cold and erection anyway."

A giggle laced into my hiccup. I swatted his chest. "Move, then."

"Hey, Bitchy?" He stopped.

"Yes, Mac?"

"You're okay with what we just did, right?" He kissed my temple, still pinning me to the ground, and I had a feeling he was still on top of me because he was afraid I'd fall apart and break, and was keeping me together to ensure I was all right.

I nodded. I wanted to do it again, naked and often. I wanted more kissing and touching and nipping and sucking. But I wanted the other stuff too. The conversations and the movies and the hand-holding. To be his. For him to be mine.

"Yeah?" He tilted his chin down, assessing me.

"Yeah."

"I just…" I started, not sure what I wanted to say. "I don't want either of us to get hurt."

Me. I don't want to get hurt. I don't want to need to collect my scattered pieces when this is all over. It took me years after Franco. Years.

Row looked away, at the ground, his ruddy, high cheekbones flaring with heat. "I'll take what you are willing to give me."

I could give him just the sex part. I could. I didn't need the boyfriend stuff. It would keep both of us protected. I nodded. "Okay."

He hopped up to his feet, then offered me his hand and pulled me up.

"Dust the snow off, Dot. Now, how many Pop-Tarts should I make you?"

CHAPTER THIRTY-SIX
ROW

McMonster: Hi.

McMonster: You can't be mad.

McMonster: I'm not even your boyfriend, I don't need to tell you where I go and when I leave.

McMonster: London is lovely this time of the year.

McMonster: You should come visit sometime.

McMonster: You should also come, period.

McMonster: It would help loosen all this pent-up rage.

McMonster: I volunteer as tribute.

CHAPTER THIRTY-SEVEN
ROW

"Heaven's sake, Ambrose, is that duffel from Target?" Tate Blackthorn, the CEO of GS Properties, leaned an elbow against his red Gulfstream G650ER, ripping his Ray-Bans off his eyes.

"Walmart," I corrected. "Nice wheels."

Tate scowled disapprovingly in his Tom Ford suit, fighting his gag reflex. "Yeah. Bill Gates owns the same model. His is older, though." He yanked off his dark leather gloves one finger at a time. "He's doing this whole green thing now. What's it called?"

"Global warming?"

"Yeah, that liberal nonsense."

I took a slow, calming breath and counted to ten in my head. At least he hadn't called it a hoax. Although I couldn't put anything past this man, mass murder included.

"Thanks for the ride." I carried my duffel bag along the tarmac of the small private airport outside of London. I'd spent the last couple of days checking in on the progress at La Vie en Rogue, my upcoming restaurant. A perfect excuse to remove myself from Staindrop and from Cal.

"I was in the neighborhood. Had business in Geneva." Tate started up the stairs. "And you're a hard man to pin down these days."

"Got this pesky little thing called a day job." I followed him up the stairway into the plane. "Takes hours of my time every day."

"Unfamiliar with the concept. I specialize in empires, not 'jobs.'"

Tate Blackthorn was a shark. The kind of New York, old-money asshole who possessed a second brain instead of a heart. He'd invested in one of my restaurants when I'd started out, and now he thought he owned my ass, even though I made him a shit ton of money. In Tate's world, anyone who wasn't born with a silver spoon and a trust fund was indebted to him if he paid them any kind of attention. And if all of that didn't make him insufferable enough, he always struck me as a raging playboy. The type to have spawn out of wedlock in at least the double digits that he didn't even know about and a string of exes who'd love nothing more than to attend his funeral.

Tate shouldered past a starry-eyed flight attendanr. "Gotta say, I wasn't expecting to be ghosted by anyone, let alone someone who's about to receive a fat check from me."

Didn't surprise me. Tate was the kind of man who was sought after, not the one doing the chasing.

"That's an observation, not a question." I entered the plane, taking a seat by the window. The interior was lavish and in your fucking face—just like its owner. Velvet burgundy seats, golden fixtures, a heavy wood bar. The place could moonlight as a brothel. Which, I had no doubt, sometimes it did.

"You want a question?" He fell into the recliner in front of me, scooting to the edge and lacing his fingers together. "Fine, I'll give you one: What's the holdup, and why don't I have this damn contract signed yet?"

I normally liaised with Tate's team—mainly because he was too busy to care about this bumfuck-nowhere side project. But since it was just the two of us, I figured it was time to face the music. "I read your official proposal, dug into the plan a little." I stuck my tongue into my inner cheek.

"And…?" He tilted his chin down expectedly.

"It's shit."

"Shit?" he asked calmly. "How so?"

"The provisions, the architecture, the structure, the brands attached to the retail project—pure crap. I'm jamming this project down people's throats, so I have to sell it to them. There's nothing marketable about your plan for Staindrop."

My shitty mood had begun the moment I'd boarded the commercial flight to London the day after kissing Cal. I found myself replaying the kiss in my head time and time again, and remembered Cal's Brain Boyfriend remark. Itching for a distraction, I had decided to dig through the blueprint Tate had sent me when he'd made the offer and nitpick every small fucking thing about it. I didn't actually think it was bad. Tate was a terrible human but a top-tier businessman. He had the talent and ability to turn the town around. But the real answer—that I didn't want to sign the contract because I wanted into Cal's pants—wasn't acceptable. Not to my business partner, and not inside my own head.

My mood had taken a further nosedive later that day when I'd checked on La Vie en Rogue. Not because the progress wasn't to my satisfaction. On the contrary—everything had gone according to plan. The stained marbled bar was pristine, the black granite walls were already up and covered in eclectic art and graffiti, the handmade upholstered leather stools were lined up over the shiny parquet floor, and the bulbed chandeliers looked like a Milky Way constellation map.

Everything was perfect, and yet I couldn't, for the life of me, find any excitement and pleasure in it.

"Let's try again." Tate sat back, lacing his fingers and tapping his indexes over his mouth. "I'm going to pretend you have the greenest clue about city planning and ask why you think this proposal, designed by three of America's boldest and most prestigious architects, is shit?"

"It's like planting the Woolworth Building in a cornfield. Completely out of character for the town."

"It's like putting a profitable high-end business in a shithole, breathing life into it," he countered, his lips thinning impatiently. "Of course it'll change the town's makeup. That's a pro, not a con. What's wrong with the retail lineup?"

Nothing. You killed it. Problem is, it's killing my chances to be with Cal. I knew she didn't like I was shoving this plan down the towns-people's throat.

"Too bougie. Prada and Gucci in a small Maine town? That's not running out of business; it's sprinting away from anything remotely lucrative, kicking and screaming."

"The town is only a couple hours' drive from the Canadian border, and there isn't an outlet or a five-star hotel in a fifty-mile radius. We've done our research. The numbers track," Tate assured me. "Rich assholes always want to put their credit cards to good use. I'm here to help."

"How gallant of you," I grumbled. "Still, this plan isn't gonna work for a town like Staindrop."

"With all due respect—which is currently at an all-time low, by the way—that's not your problem, is it?" Tate sat back, crossing his legs. Both of the flight attendants he'd hired stole glances over their shoulders at us.

"Can we get you anything, Mr. Blackthorn?" one of them cooed.

"A logical business associate would be nice." Tate unbuttoned his blazer, eyeing me like he was dying to throw me off the plane.

"I'm all but illogical," I countered. "You know numbers, but I know Staindrop. And I'm telling you, a mall this big and a hotel this glitzy is the wrong way to go."

"You're here to sign the dotted line and hand over control, not to make suggestions. Staindrop is gonna be in good hands, trust me."

"No offense, Blackthorn, but I'd sooner trust a broken condom." I folded my arms over my chest. "And when this all goes to shit and you move on to your next venture, you're going to leave my hometown with two huge-ass structures that are unusable and ugly as sin."

"And you care because?" He lifted one eyebrow.

He had me there. Giving a shit wasn't in my nature. It wasn't like I was going to stick around. Dylan and Mom would still live in Staindrop, sure, but their future was secured. Cushioned by my never-ending stream of cash and quarterly visits.

I didn't have any reason to care, other than the fact that Cal didn't like this idea.

"Takeoff in two," echoed the pilot's announcement above our heads.

"Whiskey?" One of the flight attendants parked her ass on my armrest, smiling down at me suggestively.

"Pass." I slid to the other side, rejecting both the drink and her.

Tate checked his phone, waving a dismissive hand in her direction. "Keeley, I'll take a double, neat. And a charcuterie board. No carbs."

I guessed he was one of those pricks who ate every single hour to keep their metabolism as fast as they were in the sack. I pulled my phone out of my pocket and checked my messages too.

Mom, asking if I was okay.

Dylan, venting about the fifty-pound baby who was currently squeezing her bladder like a WWE contestant—her words, not mine.

Rhy, telling me he sincerely hoped I spent my time in London buried in women who weren't my childhood fantasy to scratch that itch.

I pushed away my disappointment. What was I expecting, Cal to send me nudes? That ship had sailed thanks to fucking Franco. I wanted to resurrect him just so I could kill him again.

Tate returned his attention to me. "Where were we?"

"I was telling you your proposal sucked, and you were throwing a fit," I said matter-of-factly, happy to be anchored back to the present. "I'm reconsidering it."

I am? Why the fuck? I needed that check. Opening a new

restaurant, building a house for my family, *and* buying a luxury apartment didn't come cheap.

The plane began takeoff, rolling on the tarmac, gaining momentum. Tate tossed his whiskey back in one gulp.

"Am I in a bidding war?" He slammed the empty decanter on the table between us.

"No," I said honestly. "I'm just trying to do the right thing here."

"No, you're not. When given the chance, you always do the fun thing, not the right one." He studied me intently. "Something's changed. *You've* changed. Why?"

"Grew a fucking conscience. Sue me." I shrugged off his attitude.

"Tempted to." He stroked his chin. "Unfortunately, you haven't signed anything yet. How about we play on it?"

"On an eight-million-dollar contract?" I snorted. "Fucking pass."

Goddamn. An old-money white billionaire was a level of thrill-seeking I'd yet to meet.

"Come." He tapped my knee fatherly, a taunting smirk on his lips. "You know you want to."

I really didn't want to, but we were going to have to burn the time somehow, and I had a feeling he was going to screw the flight attendant right in front of me if I didn't keep him busy. "Fine. What are we playing?"

"Your favorite object, Casablancas—*knives*."

CHAPTER THIRTY-EIGHT
ROW

"Way I look at it, selling is your only option." Tate sent a charcuterie knife careening toward the target hung on the wall in front of us. The blade sliced through the bull's-eye so deep, it probably left a dent in the interior.

So. Tate Blackthorn was a sociopath. *Just my fucking luck.*

We were a quarter of the way over the Atlantic Ocean, and I was wrong—he had fought off the flight attendant's advances several times, between picking up the phone and screaming his throat out at his PA, a woman named Gia.

"Oh yeah?" I unpinned the knife from the target, walked over to him, and hurled it at the bull's-eye, unblinking. "How so?"

He took a sip of his second drink, putting it down on the table. "Everyone in Staindrop already hates your guts. You've got nothing to lose. This community you were a part of—the old-timers, local artists—they're not your tribe anymore. Now you're one of us. The suits, the hustlers, the capitalists. Admit it, Casablancas. You sold your soul to the devil. Your place is in hell, right along with me."

"Hell is my playground. I'm no newcomer to the zip code." I ran the blade of the knife along my finger, watching the edge glint along my skin. "See, I'm a hedonistic creature like yourself, Tate. And right now, there's something I want far more than your millions, and you're standing in my way."

"Finally, the cat's out of the bag." He laughed sarcastically.

And the pussy's fucking worth it. Though I was interested in much more than fucking her raw, and that was a problem.

"However lovely she might be, my ability to pad your bank account is even comelier. Plus, I don't like being jerked around."

"Why not? Must feel right at home, seeing as you're a first-rate jerk."

"Buddy, no offense, but you are not rich enough to entertain second thoughts," he quietly seethed. I had a feeling most people, people who weren't forged under the abusive hand of a raging alcoholic, found him frightening. "You need the money. You just bought a bachelor pad in London and built your family a mansion. Spoiler alert: King Charles is not as lax on taxes as Uncle Sam. You'll swim in debt if you don't sell. Not to mention, I'm an investor in La Vie en Rogue, and I'll be feeling very *un*invested if you shit all over our deal."

"I'll chance it," I hissed.

His eyes raked over my face. "Is she worth it?" he asked finally.

"She is worth much, much more."

My phone pinged with a notification, and I fished it out of my pocket. Tate grabbed a knife from the holder, but instead of hurling it at the target, he whipped around quickly and threw it at me. I caught the knife by the handle without lifting my eyes from my phone, still reading the weather forecast.

"Good instincts." He whistled low.

I looked up nonchalantly. "You missed."

He gave me a pitiful smile. "No, Casablancas, I *spared*. I won't be so charitable next time. Sign the fucking contract."

I advanced toward him, suddenly feeling trigger-happy. This man could've cut my throat half a second ago. I wasn't one to respond well to threats, even from people who were used to getting their way. Tate didn't cower, just watched me with lazy amusement as I wrapped my fingers around his neck and slammed his back against the wall. The two flight attendants gasped and rushed toward us, but Tate held up a hand to them. "Sit back. This is finally getting interesting."

I pushed my face into his. "Let's make one thing clear. Whether I sign this contract or not, this is the first and last time you threaten me. Next time that happens, you'll be enjoying a skydiving session sans the parachute."

He smirked. "Proud of you, son. You're no pushover."

Son? I was maybe two years younger than this fucker.

"Keeley?" I asked, still staring at him with my hand on his throat.

"Y-yes?"

"I'm ready for my drink now."

CHAPTER THIRTY-NINE
ROW

oBITCHuary: This is a message for McMonster, not Row.

McMonster: Okay.

oBITCHuary: I have a problem.

McMonster: Just the one?

McMonster: Jk.

McMonster: What's the problem?

oBITCHuary: Boy problem. There's a guy who kissed me and left town without a word. I'm extremely annoyed about this. What should I do?

McMonster: How was the kiss?

oBITCHuary: Eleven out of ten.

McMonster: Liar.

McMonster: It was at least a twenty.

oBITCHuary: Can you stick to the point?

McMonster: You're mad because you're interested. He'll be back soon.

oBITCHuary: Not interested in seeing him again after the way he went off the radar so suddenly.

McMonster: You'll forgive him.

oBITCHuary: How do you know?

McMonster: Because he's willing to grovel.

CHAPTER FORTY
ROW

The taxi driver spent the entire drive to Descartes trying to convince me to invest in crypto through a company he worked for. I didn't think he realized he was a part of a pyramid scheme, and I wasn't in a charitable enough mood to break the news to him.

A snowed-in Maine zipped by, with the car slowing down as we maneuvered into the narrow streets of Staindrop. My knee bounced against the passenger seat the closer we got to the restaurant. Cal didn't have a shift today. Two days ago, she'd spread her dad's ashes. I'd prepared the meal for her in advance: homemade chocolate cake–flavored toaster pastries, triple-fried panko onion rings, jalapeno-honey corn dogs, and spicy apricot soy burgers. Basically, I'd made all of her favorite junk food but put my own twist on it. Strangely enough, it had felt good, depositing the three laden paper bags outside her door. I wasn't used to making people happy, but with her, it seemed like an instinct.

"…all I'm saying is that diversification is key in this world. Just like you'd invest in gold, bonds, real estate…" The taxi driver droned on. He rounded the curb toward Main Street, where Descartes stood proudly. "You should give it a go. What's the worst that could happen?"

He slowed down to a stop in front of my display windows, and that was when I noticed it.

Descartes was *trashed*.

About two dozen broken eggs were smeared across the windows and doors. A pile of garbage spilled at the door. *TRAITOR* was graffitied across the length of the restaurant in black. The double-glazed glass door had been smashed.

"The fuck?" I pushed the taxi door open, throwing a wad of cash in the driver's general direction.

Taylor stood outside, a stunned look on his face. He wore jeans, sneakers, and a checked hoodie, and it occurred to me I couldn't remember him wearing anything other than his chef clothes because he always clocked in hours before I did. I had never grabbed a drink with him and asked about his life.

Which was a weird thought to have right now, when my restaurant was demolished.

"What happened?" I stalked his way, dropping my duffel bag on the ground.

Taylor shook his head. "Just got here and saw this. I called Rhy. He's on his way. We have surveillance cameras, right?"

We did. And I had an app on my phone with access to the footage. I shouldered past him, entering the restaurant. Broken glass crunched under my feet. The place looked unspoiled inside, but the outside had at least twenty thousand dollars' worth of damage, and shit knew how long we'd be closed. We were already overbooked. We'd have to cancel every single reservation for the next three days, minimum.

"Who could it be?" Taylor's voice followed me from behind.

"Randy," I said, even though I didn't know if I believed it myself. "Melinda and Pete. Allison. Lyle."

At this point, it could have been anyone. Could have been Cal, for all I knew. This whole thing had started after she'd arrived.

Someone was sending me a message, and the more time passed, the bolder they got.

Curious onlookers began gathering outside the restaurant,

peering inside, taking pictures on their phones. I ran a hand through my hair and slowly felt my patience evaporating through my pores. I fucking hated this place. Always had. Staindrop's only redeeming quality was Cal, and she was about to leave in a few weeks.

Should've signed Tate's contract a few hours ago and gotten it over with.

"Called the police." Rhyland's voice made both Taylor and me whip our heads toward the door. He elbowed a dangling piece of glass to clear his path into the restaurant, his phone pressed to his ear. "Shit. That's gonna be a lot of cancellation calls."

He said it with such indifference, I began wondering if *he* was the one who had done this. Fuck, I was becoming paranoid. Tate was right. This town would make my death day a national holiday. I shouldn't give a crap about handing it over to him.

Pulling my phone out, I checked the surveillance camera app. Coast looked clear until about five thirty in the morning, when I spotted car headlights entering the frame, then quickly turning off. I couldn't tell the car's model or make, since it was just the edge of the headlights. A black-swathed figure in a balaclava got out of the car and sauntered to the surveillance camera with confidence, knowing exactly where it was. He had a stool in his hand, which he used to step on to reach the camera, and then smashed the camera with a hammer.

"Whoever did this broke the camera." My teeth ground together so hard I could feel them crumbling into dust.

Taylor frowned. "Can you see who it was? Anyone we know?"

"Yeah." I shot him an annoyed look. "Just keepin' you assholes guessing for the suspense of it."

Rhy clapped Taylor's shoulder. "Don't worry, buddy, you get used to the verbal abuse."

"They broke it for funsies," I said, mostly to myself, replaying the video. "The guy was wearing a balaclava and parked way out of the frame. Knew he wouldn't get caught."

"Well, *whaddawe* have here?" Sheriff Menchin strode into Descartes, tipping his hat down in my direction. Theo Menchin was a thirtysomething, young-Brad-Pitt clone with a no-bullshit attitude I'd have admired if it hadn't been directed at me. He slung a thumb into his belt and peered around. "Looks like some rich folks are gonna go hungry tonight."

Behind him, a meaty young officer snickered at his joke.

"Got a call in saying someone at this address wants to file a report." Menchin popped one blond eyebrow. "What for?"

I threw my hand at the door. "This little vandalism stint is gonna cost me twenty K at a minimum. That's before the loss of income."

"Tough sale." Menchin clucked his tongue, unimpressed. "All I see here is a second-degree misdemeanor. A couple broken eggs on your window…"

"They broke the door."

The sheriff smirked. "You sure? 'Cause I just saw our old buddy Rhyland here breaking a piece to walk in without opening it."

"You serious right now?" My fists tingled, ready to plow into his smug face.

Menchin didn't back down, eyeballing me right back. "I'm always serious, Casablancas. And I'm seriously pissed off about what you're doing to this town. Allison says crime is gonna get out of control. My department doesn't have the budget or capacity for this kind of crowd."

"Regardless of what you think about me, you need to investigate this shit."

"I'm not telling you how to flip a burger, so don't tell me how to run this town."

He knew damn well I wasn't flipping burgers. It was just his way of flipping *me* off. "Fine," I bit out. "I'll talk to my guy at the FBI. Tell him how you handled this case." I had no guy at the FBI. In fact, I was so antisocial, the inn's cleaners barely knocked on my door.

Menchin sighed. "D'you have any clear footage of who did this?"

"No, but—"

"Shoot," he said sarcastically. "Investigation closed." Ambling deeper into the restaurant, he took in an eyeful. I could tell he'd never been anywhere this fancy. Never tasted food like what I served. He was antagonized by everything this place represented. Wealth, power, sophistication. Menchin ran a finger over the corroded stone wall. "Gonna be real honest with you, Casablancas. We're a little understaffed right now, what with Thanksgiving and Christmas comin' up. My to-do list is long and growin' by the minute. We don't investigate petty crime unless we have a clear lead."

"This shit's beyond petty. I have a stalker. The same vandal also left a dead coyote on my property and slashed my tires."

Menchin sucked his teeth. "Sounds real romantic, Casablancas, and we'll sure keep an eye out for a bunny boiler with a crazy zing in their eyes. Someone who buys eggs by the dozen. Now, who might that be?" He tapped his chin, turning to his sidekick.

Sidekick beamed, delighted to be acknowledged. "Mrs. Summerford buys three cartons every other day."

Mrs. Summerford was seventy-two. And a baker.

Menchin snapped his fingers Sidekick's way. "Can you pin her picture in the center of our suspect board?"

"We don't have a suspect board." Sidekick slanted his head like a confused dog.

"Humor me, Dalton." Menchin clapped his shoulder fatherly. "Oh, and add all those fancy red lines too. Nothing but the best for our famous friend."

This was my cue to give Menchin a piece of my mind, but Taylor beat me to it.

"You can't just brush this off." The kid stepped forward, looking upset on my behalf. "This man is a taxpaying citizen, not to mention one of the most critically acclaimed CDCs in the world."

"Not sure what CDC is, but I know he's an *A-S-S*." Menchin tsked. "Which reminds me, that fancy-lookin' guy with the tight suit and brick-sized teeth was doing the rounds the other day, passin' around a petition to build more roads. Including a highway."

Jesus. Tate was such a douche, he was practically a bidet. I hadn't even signed the contract and he was already trying to build roads here.

"I'll handle it," I hissed through clenched teeth.

"Good. You do that, and I might sniff around for that eager admirer of yours." Menchin winked, flicking invisible lint off my shoulder. "You scratch my back; I'll scratch yours. Ain't nobody needs roads here."

I was left simmering in my rage, in an out-of-commission restaurant.

CHAPTER FORTY-ONE
CAL

oBITCHuary: I was promised groveling.

oBITCHuary: Hey, are you dead?

oBITCHuary: Please don't be dead.

oBITCHuary: I hate to admit it, but...I've gotten a little attached.

CHAPTER FORTY-TWO
CAL

"I Will Always Love You"—Whitney Houston

"Wakey, wakey! Time to put those hideous leggings to good use."

I knew that voice.

That voice berated, belittled, and bewitched me at times.

It was the voice of a man who had run with me every morning—until recently, at least.

Of someone who'd kissed me to the point my knees were still weak and my heart still beat irregularly every time I played the moment in my head, and I played that moment in my head at least twice a minute.

Now, my stomach flipped at the memory of being pressed against the snow beneath Row three nights ago, of that kiss that had electrocuted me, before he'd disappeared to London without as much as a goodbye. I'd had to hear through Dylan that he was on another continent.

"Go away," I groaned.

Semus, beside me, doubled down with a loud, dismissive *meow*.

"You're welcome for the free catering," Row growled beneath my window. He appeared to be in a great mood. Had he murdered someone? *Not* that I condoned that type of action, but I hoped that Allison was the victim.

I buried my face in my pillow. It was too early, too cold. Plus, I felt under the weather after spreading Dad's ashes in Moxie Falls a couple days ago.

One promise down, another one to go.

"Dot, I'm counting to ten."

"Good for you. What a milestone to celebrate just shy of your twenty-seventh birthday."

"Joke's on you when I get up there," he threatened.

"What will you do to me?" I raised my head from the pillow, my curiosity piqued. *Please let it be filthy. And naked. And full of bodily fluids.*

There was a beat of silence. What, no comeback from Mr. Sarcastic? I stared at my window with my heart in my throat.

"Just come down, will you?" His voice sounded tired and… defeated? Could it be? "*Fuck.* I'm trying to be there for you, but I'm out of my depth here. The restaurant is closed down for the foreseeable future and I have a crazy stalker running around freely. Quit being difficult and come down already."

"Oh. Shit. Are you okay?" I bolted upright, brushing my hair with my fingers, running to the window. The mere sight of him soothed my soul. Oh God. I was so freaking screwed.

"Yes. No." He scrubbed a hand over his face tiredly. "I don't know."

"Give me five." I dragged myself out of bed. Semus stayed there, squinting at me patronizingly as I collected my hair into a bun and slammed my feet into sneakers. "Yeah, I know. You get to sleep in *and* lick your own balls. Such a winner, Sem."

After splashing my face and brushing my teeth, I threw my door open and came face-to-face with Row.

He was wearing a black hoodie and gray sweatpants, his usual attire for our morning runs. As soon as he saw me, his frown melted into something else entirely. I loved that he looked at me in a way he never looked at anyone else. Like I wasn't just a person but an experience.

"What happened?" I asked.

Row shook his head. "Been freezin' my ass off here waiting for you. Let's start running and I'll tell you."

"Fine, but I'm going to yell at you at some point," I warned.

"What for?" He glowered.

"Kissing me—we can't do that again, by the way. And leaving without a word. But first, tell me what happened to Descartes."

Usually, we spent our runs teasing each other, Row's way of making sure I wasn't inside my own head or replaying my flash-backs with Allison. Maybe it was because Row looked pissed off or maybe it was because Dad was somewhere beautiful right now, floating in the wind, being the freest he'd ever been, but for some reason, I didn't concentrate on the running or my trauma when we started making our way down my street. We jogged lightly, minding the slippery sidewalk with the leftover melted snow.

Row brought me up to speed about what has happened to his restaurant as our feet pounded the pavement. I didn't know what part annoyed me more—the way people in this town were treating him or how callous Sheriff Menchin was about it.

"I'm not even sure how long Descartes will be closed for. We have media appearances booked, food critics scheduled, a whole farewell party… This was supposed to be a fucking celebration. Not a hastily closed business," he grumped.

"It'll be open for the last week before Christmas," I heard myself say. God knew who had given me the authority or knowledge to make such a prediction. "You'll close it with a bang, and it will be legendary."

We made it to downtown before I even realized I had run all that way. Something compelled me to announce, "Come on, coffee on me at Dahlia's Diner."

He used the hem of his hoodie to wipe the sweat off his forehead, revealing a freakishly defined six-pack. Or was it an eight-pack? I was usually good at math, but not when my entire blood flow rushed to my vagina.

"Nah." He shook his head. "Don't feel like another horror show."

"Don't let them win," I chided.

"I'm about to bulldoze over their town to get cut a nice check. I'm the one who is winning. Don't see a point in rubbing it in their faces, though."

"Fine. Wait here." I marched into the diner, returning after a few minutes with two steaming cups of coffee and a box full of pastries. I led him to a bench overlooking the harbor and flipped the box open. He reached for a custard-filled donut. I slapped his hand away. "You're going to have to earn your food, mister."

"Sexual favors?" His gaze swung to mine, one eyebrow quirked up. "You *did* say we're inevitable."

"Ugh. You and your one-track mind." I shook my head. "I'm going to ask questions; you're going to answer them. Question number one: Why are you helping me run?"

"Because I like you despite my better judgment. Next question."

I was somewhere between deliriously flattered and completely crushed. "Well, nothing can happen between us."

"Why?"

Because I like you, too, and I can't put my heart on the line. I have been hurt before. I cannot afford another public demise.

"Because of Dylan." This wasn't a lie. It was my number one reason. My idiot heart came a close second. "Question number two: Why didn't you tell me you were going to London?" I couldn't keep the hurt from my voice. I had been off the entire drive to Moxie Falls, after Dylan had casually mentioned Row was away when I'd visited her to drop off more secret cupcakes.

Row looked puzzled. "Didn't think you'd give a shit."

"I do. I am. I…I care," I admitted chokingly. "It's also basic courtesy."

"Duly noted. I'll work on my manners. Anything else?" he asked, patiently impatient, eyeing the donut.

"What are you going to do about your stalker?"

"Kill them, once I catch them."

"Be seri—"

"Nope. Earned at least one pastry." He snuck his hand into the box and grabbed a donut, taking a big bite. He grinned at me, his straight white teeth covered in green and red Christmas sprinkles. "You were saying?"

The green reminded me of something. "Did you ever send me a broccoli cake for my birthday?"

"No." His cheekbones pinkened, and he dropped the donut back into the box.

"Row."

"It was the culinary challenge, okay?" He trained his gaze on the ships anchored by the harbor, releasing a quick breath. "I was in New York for a conference and remembered your stupid birthday wish. Marcus, the executive chef of the restaurant you worked for, is an old friend. He told me you'd have a shift."

"Dude, it was actually delicious. Do you have, like, a secret sauce?"

His eyes traveled down to his groin, and I laughed, pushing his muscular arm playfully. Row grabbed another pastry, shoving it past his lips. "My turn to ask questions—why red?" Sugar-powdered fingertips reached to tuck a tendril of my flame-hued hair behind my ear.

Because that's the color I've been seeing ever since you left without saying goodbye.

"It's that time of the month," I lied. I wondered if we were ever going to stop lying to each other. If we were capable of simply saying the truth when it came to us.

He narrowed his eyes. "You're bullshitting me."

"Wanna check?" I snorted.

"Yes."

The laughter that fizzed out of my mouth sounded like two whales trying to communicate from different oceans. He stared at me stoically. The idea of him giving me a physical exam made my heart race and my insides clench with need. "I have another question," I announced.

"Yay," he said flatly, his eyes on me. "Hit me."

"Why did you really cut out my head from all of my pictures with Dylan when we were kids? My seventeen-year-old self was deeply offended." *Not to mention creeped out.* I had never, for one moment, believed that it was Dylan. She had no motivation to do so.

"Tell her my twenty-one-year-old self cut your *face* out, not your head." He paused. "Because I wanted a reminder of you, and taking a whole-ass album was out of the question. I could only afford the one suitcase."

"You could've taken two or three pictures."

Headshake. "One thing you should know, Dot, is that I'm greedy when it comes to you."

We stared at each other silently for a beat, an entire ocean of words raging between us.

Oh crap. He was right. He was going to screw me at some point.

"One last question." I wanted to grab the drawstrings of his black hoodie. To loop them around my fingers. To tug him to me and kiss him until we were both out of breath.

"Shoot."

"Do you think I'll be able to complete the 10K for Kiddies?"

And there it was. The smile that made my heart melt. "Dot, you are going to kill it."

CHAPTER FORTY-THREE
CAL

oBITCHuary: Are you okay?

McMonster: Clearly not. When have I ever been?

oBITCHuary: LOL.

oBITCHuary: I mean mentally. Bc of the restaurant.

McMonster: Hanging in there.

oBITCHuary: You might need a bodyguard after what happened.

McMonster: The position is vacant.

oBITCHuary: Hmm. I do need a job...

McMonster: My bodyguard will need to be naked at all times.

oBITCHuary: Hmm, what? WHY?

McMonster: It's my process as an artist. Don't question it.

oBITCHuary: What if it gets cold?

McMonster: Why would it get cold, silly? We'll never leave the bed.

CHAPTER FORTY-FOUR
CAL

"Human Nature"—Madonna

"Know what you should do?"

"Don't say find a serious job. Being a server is a perfectly good occup—"

"Get laid." Dylan's eyes were covered with sliced cucumbers.

She wore a purple face mask. Pregnancy-friendly whitening strips braced her already pearly teeth while she lay in her bed next to me. I'd set the white noise machine on water gurgles and bird chirps, and we were both in bikinis, pretending she was enjoying a babymoon in the Seychelles.

I was in a face sheet and a hair mask secured with a nylon. I choked on my dill pickle chips, sitting up straight. "What makes you say *that*?"

"Hmm. Let me think." Dylan reached for a grape in a bowl by her nightstand. "The fact that you've been uptight ever since you came back home?"

"I just lost my father. I'm sad."

"Sex releases endorphins."

"So does exercise," I pointed out.

"Yeah, but I'm being realistic about things you are actually willing to try out." Dylan spat out the grape, along with the whitening strips she'd forgotten were in her mouth. "Pregnancy brain sucks, man. Luckily, it will be worth it, because I plan to tell her three times a day, *Just remember I made you.*"

"Totally functional." I readjusted the nylon in my hair. "And I'll have you know I've been running for two weeks straight."

My muscles were sore, and my feet were blistered. Row showed up under my window every day. We'd laugh, tease each other, and talk about our future plans. Row would give me business advice about my nonexistent podcast. He made me think of it as a possibility, not just a dream.

He'd shown admirable restraint for someone who'd found out his restaurant was going to be out of commission for three weeks. There was no doubt that the glazier he'd hired—Melinda's son-in-law—was dragging his feet about fixing the broken glass door because his in-laws had pulled some strings, but my grumpy boss barely even snarled and complained about it.

"You have been?" Dylan acted surprised, yanking the cucumbers from her eyes and frowning at me. "I thought you were triggered by running."

Row didn't tell her?

"Pushing through it. I'm planning on doing the 10K for Kiddies this Christmas."

"Holy shit. I hope you survive it. I've kind of gotten attached since you came back."

I gave her a look. "Thanks for the vote of confidence."

"Oops, what I meant to say is—yay! You're almost certainly going to survive it." She grabbed her Stanley cup and clasped her lips around the straw. "Anyway, running doesn't do the trick. You still need a banana in your fruit salad."

"Even if I wanted one, there are no bananas in the...erm, market." I shoved another chip into my mouth.

"Of course there are!" she said perkily, sitting up so both our backs were plastered against her headboard, and cradling her stomach. "Aw! She just kicked. Sorry, I've yet to teach her not to eavesdrop. She *loves* bananas. Figures. She's not the one who has to deal with the constipation." Dylan snatched my hand and pressed it against her bare belly. Something hard and tiny dragged across her stretched skin, *tap-tap-tapping*, and my emotions were somewhere between extremely thrilled and completely freaked out.

"Is it true that they go nuts if you give them sugar?" I rubbed her belly gently.

She reached for a frosted cookie I'd brought over, took a bite, then chewed thoughtfully. "Totally. The sugar wakes her up. But we're not changing the subject. Back to the banana part. What about Kieran?"

I shook my head vehemently. "No."

She gasped. "Why? He's too dreamy."

"Exactly. He looks and feels like somebody else's fairy tale. Like a Disney prince. You know—too perfect to be attractive."

"Speak for yourself. I'm in my Prince Naveen era." Dylan took a bite from a cookie, then a bite from a grape. I didn't want to tell her Kieran also gave off intense hiding-something vibes. No man could be *that* perfect. It was all an act.

"Sheriff Menchin?" she suggested. "Some would call him... *unlawfully arresting.*"

"Dude, no way." I made a cross with my fingers, as if to ward him off. "He is too G.I. Jock."

"What does that even mean?"

"He feels like the type to wrestle a bear bare-chested...then steal its wife. The man hunts for fun and goes to gun shows."

"That's not a crime."

"Sure, but it's not my type either."

"Rhyland?" Her eyes lit up. "Rhy's *everyone's* type. Hot as Hades, all charm and style. I've yet to find one woman who'd turn him down. Taken or not."

"He's too...obviously attractive."

"Sure, we don't want that. Nothing turns me on more than missing teeth and some nose hair. Really brings out the allure and mystery in a man." My BFF's eyes almost bulged out of their sockets. "Hey, what about Row?"

I was just taking a sip of my mocktail, so of course I sprayed it all over her bed, proceeding to cough in horror. "My goodness, Dylan, I'd never—"

"Oh stop. You would because you *did*. You can't tell me he isn't your type. I've got receipts."

Our eyes met, and she looked somber all of a sudden. We were both transported back to the night she'd caught us together. "I'm not doing anything to jeopardize our friendship ever again." I swallowed hard.

"You wouldn't be jeopardizing anything. I hereby give you permission to pork my brother. Just please spare me the details. I'm dealing with awful reflux as it is."

I thought back to Row saying Dylan had told him she wouldn't mind if we hooked up. My stomach twisted, I was running out of excuses not to act on this attraction.

"He seems like a player." I began scratching away the cool, damp sheet on my face. "And even if I went for something casual, I'd only be down for exclusivity."

"If Row's a player, his game is hard to get." Dylan snorted. "And he's really good at it. Don't believe what all the tabloids say. He isn't much of a man-whore."

"So you wouldn't be mad if we…?" I left the rest hanging.

Dylan stood up, waltzing over to the bathroom and returning with a damp, warm cloth, scrubbing away at her mask. Seeing her in a bikini was jarring. She looked like a pregnant supermodel. "Nope. Cross my heart and hope Tuck dies—I promise I'll be totally okay with that."

"Why?" My nose twitched.

"I love you both and I want to see you happy."

"Can your brother really ever be happy?" I asked, thinking about everything Row had been through.

"I don't know." Dylan gnawed on her lower lip. "But if anyone can make him happy, it's you."

"Well…banana gives me heartburn." I pursed my lips.

Dylan tipped her head back and laughed. "Just as long as it doesn't give you heartbreak."

CHAPTER FORTY-FIVE
CAL

Cal: Hi.

Row: Hey.

Cal: Can I show you something?

Row: Is that something going to end up in my spank bank or with me bailing both of us out of jail?

Row: Either way the answer is yes. I just like to be prepared.

Cal: It's a rough draft for one of my podcast episodes. I wrote the layout, bullet points, etc.

Row: Show me.

Cal: Will you tell me if it sucks?

Row: Abso-fucking-lutely. I made a career out of putting people down.

Row: It's the sole reason for my success. I actually barely know how to operate a microwave. Best kept secret. Don't tell.

Cal: <sent an attachment>

Row: BRB.

Cal: It's twenty pages. Obviously, take your time.

Row: I'm done.

Cal: ???

Cal: It's been twenty-five minutes and it's the middle of the night.

Row: Sucked me in. Your fault, really.

Cal: Are you saying that it's good?

Row: I'm saying that it's perfect.

Row: Exhilarating, funny, sad, heart-wrenching. Should I continue?

Cal: Really? Because I plan to use it for one of my first five episodes.

Row: Record the podcast, Dot, and I promise you I'll be your first listener.

CHAPTER FORTY-SIX
CAL

"All I Want for Christmas Is You"—Mariah Carey

The Christmas lighting in the town's square was the grandest event in all of Staindrop. Even as a kid, I remembered it as a monumental occasion.

There were always food trucks, visitors from neighboring towns, a countdown, and one time the mayor had even managed to bring an actor who body-doubled for Sharon Stone to flip the switch.

Skipping didn't even cross my mind. Even though seeing Allison Murray always guaranteed an internal meltdown for me. The only reason I'd survived Row's town hall meeting with her sitting up there on the podium was because Dylan had held my hand through it.

But Mamushka loved seeing the lights go up, and she'd knitted us matching red and green mittens for the occasion. Besides, Dylan had gotten the all clear from her ob-gyn to attend, and I knew she wanted me there.

"Your father came to me in a dream," Mamushka announced as we strolled toward Main Street. Our arms were linked, and we were wearing big faux-fur ushankas and puffy coats.

"He did?" My mouth quirked into a smile. "What did he say?"

Mom pressed her lips together, fighting a grin. "Know how I've been debating whether to start my mitten business or go back to teach another year?" she asked.

I nodded. Mamushka taught math at the local high school.

"Well, I didn't tell you this, but when we went to spread his ashes in Moxie Falls, I asked him to give me a sign. Something to let me know it's time."

"And?" Our feet crunched the thin layer of ice on the pavement.

"And when you went to pee behind the bushes, a feather landed in the palm of my hand. I tucked it into my bag. They say that when feathers appear, angels are near."

It was just like me to miss this monumental moment because I'd overindulged with a venti pumpkin spice latte and nature had called.

Mom continued. "The feather felt meaningful, but I couldn't tell for sure. Well, yesterday, in my dream, your father told me it was a stork's feather. And that storks represent new beginnings. Like the one I should have. I googled stork feathers and compared the one I kept. It matched."

We both stopped on the corner of the street. We were still a few feet away from the crowd milling around the square. Food trucks, generators, and people were everywhere. There was a big red button hooked up to a generator barricaded by orange construction barriers.

"What are you saying, Mamushka?" I squeezed her fingertips.

"I'm saying I want to quit and sell my mittens. I'm saying I'm opening an Esty shop. If you could help me, that is. You know I'm useless with technology."

"Etsy." I grinned. "And it'd be my honor. We're going to open you one first thing tomorrow morning, and I'll even take pictures of your inventory. Make it look legit." I was pretty good with Photoshop. Had taught myself in college. I was sure I could make her something presentable.

"Thank you. What about you?" She frowned. "When will you record your podcast?"

"Soon, Mom," I lied. *Again.* "Very soon."

"You know, when I was your age, I really wanted to be a news reporter." She smiled grimly. "Your father and I had already moved to Staindrop. I got accepted as an intern for a local newspaper. I said no."

"What? Why?" I hadn't even known Mom had wanted to be a reporter. It fit her much more than being a math teacher, though.

Mom shrugged. "The possibility of failing scared me more than the prospect of succeeding thrilled me. I was a scaredy cat. I didn't want to get hurt. Another opportunity didn't come along. In fact, I was too scared to even apply to anything else. So I just took the job I thought I deserved and went along with it. If there is one thing I can guarantee you—your dreams don't wait around for you to get to them. That's why it's called *chasing a dream*. We keep running out of time. Don't postpone for tomorrow what you can do today. You're brilliant, passionate, and hardworking. Run after your dream, Callichka. Or you'll never catch it."

She opened her arms, and I stepped into a Litvin hug. Usually it was a three-way hug with Dad, but for the first time since he'd been gone, the space he had left didn't feel like a wound between us.

"Lookie here! It's my BFF and her MILF!" Dylan's voice singsonged from behind my shoulder. I turned around to look at her. She was wearing a huge rainbow faux-fur coat I had made for her when we were teenagers, hot pink heels, and a pair of skinny jeans. She approached us with her mom holding her hand to keep her balanced.

"What's a MILF?" Zeta frowned with suspicion.

"Mother in lovely fur!" I said with flourish, gesturing to Mom's coat.

"Now, that's a nice abbreviation." Zeta snapped her fingers, pointing at me. "I think I'll use that."

Dylan's eyes lit up further. "Please, Mom, feel free to. Any chance you get."

The four of us exchanged pleasantries before I dove into the thick of the crowd to find a chair for Dylan to sit on. When I came back with one I'd stolen from a vendor, Kieran was there. He was wearing one of those long preppy coats, his hair tousled to perfection, chatting with Dylan, holding the small of her back casually to support her posture. She looked up at him, her smile so blindingly bright, my heart was ready to explode, and I realized…

Dylan was truly happy without Tucker.

I didn't want to see her smile dim when he returned.

Mom and Zeta were deep in conversation, cradling steaming cups of chai. Kieran was holding little cardboard plates with food samples. As soon as I put the chair on the sidewalk for Dylan to sit, he handed one to me. It looked like a human liver. Red and grainy, swimming in its own blood.

"Are you, uhm…in the organ-trafficking business?" I quirked an eyebrow.

Kieran smiled, but his eyes were still trained on Dylan's face as she took her seat. "Beet kofta. Supposed to be really good."

"Beets, you say? Well, they were my father's favorite root vegetable." I shoveled some onto a plastic fork and took a big bite. It *was* delicious. "Hey, Dylan, remember that time we had beet salad and you peed in the public pool—"

"Cal!" Dylan shot me a murderous look. I stared at her midbite, confused. Dylan wasn't familiar with the notion of shame, not to mention mortification. Yet she was precisely the color of the kofta I was eating, jerking her head toward Kieran with arched brows.

Oh.

Oh.

Kieran looked between us. "Care to finish that story?"

"I…uhm, it's a gross one." I smiled, still staring at Dylan.

"Don't hold back on my account." He chuckled. "I like a good gory story."

"I was just reminiscing about that time *I* ate beets and peed in the community pool." I twisted my red-tipped hair.

Kieran scrunched his nose. "How old were you?"

"Seventeen." I raised my eyebrows at Dylan. "Old enough to know better, wouldn't you think?"

"She was in her staying-a-virgin-forever era." Dylan turned to Kieran, sighing exasperatedly. "I tried to civilize her best I could. But there's only so much one woman can do."

Kieran's lips twitched, and his blue eyes turned warm and soft. "Cut yourself some slack. Cal's a lost cause."

"So happy you are bonding over my shortcomings." I made a heart sign with my fingers.

"Oh, shush." Dylan patted my arm, a wide, toothy smile stretched across her face, eyes never wavering from her target. "You're still atoning for your sins."

I wondered if Row was going to show up. The restaurant had just reopened the previous day, and he was busy doing press for his London gig and inviting food critics for a last-minute meal at Descartes.

"Oh, by the way, you kind of have to finish your 10K now." Dylan elbowed my side, back up on her feet. Why wasn't she sitting down? But I already knew the answer to that question. *Kieran*. And his smoldering looks. And his big adoring smiles.

Row was wrong.

Kieran didn't want me.

He wanted *Dylan*.

I didn't know what to make of it. Dylan was pregnant and in a relationship with another man. And Kieran? He was one of the most famed, worshipped men on planet Earth. He was ridiculously photogenic. A filthy rich jock whose life was so private nobody really knew who or what he was. And...hadn't his last girlfriend been a Victoria's Secret model? What would a relationship between them even look like?

"You're running the 10K for Kiddies?" Kieran turned to look at me, finishing his last kofta in one bite.

"Planning to." I gathered my hair into a messy bun. "It was kind of my dad's last wish."

"Mine too." Dylan raised her hand in the air, like she was in class. "Now that I placed a bet that you would complete it and be one of the first ten to finish, you can't let me down. There's nothing I hate more than losing." She paused to think about it. "Other than a bikini wax. I *loathe* bikini waxes. No man is worth that kind of pain."

"Me too," Kieran volunteered. "It's the worst."

"You get waxed down under?" Dylan's eyes nearly bulged out of their sockets.

He nodded. "Helps with the running. Most soccer players shave, but I'd hate giving my lady friends third-degree carpet burns when we hit the sack just because I'm scared of getting my crotch hair plucked."

Dylan pressed a hand to her heart. "And they say romance is dead."

"If it is, I'll gladly resurrect it." Kieran flashed a winning smirk.

"*Whoa.* Hey. Back up now." I snapped my fingers, waving a hand in Dylan's face. "Who did you bet with on me? And why?"

If she said Row, I would have such a great excuse to touch him when I punched his face.

"The girls from your high school track team." Dylan braced the back of her chair to support her weight. My stomach lurched painfully. *Of course.* She had no idea they were the ones who had broken my ankle. She only knew I hated Allison. "Becky stopped by with some undercover churros the other day. I told her you were in town and doing the run. She bet me a Benjamin you won't finish."

I bet you a Benjamin she is the one who has trouble finishing, judging by how bitter she sounds.

"Is she still with Derek Sutter?" He was a douche and a half, who had body-shamed girls and belittled them on the reg while we were in high school.

"Yup." Dylan nodded. "He's good friends with Tuck, actually."

"You don't say." My eyes roved the square, hunting for Dylan's brother. "I'll complete the run, and you will get your Benjamin."

"Good. Because they're all going to be there."

"They're running too?" I was about to faint.

"God, no." She laughed. "They're doing the baking competition for the charity."

I bet Allison was going to be all over that event. She was the mayor, after all.

A loud shriek came from my left. I whipped my head to see the source of the laughter, and my heart sank to the pit of my stomach. *Speak of the devil.*

Allison was enveloped in a luxurious white cashmere coat and a black Gucci belt, sporting an elegant updo with tendrils of scarlet hair framing her face. She was standing next to Row, giggling at something he said.

Row's face was as blank as a white page. Then again, Row always had the flat, disinterested expression of a man who deemed anyone and anything around him unworthy. Unfortunately, his reluctance to be next to her did nothing to soothe the anger and jealousy swirling inside me. I'd confided in him about Allison. Told him what she had done to me. I didn't know what outcome I expected. For him to ignore her existence completely was impossible—she *was* the mayor of this town.

Technically speaking, they had a lot to discuss, what with him being about to sell his land and everything.

And yet.

And yet.

Allison placed a hand on Row's chest, batting her lashes with a beaming smile. She rose on her tiptoes to whisper in his ear. His stone-cold expression didn't change. His eyes scanned the square relentlessly.

"My dear summer child." Dylan put a hand on my shoulder, her voice sympathetic. "You're making a rookie mistake. Allison knows you're staring, and she thrives on drama. Look the other way and pretend you're having fun. Don't fall into her trap."

I ripped my gaze from Row and Allison, refocusing it on the crowd. I tossed the empty kofta plate into a nearby trash can, feeling silly all of a sudden. In my weird hat and cheap coat and... *No, you are not allowed to be embarrassed about your mittens. Mamushka made them.*

But hell, Allison looked like a movie star and I looked like...a production assistant who was about to get fired for being an eyesore.

"What they do together is none of my business." My voice barely quivered.

"Jesus, Cal." Kieran's eyes ping-ponged between me and Row. "Don't tell me you like that prick."

"That prick is my brother," Dylan reminded him through pursed lips.

"That's literally the only positive trait he has going for him," Kieran informed her with a snarl. "Sharing DNA with you."

"Don't be salty because he hates you." She wagged a finger his way. "You were terrible to him in high school. He told me."

"I've grown up since. He should too."

"Why does it matter? Not everyone is going to like you." Dylan flashed him a curious look.

"It matters because there is something of his that I want." His jaw ticked, and he turned serious. *"Badly."*

They stared at each other for a silent beat.

Oh no. They couldn't fall in love, could they? Not with Dylan about to give birth to someone else's baby in a few weeks. Disaster clung to the air like a stink bomb waiting to explode.

"I'm going to get us more food!" I announced, not that either of them registered my existence at this point.

I stumbled to the nearest truck and ordered pineapple pizza. If I was in a bad mood, everybody had to suffer with me. Melinda, Pete, Lyle, and Randy were standing by the side of the truck, munching on a deep-dish pizza and talking amongst themselves.

"…will do anything for that man. The woman has no self-respect," Melinda complained. "He dumped her so fast, I didn't have time to blink."

"Allison is a capable woman," Lyle disagreed. "And I ain't buyin' that she wants to get back with that heathen. She is probably going to convince him to give up the idea the old-fashioned way. The woman knows how to work her charm."

They were talking about Allison and Row. I was going to throw up. I tapped my foot on the cement, waiting for my pizza. My gaze flickered back to Row and Allison. He was now staring at Dylan and Kieran, while Allison continued nuzzling into him, trying to get his attention.

Since when was I jealous? Why did I *care*? But the answer was clear—I had always cared. He hadn't been just a crush back when we were kids. He had been…*everything*. And I had been so scared to admit it to myself after what had happened to me that I'd chalked up my feelings to a harmless crush.

Those wicked lies are going to kill you one day, Calla Litvin.

"Your pizzas, ma'am!" A pimply teenager shoved three paper plates with greasy pizza slices on them toward me.

Great. I was a *ma'am* now. Could this day get any worse?

I mumbled a thank-you, tipped hard to rearrange the universe so my karma wouldn't suck, and went back to Dylan and Kieran, who were now—thank goodness—discussing the safe topic of jock itch creams.

"I have a prescription for hospital-grade stuff," Kieran boasted. "Itraconazole. You could run a marathon and chafe your thighs to death and not feel it. You know, if you ever need it."

"Thanks for the offer, but it's been weeks since I could reach my thighs," Dylan grumbled. "Longer for my ankles. The only proof I still have them is that I can walk. If you can call my wobbling walking."

"Oh. Right." Kieran pinkened, scratching his jaw. "Well, I can always help out, if you need a…hand."

Her luscious lips tugged in a sly smile. "My brother would murder you."

"I can take him."

My God. Had they just made jock itch romantic? I shoved the pizza plates in their faces, not in the mood to see other people enjoying themselves. "Here ya go."

"Pineapple?" Kieran frowned. "What the fuck, Cal? Is this a call for help?"

"Dot, why do you look like you're about to cry?" Dylan dumped her pizza plate on top of Kieran's as soon as she took one look at me. The playfulness disappeared from her face. "What happened?"

"Nothing." I let out a pathetic attempt at a laugh, glancing around me. Mom and Zeta moved closer to the barricades surrounding the generator. They had found a few of their bingo friends and were chatting with them. "When is this thing starting? I need to wake up early tomorrow."

Kieran gave me a blank stare. "It's six thirty."

Over his shoulder, Row finally spotted me. Allison was still talking his ear off. He raised a hand and offered me a wave. I looked the other way, clenching my teeth. Childishly, I was mad at him. He was standing with the girl who had helped break my ankle, who had broken *me*.

An angel and a devil rested on each of my shoulders.

The angel said, *You don't know what they're discussing. Let him explain.*

But the devil said, *If someone shows you who they are, believe them.*

Kieran turned his head to see what I was looking at, then pierced me with a pointed look. "Still can't believe you're into him. He looks like the kind of asshole to kill you, then join the search party."

"My guess is Row is shitting bricks right now." Dylan stroked her belly distractedly. "He's been spending too much time in forced proximity with Cal, so now his self-destruction urge has kicked in and he is trying to push her away by paying attention to Allison. Classic bad-boy mechanism."

"You're just trying to make me feel better," I said.

Dylan let out a small laugh. "I'd never spare you the truth, Dot. I love you. Good friends never blow smoke up your ass."

Allison grabbed Row's hand and dragged him toward the center of the square, past the barricades. He followed with all the enthusiasm of a war prisoner. She stopped in front of a microphone and tapped it with an excited grin. It made a loud screeching sound. "Oopsie. Sorry!"

People quieted, watching her and Row with interest. Tears needled my eyes. Jealousy festered inside my body like poison. It was a medical miracle I could still function with the havoc watching them together wreaked inside me.

"Hello, everyone, and thank you *so* much for gracing us with your presence as we light up the Christmas decorations for the year!" Allison gave a big smile. "Traditionally, mayors in town have always tried to bring a celebrity to help turn on the lights. Most of the time it's people who have no affiliation to the town and don't know our customs and traditions. So this year I thought, why not bring *our* most famous citizen?" She flung her arms to the side, giggling girlishly. "But then Kieran Carmichael politely declined." She gestured toward our corner.

Everyone whipped around to look at us, laughing at her fantastic joke. Kieran *was* more famous than Row. Kieran stood shoulder-to-shoulder with Jesus Christ. In fact, the latter was marginally less popular, even in Catholic countries. There was a Brazilian city named after him. Kieran saluted Allison snidely.

"You said no?" Dylan's brows furrowed. "Why?"

"Wanted to go incognito and not have the paps follow me here. It was one of the things I'd agreed to when Ashburn let me do my physical therapy in Staindrop and take some time off. Too fucking late for that, thanks to Ms. Murray here."

Oof. It was the first glimpse I'd had of the old Kieran, the one who was mean to people sometimes, and it made me wonder if his good-guy act was all a persona he'd adjusted to, now that he was famous.

"And so I had to settle for this guy." Allison gestured toward Row like a *Price is Right* girl. "Which was all right with me, considering I know how to butter him up." She winked suggestively.

I was going to be sick. Row stared directly at me, his eyes burning with something unreadable. Hopefully acid. That prick.

People chuckled, enjoying Allison's schtick. I felt as small and meaningless as I had all those years ago when Allison had hurt me.

"*Soooo* without further ado." Allison tugged Row closer to the red button. "I present to you Ambrose Casablancas! Chef, celebrity, and reality TV star with a combined twelve Michelin stars, and the holder of the Guinness record for fastest sushi ever rolled."

Row stepped forward, nodding stiffly at the crowd as I treaded behind Kieran and Dylan. I didn't want him and Allison to see me cry. They didn't deserve my tears.

"Well, big man, now's your time to shine." Allison draped a hand on Row's shoulder, leaning into him intimately. "All you have to do is press that button right here. Even though he is a man, let me tell you, he has no problem finding these things." She winked again.

Laughter rang across the square. I shivered in my coat.

"Ready for the countdown?" Allison flung her arms in the air. They looked perfect together. Perfect. These tall photogenic people. With their successful careers and superior bone structure. I was mad at myself for telling him what Allison had done to me. For believing him when he'd said he liked me. How stupid could I have been?

"Yes!" the crowd cheered in unison. The first tear rolled out of my eye down my cheek, freezing an inch before it reached my jawline.

"Ten!"

Row's mouth quirked one way, revealing a dimpled smile.

"Nine!"

I bet he'd run to tell her I'd snitched on her after that night we'd kissed. That Allison had found a way to explain everything to him. Maybe he was taking her side now.

"Eight!"

Another tear ran down my cheek. Kieran and Dylan stepped away from each other, bracketing me on either side, shielding me from view. Dylan rubbed my shoulder, pressing a kiss to my cheek. "Don't, Dot. You know I'm your no-bullshit friend, and I'm telling you as someone who can see the bigger picture here—there's nothing between Row and Allison."

"Seven!"

But even if Dylan was right, tonight proved I couldn't chance a heartbreak.

"Six!"

"Stop looking so miserable," Kieran ordered through gritted teeth. "Allison is having a field day watching you."

"Five!"

Row was staring at us with an intensity that burrowed into my bones.

"Four!"

"Argh." Kieran ran a hand over his hair. "I hate being a good guy."

"Three!"

Allison shimmied her shoulders in anticipation, giving me her best Ursula-in-human-form smirk.

"Two!"

"Fuck," Kieran muttered, bending forward to catch Dylan's eyes. "Just so you know, the next thing I'm about to do doesn't mean anything and is solely done to impress you."

"One!"

Kieran grabbed me by the waist, tipped me down, cradling the back of my head, and pressed the coldest, driest, most platonic kiss I'd ever been given to my lips. One of my legs tipped in the air, like in the iconic V-J Day nurse and sailor smooch.

My breath caught in my throat. My eyes were wide with horror.

Kieran. Kissed. Me. And I was cold all over. Humming with terror and dread. Scared down to my tiniest bone.

Stop touching me, my mind screamed. *Let me go right now.*

I noticed the sky was ink-black save for a few lonely clouds. No Christmas lights were turned on. Row had never pressed the red button.

The next thing happened very fast. Kieran grabbed me by the waist and the back of my neck, mumbled *shit*, and tipped me down so my hair nearly touched the ground. He pressed his lips to mine, and my heart stopped in my chest. Panic clawed through my flesh, and I felt like four invisible walls were closing in on me.

"Motherfucker."

He is touching me.

This man *is touching me.*

My mouth fell open, the beginning of a scream making its way up my throat. But before I could yelp for help, Row was pulling me upright to stand on my feet and shoving me into his sister's arms.

In a flash, Kieran was flush against the back of a food truck. Blood gushing from his nose. Row had murder in his eyes, and I didn't know if it was because he knew I was scared of men, he was jealous, or both.

Kieran tipped his head back, chuckling. He didn't bother wiping his nose, even though his designer coat was marred red. "You're welcome, asshat."

"Welcome?" Row seethed, balling Kieran's shirt, pressing his nose to Kieran's, pupils dancing in fury. "I'm about to give you your farewell, and you're telling me I'm *welcome*?"

"Jesus Christ!" Dylan dumped me on the plastic chair I'd brought for her. She thundered toward the two men, shooing Row away like he was an aggressive duck trying to steal a sandwich. Row retreated, probably because he didn't want to take any chances with his heavily pregnant sister. She plucked a handkerchief from her purse and pressed it to Kieran's nose, tipping his head back and brushing his hair away from his face. "I'm so, *so* sorry. My brother is a world-class idiot and I'm probably going to write a tell-all and throw him under the bus after this."

"Don't forget to mention that time he sold weed on school grounds and got suspended for two weeks." Kieran grinned down at her, towering over my friend, who normally dwarfed all men other than her brother. He clasped a lock of onyx hair that fell across her eyes, rubbed it between his fingers, then slowly curled it around her ear. They both ceased to breathe, and I had to blink to make sure I wasn't hallucinating the entire thing.

"Not done with your ass by a long shot." Row pointed at him, his cheeks ablaze. He took advantage of Dylan stepping aside and balled the collar of Kieran's shirt, bringing him closer. *Everybody* was staring, inching toward us. This didn't bode well for Kieran's quest for privacy. Our pineapple pizza had been discarded on the ground.

Row raised his finger in warning, his nose almost touching Kieran's. "Now you listen carefully, pretty boy. If I see your ass—let alone your lips—anywhere near Cal, I—"

"You what?" Kieran snarled in his face cockily. Kieran might know how to play the good-guy role these days, but he still had that villainous spark. "She is just your employee, right?" Kieran tilted his head sideways, popping a toothpick into his mouth. "Running partner, maybe. Any other titles that I'm missing?"

"Let him go right this minute," Dylan demanded, wiggling a finger at Row. "Or I will strangle you with all the wrath of a woman who has not seen her knees in five months."

"Ambrose!" Zeta gasped from the depths of the crowd, shouldering the throng as she made her way to us. She pushed through curious bystanders. "What in the world are you doing?"

"Making a headline we both don't need," Kieran answered indifferently, staring Row down.

Finally, I snapped out of the weird haze Kieran's kiss had put me in and stood up, stepping between the two men. I blocked Row's way to Kieran, giving his chest a push. "Don't you dare go anywhere near him," I seethed.

Movies and books had taught me that this was the part where Row would soften, explain himself, calm down. False advertisement. In reality, he stared at me like *I* had betrayed *him*. Up close now, I could read his face. The words written across it, in invisible scars.

Pain.

Damage.

Despair.

Distrust.

Distrust.

Distrust.

The edges of his snakeskin eyes turned scarlet, his jawline tensed, and he was panting like a wounded beast.

"Ambie?" Allison purred behind my back, brushing past me as though I were air. To her, I probably was. "Are you coming?"

But he ignored her completely, shoulder-tackling my midriff and hoisting me over his shoulder. "Privacy," he clipped out shortly, pushing through the crowd as he made his way up the street and toward an alleyway between Dahlia's Diner and an auto shop. "Showtime's over."

"Put me down before I destroy the crown jewels." I thrust my legs desperately, trying to get to his groin while raining my fists on his back and shoulders.

"That would be on brand. You seem to destroy every other fucking thing in my life." He put me down carefully, my back pushed against a redbrick building. His mouth was twisted into a scowl. We stared at each other, panting. I wasn't going to say something first. Not because I didn't have anything to say—I did, and the words were plentiful—but because I wasn't sure if I was touched by his concern for my phobias or enraged by his uncalled-for possessiveness. My ancestors had not burned bras on the street so he could treat me like a prize he could knock over the head and drag into his cave for a good time.

"You know, it's my fault." He sucked his teeth.

I sighed, relieved. "*Finally*, we're on the same page. If you want to remain friends, an apology would be accep—"

"I promised myself I'd never give you the pleasure of making me feel like shit again." His nostrils flared, his words cutting me like a dagger. "Yet, here I am, doing this song and dance with you again."

My mouth fell open. "*What?*"

"I let you in, and you let me down," he gritted out. "I told you I liked you, and you're giving me mixed signals. I told you I want to take you out, *eat* you out, and you're friend-zoning me even though your nipples are harder than stones whenever we're in the same zip code. I told you how I feel about Kieran, and you went and kissed the crap out of him the first time we are all together."

"First of all, he kissed me, not vice versa. Second, I told you how I feel about *her*," I hissed, my voice pained. I was glad Allison wasn't around because I wouldn't be able to speak freely otherwise. Pathetically, I was still scared of her.

"And I listened carefully. Stayed the hell away. If you let me explain—"

"No need to. I have eyes. You guys seemed chummy enough. A picture is worth a thousand words."

He ran his fingers through his hair, messing it further. "*Fuck*, I keep making the same mistake, expecting different outcomes."

He was being so hypocritical. We'd both confided in each other before we'd started hanging out, and we'd both kept a cordial relationship with the people who had hurt the other person. Besides, there was no symmetry between Kieran being a dickhead and Allison *trying to kill me*. Row was acting like some kind of saint, not a man who'd let his ex—my *enemy*—dry hump his leg a second ago. "Don't try to gaslight me. I have eyes, you know. You two came here together—"

"I came here alone." He sliced through my words. "I was planning to join you and Dylan. I was gonna ask if you wanna grab dinner afterward. At Descartes."

"As a friend, a worker, or…?"

"As a *date*." His cheeks flushed, and he looked ready to murder himself for the confession. He had been going to ask me out? Misery slammed through me. I wished things hadn't gone so sideways tonight. The idea of doing something so normal and mundane, such as going on a date with a man without being deathly scared, appealed to me.

"Well, you hung out with her." I prickled, remembering he hadn't even approached us to say hello.

"I had my reasons."

"Which were?"

He shook his head. "Doesn't matter now, does it?"

"If you say so." I wanted to fight for his words, to explain that Kieran had only kissed me to piss him and Allison off, but the words perished on my tongue. I was too chickenshit to fix the situation. Showing him I cared made me feel raw, panicked. Like I was peeling off my skin right in front of him, giving him a sneak peek at everything that was inside me.

"You had no right to hit Kieran." The words stumbled out of my throat messily, spilling between us.

"I had every right to hit Kieran." Row stepped back, turning away from me, about to leave.

"Why?"

"Because I knew you didn't like it." He spun on his heel, walking backward but looking at me. "And I am utterly fucking incapable of letting you feel the slightest discomfort without doing something stupid and over the top. And there's something else." He was getting farther and farther away from me, and I was feeling the loss of him everywhere. I wanted him back. His warmth. His smirks. His grumpy attitude.

"What's that?" I whispered.

"You weren't his to kiss."

CHAPTER FORTY-SEVEN
CAL

oBITCHuary is Online.

McMonster is Online.

oBITCHuary is typing...

oBITCHuary is deleting...

McMonster is typing...

McMonster is deleting...

McMonster is Offline.

oBITCHuary is Offline.

CHAPTER FORTY-EIGHT
CAL

"Lovefool"—The Cardigans

Later that night, I tossed and turned in bed.

Semus was vying to snatch the International Asshole Award from Row. Not only had he peed in every single pair of shoes I owned today, but he'd also decided to attack my feet whenever I had the audacity to shift in my own bed.

I couldn't stop rewinding the disastrous Christmas lighting event in my head. Thinking about Kieran's dislocated nose, which had been promptly relocated by Randy, who'd reassured him by saying, "No one has the right to look as good as you did, son. Wasn't it Shakespeare who said that you need your face to be a li'l messed up to be truly beautiful?"

"I believe the quote is, '*There is no exquisite beauty without some strangeness in the proportions*,'" Kieran had muttered, hissing as his nose bone was jammed back into place. "And that was Edgar Allan Poe."

"What a fancy pansy name," Randy had mumbled into his gin bottle, which had been bundled in a brown paper bag.

I'd twisted my hair into a braid to do something with my hands. "Did you know that Edgar Allan Poe allegedly died of cholera, influenza, rabies, syphilis, *and* hyperglycemia?"

"Wow." Dylan's eyes had nearly bulged. "Clean living was obviously his passion."

Allison was the one who had ended up hitting the button once Row had stalked off, disappearing in a cloud of anger. Yellow lights had engulfed Main Street. Allison had slipped into her Escalade soon after, accompanied by her assistant, Lucinda.

Mom and I had retired early. She'd asked questions about Row, so I'd had to pacify her by lying and saying Row and I were sort of dating.

Alexa, play "Little Lies" by Fleetwood Mac.

This lie wasn't even a white one. It was a glaring, neon lie. One that collapsed onto your head and killed you. But I'd had to find an excuse for why we were so intense together, and *We want to have sex together but also want to kill each other* was a pretty weak explanation.

That kiss with Kieran had hurt him, and to add salt to the wound, I had done what I always did when I felt threatened—I'd bricked up with anxiety, refusing to give him an inch or show him that I cared. Just like the night he had taken my virginity, I'd made him feel disposable and meaningless.

And the thought of Row feeling those things made me feel nauseous with guilt.

I needed to make this right. With the boy who'd made me a broccoli birthday cake. Who had taken my virginity because I'd wanted to get rid of it, even though he had wanted so much more than just that. Who had helped me face my trauma and fear in neon attire, just to make me smile. Who had an excellent track record of giving me employment, rides, and irresistible kisses whenever I needed them.

Flinging my legs off the bed, I raced downstairs, shoving my feet into my sneakers on my way to the door. I stopped by the ugly key bowl, squeezing a Juicy Tubes gloss to my lips and extracting Mom's keys to her Subaru Crosstrek. I was sure she wouldn't mind.

Sixty-six percent sure, to be exact.

I drove to the Half Mile Inn, my heart in my throat. I didn't know what I was going to tell him. Only that it was time to lay it all out. I parked in front of the farmhouse-turned-inn. It was white, black-shuttered, and devastatingly charming. Pots and plants spilled out of every windowsill in vivid colors, and a handful of snow covered the roof, like a little hat. Dim yellow light danced from beyond the windows upstairs.

I got out and looked up at the moon. It glowed like a shiny pearl, round and full, achingly perfect against the dusky night. I swallowed hard, took my phone out, and put Row's favorite song on. "You Really Got Me" by The Kinks.

The song flooded out of my phone. I raised my arm and held it toward the windows, waiting for Row's face to appear.

It did appear.

But it did *not* appear happy.

He wore a white tee that clung to his tan tatted arms as he slid the window up. "Christ, Dot, it's two in the morning!"

"Time is an abstract concept!" I yelled back, grinning.

"Jail isn't, and Gertie lives down the hall and is very trigger-happy. Turn that shit off."

I did so dutifully, swallowing my mortification. *Oops.* Hadn't thought that one through. "Sorry," I winced.

"Is this retaliation for punching your little boyfriend?" His scowl deepened as he watched me from above.

"What? No!"

"Why are you here, then?" His eyes swept over me suspiciously.

"I couldn't sleep." I let out a huff, hugging myself. "You said if I can't sleep, I can talk to you."

He blinked, surprised but not completely thawed. "I take it Kieran was busy."

"Kieran…" I trailed off, exhausted from pretending Row was just a friend. "Kieran is not in the race."

His throat moved with a swallow. "Is that right?"

"Honest to God truth." Then, because it was time to fess up, I added, "Look, I'm tired of running away from this."

"From what?"

"From us."

That seemed to smooth out his frown. He parked his elbows on the windowsill. "Allison ambushed me to turn on those stupid lights this afternoon. I told her to take a hike, but then she said it might be good to show people I still care about this town—"

I shook my head. "I should've cleared the air before I got mad."

"No," he insisted. "I should've...I don't know. Called. Texted. *Explained.*" He worked his jaw back and forth. "As soon as I showed up, she dragged me there in a panic. I wasn't doing her a favor, Dot. I was trying to show people in this town I'm not a villain because..." He sighed. "Because I know it is important to *you.*"

"Row," I croaked, hanging my head down shamefully.

"I'm sorry you saw us together, but our entire conversation was her sucking up to me, and me telling her I'm fucking crazy about you and complaining you keep turning me down. I wasn't above wounding her ego to make you happy." Pause. "I'm not above doing *anything* if it makes you happy, if I'm honest."

I nodded, wishing he were next to me. That I could touch him. "I'm sorry too."

"What for?"

I shrugged. "Being so irresistible you had to punch Kieran in front of a full audience."

He chuckled, shaking his head. "I'd have taken any excuse to punch Kieran."

"You dislocated his nose, you know." I toed the frosty ground with the tip of my shoe.

"Dylan brought me up to speed." He kept his gaze locked on mine. "Anything else you want to tell me?" Row quirked an eyebrow, one hand propped against his window.

Yes. No. Just come downstairs so we can talk.

"Jeffrey Dahmer gave his neighbors meat sandwiches, which some believe contained his victim's human flesh," I blurted out.

Nice one, Cal. Super seductive.

Row's lips twitched. "I know someone who ate their own knee cartilage. Said it tasted like pig."

"Really?" I rubbed my palms together to gain heat. "I heard it tastes like chicken or tuna."

Row shook his head seriously, and I suppressed a laugh. No one rivaled Row's ability to handle my quirkiness. "Straight-up pork. She cooked it too. Minimal seasoning."

"Huh," I said.

He raised his eyebrows in question. "Anything else?"

"Nope." I gulped. "Glad we straightened it all out."

"Great. Thanks for that before-bed tidbit."

"So…" I walked back, jerking my finger behind my shoulder, to the car. *Cal, you coward.* "I'll see you tomorrow, then. For the run."

"I'll be there."

"And work."

"I'll be there too."

I forced myself to turn around and cross the street to my car.

Do not look back. He sent you on your way. You couldn't have been clearer.

Couldn't I, though? I had spoken to him about cannibal sandwiches. Maybe this wasn't how one usually expressed their longing toward another.

With a sigh, I fumbled for the car key in my sweatpants, unlocked the Subaru, and reached for the driver's door handle. I pulled it an inch before a hand slammed it shut behind me, grabbing my waist and whipping me around.

It was Row. And he looked *raw.*

"Moonlight. Music. Chin tilt. You came here because you wanted me to kiss you, didn't you?" His tiger eyes gleamed like a thousand fireflies in the dark. My knee-jerk reaction was to deny, deny, deny through my teeth. Damn anxiety. I plowed through that instinct like swimming against a heavy stream.

I gulped. "Yeah."

"*Fuck.*" His shoulders sagged with relief. "I'm so glad I'm just slow, not completely dumb."

His mouth fused with mine, sucking away my oxygen and all rational thought.

This time, it wasn't awkward and apologetic like the first time. Not explosive and frustrated like the second time either. This was new, hungry, and perfect.

His tongue swept across the seam of my lips before prompting them to part with a flick. I opened up for him, our tongues tangling in an erotic dance. Row cupped the side of my face, groaning ferally, digging his inked fingers into my hair. A tide of heat crashed inside my belly, sending currents of warmth to my nipples, spine, and the back of my skull. I clutched his shirt, burrowing into him as he deepened the kiss, tilting my head back, pinning me against the car.

"Dot."

He tasted divine. Of toothpaste and a shot of whiskey and something unapologetically male. Primal, hot, uncontained. My fingers wound tighter around the fabric of his shirt, and I felt the defined, tight ridges of his pecs and the dusting of hair on his chest. My toes curled and I whimpered into a hot, wet kiss that didn't have a beginning or an end. It felt like we were fused together, a hotwire of mini-orgasms.

I needed more. I needed *everything*. I wasn't even sure what everything entailed. I ran my frigid fingers down his arm, lacing my fingers in his and guiding his hand to cup one of my breasts. I wasn't wearing a bra, and my nipple was tight and puckered, begging to be teased.

"Missed your tits," he hissed out huskily, sounding almost pained, as his thumb rubbed and flicked my nipple through my shirt.

"Do you remember them much?" I explored his mouth like it was a forbidden fruit, devouring its juices, seeds, and flesh.

"I remember every inch of you." A satisfied growl made its way from the back of his throat, and he pinched my nipple teasingly, just south of inflicting pain. "Each individual cell."

His hand skimmed my rib cage, running down my belly, stopping at the hem of my sweater before snaking underneath it. He swirled my skin with his fingertips, all while angling his head to kiss me deeper. My knees gave out and I clawed his shoulders to stay upright, heat racing down my body to the apex between my thighs. I could feel my pulse in my clit. My blood pumped inside it, making it unbearably sensitive and swollen.

This was too much, and yet entirely not enough.

His hand hiked up under my sweater, the pad of his finger rubbing my nipple, and I melted into him, sucking the bottom of his lower lip greedily into my mouth with a desperate moan. "More."

"How much?" He kissed a path down my jaw, then neck, then collarbone. It was a sticky kiss, full of my lip gloss and its fruity, sweet taste.

"All of it. I want you," I said.

"I *need* you," he hissed.

He buried his face in the crook of my neck, thrusting his kraken-sized erection between my thighs. My clit pulsated against it through our clothes, and I swore he could feel it. His cock jerked, *tap-tap-tapping* it, bringing me closer to the edge.

"Row?"

"Dot?"

"Jail isn't an abstract concept." I pulled away from our kiss, clearing my throat. "We should go upstairs before we get arreste—"

I didn't get the chance to finish the sentence because Row scooped me up and turned around, carrying me into the inn. The lights were off in reception. A security guard snored peacefully in his chair in front of the monitors, his ranger hat tipped down to cover his eyes. I giggled in Row's arms, kicking my feet up.

"Shh. You'll wake up the dead, and I'll be too busy with your ass to fight zombies." He shoved two fingers into my mouth to shut me up, and I sucked them immediately, my thighs clenching with need as he took the stairs two at a time.

He kicked the door to his room open, and I tore away from our kiss to register the place he'd called home for the past year.

Freshly painted. Crown moldings. Heavy wooden furniture spaciously peppered across the room. Zero personality inside it. Row was ready to up and leave at a moment's notice.

We are just two passing ships. You can't handle more, Cal.

But it was too late to back down, even if I knew my heart was about to sink like the *Titanic.* He placed me on his bed, then stepped back, as if admiring his handiwork. I knew he was memorizing me between his sheets because he had no intention of keeping me there.

I should have felt self-conscious in my sweatpants and Cookie Monster sweater, but I didn't. I felt beautiful. Irresistible through his hooded eyes, like a flower in bloom, kissed by the unrelenting sun, on a flawless summer day.

Happy. Alive. *Home.*

Row rounded the bed, trying to work out what he wanted to do first. I was wide-eyed, a little scared, but mostly excited. I had gotten Dylan's okay. I could do this without any fear or doubt. He stopped in front of the foot of the bed, reached to grab the backs of my thighs, and dragged me to the edge. I gasped as he brought one of my legs up to rest on his shoulder, pressing a hot kiss to my inner ankle as he plucked my sneaker off. "You sure you want to do this?"

"Never been this sure in my entire life," I admitted. This time, not a lie.

"If you feel uncomfortable and scared…" he started.

"I won't," I promised, and our eyes met across the length of my body.

"Good. Because I'm going to eat your cunt like it's fucking ice cream, and come for seconds and thirds," he informed me, businesslike, swirling his tongue over my ankle bone, my heel clasped inside his rough hand.

A ticklish, delightful sensation traveled up my leg like a spark, detonating at my center. "Ahhhh. So, unfortunately, I didn't actually shav—"

"Don't care." He reached to remove my other shoe, repeating the process of kissing my ankle, my foot, down to my little toes.

"No, seriously. There's a lot going on down ther—"

"Sounds like fun. I'm eager to explore." My sneakers fell to the floor with a thud, and he tugged my sweatpants off, revealing my black cotton panties. His lips quirked with a smile as I lost all decorum, spreading for him, wide and eager. "Yeah, open those beautiful thighs. I want to see your pink cunt dripping for me. That's my girl."

My. Girl. Heaven was a place on earth and it was Row Casablancas's bed.

He rolled his hot tongue along my leg, inching north into my inner thigh, lowering himself to his knees inch by inch as he tasted my skin. When he reached my apex, he buried his face in my slit through my panties, inhaling deeply. A rush of heat ran between my legs, making every muscle in my body tense with anticipation. My breath hitched as Row began kissing my inner thighs like they were my mouth, swirling his tongue, nuzzling his nose, making me open my legs wider. I grabbed one of his pillows and moaned into it loudly.

A hand reached from between my legs, grabbing the pillow and tossing it on the floor. "No fucking way. I want eye contact."

"But I'm embarrassed," I whined.

"Being perfect is a lot of pressure. I get it."

"Row." I grabbed a fistful of his hair, tugging him closer, arching my back, my pussy quivering with anticipation. "Why'd we wait so long?"

He raised his head from between my legs, scowling at me. "Because you are stubborn, annoying, indecisive, flak—"

"Okay, okay." I pushed his head back into my crotch. "Go back to doing what you do best."

He took his sweet time, kissing me through the fabric of my panties torturously slowly. "You smell like heaven." One of his palms pressed against my inner thigh, his pinky hooked into my panties so that he tickled my tight hole. Not penetrating, but teasing it enough that it added more pressure to my building orgasm. His other hand snaked up my body, pushing my sweater up until it was rolled halfway on my breasts.

"Dot?"

"Hmm?" I moaned and thrashed, close to climaxing before he'd even paid my pussy attention.

"Play with your pretty tits for me."

I reached for one of my breasts and plucked a nipple, a shot of electricity running from my spine to between my legs. I hadn't realized how full and delicate my boobs felt.

"Yeah, baby. Just like that. So beautiful. So innocent. So mine." He sank his teeth into my flesh through my panties, biting and dragging his upper teeth all the way down to my crack. I shuddered, my muscles burning, the desire so intense I forgot to draw a breath.

"Slap your tit, Cal," he instructed. I did. Oh crap. It felt good. Another rush of heat moved between my legs, and I knew he could see and smell how soaked I was. My panties were drenched. "Row, please."

He scraped the edge of my panties away with his teeth, removing them bit by bit like a curtain being drawn. "Say it," he demanded hoarsely. "Give me your words. For once in this goddamn life, *you* come to *me*."

I was about to come to him, at him, and *on* him. I popped my head up, and our eyes met through the valley of my breasts. We were both panting hard. "Please shove your tongue inside me before I die."

"Good girl."

"Say that again."

"You're my good, obedient girl. As such, you'll get rewarded accordingly. Eyes on me now. I want you to see the filthy things I do to you."

He pressed his thumb to my clit and pulled upward, dragging his tongue across my slit, bottom to top. His lips clasped around my clit. I flung my head back and groaned. My entire body was shaking as he pried me open, strong fingers spreading my ass cheeks and cunt, fucking me mercilessly with his tongue, in and out, in and out, his pinky stroking my anus playfully. Every time I squirmed or tried to move away from the intensity, he'd let go of one of my ass cheeks and slap one of my nipples. The pleasure was so intense, and there was nowhere to escape. I never thought I could be so open with someone, so trusting, so bare again.

I was leaking juices all over his mouth, his chin, and I felt my own wetness against his face every time his tongue drove into me. "You're so fucking wet, I'm about to come just from eating you out," he grunted, pushing his index finger inside me right along with his tongue, curling it to that coarse, deep spot inside me that made me go wild every time my vibrator hit it. My whole body clenched and soared, and I convulsed around him.

"So fucking tight. Look how good you're taking my tongue and finger. That's my girl. Letting me stretch you out like that. You'll be taking my cock so well, baby."

His praise licked at my skin like rays of sun. The pleasure was so intense, I felt like I was floating on a cloud.

When he picked up speed, I couldn't take it anymore. I grabbed his head with both my hands and began grinding against him shamelessly, riding his face like I was at a rodeo. He laughed devilishly as he added another finger, as his mouth sailed up, clasping my swollen clit and sucking it hard.

The sound of my juices slicking his fingers rang around the room. My nails dug harder into his scalp. "No one told me sex could be this good," I moaned, every bone in my body deliciously heavy under the weight of an impending orgasm.

"This isn't sex. This isn't even foreplay." Lick. Suck. Bite. "This is merely an appetizer. By the time you get to dessert, you won't be able to stand straight."

Oh.

My.

God.

"You've...become better at it," I noted.

"No, Dot." His mouth moved against my clit, scraping it with his teeth. It was literally the hottest thing I'd ever experienced. "We were always dynamite together. You were just too wrapped up in other things to notice."

He flipped us over quickly, him flat on his back now, with me straddling his face. "Hold on to the headboard, Dot."

"Why?"

"I'm about to tongue you to oblivion and back."

Deciding once again to be a good girl, I curled my fingers over the upholstered headboard and sank my pussy directly onto his tongue. He groaned with pleasure when I was fully seated on top of his face, and I was seriously concerned for his ability to breathe. "Are you okay down there?"

"Perfect. Ride my tongue, Dot."

"What if I break it? Your tongue is a muscle too."

"Worth it."

"Are you su—"

"I said what I said, baby."

I rode his face like a cowgirl, his fingers sinking deep into my ass cheeks as he guided my movements and feasted on me like I was his last meal. Soon, heat bloomed over my skin, my muscles tightening, my mind becoming deliriously empty and clouded. The climax slammed into me with force, shaking me to the core. The little hairs on my arms stood on end, and my breath hitched as wave after wave of pleasure hit me. Tears stung the sides of my eyes before I collapsed on top of him, boneless and spent.

He was still beneath me, breathing hard. He kissed the side of my thigh before gently raising it so he could roll out from under it. A moment later, his heavy body dropped next to mine. Our faces were aligned. And he was beautiful, always, but especially now, when he appeared drowsy and content, his lips swollen and wet with my juices.

"Kiss you?" He grinned, asking for permission. I nodded. He reached to give me a peck on the mouth.

"Row," I rasped, rolling my finger over his full bottom lip, the earthy, musky taste of my own arousal invading my mouth. "That was the best orgasm I've ever had."

"Yeah." He caught the tip of my finger between his straight teeth, nibbling playfully. "Mine too."

"Hmm, what?" My eyes flared. I tilted my chin down, trying to peek, but he pounced quickly, kissing the living hell out of me, blocking the view of his crotch.

"I said what I said."

He'd had an orgasm from *eating me out*? I needed to put a ring on it.

"Whoa. That is so—"

"Embarrassing?" He rose up and patted the nightstand, finding his pack of cigarettes and lighting one up.

"Amazing," I breathed out.

"Yeah. You certainly are." He puffed on his cancer stick.

The words pierced through my skin, soaking into my soul.

"What now?" I eyed him eagerly. Were we going to have sex? Was I going to redeem myself after that night four years ago?

"Well." He reached with the hand that held the lit cigarette, using his thumb to brush residual lip gloss from the corner of my mouth. "I've been dreaming about your glittery pink lipstick smeared all over my dick."

CHAPTER FORTY-NINE
CAL

"Truly Madly Deeply"—Savage Garden

I was fully prepared to give Row the best blow job to be recorded in the history of humanity.

There was only one problem.

Okay, two, if you consider the Guinness World Record people never actually timed blow jobs for their books.

Row fell asleep like a sack of bricks not even a minute after he made that sexy declaration. I went to the bathroom to pee, and when I came back, the cigarette was in the ashtray, still not put out all the way. He was snoring, his cheek smushed against a pillow, his long curly lashes casting a shadow over his cheeks.

Hello, awkward, my old friend.

I put out the cigarette and emptied the ashtray, then slipped into the bed and turned my head to his nightstand. The clock said it was three in the morning. He'd had a long day. So had I. But since not getting sleep was my new norm, I hardly ever felt tired anymore.

It was time to do the walk of shame. If I still had any muscles in me, that was. That orgasm had sucked the energy right out of me. If this was an appetizer, Row was right: full-blown sex with him would leave me in a puddle of bodily fluids and a tattoo neck choker.

Dylan would have a field day delivering the obituary.

She died doing what she loved—fucking my older brother.

But she was wrong. Privately, I knew, Row had never been just my best friend's older brother. He was the boy I'd confessed to that I had never learned how to slow dance before prom. It had been in his kitchen, while Dylan was upstairs making out with Darren from the lacrosse team. I had been supposed to distract Row by talking to him. Row had regarded me with a frown, arm still slung on the open fridge door. "You don't need to know how to slow dance. Boys are assholes and you should stay away from them."

I had given him a pointed look. He'd rolled his eyes in exasperation, slamming the fridge shut and rummaging in his front pocket for his phone. "It's really not that hard." He had scowled, choosing a song. "Truly Madly Deeply" by Savage Garden. My all-time favorite nineties song. I had thought it was a coincidence. Kismet. He'd tossed his phone on the table and opened his arms. "Come in."

Entering his embrace had been like walking straight into home. He'd slung my arms around his shoulders—I'd had to stand on my toes to get there—and wrapped his hands around my waist. We'd swayed to the music, staring into each other's eyes, and in that moment, he had broken my heart. Because I had known I would never experience anything remotely as perfect ever again.

Now, I gingerly scooted toward the edge of the bed. As soon as I moved an inch, Row's heavy arm fell directly on my chest like a tree, pinning me in place. That thing was at least five hundred pounds *before* the fancy Rolex. I exhaled, toying with the idea of waking him up. But he looked so peaceful and tranquil. Almost childlike.

I patted the nightstand behind me blindly, grabbed my phone, and texted my mom that I was okay, alive, and sleeping at the inn, then put my phone down. I was fully prepared to stare at the ceiling until dawn.

Blinking back at the darkness, I began sailing down the river of my thoughts. But something about Row's deep, calm breaths, the weight of his arm against my chest like a heavy blanket, and the way I felt just right—like I was exactly where I was supposed to be—stopped me from overthinking.

Then, something truly wonderful happened. A switch flicked in my head. Something shifted in my chemistry.

And for the first time in a long time, I fell asleep.

Rays of winter sunshine filtered through the windows.

But they weren't what woke me up. No. That was Row's snoring.

I rolled to my side, eyeing him. Joy spread across my chest, filling it with giddiness. His arm no longer imprisoned me. It was now tossed over his eyes, blocking the sunlight from his face.

"I've been dreaming about your glittery pink lipstick smeared all over my dick."

I took it as consent. It was time to return a favor.

I reached for my pants on the floor and rummaged through the pockets, producing my Juicy Tubes gloss. I always kept one with me. You never knew when you needed to look fabulous. I applied a generous coat, smacking my lips together. I ran my fingers through my hair before flinging the duvet off him. His black sweatpants displayed his morning wood, and my mouth watered at the idea of him filling it.

I peeled his sweatpants down an inch, glancing up to check if he stirred. He was still dead to the world. I inched his pants farther down. His dick sprung out. As far as penises went, this one was gorgeous enough to be on the cover of *GQ*, wearing a cowboy hat and a serious frown. It had a smooth crown, a long, veiny shaft, and just the right amount of trimmed groin hair.

I wrapped my fingers around the root, licking my lips. He smelled earthy, warm, and delicious. Dry cum covered his tip from last night. His cock jutted in my hand, awakened by the sudden intrusion.

Leaning forward on my knees, I took his tip in my mouth and suckled softly, the smell of my lip gloss filling the air. I swept my tongue across the tip, scooping up fresh, salty precum, before taking his entire crown in my mouth and sucking hard.

A sharp intake of breath filled the room, and his thighs jerked forward with a pained hiss. "Dot?" he croaked.

My head shot up. Sleepy, gorgeous golden eyes stared back at me.

"Who else? Do *not* say Allison, I have your dick in my hand."

His chest rumbled, and he sent a hand to stroke the nape of my neck. "Jealous?"

"Should I be?"

He shook his head. "Whether it's to have sex, go to a funeral, or start a heist, I'd always choose you over anyone else."

"Why?" I probed.

"Because you're it." He flashed me a sexy grin.

"What's *it*?"

"Everything, baby."

My heart was drumming so fast and hard, I became a little nauseous.

"You're just saying that because my teeth are very close to your phallus."

"I'm saying that because it's the unfortunate, infuriating truth." Row brushed my hair from my face with his thumb. "And because I *really* want you to keep doing what you're doing, not that I'm not enjoying the conversation."

I tucked my hair behind my ears and dove down, taking his penis in my mouth again. The tip was engorged, almost purple, a pearl of cum on its edge. His shaft was thick and long, veins running through the tan, velvety skin. I could feel his eyes on the crown of my head, and his thick, briny precum coating the walls of my mouth. Heat flooded my insides, and I started rolling my hips, humping against nothing as I curled my fingers around his shaft, taking him deeper into my mouth. I held my breath to tame my gag reflex when his tip brushed the back of my throat, feeling my eyes water as I made delighted noises, sucking him off. It felt so good to please him. I didn't know why, but making him happy was the biggest turn-on I'd ever experienced.

Row kept stroking my hair, his voice ragged and strained. "Fuck. Dot, what are you doing to me?"

Nothing in comparison to what you're doing to me.

I was a novelty, but him? He was magic.

Only one of us had a fulfilling, glamorous, and exciting life to return to when this was all over. All I had to show for myself was disabling social anxiety, a fear of men, a shoebox apartment, and unresolved issues.

Trying to focus on the here and now, I curled my tongue into the shape of his shaft, licking him like a lollipop, jerking him off while swirling the tip of my tongue around his crown. He grabbed my hair from the back, twisting its length around his fist like the reins of a horse, and tipped my chin up just so, making his shaft grind against the roof of my mouth as he began fucking it mercilessly. "Is your little cunt aching for me, baby?"

I nodded eagerly, my jaw straining as the tip of his cock hit the back of my throat with each thrust. He picked up speed.

"Is it dripping for me?"

Another nod. Hell yes it was. My head was spinning, I was so drunk with desire.

"Can I check for myself?"

Tears prickled my eyes as he pounded harder and faster into my mouth, pressing to the hilt. He was an aggressive lover, and I liked that he didn't treat me like a fragile little thing. Like damaged goods. I nodded eagerly.

He kept one hand holding my hair in a death grip and continued fucking my mouth as he reached past my breasts, giving them an appreciative squeeze before gliding his big tough hand down my belly. When he reached my legs, he slapped my knees open so I was spread as wide as I could be in this position. Curling three fingers, he brushed them along my pink, dripping pussy. *Oh God. I am going to combust.*

"Fuck. Maybe you can take it this time like a good girl. What do you say?" He picked up more speed, and it felt incredible, him in my mouth, his fingers in my pussy, filling me everywhere. Well, *almost* everywhere.

As if reading my mind, a low rumble trembled through his abs. "Are you gonna come just from sucking me off, Dot?"

I looked up, pinning my tear-filled gaze on him, and nodded. I could. I really could.

He removed his hand from my pussy and used it to trace the edges of my jaw gently, still fucking my mouth. "May I play with your ass, sweetheart?"

I gurgled the saliva and precum in my mouth as answer, gathering my breasts in my hands and using them to massage his balls with a small nod. I writhed, empty and desperate for my own release, grinding against the flat surface of his mattress.

Please. Please help me. I need this. I need to come.

"I got you, Dot." He grabbed me by the ankles, scooting me closer so my face was in his crotch, still sucking him off, while he grabbed one of my ass cheeks in one hand and slipped his index and middle finger into my pussy with the other, and fit a pinky into my tight hole. He began playing with me, the slurping sounds my body made filling the room. A spasm volleyed through me, and I cried out, choking on my own saliva and his cock, stars twinkling underneath my eyelids as ripple after ripple of an orgasm washed through me. What was happening? Since when was I a sexually liberated woman who loved to suck cock and get her ass fingered? What was this man doing to me?

"Gonna come now, baby," Row said huskily, wrapping my hair around his fist and tilting my head up to pull me off him.

I stayed glued to his dick, nodding my head. "Go for it."

"You mean…?"

I nodded, not ready to part ways with his cock.

He grunted. "Shit, I knew you were perfect. Perfect." He thrust into my mouth. "Perfect."

With this praise, he came undone. A flood of hot, thick cum rushed into my mouth. I swallowed every drop, closing my eyes with his hand clasping the back of my head, his entire body shuddering. When the trembling subsided, I looked up at him.

"Row?"

"Yes, Dot?"

"Your dick is covered in my lip gloss."

He sat up straight, this smooth large Adonis of a man. He looked down at his cock—still half-hard—and the pink, glittery smears around it, and smiled. "I think I might skip my shower today."

"Bad idea. Here." I rolled his sweatpants back on, tucking my lip gloss into his waistband. "Just put some on your dick instead of lube next time you feel horny."

His hand clasped mine before I could remove it from his waistband. "Next time I feel horny, I know who to call."

Calm your tits, and the organ beating wildly behind them, Cal. You cannot afford to fall in love. Last time you opened up to Franco, he detonated your life.

"So." I licked my lips. "Now that we're done with third base, I guess it's time for…" I trailed off, raising my eyebrows meaningfully.

"Our morning jog," he finished for me, jerking his head sideways, to the clock. "Almost seven. Better hurry up."

"I was thinking about doing a different kind of cardio." I cleared my throat.

"I've been thinking about that kind of cardio with you since I learned my dick is good for more than just peeing. Are you sure you're ready, though?"

I loved that he asked. Loved that he was considerate and, at the same time, still treated me like a sex kitten and not some fragile, little ditzy girl while we were intimate. "I'm ready," I said.

He grabbed the back of my neck, tugging me forward to plant a kiss on my lips. "Now let's fuck the attitude you gave me this past month out of you. Be a good girl and go bend—"

A rap on the door cut him off.

Noooooooooooooo.

"Casablancas!" Gertie's voice screeched. "Cleaning's in ten minutes. You better get your ass outta there by then, or you'll have to wait until after the weekend."

"Did you not see the *Do Not Disturb* sign on my door?" he called out, tucking me under his arm protectively, like she had caught us. Such a stark difference from how Franco had treated me. My heart crumbled like a cookie.

"Sure did," she confirmed. "Ruining your day is my only source of joy these days, seeing as your little deal is about to run me out of business. Eight minutes now."

There was a thump, indicating the woman had left. Row and I looked at each other for a beat. "Honestly, I don't think I'll last more than ten seconds once I'm inside you, but preferably, I'd like more than eight minutes to make sure you come too."

"Fine, we'll jog." I pouted.

He kissed my puckered lips. "That's my girl."

CHAPTER FIFTY
CAL

"Desert Rose"—Sting

Since I didn't have any running gear, we made a pit stop at my house.

Mamushka was drinking her morning tea at the kitchen table, mindlessly flipping through a newspaper and humming to herself.

"Hello, Ambrose, how are your knuckles doing?" She grinned behind the rim of her mug as soon as we walked in, not bothering to raise her gaze from the paper.

"Better than Kieran's nose, I hear." Row leaned down to kiss the crown of her head. "Good morning, Mrs. Litvin."

"It certainly seems to be, at least for you two."

"We brought pastries." He slid a box of Dahlia's Diner's finest across the table. It was his idea not to come empty-handed. *Suck-up.*

"Come, sit down. I'll pour you a cup of tea and ask you inappropriate questions about your relationship with my daughter while Cal gets ready for her run."

"You knew we've been running together?" I asked, surprised.

"You weren't very discreet about it." Mom flipped open the pastry box, settling for a white chocolate croissant. "I can hear your bickering from all the way down the street."

I felt my blush charring my skin to the point of third-degree burns. "Row, please don't feel obligated to answer any of her questions."

"Don't worry." Row smirked at Mamushka. "You can ask me anything you want, and I'll answer with unnecessary detail, explicit examples, and time stamps."

"I hate you." I picked up a powdered-sugar donut, licking the sugar.

"Got a weird way of showing it." He snaked an arm around my shoulder and dropped a kiss to my temple.

Oh my. We were flirting. In front of my *mother*. My head snapped up to look at him, shocked by the semipublic display of affection.

"Is this okay?" He scanned me, his question barely audible.

I nodded quickly. *It's more than okay. It's a dream I don't want to wake up from.*

Eventually, it was Mom who broke the spell by fanning herself with a huff. "Is it just me, or is it getting really hot in here? Row, you can take off your shirt if the heater is too much."

"The heater is not on." Row frowned.

"*Mamushka!*" I chided, frowning at her.

"He finds it funny." Her innocent eyes clung to my face. "See? He is laughing."

Row was, in fact, laughing. A low, husky rumble that dripped like warm honey into the pit of my stomach.

"He's just being polite," I said.

"I'm never being polite," Row retorted. "Not unless I can help it."

"So." I cleared my throat. "I'm going to go get dressed now."

Row nodded, taking a seat next to Mom and looking completely at ease. "Not my favorite state of you, but go for it."

"Row!" I gasped.

"Oh, come on." Mom laughed. "We both know you weren't playing Monopoly when you spent the night away from home."

"The emotional scars from this conversation will never heal," I mumbled as I made my way to my room. Once there, I decided to take a quick cold shower. Mainly to calm my raging hormones down. Then I slipped into my sports clothes.

"Callichka, sweetie, I'm off to the supermarket, and I'm taking the car!" Mom called outside my door.

"'Kay, Mamushka. Love you."

"Love you too."

I blow-dried my hair quickly and put on minimal makeup, trying to atone for my *Full Metal Jacket* look yesterday when I showed up at the inn.

From the other room, I heard Row dropping his voice to a threatening whisper. "Now, you listen to me, Semen." *Semus, not Semen.* Also, was he…threatening my cat? "You're gonna stop pissing in Cal's shoes, or I'll come here personally every day to take a shit in your litter box. Now how would you like that?"

My educated guess was that Semus wouldn't like it at all. But it was incredibly sweet. He had stood up against my bully. My bully just happened to be a seven-pound furball.

Semus meowed his response, and that was when I decided to walk out of my room. Row gave me a slow, appreciative once-over, his gaze heating.

"How's my outfit?" I twirled in place.

"Hate it."

"What? Why?"

"Blocks all the good view."

"Behave yourself, Mr. Casablancas."

"That's not on the agenda today, baby."

We both walked outside, hit by the frigid air.

"Hey," I said. "Are you coming to the Thanksgiving parade on Main Street next week?"

"Absolutely not." Row made a face. "Filled my quota for Staindrop events after the Christmas lights incident."

"It's not like it's gonna happen again," I said, realizing that I really, *really* wanted him to come. "For starters, Allison is not going to ask you to cook the turkey she'll pardon, and I won't be kissing Kieran."

"If Kieran wants to keep this pointless life of his, he better not be on the same side of the street as you. Still, I'm not coming."

"Shame." I shook my arms, cranked my neck, and feigned nonchalance. "If you isolate yourself, you'll be missing out on all the good parts."

"Impossible." He scooped my jawline in his palm. "The best part is right in front of me."

Then he dipped his head down and kissed me.

CHAPTER FIFTY-ONE
ROW

McMonster: Can I tell you something?

oBITCHuary: Yes.

McMonster: You remind me of those paintings of anatomical hearts with flowers bursting out of the arteries and veins.

oBITCHuary: I think that's the most romantic thing anyone has ever said to me. How sad is that?

McMonster: Not sad at all.

McMonster: To me it sounds like a happy beginning.

CHAPTER FIFTY-TWO
ROW

I hated running.

Or any other type of cardio that didn't involve Cal's legs wrapped around my waist, to be honest. I didn't need a workout. I worked a physical job, hurling a shit ton of food crates from one place to the other, chopping, slicing, tossing, flipping, glazing, grating, all in a kitchen of about thirty thousand degrees.

I needed this morning run with Cal like I needed a second tailbone.

Only reason I did it was so I could have an excuse to spend one-on-one time with her. My patience and virtue had paid off, because this morning, I'd had my dick inside her mouth and my pinky up her ass. Blood rushed to my dick just thinking about the things I was going to do to this woman. I was going to live inside that pussy every waking moment until I had to pay fucking rent.

Too bad now that I'd had a taste, there was no way I was ever going to settle for just another meaningless, faceless hookup. She was exquisite, and she was all fucking mine.

"You look happy." Rhy eyed me accusingly when I walked into my upstairs office at Descartes, his pen still hovering over his bookkeeping ledger.

"Is that a crime?" I slid a bottle of beer across the desk and took a pull of mine. We opened service in two hours, which meant that Cal wouldn't be here for another hour and a half. Not that I was keeping tabs or anything.

"Depends on what lifted your mood." Rhy sipped his beer, lounging back. "Is Kieran dead?"

"Alive as far as I know, much to my chagrin." I fell into the chair opposite him, crossing my ankles over the desk—*and* his ledger. "How're the numbers lookin'?"

"Great. Insane profit margin. But selling the land was the right thing. This place is fucking toxic after the bullshit Allison pulled on us."

If I'm selling. I'd been blue-balling Tate Blackthorn for weeks now. It was like ignoring a tumorous growth, though. I needed to sign the dotted line if I wanted him to release the funds for my new restaurants and the new mortgages I'd taken on. Blackthorn was right—I was in no position to fuck around and find out.

"Toxicity is where I thrive, so no complaints there." I shrugged.

"Don't change the subject. What's with the perpetual smile?" Rhy frowned. "This wouldn't have anything to do with a certain green-haired girl, would it?"

"Her tips are purple now," I informed him. "And I don't kiss and tell."

"You don't have to. Your dumbass smile told me the entire story, including the graphic details. Shit, dude, the ass too?" He uncrossed his legs and put them down.

I stomped his foot under the desk, and he let out an agonized yelp. "Watch your mouth when you talk about this woman." How could I let her walk away? More importantly, how could I make sure she didn't run off? Calla was so good at running off.

"Does she know how you feel yet?" Rhy accepted his beer, tipping it over his lips and taking a big drink.

Hard no. If she knew how I felt, she'd sprint to the fucking hills. She loved New York. Loved her independence. Loved being alone.

Any hope I entertained about her developing feelings for me in the process was bound to kill me faster than the smoking habit she hated so much.

There was a knock on the office door. He pushed up to his feet, downing the beer and slam-dunking it into the trash.

"Pissed off with this town? Yeah," I said.

"In love with every cell in her body." He advanced toward the door.

"I'm not in love with her," I murmured into my drink.

Rhyland stopped with his hand on the doorknob, cocking a brow. "Cut the bullshit. What are you, five?" Another, sterner knock. "Just remember she has ten tons of baggage. Her anxiety issues always stand in her way, and I doubt she can form any sort of serious relationship with anyone, even you."

"What the hell does that mean, even me?"

"Even someone who'd accept her exactly as she is—flawed to the core—and won't ask her to change."

Damn straight. Her flaws were some of her best features. Protective anger simmered inside of me. I was about to give him a piece of my mind when he opened the door. Kieran stood on the other side.

The universe must've picked up on my good mood and decided to shit all over it. The bastard waltzed in, looking like a trillion bucks with his stupid peacoat and even stupider smile, and a nose that— unbelievably—*did* make him look more ruggedly handsome. Young Clint Eastwood looked like a dumpster fire next to Fuckface.

"Hey, man." Rhy and Kieran exchanged a handshake and a bro hug. "I'll leave you two to kill each other." Rhy exited the office. I kicked the floor to turn around on my executive chair, narrowing my eyes at Rhy as he added, "Just watch the carpet. Been meaning to take it with me to New York when we close this place up."

"Fuckface," I said.

"Asshole," Kieran replied.

"What heinous crime have I committed in a previous life to

deserve this social call?" I picked up a cigarette, rolling it between my fingers.

"Don't be so humble. I'm sure current-life you is on karma's shit list too." Kieran strode in, debonair and cocky as a man who earned a hundred million pounds a year should be. "Apology accepted, by the way."

"Apology not issued." I tucked the cigarette behind my ear. "Do I need to call security, or do you want me to kick you out myself?"

He sauntered deeper into the room, over to the drink cart behind my desk, to fix himself a whiskey. I'd never seen Kieran Carmichael drink. He always struck me as a Patrick Bateman type. Someone who was too busy shoving decapitated heads into freezers to have a stiff one with a buddy. So this gave me pause.

"You should be thanking me, you know. My fake-kissing Cal snowballed into your hookup." He poured himself two fingers of Hibiki, then raised the glass to his lips. "Had to give Lady Faith a little push. Neither of you had the balls to make the first move."

"And you know Cal and I are together because…?" I tilted an eyebrow.

"She left me a three thousand–word text message relaying your entire night together, lip gloss flavor included." He sipped his drink calmly.

"She didn't," I said, even though it sounded *exactly* like something Cal would do.

"Prime reading material, highly recommended," he continued, picking up random shit on my desk, snooping in my stuff. "Probably wanted to send it to Dylan."

Classic Cal move. For a moment, I allowed myself to imagine what life with her would be like. A ton of trips to the ER, foot-in-mouth scenarios, and spontaneous sex in exotic places. I'd sign on for this kind of life in a goddamn heartbeat.

"Now that you know she's not up for grabs, stay the fuck away." I itched to stand up and assert my power but also didn't want him to see how territorial I was over Cal. She was a weakness, a blind side, a cruel reminder of my mortality.

"Trust me, Casablancas, there's nothing I'd like more than to ignore your meaningless existence." He finally propped against the doorjamb, looking bored with the entire situation. "Unfortunately, I can't do that."

"Because?" I rose up to my feet, treading toward him until we were face-to-face.

"First of all, I hear we'll be neighbors next year. You're moving to London."

"London's big, and my hate for you is even more infinite. Don't worry, I won't knock on your door asking for sugar."

"Good. That shit's toxic and I don't consume it." He plucked the cigarette from behind my ear, snapped it in two, and tossed it into the garbage. When Cal and Dylan weren't around, he really let his real asshole self come out. Strangely, I felt more comfortable with this version of him. The one that was mean to me growing up. At least I knew what I was dealing with.

"See, I needed to give you a good excuse to punch the daylights out of me yesterday," he said, a grin spreading across his lips.

"Because of what happened when we were kids?"

"No, because I'm about to hit on your sister, whether you like it or not."

I was torn between dislocating his nose again and fist-pumping the air.

He wanted *Dylan*? Was he fucking insane? I loved my sister, but she was a headache. Unruly, fiercely independent, mouthy as all hell, and impossible to manage. She was the hard to Cal's softness. The ruthlessly bossy to her soft quirkiness. I was the first to like a challenge, but Dylan wasn't a challenge. She was a *Squid Game* obstacle course that ended with you speared to a wall by rusty metal spikes. Plus, I knew she'd never go for a guy like him. He was too smooth around the edges, too well-mannered, too rich. Dylan would never go with the obvious choice. Her favorite ice cream flavor was butter pecan.

"She is engaged and pregnant," I pointed out.

"And he is absent and stupid," Kieran deadpanned, in the same businesslike, flat tone. "I remember Tucker Reid. He used to burn insects with a magnifying glass and wedgie your sister. She deserves better."

"Agreed, but that applies to you too." I pulled at his ridiculously ironed shirt. "You were a shit kid who spent every waking moment reminding me that I was the poor son of an alcoholic."

"Are you ever going to let the past go?"

"Why would I? The past tells us a lot about what we should expect from the future."

"Ever wonder why I was the way I was?" he snapped, growling at me. "I was cruel because I was *weak*. My dad rode my ass six ways from Sunday about soccer, about becoming a star, being drafted to a European team in my teens. We weren't as rich as you probably thought we were, and most of the money was poured into my sport anyway. I was under an immense amount of pressure. And there you were—popular, hot shit, straight-A student, and already interning at a Michelin-starred restaurant outside of town. You had it easy. Or at least, your nightmare wasn't as elaborate as mine. Nobody put all their chips on you. Nobody told you that if you didn't make it, your family would fall apart."

He was jealous of *me*? Hadn't seen that one coming.

"Yeah, life was just a piece of fucking cake," I snarled.

"My dumb teenage self thought so."

"So what, you want my forgiveness now?"

"No offense, but I really couldn't give two shits about whether you forgive me or not. I want your understanding." He pushed off the wall. "Mostly, I want you to be out of my fucking way when I court your sister. Because let me tell you—if I don't get around you, you bet your ass I'll get *through* you. Understand?"

My nostrils flared, and I stepped forward. Our pecs bumped into one another. "You have some nerve coming into my establishment, running your mouth like you deserve anything more than another sucker punch."

Kieran met my gaze head-on. "I'll allow you one more punch to get it out of your system. After that, I'm throwing fists too."

It had been a long time coming. My entire adolescence, I'd wanted to beat the crap out of him.

I sent a knockout punch right into his abs. He folded, staggering backward, bracing himself against my desk. He pushed off the furniture, barreling into my side, tackling me with his shoulder to the floor.

"For fuck's sake, Casablancas." He planted a knee on my rib cage to paralyze me, grabbing me by the jaw and squeezing until it almost snapped. *Shit*, he was strong. And I was rusty, having avoided bar brawls since I'd gotten famous and my lawyers had told me each altercation was a potential seven-figure settlement deal.

"How long have you had a thing for her?" I caught his wrist and bent it, forcing him to follow my movement and flipping us so I was on top.

"Since I came back. I never paid attention to her before." He pounced up, grabbing my neck and putting me in a headlock. We kicked and thrashed, each trying to get on top of the other.

"Is this a fucking pregnancy kink?" I growled. "You sick fuck."

He plowed a sucker punch straight to my jaw. "Don't reduce her to a fucking kink, you son of a—"

"Don't complete that sentence."

"Right. Zeta birthed my favorite human in the world. Better not."

For whatever reason, I believed that he genuinely liked my sister. But that didn't stop my fist from connecting with his mouth. His lower lip popped, blood running down his chin and neck.

"Goddammit. This is the second Givenchy coat you've ruined."

"Stop being so damn punchable, and I'll stop punching you."

We were on the floor, bloodied and flushed, when I heard a knock on the door.

"Busy. Fuck off!" I snarled, trying to scratch Kieran's eyes out.

"Fine, but we'll have a real conversation about your attitude next time I see you!" I heard Cal on the other side.

"No. Wait." I dumped Kieran's limp body on the floor, scrambling up to my feet, stumbling to the door. "Wait. Don't go."

Kieran lay on the floor, shaking his head and chuckling.

I threw the door open. Cal's big blue eyes flared at the sight of my beaten-up face. She peered over my shoulder, catching a glimpse of Fuckface lying in a pool of his own blood. Her mouth slacked.

"Don't worry, Cal. This was a therapeutic session." Kieran gave her a little wave behind me. "Everything is under control."

"Completely consensual." I forced out a grin. Shit, he had given me a black eye. I could feel it swelling. "Need anything, baby?"

I was calling her baby now, while my dick wasn't shoved in one of her holes. Rhy was right: I was a goner, and the place I was headed to was right into a deep depression when she bailed on my ass.

"Hmm, I came in early to help Rhyland do some filing..." She trailed off, still looking unsure. "And ended up scrubbing puke off the bathroom floor because Katie has food poisoning. Been doing that for thirty minutes."

Who the fuck was Katie?

"Your maître d'." Cal frowned, as if reading my thoughts. "She's been working here since the day you opened." Eh.

"Poor Dot." I tugged her by the shirt, wrapping her in a hug. "Next time let me know and I'll send someone else to clean that up."

"Are you sure you're okay?" She frowned.

"Never been better."

"Cool. So...whose dick do I have to suck to get a margarita around here?" She sniffled into my shirt.

Kieran and I answered in unison.

"Mine," I growled.

"His." He swallowed. He scraped himself off my floor, limping his way past my door while keeping his distance from Cal. He was bleeding all over my engineered hardwood. "See you later, folks. Enjoy one another."

Maybe Fuckface wasn't so bad after all.

CHAPTER FIFTY-THREE
CAL

oBITCHuary: What's your favorite fantasy?

McMonster: You, taking it from behind while I fuck you so hard against my chef station your pelvic bones almost snap.

oBITCHuary: Dirtiest fantasy?

McMonster: Same thing, but we accidentally spilled lukewarm bone broth all over ourselves. That shit stinks.

McMonster: Your turn.

oBITCHuary: You, fucking me in a recording room.

McMonster: Into it. Why a recording room?

oBITCHuary: Because that means that I've made it.

CHAPTER FIFTY-FOUR
CAL

"Doll Parts"—Hole

Row fed me brown sugar mooncakes and passionfruit margaritas my entire shift, which was lovely, because the place was so busy, I definitely needed the pick-me-up. We all did, to be honest, which was why I snuck some of the margaritas to other servers and busboys each time I made a pit stop in the kitchen.

When I came in for my eighth margarita in two hours, Row curled his fingers around my wrist with a frown, my hand holding the fancy drinkware, the pink Himalayan salt gracing the rim. "How are you not shit-faced?"

We both leaned against the butcher block of his station, his body pinning mine.

Everyone in the kitchen was watching us curiously, unused to seeing Row giving anyone special attention. My chest blossomed with pride.

"Us Russians can hold our drink." I smiled innocently.

"Us Italians can smell bullshit from three states over." He touched his nose to mine. "No intoxicating my staff, little Dot."

"It's not fair that I'm the only one who gets to drink while on shift."

He dipped his head down, his lips grazing my ear. "It's not fair that you'll need to accommodate eleven inches after spending the entire night on your feet."

I gasped. "I thought Rhyland was supposed to leave early today."

He bit the tip of my ear teasingly, giving my ass a smack. "Brat. Now get off my station. You're contaminating it with your germs."

Rearing my head back, I flashed him a pout. "Thought you liked my germs."

"I do. I'd keep them as pets if I could. Unfortunately, my customers don't share the same level of obsession."

"You mean admiration?"

"I said what I said." With another pat on my ass, he sent me on my way. The rest of the shift was a hectic blur, which was how I forgot to hand over the check to one of my tables. It was only when I zipped past the two patrons—thirtysomething, sharp-looking businessmen who appeared out of place in Staindrop—and saw their pissed-off faces that I realized they had asked for the check ten minutes ago.

"My apologies, gentlemen. I'll be right back with your check." I bowed, swiftly making my way to the register to produce their bill. I came back with a complimentary raspberry soufflé and an apologetic smile.

"Here you go. On the house." I put the bill down, along with their treat. One of them wrapped his fingers around my arm, stopping me from leaving.

"Really? You keep us stuck here for forty minutes and all you have to show for it is a pink biscuit?"

My eyes widened, and my skin burned where he touched me like he was putting live fire to my flesh. White-hot panic coursed through me. I tried to jerk out of his grip, but he held me more firmly.

"This pink biscuit costs more than your suit," I blurted out. It was the first thing that came to my anxious mind.

He laughed. He had a terrible laugh. And way too much gel for something that wasn't an ultrasound stick.

"Let go of my arm." My voice trembled, and so did the muscles around my eyes as I began blinking excessively.

"Not before you give me your number, funny girl."

My breath hitched, and I was about to do something I'd seriously regret, like toss his red wine in his face, when a growl came from behind me.

"I strongly recommend you remove your hand from my girlfriend's arm unless you want to play scavenger hunt finding your own fucking fingers on the floor."

Row.

My panic turned to hysteria. Because Row was the same person who'd rearranged Kieran's face for giving me the coldest, friendliest peck in front of him.

Also: Girlfriend?

Girlfriend?

The man released me like I was made out of fire, sitting back and smoothing his shirt down. "Hey, Casablancas! I know you from TV."

But Row was not in the mood for a picture and an autograph. In fact, as soon as the man flicked his gaze up to meet his, Row bunched the collar of his shirt in his fist and shoved him backward. His chair dangled on its two back legs, with only Row to keep him from falling. My *boyfriend* shoved his face in the businessman's face and growled, "Apologize right fucking now."

The man's eyes were as wide as saucers, and a sheen of sweat covered his entire face. "Sorry, man, sorry!" He raised his palms up. "I had no idea she was your girlfriend. I thought she was just a waitress."

"And that made it okay?" Row stared at him incredulously.

"No!" the businessman shrieked, high-pitched. "I was just messing around."

Row's fingers tightened around his collar, and I had a feeling he wasn't in complete control over himself.

"Man, please let him go," the other guy said. "We're just two lowly paralegals. Came here for you, actually. We work for Tate Blackthorn."

"Don't care if you work for the pope." Row let go of the businessman, who fell to the floor, letting out a small screech. "Get the hell out of here." He turned to me, putting his hand on my shoulder. "You okay, Dot?"

I nodded, flushed and grateful and still a little distraught. "They work for the guy who is buying the land from you?"

"Apparently. But I don't know them." He raked his hands over my face and hair, as if taking inventory. They were shaking a little, but so was I. What were we doing, pretending like this could end in anything but heartbreak?

"Row, I'm okay. Rude customers are nothing new to me." I laced my arms around his neck, itching to kiss him but reminding myself that this was just a fling.

"You have to change jobs," he concluded.

I laughed. He didn't, his nostrils flaring ruefully. *Oh.* He was serious. "I'm not changing jobs."

"Why not?"

"The tips are great."

"Become a stripper. The tips will be better."

"How will becoming a stripper be *better*?" My eyes nearly bulged out of their sockets.

"I'll be your only client. The pole will be in my room."

A giggle ripped from my throat. "Be serious!"

"I *am* serious. I'll throw in great dental insurance. At least think about it."

Rhy materialized behind us. "Taking the trash out. Be right back." He put one hand on each of the men's shoulders, escorting them through the door. He had seven inches and a hundred pounds minimum on each of them, and looked like a bodybuilder picking up his toddlers from school.

"So…" I bit down on my lip.

He raised his eyebrows.

"You called me your girlfriend."

"Right." His sharp cheekbones stained pink, and he dipped his head to hide his embarrassment. "Wanted to scare them off. Did I do the same to you?"

"I'm not scared," I lied. I was petrified. And not just because of the word but also because of how I'd felt when he'd said it. Like he'd put a crown on my head.

"Yeah?" His face softened.

"Yeah. In fact, I'm the opposite of scared. What would that be?"

"Brave."

I swiped my tongue over my lower lip. "Sounds about right. I'm feeling pretty brave recently." *With you around.* "But…Row?"

"Yes, Dot?"

"I wasn't in your plans."

"Plans change."

"People don't, though."

"I don't know about that. I think the good ones do. It's called growth."

He drew a ragged breath and opened his mouth, about to say something more, then clamped it shut, like he'd thought better of it. "I have a call with Blackthorn after service ends. Wait up? I'll make you dinner and we can stay at the inn."

"Deal."

CHAPTER FIFTY-FIVE
CAL

"All That She Wants"—Ace of Base

I hated Tate Blackthorn.

Okay, fine. I didn't actually know him, but it was half past midnight and Row was still on the phone with him in his office upstairs. The kitchen was the kind of squeaky clean where you could eat off the floor. Pans and pots gleamed, the air-conditioning was on full blast, and the only audible sound was the loud humming from industrial fridges.

After I slipped out of my work clothes into a pink wooly dress, I allowed myself to sit on the butcher block counter, dangling my feet. Sweaty, tired, and in desperate need of one more drink, I scrolled on my phone through old notes I'd made for murder-mystery podcast episodes that I'd never had the courage to record.

There was a good chance Row was going to kill me. My ass was on the surface where he made ludicrously expensive, microscopic food. In my defense, there was nowhere else to sit. His face was nowhere in my vicinity, there were no chairs, and the dress was brand-new.

"Sorry it took long." Row waltzed in, slapping the door open and moving toward me with the sleekness of a feline zeroing in on his prey.

"Heyyy. How was the phone ca—" I was about to jump off the counter but stopped cold when he cut into my words.

"About the attitude you've been giving me ever since you returned to Staindrop."

"Yes?" I blinked innocently, heart almost thundering out of my chest and humping his leg.

"I'm about to fuck it out of you."

He rounded the pastry station and slid between my thighs, making me spread my legs wider to accommodate him. I was surprised I could still breathe. The heat rolling off his body alone made my mouth water and my skin buzz with excitement.

"I—uhm, if you must." I tried to downplay my own desire for him.

"I'm afraid I must. Permission to push your limits?" he asked, and I loved that he did. That he put my consent above all else.

I nodded, my chest expanding with fuzzy heat. "Granted."

"How far?"

"The farthest." I was feeling reckless and full of bravado, secure in the knowledge he would never ever hurt me.

"Your safe word is *bumfuzzle*," he informed me. Rather than fear, all I felt was excitement.

"Why *bumfuzzle*?"

"Because one would never be tempted to use it as part of dirty talk." He frowned. "Though with you, I'm not so sure."

A nervous laughter escaped me, and I bit my lower lip. "I forgot you said only food goes on your butcher block."

"No, you didn't." He leaned forward. I closed my eyes, bracing myself for a kiss, but the kiss never came. Instead, a sharp snapping sound filled my ears. My eyelids ripped open and I realized… *What the fuck?*

He had pinned one side of my dress to the butcher block by sticking a knife into it. I repeat: he had tacked me to his butcher block with a chef's knife. "This is not the way I expected to be nailed," I piped up.

I was aflame, burning with sweet ache and decadent desire. But also…was this going to turn into one of the cases I listened to on *Morbid* and *My Favorite Murder*?

No. He wouldn't.

…would he?

If so, I was a willing victim. Dying in his hands was a lovely way to die.

"Trust me." His eyes held mine, and I had a feeling this was an exercise in letting go. A trust fall of sorts. He wanted to bring me to the edge and show me that I was safe with him, no matter what.

"I trust you." My voice was steady, leveled. Row grabbed another knife—just as big and scary—and pinned the other side of my dress to the block. I was now essentially glued to this board, completely at his mercy.

My mouth hung open. His eyes were hooded, clouded with desire and determination. He grabbed a third butcher's knife from the neighboring station without moving an inch from his spot between my thighs and used the tip to tilt my chin up. Adrenaline zipped through my veins, making my entire being sore.

"I said only food goes here," he growled, baring his teeth. Yet somehow, I wasn't scared. "So now, Dot, I have no choice but to eat you alive. Now how does that sound?"

The pressure between my legs became almost impossible. My panties were *soaked*, my heat dripping a thin river down my thigh. He was pushing all my limits, pressing all my buttons, and showing me that I wasn't scared. That I knew how to trust. Him. Myself.

"S-sign me up," I said breathlessly.

"Do you like fluorescent lights, Dot?" He slid the tip of the butcher knife from my chin, down my neck, and toward the top of my dress. An excited tremor moved through me, my skin exploding with goose bumps. I hadn't even known I liked knife play. Wait, *was* this knife play? The blade barely touched me. There was a lot of googling to be done when I got home.

"Big fan. Huge."

"Good, baby." With one swift motion, he tore the front of my dress with his knife, revealing my embarrassing gray Calvin Klein sports bra and my strained nipples behind it. "Because you're about to be looking at them for some time."

He dumped the knife on the board, flattened a hand over my rib cage, and pushed me down to lie firmly on the surface. I was pretty sure the majority of my blood flow ran straight to my clit, making me lightheaded. Fisting my panties (also gray Calvin Kleins), Row slid them down my legs and discarded them on the floor.

I couldn't believe we were doing this in his kingdom. In his *kitchen*. He grabbed my left ankle and pressed my thigh down with his strong, capable hands, looping the back of my knee around the knife holding my dress. Then he did the same thing with my right leg, so I was spread eagle, awkwardly open wide right in front of him.

"Do you have any idea how many times I've fantasized about fucking you like this?" He trailed his rough knuckles along the soft flesh of my dripping slit leisurely, taking a long, unhurried look at my cunt. My inhibitions popped like buttons after Thanksgiving dinner. *Pluck, pluck, pluck.* He used the tip of his finger to stroke the seam of my pussy back and forth, teasing me lazily, his hand quivering to stop himself from ravenously devouring me. My inner thighs were wet and sticky with my need for him, and I bucked my hips forward, begging for more of his touch.

"A lot?" I purred, barely capable of producing words. What were thoughts anyway? I had no recollection of having formed any.

He lowered his head between my legs, pressing his entire mouth onto me and sucking my pussy whole. The pleasure was so sharp and maddening, I arched like a crescent moon and whimpered ferally at the foreign sensation.

"The answer is every single minute of every single day, of every single month, of every single year of my fucking life since you turned seventeen," he growled, his hot tongue swirling and teasing, licking and penetrating.

My mouth fell open, my head lolling on the butcher block as I stared up at the ceiling while Row's tongue disappeared between my folds, entering my narrow channel. A violent shudder ran through me. I fastened my fingers in the thick dark strands of his hair, shuddering not only with pleasure but also with glee. I'd never been this intimate with a man before. This comfortable in my own skin.

I didn't trust people.

I *did* trust Row. With my body. With my life. Just…maybe not with my heart.

That was the only organ I wanted to keep for myself.

He fucked me raw with his tongue while swirling his thumb over my clit. I gasped, tightening my grip on his hair. My muscles began to spasm, both from the way my legs were stretched open and an impending orgasm.

"So delicious. So fucking tight." He kissed my inner thighs, biting softly, spreading my wetness over my skin, then diving back for another lick. He began kissing his way up my body, nibbling, kissing, and tonguing, toying with my clit using his thumb. "That first time I fucked you, I thought I was going to come before I was halfway in. I couldn't believe my luck."

My eyes prickled with tears because I knew how I'd treated him not even minutes later. How I'd discarded and belittled him because I couldn't admit my feelings toward him to Dylan—to *myself.*

"Row…"

"Shh." My orgasm seized me, a yelp of joy tearing through my mouth as my entire body tightened and froze, hardening like a clenched fist, and then all of a sudden, heat spread over my entire body as my muscles relaxed.

His lips skimmed up my stomach, tongue dipping into my belly button and swirling playfully as his fingers kept playing me like a piano, knowing all the chords, breathing life into me with music only we could hear. "I don't want to talk about the past. I want to focus on the present. And what a lovely fucking present you are." He tugged the thin strap of my sports bra, dragging it with a trembling hand until the sound of fabric tearing assaulted my ears. Every nerve ending in my body was ablaze, my core achingly empty, begging to be filled with him. He covered my puckered nipple with his mouth and traced the areola with the tip of his tongue. Christ almighty, I was going to combust right there on his station and win him a C from the health department for unsanitary conditions.

My eyes rolled in their sockets, stars exploding on the backs of my eyelids.

A knock on the door snapped us out of our trance. We both froze, bolting upright, our eyes meeting in horror.

"I…Chef?" I could practically hear Taylor awkwardly drawing circles with the tip of his shoe on the floor on the other end. "I forgot my headphones." The door shook back and forth as Taylor tried to open it up, but it was locked from within.

"No fucking way I'm waiting another *second* to fuck you," Row said, his eyes murderous. He flattened his entire palm against my pussy. My cunt dripped so much, it slicked his hand, making it slippery. That was when I realized…he had put something in me. In my pussy. A…small zucchini?

"We're closed," Row grumbled, eyes still trained on me as I writhed and rocked back and forth while he slid the zucchini in and out of me, a sweaty, horny mess in his Adonis arms. "Fuck off, Chef."

"But I—"

"Fuck. Off. I cannot stress this enough. If you value your job, you'll get out of here," Row barked. After a pause, he added, "I can still hear you breathing. I said get out!"

The squeaks of sneakers running along the oak floor sounded, evaporating as Taylor exited the restaurant. Row picked up a candy cane from his station, pushed my legs farther open, and grabbed my waist, scooting me to the edge. "I don't like these." He played with the candy cane like it was a pen between his fingers. "I find them culinarily offensive, but Rhy gave me one."

"I like them." I licked my lips. Did I, though? I had officially been reduced to hormones and flesh.

"Want to experiment?" Row cocked one thick dark brow.

"Yeah," I groaned. "I do."

With our eyes still holding one another, he began slowly pushing the candy cane through my tight hole while still shoving the zucchini into me. It was peeled, so it felt sleek and lubed as it slid in and out of me effortlessly. I chased the cold, sticky sensation of it. "Just stretching you out, baby." Row leaned between my legs to steal a dirty kiss full of tongue. "I want to make sure it fits. Can't hurt you like last time."

I nodded enthusiastically, wanting to be a good girl for him. To please him. The candy cane was now firmly inside my rectum, the hook poking outside for easy removal, like a tiny tail. The pressure felt delicious inside my ass. I was going to combust. I was sure of it. He moved the zucchini in and out of me, stretching my pussy, helping me get used to something bigger than my vibrator. "Is this okay, sweetheart?" He held the zucchini by the base, angling it up to hit my G-spot, making me shamelessly scoot down and chase more of it.

"It's perfect."

"Good, sweetheart. You're almost ready." Row lowered down to a deep squat and fastened his teeth around the hook of the candy cane, slowly prying it out of my ass. The sensation was heavenly. I couldn't stop moving, squirming, moaning loud enough to be heard from space.

"I'm coming," I panted.

"Not until I tell you to." His teeth were locked over the hook of the candy cane, but I was moving and thrusting, not wanting him to withdraw it all the way. If it broke off and I had to spend the night at the hospital, removing seasonal sweets from my ass, I was going to kill him.

"Row, I don't think I can—"

"Ask *nicely*," he murmured into the seam between my pussy and my ass. "And I'll give it to you. Ask not so nicely, and I might take it from you. Understand?"

Row was always controlling at work, so it shouldn't surprise me he was the exact same way in bed.

"Please, can I come? I can't hold it anymore." Though I sort of could. And it felt really good too. Riding that just-before-orgasm train a tad longer.

"Who owns you?"

"You do." My breath caught as pressure built between my legs again. I would give him everything in my bank account and a large portion of my nonvital internal organs at this point to be able to come.

"That's right. Cum all over the zucchini, Dot."

The orgasm washed over me, and I went under willingly. Every cell in my body blossomed. He withdrew the zucchini from inside me, slam-dunking it into a nearby trash can. He then used his fingers to scoop my cum from my pussy, slowly trailing them between the lips until he produced sticky, gooey cum. He popped his fingers into his mouth, devouring my desire for him, rubbing his fingertips over his teeth like my scent was pure cocaine. Row then trailed his hand up my stomach and gave my tightened nipple a gentle slap. Delirious with pleasure and glee, I grabbed his wrist and hoisted myself up, pressing my lips against his.

He opened immediately for me, whirling his tongue against mine, and we kissed deep and slow and passionate. The kind of kiss that made wet noises. The kind of kiss that tilted the world upside down and spilled its entire contents to the universe's floor.

"So, that sounded very unhygienic." Taylor sighed behind the door. "Still here, by the way. Really need those AirPods."

My eyes widened in alarm. He came back. We must've not heard him.

"I will buy you three pairs of AirPods if you just fuck off!" Row growled into our kiss.

"Third generation pro?" Taylor stressed. Little fucker. He sure knew an opportunity when he saw one.

"Yes!"

Taylor chuckled. "Deal."

Row's lips rolled along my jaw, down to my neck, kissing every inch of my torso, marking me all over. He gave my nipple a tug with his teeth. "Row," I moaned. "I want you to fuck me."

He popped his head up, looking flushed, surprised, and ruggedly gorgeous. "That's what I'm trying to do here. It's called foreplay."

"Foreplay?" I blinked, confused. "I've been ready for you for at least five weeks now."

He chuckled, plastering his forehead against mine, kissing me hard. Our teeth clashed, and I fumbled with his Henley, jerking it desperately off him. As soon as it landed on the floor, I pushed him back, panting. "Let me take a look. I've been wanting to ogle you peacefully since I was fourteen."

He unpinned me from the knives and stepped back, his pecs and abs so taut they looked hand-drawn. Almost every inch of him was inked, covering sculpted muscles and skin. Macabre tattoos of Cambros, and a skull with a chef hat, and more. I now knew they were all designed to hide the scars his father had left behind. A constant reminder of what Row had had to endure as a child.

It was that last tattoo that gave me pause, though. Of an anatomic heart with flowers spurting out of it. I remembered him telling me I reminded him of such a thing. And now I understood why.

Because the flowers spurting from the heart weren't just any flowers.

They were callas.

I swallowed hard, burning the tattoo into memory. He ran a hand over the tattoo self-consciously, obstructing it from view. "Not getting any younger here, Dot."

But I couldn't brush it off. I hopped off the counter, standing next to him. His eyes followed me as I lowered myself and pressed a kiss to his tattoo silently. Words weren't needed. Just the silence between us that told him I heard his message, loud and clear.

I rose up to my full height. Which still barely reached his belly button. "Turn around."

He frowned. "Wh—"

"Trust, remember?" I raised my eyebrows.

He did, spinning on his heel, his face toward the door. His back was tattooed too, but I could still see the white jagged belts of scars on his skin. I pressed a kiss to a bumpy wound between his shoulder blades. His skin budded with goose bumps. A small hiss escaped him. "You're so beautiful," I murmured, my lips chasing the constellation of scars under his ink. "Not just handsome, *beautiful*. In a dark, terrifying way."

He was very quiet as my hands roamed his muscular arms, as I kissed every scarred inch of him. He looked like his body was dipped in gold, and still, he had no idea how beautiful he was. I had a feeling Row didn't know how to accept love. He only knew how to give it to Dylan and Zeta. When I was done, I pressed my forehead between his shoulder blades and rasped, "You can turn back now." He did, his eyes molten, burning with something I recognized because he kindled it in me too.

"I want us to fuck," I admitted, somehow full of confidence and resolute. "I don't want it to be sweet and soft. I want it to be frantic and all-consuming."

He said nothing, giving me a moment to change my mind. I wasn't going to. I knew what I wanted. "I'm clean." I arched back, my center pressed against his erection.

"Yeah? Well, I'm about to dirty you up."

He grabbed me by the waist, flipped me around, and pushed me against his cooking station. Bending me over the surface by holding the nape of my neck, he flipped my dress up and ran his hand between my legs. "Palms against the butcher block, Dot."

I complied without question.

Row reached to move a hand over my glistening center. "Look at that delicious pussy." He fisted his cock, running the tip in circles around the tender, swollen lips. "Begging to be fucked."

I pressed my forehead to the surface, unsure how much more teasing I could take. "Row, please."

"Close your legs for me." He caught my waist from behind, kissing my neck and running the fat crown of his cock up and down my slit. It was damp with warm precum. "Aren't you going to ask me if I'm clean too?"

I would, if I were able to form one coherent thought. I pressed my thighs together, choking out, "Are you?"

His nose disappeared in my hair, and he slid halfway into me from behind. Already, I felt unbearably full, the combination of his size and my position with pressed thighs making him almost too much to handle. "Yeah. I'm clean."

He drove into me all at once. And he was so much. *Too* much. I cried out, clawing my fingernails on the counter. "Ahhhh."

"Very eloquent, baby." He bent his knees to accommodate my height when he pressed into me again, pushing to the hilt this time. He was so big, his tip probably tickled my kidneys. He covered my palms on the counter, lacing his fingers in mine, and a dangerous zing of heat ripped through me.

"So fucking tight," he groaned, beginning to thrust inside me. The walls of my pussy resisted his size, his width, but he still pushed through. Through his roughness, I learned my ability to endure.

"That's exactly what I said when I tried to squeeze into my high school jeans this morning." My head lolled in elation.

"So sassy." He gave the back of my shoulder a tender bite. "Your smart mouth always made me make stupid mistakes, Dot."

I grunted each time he drove inside me, the position making my hip bones dig into the hard surface. Each time they ground against the butcher block, I hissed out as my skin chafed. We were acting out his fantasy, and more than I was delirious with joy about getting fucked, being full, I enjoyed that he'd finally gotten his wish.

"Poor little Dot. Here. Let me help." He grabbed me by the hip bones, sliding me up the surface so I was flung over it, feet in the air. There was something about that angle that made it so much filthier and wilder and hotter. Like I was a ragged, inflatable doll he'd haphazardly tossed on a piece of furniture so he could plow into it.

The friction was insane.

His cock swelled and grew even more inside me.

The orgasm ripping through me threatened to ignite me.

"Fuck, Dot. Gonna come now."

"I'm close too."

We both fell apart together, groaning and gasping, my nerve endings on fire. He rolled off me, his breath tickling my neck when he gently turned me back around to face him.

"Hey." He kissed the tip of my nose, a shy smile gracing his lips.

"Hi," I said breathlessly, still amazed I had been a part of that intense, sexy, brazen scene.

"Social anxiety level?" He tilted his chin down.

"Minus thirty."

"That's my girl."

That's my girl.

That's my girl.

That's my girl.

But his girl currently had a huge problem on her hands.

Because this didn't feel temporary.

It felt like forever.

CHAPTER FIFTY-SIX
ROW

oBITCHuary: Good night.

McMonster: Turn around and tell me this. You are right here, silly.

oBITCHuary: I still want to say good night here.

McMonster: Why?

oBITCHuary: Because I'm not ready to let McMonster go.

McMonster: I'm still me.

oBITCHuary: Yeah. But when we say goodbye, Row will leave. But McMonster? He might stay.

CHAPTER FIFTY-SEVEN
ROW

The next morning, Tate Blackthorn was standing at my doorstep, holding a Starbucks coffee and an iPhone I was pretty sure wasn't out on the market yet. I slammed the door in his face, but he slid his foot in the gap of the doorframe just in time.

"Nice to see you too, Casablancas." He ripped the sunglasses off his eyes, barreling into my room at the inn without an invitation.

"What the fuck are you doing here?" I followed him inside reluctantly.

"Came here to finish our little chat from last night. Had to pick up a coffee in Connecticut, though. This place is barely civilized. Hold on a minute." He raised a finger, putting his phone to his ear. "Gia. Where the fuck are you?"

Pause.

"Seventy texts are completely acceptable when my assistant has been MIA for an entire night."

Pause.

"So what if it's lost? It's a cat, not a fucking kid. Get a new one. Now where are those files?"

I didn't think there was an amount of money in the world that was worth putting up with this sociopath. Whoever Gia was, she needed that paycheck to be willing to work for him.

Tate hung up but not before showering his assistant with yet more orders and scolding. The only reason I'd let him in was because Cal wasn't here. She had gone to pick up my Silverado from the shop—it was finally fixed—and had driven down to Portland with Dylan to shop for the latter's hospital bag.

I still hated letting her do shit alone, worried she was gonna get picked on, but I had to let it go. I wasn't going to be there to protect her when she moved back to New York. Just the thought of patrons snatching her wrist or men catcalling her made a vein pop in my head.

"Well, this is quaint." Tate looked around, nose screwed to the side like the place smelled. I could see why he'd be angry. I'd dropped off the face of the earth and left him with his dick in his hand for weeks on end, because I was having second thoughts about a deal we'd already verbally agreed on. This followed by yesterday, when I'd spent an entire hour giving him all the reasons he should fire the paralegals who'd harassed Cal if he wanted to ever be in business with me again.

"Did you have company?" He sniffed the air. "Smells like green apples and white musk. And…is it cat piss?"

Fucking Semus. "Pretty sure there are more pressing matters than my girlfriend's fragrance."

"Is cat piss a fragrance now?" He scowled. "Middle-class people are so fucking basic."

I had to stop referring to Cal as mine. She was headed to New York in three weeks. I was moving to London. We had an expiration date. Too bad it wasn't enough for me to be her first…I also wanted to be her last.

"I'm trying to do this thing where I pretend to care." Tate ran a finger over the old-school air conditioner on the wall like it was a prehistoric piece. "It's exhausting. Those asinine conversations… forgot what they're called."

"Small talk?"

"Yeah." He glowered. "They're pointless and last forever."

"Agreed." I nodded. "No need to pretend with me. We can't stand each other."

Tate looked relieved. "Let's have coffee in that diner down the street."

"You already have coffee."

He tossed the still-full Starbucks cup into my trash can. "Now I don't. Put your shoes on."

I grabbed my jacket and we went down to Dahlia's Diner. There, I was reminded of my social pariah status. Everybody knew who Tate Blackthorn was. And *everybody* knew this wasn't a social call. But I think they were all too scared not to serve me because his presence reminded them I had their dicks in my hand.

"Can I get you anything?" Dahlia herself arrived at our table, popping her gum loudly. "Coffee? Breakfast? A one-way ticket outta this town?"

"Don't tempt me." Tate glanced at his watch, completely unfazed by Dahlia's death glares. "I'll take a small triple macchiato, one inch of foamed milk."

Dahlia blinked once. "Sorry, I should've clarified. This is the only coffee we serve." She slammed a pot of coffee on our table. "Anything to eat with it? *Don't* say halloumi and zucchini organic bites. It's either eggs, pancakes, or the door."

"See?" Tate flashed me a look, gesturing around us. "This place is begging to be cultured. Help me help you, Row."

I plucked the sticky menu from his hand and handed it to Dahlia. "We'll take two coffees and two plain egg white omelets. No bread."

She walked off with a huff. Tate sat back, flinging an arm over the booth as he took in his surroundings. "You know what I really hate, Casablancas?"

"Integrity?" I folded my arms and eyed him with distaste. "Puppies? Babies?"

Dahlia returned, pouring coffee into our mugs. Tate looked at me past her stern frown. "People who jerk me around."

"I've been preoccupied," I said, which was partly true. I had been—burying myself inside Cal. But that had nothing to do with the contract. I'd been low-key sniffing around other investors. Nobody had bitten yet.

"Allow me to refocus you." Tate leaned forward, his eyes twinkling with barely contained wrath. "I have staff I need to pay. People attached to this project. Investors. Builders. A whole operation to oversee. The contract was the last hurdle before demolishing the train station and breaking ground. As it stands, you're pushing the completion date. Now, let me tell you what happens when people fuck me over." He laced his fingers together on the table. "I fuck harder. Sans lube. In holes you never knew were even in your body. I am no lover, pretty boy. Thrice divorced, and my blood sport is hostile company takeovers. I will demolish you if you cross me."

He took a sip of his coffee, then promptly spat it back into the cup. People eyeballed us from every corner of the diner, the silence humming in the air violently. "What the fuck is this, tar? Don't worry." He leaned back, glancing at the onlookers. "I'll make sure we open Starbucks, Costa, and Peet's here."

Dahlia gasped, clutching her chest.

"And you." Tate slipped out of the booth, staring me down. He didn't wait for our food. "Sign the damn contract. If I have to come here a second time to give you a nudge, I won't be so fucking nice about it." He plucked his coat from the back of the booth, turned toward the door, and disappeared.

CHAPTER FIFTY-EIGHT
ROW

McMonster is typing...
McMonster is deleting...
McMonster is typing...
McMonster is deleting...

CHAPTER FIFTY-NINE
ROW

When I returned to the inn, the first thing I did was throw doors and windows open, calling Cal's name. She should have been back from her errands by now. I flung the duvet off the bed and tossed the closet doors open. Nada. I rummaged in my front pocket for my phone, and when I found it, I realized there was a note sitting on the nightstand, glowing under the buttery light of the lamp. Pocketing my phone, I advanced toward the note, ripping it from the wooden surface, my heart somersaulting, landing wrong, and breaking every fucking bone in its body.

Row,

Meet me at the back of the parking lot.

—Dot

I grabbed my key card and took the stairs two at a time, wondering if I was too late, if I had missed her. It was a fucked-up train of thought. I'd wait an entire lifetime and some change for Cal, no questions asked. Then why was I so worried she wouldn't reciprocate it?

Because she is the loveliest, flightiest person you've ever met. Because

Franco broke her, and now that you are gluing back the pieces, you see that some of them are missing. Shattered beyond repair.

Looping around the wooden stairway, I pounded the carpeted floor to the back of the inn, passing golden-framed pastel paintings, arched rooms, and striped wallpaper. Admittedly, it was a lovely inn. I could see why people loathed me for running it out of business with the monstrous hotel that was going to open in this town.

"See you later, Mr. Rogers," I called out to the receptionist.

"Eat shit, asshole," he greeted me back.

Undeterred, I pushed the back door open, spilling out to the small parking lot. It was completely empty, save for an unfamiliar black Mustang. My pulse shallowed, and I growled in disappointment, eyes skimming the immaculate bushes surrounding the empty lot. I looked down to take out my phone when a horn blared in my vicinity. Cal's head popped up from the driver's seat of the Mustang. Her grin was so wide, you could have fit a banana horizontally into her mouth.

"Get in, pretty boy." She blinked five, six, seven times. Fast enough to show me she was nervous.

I grinned, gliding her way while expertly flipping the key card between my fingers. "What are you wearing, Dot?"

"Not much, and it's about to be taken off very soon." She adjusted the horrid yellow plaid jacket with one hand. "Now get in. I managed to rent this thing on an hourly basis and I really want to bring it back before the beginning of our shift."

"Romantic." I slid into the passenger seat, staring at her with what must have been the goofiest, stupidest smirk to ever grace my face. "I'll ask again—what're you wearing?"

She turned her whole body to face me, her plaid yellow skirt riding up her smooth thighs. "Recreating the first night we were together. Only..." She bit her lower lip. "Making it right. Making it good for you, this time. For both of us. We deserve it, don't you think?"

I nodded slowly, my heart in my goddamn throat. "Yeah, Dot. We do."

We spent the drive to Make-out Mountain discussing the fascinating subject of whatever the fuck. I wasn't really paying attention, instead laser-focused on the fact that Dot had rented a sports car and slipped into the outfit she'd worn that night, down to the knee socks and Mary Janes, for a do-over. That meant something, didn't it?

We weaved through a thick forest, uphill on a gravel path toward the top of the mountain. The car groaned in protest, too old and rusty for the journey. The windows were rolled down, the freezing cold barely registering from the adrenaline coursing through me. She parked at the exact same spot I had last time, turning off the car and leaning back in her seat. Her throat worked with a swallow, and she closed her eyes. I stared at her intently.

"What now?" she asked. I grinned. I had asked her exactly this question five years ago, after she'd asked me to drive up the mountain when I'd picked her up from that bonfire party. Back then, she hadn't known it was a dream come true. That I had been shitting bricks, worried I'd somehow say the wrong thing, act the wrong way, and blow this.

So I answered her with the exact same words she'd used on me. "Now, we sit on the hood of your car and watch the view."

We slipped out and rounded the car, hopping on the still-warm hood. Our pinkies knotted together as we stared at the Atlantic Ocean stretching like a tight canvas in a million shades of blue. I closed my eyes and breathed in the briny air, Dot's voice drifting into my ears like a lullaby. "You're right. I wasn't drunk that night. But I knew it'd be the last time I'd see you in months, years even. And I panicked. Panicked that there would be no one else like you. Someone I'd be attracted to and feel safe enough around to let my guard down. I'd never been selfish before. It was a foreign feeling. I always put my parents' feelings and Dylan's wants and needs before my own…" She trailed off. "I just wanted to get rid of my virginity. To go to college not feeling even more of a loser than necessary. I made peace with being another notch on your freakishly long belt. I never thought you could have feelings for me."

"I know," I said, frowning at the view, our pinkies tightening around one another.

"I spent the entire four years apart from you and Dylan hating myself for how I treated both of you." Her voice cracked like crème brûlée.

"There was no need for you to do that," I growled, hating the idea that I had caused her so much pain, even if she had done the same to me. "We both love you to death, through thick or thin."

"W-why?" I didn't see her face but still knew she was blinking excessively.

"Because it's impossible not to," I admitted brokenly, tearing my gaze from the ocean and fixing it on her. I captured her chin between my fingers, tilting her face up to mine.

She pawed at my face, her long lashes fluttering as she took me in. "Do-over?"

I nodded. "Do-over."

One of her palms slid down my neck, down my chest, and across my abs, settling on my erection, which was already throbbing. She unzipped my pants slowly, making my lungs sear with whatever oxygen was left in them. I opened my mouth to tell her something—fuck knew what, because I sure as hell didn't—but Dot pressed her lips against mine, hungrily devouring my tongue, sucking it into her mouth with a sexy purr. She undid the first two buttons of my denim, slipping her hand inside, rubbing it against my hard ridge. She used the friction of my briefs to gather heat into her cold palm, and I bucked forward, chasing her touch as I grabbed the back of her head and kissed her with everything I fucking had in me. My hand slipped under her skirt, and I used my thumb to brush her clit through her panties, which were already drenched and ruined. My mouth dragged from her lips to the sensitive junction between her neck and jaw.

"I wanted to eat you out so badly," I recalled, my dick jumping and jolting in her hot palm as she played with it inside my pants. Rubbing it, thumbing at the slit, milking it with her tight little fist. "I knew you'd be my favorite dessert before I even had my first taste."

She clung to my neck with one hand, jerking me off with the other. The wind whipped and swirled, dancing around us, striking at our faces. Her thighs were freezing, and I wanted to cover her whole body with mine. Shield her from the cold.

"We should hurry about it." Dot dropped down to her knees, tugging my dick out and covering it with her mouth. "We could get caught." The mere idea of being caught with my cock shoved deep inside her mouth made my balls tighten with lust and pleasure. I threaded my fingers in her hair, pushing it off her face as she gurgled and sucked my cock happily, fisting its base and slipping her mouth down to suckle my balls, her tongue licking the seam between my ball sack and my ass. My fists tautened around her hair and I hissed, the desire unbearable. I knew I wasn't going to last more than a couple minutes. This time, though, I was going to make her come until she couldn't walk straight through April.

"Up, baby." I pulled my dick out of her mouth an inch at a time, the cold biting into the wet flesh. "Already halfway coming," I grunted. I flattened my hand over her stomach, pinning her down on the hood until her upper body lay there, and pushed my thigh between her legs. They fell open willingly, my upper knee pressing against her swollen clit. I could practically feel it pulsating against my leg through her underwear. She moaned, trying to rub herself against me.

"Row," she begged. Brushing her panties to the side, I fisted my dick, guiding it to her opening. It was glistening and pink, dripping down the hood just for me. I realized she was coming, panting and convulsing before I had even entered her. I pressed home deeply and all at once, meeting zero resistance—all sleek and velvety folds, wet and ready to take me. Her walls instantly constricted around me, milking my dick. She tipped her head back, eyes closed, giving in to the moment as I thrusted into her, grabbing the backs of her knees and hoisting her left ankle over my opposite shoulder to increase the friction.

Our moans echoed over the cliff and, realizing there could be people nearby, I placed one hand over her mouth to keep her quiet. Somehow, this ended up turning both of us on even more. I was hard to the point of misery, my cock spasming inside her.

"Getting too fucking close now," I grunted, leaning down and uncovering her mouth, pressing a dirty, wet kiss to her lips.

"Me too. I feel like you lit a match inside me and let the heat spread everywhere. I love this."

I love you.

I kissed her again, pushing deeper into her. She cried out, breathlessly clawing my arms as the orgasm sprinted through her. Just in time, as my own climax was rippling through my body, making goose bumps run all over my skin. I poured my seed into her, clamping my jaw to stop myself from goddamn whimpering. This woman brought me to my fucking knees, and I wanted to stay there for eternity so I could eat her out. I stayed inside her even after we both stopped trembling, our foreheads pressed together, our hot breaths fanning over each other's faces. I was out of breath and out of my depth and *fuck*, I had not signed up for this. It was supposed to be scratching a decade-long itch. Nothing more.

The sound of a roaring engine purred from our left, signaling an approaching vehicle. Dot reached between her thighs, sticky from our cum, to rearrange her panties along her slit. She pushed down her skirt, reaching to tuck my half-mast dick back into my pants and button them. I watched her through heavy-lidded eyes, mesmerized.

"Please forgive me." She cleared her throat, her big blue gaze clinging to my face.

"Already did, silly." My eyes raked along her body to make sure she was all right.

"No, not only for what I did." She shook her head. "But for what I might do in the future. I have the tendency to reject happiness whenever it finds me. A self-defense mechanism, I suppose. I don't trust myself with a good thing, Row. And you? You are the best thing out there."

———————

Later that day, I hurled two garbage bags into the trash can outside Descartes.

I played the conversation with Tate in my head. His little speech hadn't made my balls shake as he'd expected, but he had a point—I needed to decide what I wanted to do before wrapping shit up here. I was running out of time and keeping the entire town hanging in the air. Either I told him to fuck off or I signed the deal.

The alleyway was frosted over; a thin layer of ice covered the ground. A stack of cardboard was piled up against a fire hydrant. The sound of the heavy metal door of the back of the restaurant clicked shut. I groaned. I had locked myself out.

I began making my way around the pavement to the front entrance, my boots crunching the ice, when an arm wrapped around my neck from behind, yanking me backward.

My back slammed against a burly chest. I sank my fingers into the arms cutting off my oxygen supply, trying to pry them open, when a dark figure appeared before me. A tall built person wearing black head to toe and a balaclava. The person behind me tied my wrists with zip ties, and the man in front of me grabbed my jaw, holding me in place before swinging his fist back with a sucker punch.

The metallic taste of blood exploded in my mouth. I spat a lump of it in the man's face, a wry laugh leaving my lips. "You're fucking with the wrong person if you think a little manhandling is going to change my mind one way or the other."

The man in front of me reached for my neck, squeezing, fingers shaking. I instantly became lightheaded as the person behind me kept digging their knee into my lower back, while the other kicked me as hard as they could. "I'm selling, all right. And the ugly-ass mall and hotel are going to be a constant reminder that I screwed you over. Even if you kill me now, my family will go through with the deal." This was true. My days of being bullied were over. By my father. By Fuckface. I was the master of my own universe.

A set of knuckles landed directly in my eye socket. I stumbled back, making the person behind me fall flat on their ass. "You better change that mind of yours. Otherwise both your arms will be broken and you can kiss your chef career goodbye," he warned, voice shaky and foreign to my ears.

Someone had hired him, I realized. He wasn't anyone from town.

"Tempted to finish you right here, right now," the man in front of me growled, balling the collar of my shirt and yanking me forward, slamming my back against the brick wall. The other attacker stumbled to the front, bringing his knee up to kick my face. Finally, I had an in. I turned sideways so I could use my cuffed hands, seizing his knee and twisting it to one side. The cracking sound it made told me I had broken something. The scream that followed confirmed my suspicion.

I kicked the first attacker in the face, leaving a nice imprint of my boot on his balaclava. Blood began filling the dark material.

"Shit!" the second attacker crouched over, nearly toppling to the ground. "Fuck, he broke my…" The fabric of his pants clung to his thigh as blood spread around it too. "Fuck this shit, dude. I'm outta here."

The two spun around, limping toward the street. I chased them down, ready to kill someone. It wasn't the pain that slowed me down. It was the blood trickling from my forehead. It scorched my eyes and made it impossible to see anything.

Actually, it wasn't even that either. My abs burned. When I looked down, I saw a dark stain spreading over my white chef jacket. *Blood.*

Fuck. They'd knifed me. The adrenaline flowing through my veins dulled the pain. Slipping on my own blood and slowing down to a limp, I rounded the corner after them. My cuffed wrists didn't help my speed. I inched closer, close enough to kick down one of the attackers. An Acura juddered to a halt in front of me. The back door flew open, and the two stuffed each other inside. The car bolted, speeding through a red light, zigzagging across the street. I squinted to catch the license plate, but my vision was punctuated with milky white dots, blurring by the second.

Which was just as well because my body decided now was a great time to pass the fuck out.

"Chef! You okay?" Taylor's voice was urgent behind me. The sound of his sneakers hitting the pavement rang through the street. "Shit! Stay awake. I'm calling an ambulance."

Before I went under, there was another voice.

Familiar. Soft. Ethereal.

"Row. Oh my God, Row!"

I collapsed into arms that smelled of green apples and white musk and everything that was beautiful and right in this world, and even though I couldn't see her, I could feel her.

She sobbed into my neck, cradling my face.

"If you die, I'm going to kill you."

CHAPTER SIXTY
ROW

oBITCHuary: Hi

oBITCHuary: This is just to let you know I told you so.

oBITCHuary: I told you that you needed to investigate, look into who was doing all those things to you.

oBITCHuary: Now I need to kill someone, and I really don't want to do that. Blood makes me queasy. And I don't even know who I should off.

oBITCHuary: But I'm going to find out. Before you even wake up. True crime isn't my passion for nothing.

CHAPTER SIXTY-ONE
ROW

I woke up in a hospital bed, wearing one of those hideous gowns where your ass is bare. I was hooked up to two different IVs, looking like a human hookah.

So it had happened. Somebody had finally tried to off my ass. I officially owed Rhy fifty bucks and a beer.

I was lying on a mattress that had seen thousands more asses in its lifetime, itching to punch my way through every face in Staindrop, minus one.

Dot's.

Speaking of my little angel, she was right beside me, stroking my hand in her lap, a worried look stamped on her celestial face. This resulted in me having a semi, which was very bad news to everyone around us, since that hospital robe covered *nothing*.

Mom's, Dylan's, and Taylor's eyeballs were all glued to my face, trying to ignore my body's priorities, which apparently put fucking Cal before survival.

"What's with the circle jerk?" I barked out, glowering at the three of them. "It was just a little scratch; I don't need an entire assembly."

"We thought you might want company," Cal started, standing up. "We'll give you some privacy—"

I pulled her back down to her chair. "Wasn't talking to you, baby. You're always welcome."

"Jesus. He's unbearable even on his deathbed." Taylor rubbed the spot between his eyebrows, standing at the door. "I thought a near-death experience was going to change him. Make him see the light."

"Told ya." Dylan smirked, opening her palm and angling it in his direction. He slapped a fifty-dollar bill into it with a groan.

She slid the note into her bra. "My brother can stand in a lamp showroom and still not see the light."

"Honey, we're so glad you're awake." Mom hurried to her feet from a blue recliner in the corner of the room, blowing her nose into a handkerchief. "How are you feeling?"

Horny. "Fine." I swept my tongue over my lower lip, and it felt like licking sandpaper. "Thirsty."

"I'll get you some ice water and call the nurse. Be right back." Mom dashed out of the room.

"What happened?" Cal asked softly, her fingertips tracing the veins and ridges of my hand soothingly. A ripple of desire zinged through my chest. Goddammit, did my craving for her have *any* limits? I would probably try to climb out of my own fucking coffin to hit on this woman if I were lucky enough to have her attend my funeral.

"It looks worse than it is." I snatched her hand up, placing it on the bed next to me and breaking contact before my semi blossomed into a full-blown anaconda. "Some punks jumped me in the alleyway when I went to take out the trash."

"Randy and Lyle?" Cal's eyes flared.

I shook my head. "They were bigger, younger, and knew how to throw a punch."

"I spoke to Sheriff Menchin. He said he was on his way." Dylan rubbed her belly back and forth. "We're getting to the bottom of this."

"Menchin will be getting to the bottom of his beer bottle sooner." Taylor snorted, shaking his head. "He's useless where Row's concerned. He hates his guts."

"Real talk, he has every reason to. Your beau is a bona fide villain." Dylan winked at Cal, and I didn't know what entertained me more—hearing Dylan refer to me as Cal's beau or the latter's face, which turned as pink as her tasty little clit.

"We'll take it to state level if need be." Taylor slammed his own thigh with his fist. "This lawless shit stops here."

"I'm not taking anything anywhere," I grunted, trying to shift to my side and immediately regretting it. "I'm leaving in three weeks and have no desire to drown in paperwork. Now, can someone call a doctor so I can get my medical diagnosis?"

"You're a jerk," Taylor provided unhelpfully. "Cureless condition."

"The best cure would be getting the fuck out of here and not seeing your face again," I answered charitably.

Cal froze next to me. I immediately regretted my words. I hadn't even thought about London these past few weeks, not since we'd spent real time together. At the same time, staying in Staindrop was not an option. I hated the place and the memories attached to it. London wasn't just my plan; it was also my reality, with all the money and means I had sunk into it.

"Should we file a complaint against Menchin?" Dylan turned to Taylor, ignoring my ass.

"No, Row would just become more unbearable, and it's already next to impossible to work with him." Taylor sighed, pointing at me. "To your question—you got stabbed, lost a shit ton of blood, and slipped out of consciousness for a minute there. Honestly? Didn't think you'd make it. Then when they ushered you here, it turned out your attackers didn't hit anything substantial. Guess there's a plus to not having a heart."

I had a heart. It just beat for a girl who wasn't interested in it.

"Doc told your mom you should be outta here in a few days," Dylan added.

I shook my head. "I gotta get back to Descartes."

"Don't worry, I've got you. I've already handled the schedule, ordered inventory, and taken over your station." Taylor flashed me an uncertain look, ducking his head in embarrassment.

"You did that?" I blinked in confusion.

He shrugged, downplaying it. "Whether you trust me or not, someone had to take care of business."

"I do trust you." As I said these words, I realized I meant them. Taylor was a damn talented kid with nerves of steel and some of the best culinary instincts I'd seen. He thrived under pressure and shared the same intolerance of idiots who couldn't tell raw from medium-well. We got along. Parting ways was gonna suck. Most people were stunningly bad at their jobs.

The door whined open, and Mom walked in, armed with a jug of ice water, a nurse, a doctor, and Rhyland.

Thankfully, the doctor, a balding man in his fifties, wasn't fond of mass gatherings when giving his diagnosis. He cleared his throat and said, "Mr. Casablancas should have some space. I suggest you choose one person to stay with you while we discuss your injuries and treatment."

Cal immediately rose to her feet.

I caught her hand in mine and tugged her to sit on the edge of my bed. "You stay."

Our stares locked, and she swallowed hard. The chatter around us stopped.

"You forgot a question mark and a six-letter word." She arched a devastatingly sassy brow.

"Stay, hot-ass?"

She gave me a chiding look.

I groaned. "Stay, please?"

She nodded, squeezing my hand in hers. "Until you're sick and tired of me."

Don't hold your breath.

I wasn't falling in love. I was galloping straight into a heartbreak for the goddamn books. Because Cal was no longer an abstract idea.

Something unattainable and faraway. This time, I knew what she tasted like, how it felt to have her lips flutter over my skin when she laughed. What it was like to fall asleep with my nose buried in her hair. How she tightened and spasmed around me when she came all over my cock.

I was addicted to her scent, to her hugs, to the way her whole face opened up with delight that first fraction of a second when she saw something she liked. She was my Roman Empire.

"Right." The doctor looked around the room, probably confused as to how my grumpy ass had so many people who cared about him. "So, if everyone else can just…"

"Fuck off?" I offered.

"Wait." Cal leaned into my face, biting down on a grin. "Are you sure you want me to stay?"

Forever. "Never been more positive."

"Negativity *is* the ongoing theme in his life," Rhyland chipped in. Dylan grunted.

"Can I ask…why?" Cal's big eyes blinked imploringly.

"Because you're…" I was trying to think of the right word.

Familiar?

Comforting?

Easy to talk to?

"Home."

"Ohhhh," Dylan moaned again, this time clutching her pearls. "Shit."

"I'm a grown-ass man," I barked at her from behind Cal's shoulder. "Shut up and let m—"

"No!" Dylan stood up, and when she did, it sounded like a water balloon burst against the floor, and her dress was all wet. "My water just broke."

CHAPTER SIXTY-TWO
CAL

"Friday I'm in Love"—The Cure

I was a little worried when Zeta commanded me to stay with Row while she headed upstairs to the maternity ward with Dylan. But I'd also been dying to get some alone time with him ever since I saw him collapse on the sidewalk in a puddle of his own blood earlier today.

He wanted me to stay. And I had a feeling he wasn't just referring to the hospital room. We were holding hands; his breathing was shallow and flat, making my own pulse thump out of rhythm with anxiety.

"You dodged a bullet with that stab wound." The doctor chuckled at his own joke. "No puns intended, yeah?"

Row offered him a glare.

The doctor continued, "It was half an inch away from puncturing your intestines. Could you imagine?"

"I'd rather not," Row deadpanned, unimpressed with his caretaker's bedside manner.

"You could've died a slow, painful death," Dr. Gorga said cheerfully. "But you didn't. You're going to be just fine."

"You're also going to be heard." I flipped my phone screen, angling it in Row's direction. "Taylor just texted. Sheriff Menchin should be here in the next hour. Seems like he is taking the threats against you seriously this time."

"And to think all he needed was an assassination attempt to wake up," Row drawled out.

I rubbed his bicep, not letting his grumpiness rub off on my sunshine. "Better late than never."

"Not hanging my hopes and dreams on this clown." He brought the jug of ice water to his lips. "So. Dot. What have you been up to while I was out?"

"Oh. You know. This and that." By *this and that* I meant freaking out about the possibility of losing him and chasing whatever leads I had to figure out who had done this to him.

Row's injury devastated me more than I cared to admit. In fact, it cemented that my worst fear had come true—I had strong, all-consuming feelings for Ambrose Casablancas. The kind that put my heart at risk. The kind that didn't go hand in hand with my promise to myself not to let anyone in.

"Articulate it to me." He fought a smile. "Using lots of words and analogies. I want the whole Cal flair."

Swiping my tongue over my lips, I considered how much to tell him. "Well, you were lying here, looking very pretty but also very boring, so I sang you some songs, mostly The Cure's stuff, because I think that's about the only band we have in common. A nurse brought over your dinner, and it had trail mix, and I remember you hated raisins, so I removed them from the mix. I also readjusted your pillows. And filed your nails. And...fine, painted them black. Because it is *so* your color. Is that creepy? It sounds creepy now that I'm saying it out loud. I swear it wasn't. I thought it'd bring a smile to your lips when you woke up."

Now he *did* laugh, then groaned and clutched his side where he'd been stabbed.

This was the part where I'd usually feel weird and awkward. Foreign in my own skin. But all I felt was...*seen*. It made me feel invincible. His gaze alone made me feel like the person I'd always wanted to be.

"Know what it sounds like?" He ignored the doctor and nurse, who exchanged notes on a clipboard in the room.

"Unhinged?" I offered with a scrunch of my nose.

"Romantic as *fuck*."

"Oh, it really wasn't." I tucked a lock of hair behind my ear, then busied my hands by scrubbing my phone screen clean with my sleeve. "Trust me. Dylan was here the entire time, complaining about her heartburn. At some point we discussed that time you broke your arm at six when you fell off a tree and were so scared you peed your pants."

His smile remained calm and praising. "The statute of limitations has passed on that particular case. Besides, I bet you peed yourself too, that very same day."

"Row, I was still in diapers."

"That's pure semantics."

"I see you have a lot to catch up on." The doctor looked between us. "Any more questions, Mr. Casablancas?"

"Yes, where did you get your degree—the School of Hard Knocks?"

"Thanks so much, Doctor!" I interjected, balming Row's rawness.

Dr. Gorga nodded swiftly. "I'll leave you to it." The nurse and doctor slipped out of the room, and now we were truly alone.

"Wanna know something?" I brushed a lock of onyx hair from his eye. It was exceptionally unfair that he looked like carnal sin even in a hospital gown.

"If it's coming from you? Sure."

"You're not a terrible boss, despite your crankiness. I mean, Taylor actually *likes* you. You should've seen him in action today. He even called his dad to ask some medical questions."

"That's a full circle right there." Row smiled tiredly.

"How so?"

"I saved him from going into premed. He fucking hated the idea."

"Taylor wanted to be a *doctor*?" I tilted my head. I couldn't imagine him doing anything that wasn't making delicious, highbrow food.

"Was expected to," Row corrected. "He walked into my restaurant to get drunk and forget about his finals. Flashed me a fake ID, but he was clearly underage. I was working the bar that evening to teach a new temp the job. I whipped him up somethin' to eat and he commented that the chicken could use some ras el hanout. I hired him as an intern on the spot."

"God. You're nice, aren't you? That's your worst-kept secret." I grinned.

"*Best kept*." He reached to press his finger to my lips. "Don't tell anyone. Everyone thinks I'm an ass."

"I don't think you're an ass," I pointed out.

"That's because I tap yours," he responded wryly. He scanned my face for a beat, then let out a sigh. "Listen, we need to talk."

My hackles rose in an instant. "We do?"

"About me selling Descartes."

I knew he was going to remind me that he was leaving, that this was all temporary, that we had tough decisions to make. My heart couldn't take it. So I leaned over and pressed my lips to his. He groaned, his body hardening into stone.

"Nice distraction, but I need more water." His lips floated over mine. I immediately pulled away, curling my fingers around the handle of his jug of water before realizing it was empty.

"I think you're out. I'll go get some, unless you want my Gatorade?"

"Fucking hate Gatorade."

"Okay, Sour Ass Kid." I rose to my feet before he stopped me.

"*Big* fan of your germs, though. Give it here." He brushed his knuckles over my cheek. I grabbed the half-finished bottle and lowered the straw to touch his mouth. He clasped his lips around it and sucked before releasing the straw. A blue drop lingered on his lower lip. I dipped my head and swept it away with my tongue. It tasted better off his lips.

I was about to straighten up, but he caught my wrist, tugging me closer. His tongue traced the outline of my mouth, the tip of it sliding down my chin and neck, until it disappeared in my cleavage, where he sucked one of my tits into his mouth through my bra. Tantalizing pleasure cascaded through me.

"Lock the door, Dot."

"You're inju—"

"It's just a little scratch. Need you now."

"It's a *stab* wound."

"Let me assure you, sweetheart, my blue balls hurt more."

I stood up on wobbly legs, like a baby zebra taking its first step, and stumbled to the door, rolling the lock with a soft click.

"Come ride my dick, Dot."

I drew the line at bursting his stitches open. "We're not having full-blown sex."

"Why?"

"Because as much as you annoy me, I don't want to kill you."

"Fine. Let me eat you out." We stared each other down, but my inhibitions were falling apart quicker than a Shein outfit. He raised his eyebrows innocently. "I'm in the hospital, Cal. I'm not gonna have anything tasty or substantial for *days*."

There was something seriously wrong with our generation— and yes, I blamed everyone my age collectively—considering what I did next. I climbed atop his hospital bed with my back to Row, peeled down his blanket, and raised his hospital robe. His dick sprung up straight as an arrow, a pearl of precum crowning the tip.

Making sure I hovered far away from his stomach, I grabbed the root of his cock, lowering my head and licking along the shaft, a happy noise escaping from the back of my throat. He tasted earthy and sweet, just right.

"Heaven is not a place, it is a person, and it is you." He arched his back, chasing my small mouth. "Fuck, Dot, how am I going to let you go?"

Keep me. My chest tightened, and I tried to push the thought to the back of my head. What was I thinking? I couldn't give my heart to a man. Couldn't risk the emotional bloodbath Franco had left behind. I had loved him. I truly did. He was my first taste of relationship, and he taught me that love is doomed, and that men would use and abuse you if you let them.

Row began working the button and zipper of my jeans, going for a sixty-nine. I kicked my jeans off eagerly, my heel colliding with his cheekbone in the process. "Oops!"

"Baby, you can stomp all over my face and I'll say thank you."

I giggled into his dick, licking it eagerly like a lollipop.

"Now put your cunt on my face before I die."

"Is that a request or an order?"

"It's a fucking plea."

I scooted backward, shoved my panties to one side, and sank onto his hot mouth, his tongue erect and ready, disappearing inside my pussy.

Row smacked the back of his hospital bed, writhing with pleasure. "Shit."

"Problem?" I sank my knees deeper into the thin mattress, mindful of his injured torso, taking his dick back into my mouth and giving it a good suck while pumping the base with my fist.

"A big one." He arched his back, gripping my waist and rubbing his straight teeth along my vagina. "You've just ruined sex with anyone else for me. Might have to keep you after all."

There was something incredibly hot about hearing his blissed-out grunts of pleasure without seeing his face as I sucked him off, as he pleasured me with his mouth and fingers, going down on me.

"Hmm." I threw my head back, bracing my hands against his knees to support my balance. "You wouldn't like that. I'm messy."

"Orderliness is overrated."

My tits were bouncing up and down joyfully as I rode his fingers and tongue like they were his cock. My thigh muscles cried out, but the rest of my body hummed with pleasure. I pumped his dick harder and faster as he jerked in my fist. "I'm too eccentric."

"You're just the right amount of chaos for me."

Were we really having this conversation *now*? While the walls of my pussy were squeezing against his fingers?

"I would bore you," I choked out, his fingertip hitting my G-spot again and again, the orgasm clawing up my spine like ivy.

"You're a lot of fucking things, Cal Litvin, but boring has never been one of them." He penetrated me deeper.

"Row?" I gasped desperately, falling down on my elbows as I jerked him off faster, my triceps burning, watching his sleek, huge dick dripping down my fist like an erupting volcano. I knew he got a good look at my ass crack from his position, and somehow, I felt entirely comfortable baring my all to him. "I'm coming."

Crashing down on his face again, I moaned when shocks of electricity zipped through me. Row grunted, and I leaned down and put his cock in my mouth, letting him cum inside it.

After we both came, I pulled my pants up and covered him gingerly. I went to unlock the door, then returned to stand by his bed, suddenly unsure what to do next.

Row looked flushed and extra gorgeous and—might I add—in perfect health. He patted the space next to him on the bed. "Hop on."

"Someone could walk in," I pointed out, before slapping a hand over my mouth. "Holy shit, what if there are cameras in the room?"

"Then they're welcome to the performance of their lives." Row's voice was devoid of emotion. "This is what I call a million-dollar cum shot."

I swatted his chest, feeling contemplative all of a sudden. Things he found funny weren't funny to me. The idea that someone had seen us made me want to vomit.

"Hey." He squeezed my hand. "You look pale."

"I'm okay," I lied. I wasn't. I was never going to be a person who was down with having sex in exotic places. Especially since some internet sites still had pictures of my tits.

"Look at me, Dot. I was just kidding. I was out of line. I didn't think... I forgot..." He raked his hair, shaking his head. "I'm not Franco. I would never put your safety and boundaries in jeopardy. I promise you that, okay?"

"Okay." I hated how small and uncertain my voice sounded. How I was falling down the rabbit hole of my trauma.

"Have you eaten anything?" Row tried to change the subject.

"Not since you were taken to the hospital," I admitted. And that was hours ago.

"There should be an Oh Henry! in my messenger bag. They brought it here, right?"

"I think so." I stood up, walking over to a small counter overlooking the window and flipping his bag open. Sure enough, there were two in there.

"Want one?" I unwrapped the bar and took a bite, groaning in satisfaction.

Row snorted. "No thanks. I'd rather chew on my own foo—" He stopped abruptly when he realized what he was admitting.

I ripped another bite of chocolate, studying him intently. "You don't like these bars, do you?" I walked over to him.

"Sure I do. Sometimes." He was quiet for a second. "No. I don't. Fuck, Cal, they're *awful*. How could you like them?"

I sat back next to him, nuzzling my face in the crook of his neck. "They remind me of a really great moment in my childhood."

"What moment?" He side-eyed me.

"Well, it was kind of...the first chocolate I ever had." I blinked five times in a row. "My parents were anal retentive about my teeth and wouldn't let me have anything sweet. Fast forward to age four, and I'm in my babushka's room—she lived with us before she passed away. So there I was, being my usual nosy self. You know, snooping and minding everyone else's business."

"Shocking," he commented wittily.

"I open her bedside drawer and see an Oh Henry! I immediately decide to eat it."

Row grinned. "Was it everything you've ever wanted and more?"

"It was…" I fought my gag reflex. "From 1992."

Row tipped his head back, plastering a hand over his face, omitting a dark chuckle. "Classic Cal."

"I remember thinking chocolate was so overrated. It was dry and brittle and tasted like sour grapes. I spent that entire weekend hugging the toilet like it was a freshly returned lover who came back from a war zone. Apparently, when my babushka got off the plane from the former Soviet Union as a refugee, Good Samaritans waited for them on the tarmac with baskets of food and blankets and whatnot. One of them handed out chocolate bars. She remembered the moment so fondly, she decided to save the Oh Henry! as a keepsake."

"You ate her most fundamental memory?" He crossed his arms in a hot-guy way. "I've never heard something so *you*."

"Even though it tasted horrible, it was technically my first chocolate. So I'm still fond of it, vomit bouts be damned. Now, for the last time, where do you get the Oh Henry! from, Row?"

"Fuck." His smile collapsed.

I watched in fascination, my breath caged inside my throat.

He trained his gaze on the wall behind my head, avoiding eye contact. "I make them."

"Hmm, come again?" *Ideally on my tits. But honestly anywhere else would do too,* I was tempted to add.

"I. Make. Them." His nostrils flared. "They're no longer in

circulation. I knew you liked them. So I found a list of the ingredients online, tested the quantities a few times, and started making them for you. The wrappers were easy to print and apply," he mumbled as an afterthought. "I saw a manual on YouTube. I did this because I…" He stopped, rubbing his face with his palm in frustration.

"Because what?" I choked back my tears.

"You've always been a picky eater and I didn't want you to faint. I'd…" His jaw squared. "I'd have nightmares about it."

Lacing my fingers through his, I said, "I'm sorry. I wish I were in your dreams, not nightmares."

"Don't worry, sweetheart, you star in both." He pushed a hand into his hair. "My dreams. My nightmares. My fantasies. The only place you weren't in was the place I wanted you to be most."

"And where was that?"

"My reality."

Our eyes met. I knew I was blinking like crazy. My heart begged me to open up, to take a chance, to dive into the deep end and try to swim, but my brain reminded me my one and only "relationship" had ended in emotional carnage I still hadn't recovered from.

"But now?" His pupils burned with darkness and determination. "Now I know what it's like to have you. And I never want to fall asleep because, as it turns out, my reality is better than anything a dream could ever conjure. Who are we kidding with this casual bullshit?" Row asked, brushing his knuckles along my temple softly. "I can't do this anymore. I'm sorry, Dot. Loving you from up close is so much crueler than loving you from afar. It reminds me of all the things I'll miss out on. All the shit that can't be mine. Because the thing is…" He wet his lips. "You *feel* mine."

"Am I your girl?"

"No." He shook his head. "You're my everything."

Everything. The word was so final.

Panic skated through me. Not because I didn't feel the same way, but because I *did*. I wanted to be with him too, consequences be damned. But if Franco had managed to break me so thoroughly with something that was puppy love at the time…what kind of wreckage would Row leave in his wake?

"We still have time to discuss this." I tried to sound chirpy and bright, patting his thigh awkwardly. "Why don't we—"

"Don't do this," he cut me off.

"Don't do what?"

"Don't run away from us. I'm telling you something important. I'm in love with you."

My stomach dipped like I had fallen off a cliff. And then I just kept on falling because the implications of that statement were going to be my ruin. "Again?"

"*Still*," he said bitterly. "Forever and always. I never stopped, and I'm tired of trying to hate you. To look for flaws instead of enjoying all the good parts. You bewitched me, and if I can't have all of you, I don't want scraps. I'm not half-assing what we are." He took a quick breath. "My heart has two rooms, and you occupy both."

I just stared at him, tucked under his big arm. What could I say to that?

He was…*Row*. Gorgeous and successful and grumpy and perfect. I was a novelty. He liked that I made him laugh. That he had my legs and mouth on speed dial. But the fascination with me would wear off as soon as we got serious.

If I could even get serious with a man without screwing it up.

Even if Row did love me, my trust issues would never let me be happy with him. After being chased to my almost death by school-mates, with nearly two decades of being heavily bullied under my belt, I wasn't so hot on the human race. Yes, Row was a part of the very narrow exception, but could I put my entire trust and hope in someone?

Bet all my chips on this one person?

Putting my heart on the line terrified me, and even though there was a part of me that was elated, there was another bigger part that told me to run for the hills.

"What are you asking?" I raked my fingers through my hair, realizing they were shaking.

"I'm asking you to fall in love with me." His eyes didn't drop from mine, clinging to my face, searching, pleading. "*Please.*"

I almost smiled. I knew how hard it was for him to use this word. "What if you don't catch me?" I worried my lip.

"I will."

"How do you know?"

"My arms have been wide-open and waiting for years." He stretched his muscular arms, with the needles poking out of the veins, for emphasis.

I dropped my elbows to my knees and held my face in my hands, trying to breathe through what was fast becoming a panic attack.

"This is the part where you say something." Row gave me a blank stare. "No pressure or anything."

There were so many things running through my head.

I want you, but I'm scared to death.

This is too soon, too fast.

But I had to say *something,* so I said, "I need more time."

He inclined his head. "I'm afraid this chef is out of that particular ingredient. Your answer determines whether I shit all over my Blackthorn deal and piss off the man who is holding the purse strings to my new restaurant, or if I push through and sign this contract."

"You're thinking of staying?" My eyes widened.

He nodded solemnly.

"But, Row…you hate this town."

"Yes, but I love you." He licked his lips. "Plus, I can always open something in New York. Probably not immediately, since I'll be fucking radioactive to investors and don't have that kind of capital on hand…" He sucked his teeth.

The thought of Row dropping everything, staying behind, here, in Staindrop, made my skin crawl. I would never forgive myself if I knew I'd held him back. But I also wasn't crazy about the idea of him putting me in this situation. He knew I always aimed to please. Having the opportunity to appease the entire town I grew up in was definitely temptation. But maybe I had grown a spine after all. Because no matter how happy I knew it would make other people, I couldn't do this to Row *and* myself.

"*Youshouldn'tchangeyourplansforme,*" I said in one breath, the words ripping from my mouth like a Band-Aid. I untangled from him, landing on the floor with an awkward thump. "Don't. Don't give up on everything worthwhile for me. I'll only disappoint you." I stood up in a rush, panicking, blinking, ready to bolt. "Please go. Live your life. The pressure of disappointing you will eat at me, and I'll end up messing it up. I'm not ready." Pause. "We can't be together, Row."

Our eyes met. I forced myself to stay. To look the damage I'd caused in the eye. I had to stand there and see the disappointment on his face. The expression of a man ripped to shreds.

It was in this moment that Sheriff Menchin decided to saunter into the room, accompanied by another cop. "Casablancas." He tucked his phone into his pocket.

"Village idiot," Row drawled, ripping his gaze from my face. "Long time no see."

Menchin tipped his head down. "Sorry about that."

"Don't be. Had a fucking blast. In fact, feel free to screw right off."

Menchin brushed his hand over his gun without realizing what he was doing. These two were going to kill each other if given the chance.

"I can…stick around." I cleared my throat.

Row's voice was stone-cold as he continued staring at Menchin. "Thanks, I've got it."

I swallowed hard. "You sure?"

"Positive."

"I'll go check on Dylan, then."

Nobody noticed when I slipped out of the room to the hallway, pressed my head against the wall, and began bawling my eyes out.

CHAPTER SIXTY-THREE
CAL

"Ordinary World"—Duran Duran

It took me forty minutes to get myself together and stop weeping.

I didn't know what was wrong with me. I hadn't cried over a boy since Franco—keeping my distance from the other sex purposefully—and even that had been *because of* rather than *over*. Friendships? Parents? Instagram reels of thirsty, wing-torn bees being saved by a kind stranger that kept on popping up in my feed because the stupid algorithm knew I'd always bite? Sure.

But never about an actual *guy*.

Using whatever little energy I had left in me, I took the elevator downstairs to a gift shop and bought Dylan treats and flowers. I then walked across to a shopping center and grabbed Dylan something to eat. I figured because Tuck was still on a ship with no way to get home in the next week, she could use some pampering. Then I went up to the maternity ward, where I was informed Dylan's room was at the end of the hall.

My feet pounded down the corridor, anxiety sifting through me. It was close to midnight, and I felt like I'd been awake since the dawn of civilization. I found Zeta sitting on a blue plastic chair in front of a door, sniffling into a ball of used tissue.

"Hi, Mrs. Casablancas!" I dropped the gifts and flowers on the floor, stacking my hands on top of her knees as I squatted down to reach her eye level. "Is she okay?"

She nodded, blowing her nose raucously. "Out of the delivery room. She had a C-section. Both mother and baby are healthy."

Phew. "Are *you* okay?" I put a hand on her shoulder.

"Yes, honey, I think I am." She looked up, resting a hand atop mine. "Just thinking. Wishing, really. That Dylan is with the right person. I love my children more than anything else in this world, but I had them with the wrong person. I always thought I needed to stay so they'd have both parents. I wouldn't wish that upon her."

I took the seat next to her, gathering her hands in mine. "You know, when Dylan and I were preteens, she used to say, 'I'm not like other girls. I'm worse.' We used to laugh about that. But what she meant was, she always stood her ground. Whether Tucker is a lesson or her forever, she will make the right decision. I know this in my bones. Social constructs mean jack shit to your kid."

"Cal! Language." She squeezed my hands in hers. "Anyway, how can you be so sure?"

"Because you make really smart kids, Mrs. Casablancas." *Lovable too.*

After convincing Zeta to go get some rest and promising to call her if Dylan needed anything, I knocked on my best friend's hospital door.

"Whoever comes in better not be the person who impregnated me," she moaned.

I pushed the door open, bearing burgers and fries from Jack in the Box, and flowers. Dylan was on the bed, barefaced, with dark circles under her eyes. There was a see-through plastic cart with a bundled baby next to her. The baby appeared much smaller than Dylan's still-huge tummy, further supporting my speculation she had been carrying triplets.

"How are you feeling?" I leaned down to kiss both her cheeks. She snatched the burger and fries from my hand and ripped into them with a feral groan.

"Hungry. Tired. Hurting all over." She paused to swallow a huge bite of a double-patty cheeseburger. "You also brought sweets, right?"

I silently held up a plastic bag laden with chocolates.

"Good. I need you to give me a baby-wipe bath, straighten my hair, and help me put on some lashes."

"Getting ready for a hot date?" I snickered, trying to push my own romantic woes out of my mind.

"Kieran texted. He'll be coming to visit me tomorrow," she said in a rush, adding, "and don't worry, nothing's going to happen between us. It's just nice to have someone around who doesn't see you as a baby-making machine that also bears the technology to make sandwiches. I know I should be trying to salvage whatever I have with Tucker, or at least break the news to him before I move on, and yes, I also know that falling in love with a soccer player is the worst idea a new single mom could have. I just don't want to hear about it right now."

She was clearly overwhelmed and hadn't completely comprehended her change of status.

"I promise I'll make you look so hot, Kieran'll weep horny tears." I shoved the flowers into a nearby vase. "Can I look at the baby first?"

Dylan paused for a second, gulping. "I mean…if you must."

I rounded her bed and peered into the little basket. And…*wow*.

The baby was a Winston Churchill dead ringer. The round face, downturned lips, and receding hairline. A tuft of black hair covered the back of her head—*and* portions of her forehead. She had many chins, and no eyelashes at all.

"She is horrid, isn't she?" Dylan sighed in contempt. "I can't believe it. Tuck had one job. *One.* To give me a cute baby. Of course he screwed it up."

"Dylan, what are you talking about?" I rushed to the baby's defense, a wave of protectiveness coursing through me. "She's totally adorable."

"No, she isn't. And she has no interest in my breasts either. It's all so horrible." Her chin wobbled. She dumped the half-eaten burger on her belly, the lettuce exploding everywhere like confetti. "And I can't even rearrange my pillows because my C-section is killing me and every slight movement makes me feel like my upper and lower body are hanging together by a thread. And someone must be cutting onions here, because...because..." She fanned her fingers over her face. "*Ugh.*"

I silently rearranged the pillows behind her back, then wiped the tears rolling down her cheeks. "You're overwhelmed right now, and for a very good reason. Breathe. Rest. Don't worry about a thing," I suggested. "Give yourself some grace and time to adjust to your new status."

"It would also honestly help if she didn't look like an old misogynist congressman." She used the foil sheet covering the chocolate to blow her nose, still crying. "How's my brother, anyway? Is he better?"

Oh, crap. "You mean, like, physically?" I cleared my throat. "Yeah. Making a speedy recovery. I'm telling you, this hospital? Top notch."

Her sobbing stopped, and she narrowed her eyes at me. "*Cal.*"

I bit down on my lower lip. "Hmm?"

She thumped her head against the pillow, immediately wincing. "Aw. Seriously, abs? I wasn't even using you!" Her head twisted back to me. "Tell me what happened."

"I don't want to bother you with my problems right now."

"Bother away. I have a feeling you're going to give me a good reason to take some of my existential anger out on you."

Fair enough. "He confessed his feelings for me." I swallowed. "And I...let him down. *But*"—I hurried to go on in my defense—"I never told him I was looking for a relationship. Not once. I was very clear about that, I swear."

"God. I really should hate you." She used her thumbs to wipe off her tears, and I shriveled inside myself. "For what you are putting him through. I knew he was still in love with you. I just thought you'd grown up and were finally giving him a chance. It's partly my fault, that it happened again. Thing is…" She closed her eyes, looking exhausted. "Even though I'm gutted that you broke his heart again, I can't even be mad at you properly because I can't afford to lose you again. You're a *terrible* love interest. Seriously. Zero out of ten. Would not recommend. One star."

"Eh…thanks?"

"But as it turns out, a pretty great friend."

Tears leaked through her closed eyes, and her nose reddened. "You'll always have me, Dylan. And Row will too, if he'll have me in his life. As a friend."

We both shed silent tears for a few seconds. Finally, Dylan spoke. "Tucker hasn't even called since he left. And he's late. He doesn't even know I had a baby. The only thing that's gluing us together is falling apart."

Had he not called because he couldn't, or because he couldn't be bothered? That was what I wanted to know. If it was the latter, I was fully ready to plot and execute his murder and face the consequences.

I kissed Dylan's forehead. "You and the baby have so many people who love you to death. Focus on them. On *us*." I smiled. "So did you choose a name?"

"I did." She reached into the plastic crate, smiling dreamingly. "Say hello to little Gravity."

CHAPTER SIXTY-FOUR
ROW

oBITCHuary: Hey.
McMonster: Hi.
oBITCHuary: Are we still good?
McMonster: Always, Dot.

CHAPTER SIXTY-FIVE
ROW

"You look awful." Tate stared me down like dog shit he had to scrape from the bottom of his Gucci loafers, clad in a Kiton cashmere suit and a chunky watch that cost more than a Hamptons getaway. "And I say that with lo... Sorry, can't fucking lie to your face. Hate your guts. You're one of the flakiest business partners I've ever encountered."

I jammed my socked feet into my combat boots, shaking my head. At least I wasn't wearing that ass baring robe anymore. I was back to my Henley and jeans, my duffel perched on the hospital bed. "There go our wedding plans," I said in a mocking tone.

"Don't be so touchy. You act like my ex after I dumped her for a French lingerie model during our Mediterranean cruise. People take shit so personally sometimes." Tate pushed off the door he'd been leaning against, striding toward me, hands tucked in his front pockets.

"Is there a reason you're here?" I stuffed my hoodie into my duffel bag, zipping it. "Other than clearly being obsessed with me."

"I'm sure you remember it's the last day of my ultimatum."

"You never gave me a date for the so-called ultimatum," I said flatly.

"Well, I'm giving you one now." He flicked his wrist to check the time. "It's right fucking now."

I hooked the strap of the duffel bag over my shoulder. "You know, I was just on my way to you."

"Really?" His eyes narrowed.

"No."

"I was hoping being stabbed by one of the village idiots would be the wake-up call you needed. The final reason to get the hell out of here." Tate linked his hands behind his back, peering out the window. He was probably contemplating building a dildo-shaped skyscraper right in front of the church. "As it happened, your hero complex has gotten wors—"

"Please stop talking." I stood up, steady on my feet. "I'll sign your damn contract."

But it had nothing to do with getting stabbed. Cal had said not to wait for her. There was no point in sticking around if she wasn't an option.

"Finally, you've retained some of your gray matter." He snapped his fingers once. In an instant, the door pushed open, and two suits carrying briefcases walked in. A third person trailed behind. A dark-skinned stunner in her midtwenties. Gia, I bet. She was beautiful. She was also very clearly human, which meant she probably wasn't down with procreating with her devil of a boss.

"Where shall I put the contract?" she asked in an elegant English accent.

"The ceiling," Tate huffed sarcastically. "There's only one surface in this room."

Her lips shaped the word *twat* noiselessly, and she arranged a pile of documents on the counter by the window, producing a pen from her purse.

"Mr. Casablancas." She motioned toward the documents with the strained smile of someone who really loathed their job. "I'm happy to go over the fine print and answer any questions."

"That won't be necessary. I really don't give one shit what's in it." Hell wasn't hot enough for most of the people in this town. I was tempted to pack up Mom and Dylan and take them with me to

London. The only thing stopping me was the slight chance Tucker was man enough to want to raise his child.

"Wish I'd known all it'd take was a little prickle to take the air out of you." Tate gave me a once-over, folding his arms over his chest. "I'd have stabbed you myself."

"Wouldn't doubt it," Gia muttered under her breath.

"Uh-huh." I plucked the pen from her fingers, jotting my signature over the dotted lines as fast as I could. "Good luck winning the people of Staindrop over."

Tate chuckled. "Not looking to make friends here."

I tossed the pen on the documents and grabbed my ball cap, pushing it down my forehead. "Anything else?"

Tate picked up the contract, grinning at it as he waved me off. "All good. When are you getting to London?"

"January first."

"Want a ride?"

"Would rather hang on to a baby-oiled airplane wing to get there."

"I'd pay good money to see that." He rubbed his chin. "I have a table booked at La Vie en Rogue on opening day. See you then."

"Can't fucking wait."

I slammed the door behind me.

CHAPTER SIXTY-SIX
ROW

"Surely she's not going to stay this ugly forever, right?" Dylan peered at Gravity, who nestled in my arms in my mom's kitchen. "Neither Tuck nor I have a Gonzo nose."

"Dylan!" Mom flapped the kitchen towel, marching toward her from the laundry room. *"Da oggi si cambia musica!"*

Dylan hopped off the counter stool, dodging the towel smacks. "My kid, my opinion! Also, I'm the one whose boob she's attached to twenty-four seven. I'm sacrificing my killer cleavage for her."

"She's latching beautifully." My mother's face softened in an instant, and she started folding the towel. "I'm proud that you didn't give up."

"How could I?" Dylan sighed. "She's not vying for a Miss Universe title with this face, is she? I have to make sure her IQ is higher than average. Apparently, breastfeeding does that."

"Come ti ho fatto, ti distruggo!" Mom was back to chasing Dylan around the house. "I should wash your mouth out with soap."

I peered down at Gravity's little face. She was sound asleep in my arms. At three days old, most of her forehead hair had fallen off, but she still looked like an old stern man. Contrary to Dylan's opinion, I thought she looked a lot like Tuck.

"She doesn't know your struggles." I nuzzled my nose in her cheek. She smelled so pure. "You're going to grow up to be beautiful and brave, and Uncle Row will be ready with a baseball bat when that happens."

Gravity stirred in my arms, sniffling. Dylan zipped toward me in a flash, already unstrapping her bra under her oversized shirt. "Shit. She hasn't snacked in two hours. She's going to maul me."

I handed my niece over to her like she was a hot potato. My life was miserable enough these days without adding *watching my baby sister flash me* to my list of unfortunate incidents.

"I'll be in my room, feeding her."

"I'll be upstairs doing the laundry." Mom planted a kiss on my forehead. "Should I stop by your room and do yours?"

"Thanks, Ma. Already done mine."

I'd moved here the minute I had gotten discharged from the hospital. There was no point returning to the inn after I'd signed Tate's contract. Word had gotten out fast, and everyone in town was officially done with my ass. Just as well, as Descartes was entering its last days of operation before shutting down.

On the flip side, it looked like Menchin had finally started taking his job seriously. When he'd visited me at the hospital, he had promised there'd be a police car outside of Descartes until we closed shop and had made good on his word.

"I'd have started inviting people over for interviews, but Mayor Murray seemed eager to lay this case to rest," he'd said during his visit. "She doesn't want small business owners and elderly women getting arrested. Can't say I blame her."

But I could. Fucking Allison. Optics meant everything to her, justice be damned.

There was a knock on the door. I wasn't in the mood to see anyone, but it could have been Rhyland, about the restaurant. I swung the door open. It was Cal.

I hadn't seen her in three days. Not since we'd had mind-blowing oral sex, and I'd declared my love to her and gotten slammed with a rejection. She had little plastic butterflies holding her hair together, coveralls, and a stripy sweater. Her glacial blues set my heart ablaze as soon as they landed on my face, blinking repeatedly to tell me that she hadn't been expecting me, that she was nervous. She stumbled backward at the sight of me, and I itched to catch and steady her.

"How are you doing?" Her voice was soft.

"Good. Better." *Shit. Worse than ever before. Why are we not together? I know you want to. You trust me. You're open with me. I make you laugh. I make you moan my name. What more can you ask for? Why am I never fucking enough?*

Unfortunately, I was too much of an ass to ask how she was doing.

"Is Dylan home?" She cleared her throat.

I stepped aside, jerking my chin upstairs. She ducked her head as she passed me, avoiding eye contact. Every second in her presence felt like a sucker punch straight to the gut. When Cal stopped in the middle of the small living area, I noticed the tips of her hair were dyed flint. Somewhere between purple and gray.

"Actually." She twirled on her boots to face me, and when our gazes clashed, it felt like a fucking car crash. "I wanted to talk to you."

"What do you need?" I asked woodenly.

I hated how transparent I was with her. An open fucking book. And a shitty one at that.

She worried her bottom lip, shooting me an uncertain look. Jesus. Had she changed her mind? Was there still a chance? "We need to get ahold of Tucker."

Why the fuck?

"We do?" I parked my elbows on the counter behind me languidly.

"Yeah. He doesn't know he became a father. As much as I dislike him, this seems unfair. And I also think a lot of the reason Dylan is stressed out is because she isn't sure where they stand."

"That all might be true, but there isn't much signal in the middle of the fucking ocean." I fished my cigarette pack out of my front pocket. It was surreal, talking to her about anything that wasn't us right now. Especially that idiot, Tuck, who didn't deserve my sister nor Gravity.

"He should be close to shore at this point," Cal insisted, ocean eyes clinging to my face. "We need to at least try. We owe it to Dylan. She went through the last few weeks without the father of her baby."

I worked my jaw back and forth, too distracted by her face to pay any real attention to the conversation. She was so fucking beautiful and the thought that, in less than two weeks, I'd return to not seeing her at all made my skin crawl. How the fuck did people live their lives not having a dose of Cal in it? Insanity.

"Fine," I bit out.

"Thanks." Cal's shoulders sagged with relief. "Do you have his number?"

"Yeah." I pushed the cigarette into the corner of my mouth and fished my phone out of my pocket, tossing it into her hands. She caught it. "What's your passcode?"

Your birthday.

"Here. I'll open it for you."

"Great. While you're at it, please refrain from spreading your cancer stick fumes inside a house where a newborn lives. Now and until you leave. *Thankssomuch.*"

I found Tucker's number and passed the phone to her. She put it on speaker. It went straight to voicemail, just as I'd expected. When I went to grab my phone back, she yanked it away. "Do you know his captain?"

"Sure do. He's one of the key service providers for Descartes."

"Let's call him. Maybe Tucker forgot to turn on his phone when they reached a signal."

She hit the search icon on my phone and inserted his name, tapping it with her finger. The line went through.

Beep. Beep. Beep.

We both stared at each other, mouths agape. The line clicked, and a croaky voice filled the air. "Row, my boy. How're you doing?"

Cal's eyebrows shot to her hairline. I thought on my feet. "Hey there, Sanders. Good. You?"

"No complaints. Filled all eight hundred traps we sailed with. Shame about Descartes shutting down. These lobsters would've earned you another Michelin star."

"Uh-huh." I traced my tongue inside my inner cheek. "When are you heading back?"

Silence. Normally, I was a fan. But I had a feeling this quiet was the result of mental scrambling on his part. Sanders gulped audibly. "What do you mean, back?"

"When are you scheduled to arrive in Staindrop?"

"We've been back for a couple days now." Sanders coughed, and I heard him fumbling with food wrappers, cracking open a can of beer. "Is Tuck not home?"

"No," I said, jaw flexing. "He is not."

More silence. My blood bubbled in my veins, reaching a dangerous temperature.

"Any idea where he might've gone?" I pushed. Cal was turning a pale shade of green.

A rustling sound came from upstairs. "Aw! Nice burp, Grav. Your daddy's daughter, indeed." Dylan whistled, impressed, while descending the stairs.

Cal gasped, pushing me out to the front yard so we could continue this conversation in private. She shut the door behind us. As soon as we were out, I lit that cigarette.

"Th-that ain't really none of my business," Sanders stammered.

"No." I exhaled smoke through my nostrils. "But it's mine, and if there's something I need to know, you better tell me now." Then, to bring my point home, I added, "Dylan gave birth three days ago. We need to find Tucker and let him know."

"The little idiot…" Sanders muttered, sighing. "Congratulations to your sister, son. Children are the greatest gift of all."

"Sure about that? Because I can think of one gift that's even better—sparing you from boycotting your business. If you don't spill the beans right now, I'll tell all my East Coast chef friends not to fuck with you because you're a flaky *sonovobitch*. Spit. It. Out."

"Look, once we arrived at shore, he got picked up by someone. I told him to go straight home to his pregnant girlfriend. That no-gooder didn't listen. I thought it wasn't my business, and it still isn't, but goddamn. The boy ain't the sharpest pencil in the pack, is he? What the hell is he thinking?"

"Who picked him up?"

"Row…" He sighed.

"Sanders." I smacked the wall of the house, about to lose my shit. Cal gasped. "Answer me."

"It was Mayor Murray."

CHAPTER SIXTY-SEVEN
ROW

Half an hour later Cal and I were sitting on either side of Dylan, who had just put Gravity down for her fortieth nap for the day. She looked exhausted and sleep-deprived. What she didn't look was devastated, heartbroken, or inconsolable.

Which was interesting, since we had just broken the news to her that her boyfriend was probably cheating on her with Staindrop's mayor.

"You mean…he is in town and hasn't even bothered to check on me?" She perked up, squeezing her own cheeks with excitement.

"Yeah." Cal squinted, studying her with alarm. "That's what we're saying. Are you high on those pain meds?"

"Nope." My sister seemed genuinely giddy.

Cal licked her lips, still confused. "Look, I know this is—"

"Wonderful!" Dylan stood up, flinging her hands in the air with a radiant smile. "Oh, this is the best news ever. Dot, I would kiss you right now if I didn't know your favorite lip gloss shade is my brother's spunk."

Cal choked on her boba tea, sending me a frightened look.

"She's not making any sense," I offered charitably.

"That's hardly news." My sister snorted, pulling at the collar of her shirt and rearranging her boobs in her bra.

"Do you have any…questions, maybe?" Cal pulled my sister's hair back, using her own scrunchie to tie it into a fashionable bun.

"Yeah. Can anyone get me some M&Ms? I've been dying for sweets my entire pregnancy."

"Check her temperature," I ordered Cal.

Cal stood up and pressed a hand to my sister's forehead. "Nope. Seems fine. Maybe it's the exhaustion?"

"Might be a brain hemorrhage." I stroked my chin. "I'll take her to the hospital; you stay here and watch Grav—"

"Don't you see?" Dylan spun in place à la Julie Andrews in *The Sound of Music*. "Now I don't have to be the bad guy. *I'm* not going to be the one who broke this family apart, who took the selfish way out. Tucker did it for both of us. In fact, he did something so inexcusable and selfish, nobody is ever going to give me shit for leaving him."

Cal stared at her in awe. "Dylan, he *cheated* on you."

Dylan shrugged. "It only hurts if you care about the person."

"You must care a little." Cal scrunched her nose. "You had a baby with him."

Dylan sat back down, sobering up slightly. "As much as I love Grav—and all jokes aside, I'm honestly freaked out about how in love I am with this tiny creature—she wasn't planned in any way. I'd been wanting to break it off with Tucker for months before I found out that I was pregnant. In fact…" She took a quick breath, glancing at me anxiously. "I had kind of…done a thing. I signed up for community college in Portland. Wanted to get a degree and start spreading my wings. I don't know, marketing seems cool. And PR. I think I could be good at it. I'm an extrovert; dealing with people fills me up."

My sister was the exact opposite of me. I felt drained just knowing humanity was still in existence.

"Of course, I withdrew as soon as I found out I was pregnant. And, sure, I thought I'd give this thing with Tucker another chance.

I owed it to Gravity. To try to give her some normalcy. But Tucker just proved without a doubt that he cannot be trusted."

I still wanted to break Tucker's nose, just for funsies, but I had to admit, Dylan had taken the sting out of my wrath. If she didn't care, I didn't care. Just as long as the oxygen waster stepped up for his daughter and performed his co-parenting duties.

Thus ensued a hushed conversation between Cal and Dylan about Murray being a homewrecker (agreed), Tucker being an asshole (ditto), and tentative plans for Dylan to go to community college once Gravity got a little older.

I tuned out and drifted to the backyard once Cal began enthusiastically researching portable breast pumps for when Dylan was in college. "Mamushka can look after her. She's been bugging me about giving her grandchildren since before I hit puberty."

Once outside, I took a seat on an axed tree trunk and pulled my phone out.

> Row: Changed your mind about joining me in London? Not a whole lot of people to fake-date in Staindrop.
> Rhyland: I love you, man. And in order for me to continue to love you, I have to cut the cord. I've met actual cunts less cunty than you.
> Rhyland: I actually really like cunts. They taste great too.
> Rhyland: And I'm moving to New York, so no Staindrop for me. Anyway, how are you feeling?

Mentally, run over by a thousand trucks. It was hard to see Cal and not be with her. At the same time, I was an all-or-nothing man. And she had made herself clear.

> Row: Like it's time to find a new best friend. One who isn't a sex addict.

Rhyland: You'll get over her.

Row: No, I won't.

Rhyland: You're right, you won't. But you'll learn how to live with that hole in your heart. Just like you did before.

CHAPTER SIXTY-EIGHT
ROW

My hopes Cal would be gone by the time I got back inside after my trillionth cigarette break were crushed when I stepped into my living room. Cal was still there, massaging Dylan's feet on the couch, watching some kind of a reality TV show with her.

"You're still here," I heard myself grunt. My default was to be mean to her if I couldn't have her. But even that was growing fucking old. Making her feel like shit no longer got my rocks off. Because making her come felt so much better.

"I was just heading back home." She stood up, readjusting her coveralls.

Don't offer her a ride. She's not your problem. She broke your heart.

"I'll give you a ride."

You never learn, do you, Pussy McWhipson?

"Thanks." She attempted a weak smile.

Dylan's laser gaze ping-ponged between us. She slowly chewed on a ZBar. "Keep your clothes on, kids. You don't want to end up like me."

Cal was already sailing across the room toward me before she glanced at Dylan behind her shoulder. "What are you talking about? You turned out to be the best."

"I did, didn't I?" Dylan flashed me a brave smile, and in that moment, I knew she'd needed it. That good word.

CHAPTER SIXTY-NINE
ROW

I spent the entire drive to Cal's house stopping myself from telling her she was being a coward while she longingly stared at my profile. I couldn't rush her. Even if she was clearly fucking both our lives up by giving up something just because she was afraid of losing it.

"I think Allison sent people to stab you," she blurted out of nowhere when I turned off the engine in front of her house. "Like, almost certain of it."

"It's possible." I reached into the glove compartment, brushing my hand over her knee accidentally while popping it open. I extracted a pack of gum and threw two sticks into my mouth. "She has a track record of wanting people dead."

"How are you not mad?" Her fingers curled around the handle of the passenger door, but she made no move to leave. "She could've killed you."

"Back at ya." I popped my gum, looking out the windshield with my signature boredom. She needed to do this. She had to face her bully if she ever wanted to step out of the shadow Allison had cast over Cal's life. I had my own beef with Allison, and I was going to go for her throat, but not before Cal found out for herself that she could handle anything, least of which was Mayor Murray.

"It's not the same," she cried out desperately. "She formed an entire movement against you."

I didn't take my eyes off her, waiting for the penny to drop.

"It's still not the same," she yelped. "What happened to me was a long time ago."

"You let your past dictate your present. Which is why you have no future." I reached to open the door for her. "Word to the wise—fight your own demons before helping other people slay theirs. Goodbye, Dot."

CHAPTER SEVENTY
CAL

oBITCHuary: I miss you.

McMonster: Then do something about it.

oBITCHuary: Like what?

McMonster: Change your mind before we say goodbye.

oBITCHuary: You can't promise me you would never hurt me.

McMonster: You're right. I can't. That's why you have to take a chance on me. Love is a high-stakes game, Bitchy. Show me I'm worth it. Because to me? You're worth the entire fucking world.

CHAPTER SEVENTY-ONE
CAL

"Never Ever"—All Saints

On Christmas Eve, I opted out of the festive dinner the Finches had invited Mamushka and me to on account that I'd have rather feasted on soiled toddler underwear than spend a minute with Melinda Finch. It was the last day of Descartes, but I didn't have a shift. No doubt Row's doing. He knew I disliked big crowds.

"I wish you'd come." Mom curled a fuzzy multicolored scarf around her neck, shoving her hands into her mittens. "Melinda makes the best mince pie in all of Maine."

"Pretty sure she makes the *only* mince pie in all of Maine," I guffawed from my spot on the couch, fluffy socks rolled all the way up my shins. A laptop rested in my lap. In lieu of a love life—of *any* kind of life, really—I had begun drafting more of my hypothetical podcast episodes. It was pretty therapeutic. And by therapeutic, I meant it distracted me from wanting to punch my own face for screwing it all up with Row. Again.

Mom propped against the door for balance, dunking her feet into snow boots. "Shall I bring you some leftovers?"

"If they don't come with a side of prejudice against Row," I murmured, typing my life away.

"What did you say?"

"Nothing, Mom. No leftovers needed. I want to keep it light for the 10K run tomorrow."

"Oh, yes." She spooned her cheek with her palm, grinning proudly. "I wish your dad could've seen you."

"Don't jinx it, Mom."

"You'll crush it. You've been practicing for weeks. Rain or shine."

She was right. But my issue wasn't the physical challenge. It was all about how I was going to handle it mentally.

As the front door clicked shut, I perched back on the armrest of the couch and blew out a breath, flipping the laptop shut.

I was going to come face-to-face with Allison tomorrow, *really* see her for the first time since I'd returned to Staindrop, and she'd be able to see me, talk to me, taunt me. Row was right. Even now, after all these years, I still let her get to me so much, I doubted my ability to complete the run. Worse than that, I think that in a way, Allison had messed me up much more than Franco did. Because Franco was firmly in my past. Allison was now a part of my present, too. She never did get her punishment. Karma didn't find her address.

My tab with Allison Murray was forever open.

She had tried to kill me.

Had possibly sent people to *stab* the man I loved.

Had an affair with my best friend's fiancé.

To top all of that off, even though it wasn't her fault Franco had done what he did to me, she had sure had a ton of fun telling me my pictures were on porn sites.

Allison Murray had tarnished every beautiful thing in my life and was going to destroy whatever was left of it if I let her. I wasn't sure why Row let her push him around like this, but suddenly, urgency speared my spine to get up and do something. I couldn't let her get away with everything she'd done. In my time away from Staindrop, Allison had obviously continued running people over on her way to the top.

A floodgate had opened: all the digs she'd thrown my way over the years that had made me doubt myself. Doubt my worth.

"No one will ever want you. You look like a broken flashlight."

"You smell so bad. Why can't you eat normal food, weirdo?"

"You little whore. Are those pictures Franco uploaded of you still on porn sites? The internet never forgets. Anyone who ever comes on to you will do it because they know you put out."

My fingers trembled, and I bit down on my lip to suppress a scream. No. I wasn't going to wait until I saw her tomorrow morning. Find out what she had planned for me. Let her control the narrative. I realized suddenly that I was the person I'd been waiting for. The heroine of my own book.

It was time to take control.

Time to stand up for myself.

And for everyone I loved.

CHAPTER SEVENTY-TWO
CAL

"The River of Dreams"—Billy Joel

The Murrays lived in a beautiful, oceanside white shingled mansion. The type of estate that curved around an eight-car limestone drive, with a fountain centerpiece and two Range Rovers parked up front.

Christmas lights wrapped around the edges of the roof and the pillars on either side of the front door. I braced myself against one of the columns, numbness blooming across my exposed skin. I had walked all five miles here. Strangely enough, I didn't feel cold or uncomfortable. Fueled by the burning fire of revenge and hate, I'd plowed through.

Golden chandelier lights spilled from the front windows, and the sounds of clinking utensils and laughter rang through the air. Was I really going to crash this family's holiday dinner? Seemed that way. Even stranger was the fact I didn't feel an ounce of embarrassment about it.

I pressed the doorbell and stepped back, willing my teeth to stop chattering. I'd spent the entire journey here thinking about what witty one-liner I was going to spew once Allison appeared in front of me.

Karma delivery service. You have a package was the front runner. But when the door swung open and an elderly man with shrewd, beady eyes appeared, all the words jumbled in my throat like clothes in a laundry machine. I blinked about a hundred times a minute, my entire face twitching nervously.

Tic, tic, tic.

"Yes?" Allison's father peered at me expectantly, clearly unhappy with the unwelcome Christmas surprise. "Are you going to sing or something? Or is this a donation thing? *Marsha.*" He turned around to bark to the depths of the house. "Do you have any cash on you?"

"I...I... No." I found my voice somewhere in the bottom of my lungs. "I'm here for Allison."

"Allison?" He reared his head back, bushy white eyebrows arched. "What business do you have with my daugh—"

"Oh, Daddy, it's fine." I heard the clink of heels on porcelain approaching. A few seconds later, Allison materialized like a mirage, a red sheath dress draped over her body, complementing her burgundy hair flawlessly. It was a shoulderless piece, paired with a white pearl choker. She looked beautiful yet, at the same time, ugly beyond repair. "I'll take it from here." She kissed his cheek, smiling. "Aw, so protective, what would I do without you?"

It was a dig, and as such, it burrowed straight into my heart, twisting like a sharp knife. She must've heard my dad had passed away. Must have known how much I missed him. Accompanying my pain was a dollop of pity. What a miserable creature must she be, to try to get a rise from a recently fatherless woman.

"Calla. You look"—she swiped her eyes over me aloofly—"like pneumonia in human form. You should really take better care of yourself. You're already...what's the word?" She tapped her pout theatrically. *"Prone to accidents."*

"We need to talk. Privately." I hated how unsure I sounded, even to my own ears—how I couldn't see her properly, my eyes twitched so badly.

Allison examined her bloodred manicure with boredom. "No, thank you. If I let you in, you'll contaminate my entire hou—"

That was it. I hadn't even been here ten seconds and she was already ripping into me. "No more than Tucker Reid would. And he's an engaged man. So unless you want tomorrow's charity event to start with a grand announcement from me about who you've been sleeping with recently, I suggest you let me in."

Her smug expression melted into horror. My hands shaking subsided, and my tics relaxed. I had cracked through her exterior. Broken the first of the many layers she had.

"I've no idea what you're—"

"I have proof," I cut her off. "And a slippery tongue. As you said, I'm...what's the term?" I tapped my lips in the same manner she had a moment ago. *"Prone to accidents."*

Allison peered over my shoulder before jerking her head. "Take your shoes off at the door."

I followed her inside, bypassing a gigantic dining table full of food and her relatives. They all stared at me, dumbfounded. Me being me, I decided to greet them with a little bow and a smile. "Merry Christmas!" And then, because I couldn't possibly contain myself, I gestured to Allison's back and added, "Ho, ho, ho."

This one's for you, Dylan.

"My apologies," Allison muttered, grabbing my wrist and yanking me toward one of the rooms on the first floor. "Urgent matter. Shouldn't take more than a minute."

She shut the door behind us when we reached a guest room. It was probably lovely, but I couldn't see past my panic and determination. I squared my shoulders. She whipped around to face me, knotting her arms over her chest with a scowl. "What on earth makes you think Tucker and I—"

I held up a hand. "I'll be the one asking the questions. If you answer honestly, I just *might* reciprocate. No promises, though."

Allison's face morphed into the exact shade as her dress and hair. She dropped her arms, her hands curling into fists. "Who do you think you—"

"I think I'm the woman who can destroy everything you've ever worked for and will probably do it no matter the outcome of this conversation. I have the receipts. I have the ammo. I have the *witnesses*. Drop the attitude, Allison. We're not in high school anymore."

The more I spoke, the less I ticked. History was on my side. I strode toward her confidently. Allison stumbled back, bumping into a credenza and knocking down a flower vase. She wagged a finger in my face. "You have no proof about the Tucker thing. Don't you dare make up stories about me."

"Sanders confirmed it," I said matter-of-factly, happily throwing the old captain under the bus. After all, all he'd done was speak the truth when he was confronted about it. "He saw you picking Tucker up from the port."

Allison paled. "He needed a rid—"

"Did you know Dylan gave birth the day before he touched land?" I slashed into her words.

Allison's nose twitched, and she faltered. "Well, I mean, what does that have to do with me?"

"Tucker was with you when we tried reaching him. Oh, I almost forgot." I snapped my fingers. "Row knows too."

That made her mouth drop in horror. "You *told* him?"

"Sanders did." I sighed, then patted her arm. "If it makes you feel any better, you didn't stand a chance even before he knew."

Damn, bestie. Look at those claws, I heard Dylan's voice cheering in my head.

"This is insane." She tossed her hands to the ceiling. "Just because I picked Tucker up doesn't mean anything."

"Listen to yourself." I shook my head. "You really think anyone is going to believe you? Tucker has his own truck; he doesn't need a ride. And he deliberately gave Dylan a different return date so he could have a little time with his mistress."

My eyes swept over her body. I was sure I looked as disgusted as I felt. "Out of all the men in town, you had to go for the engaged father-to-be one? And you have the audacity to call *me* a slut?"

I hated the s-word. Had never used it before. But to hurt Allison, I afforded myself this one-off.

Allison's entire demeanor changed. She sneered, trying to seize back control. "Tuck and Dylan don't even like each other!" she growled ferally, tossing her glossy hair over her shoulder. "They never stood a chance. Tuck and I are childhood friends. Our families went on vacations together. We babysat each other's siblings. She was an elaborate booty call that…that…got out of hand! A plaything—"

"It must be so hard to forever come in second place." I jutted out my lower lip, feigning sadness. I wasn't going to stand there and listen to her talking shit about my best friend. "Not with Franco at the time, not Row. Now Tuck made you his sidepiece…" I trailed off, watching her wincing again, getting ready for a blow. "I'm sensing a theme here. Wanna know why?" She didn't, but I was about to tell her anyway. "You're always so busy tearing other women down, you never stop and work on becoming a better one yourself. No one in this town is going to forgive you for running around with an engaged man and a new father. You and Tucker will be written off for good. You will no longer be seen as a pillar of the community. But that's the least of your concerns."

"What do you mean?" Her eyes narrowed into slits. "What other concerns do I have? And just so you know, I'm going to deny it through my teeth and so will Tuck. Besides, there is no such thing as bad publicity. People will play the did-she or-didn't-she guessing game before letting it go and moving on."

"All right." I shrugged. "Let's say you can survive the reputational damage—nice delusion, by the way, really complements your dress—you still have the small problem of having to defend yourself from the criminal charges that will be pressed against you for sending people to stab Row."

Allison tipped her head back, laughing manically. I hoped she was a better mayor than she was an actress because she wasn't about to win any Oscars for this performance. "You're making some grand accusations here, don't you think, little Calla? Seems like you forgot your place in the world—you're the girl with the tics and social anxiety who is so scared of her own shadow, she can't even look people in the eye. No one will believe you."

"Why wouldn't they believe me?" I placed a hand on my hip. "After all, it's not the first time you tried to have someone killed." I motioned toward myself for emphasis. "Although, I have to say, you do a really bad job of offing people. I'm glad you didn't choose it as a career path. Your Yelp page would be a disaster."

Allison rolled her eyes, which glimmered with unshed tears. She shook her head. "Don't be so dramatic. We were dumb kids. No one tried to kill you. We were just messing around."

"You let me crawl back to safety with a shattered bone, covered in mud and dirt."

She stomped. "You survived, didn't you?"

"No thanks to you. And your little minions are grown women now. If I drag them to trial and make them testify, they'll sell you out in no time. The statute of limitations hasn't passed for our case. I checked."

Every night before I'd gone to bed for the past eight years, to be exact. My true crime love was partially due to the fact I had almost gotten killed myself. I had nearly become a statistic. Something you heard about in podcasts. That had inspired me to look closely into my own case.

Every obsession had an origin. I suppose I owed this to Allison—she'd helped me figure out what I really wanted to do with my life.

Allison's back was plastered against the door now. I hadn't even realized I was ambling toward her and she was retreating farther away from me.

"Good luck stitching this case up." She gasped, a thin layer of sweat covering her face. A knock came from the other side of the door, making her jump in surprise.

"Everything okay in there, ladies?" a female voice—her mother?—inquired in a fake singsong voice.

I arched an eyebrow toward my nemesis, who inhaled a greedy breath. "Yeah, Mom. Fine."

"Do you need me to—"

"Leave me alone!" Allison barked, looking and sounding like a mean teenager again. "Just go away."

At least now I knew Allison didn't discriminate when it came to being a brat. Everybody got the same treatment. She waited until the padding of feet on carpet diminished before picking up where we'd left off. "You were saying?"

"I'm saying you sent people to threaten and stab Row," I said calmly.

"And how did you reach this conclusion?" She barked out a laugh, folding her arms.

"Glad you asked." My eyes bore into hers, and I was no longer nervous. I'd found my strength. It had been there all along. Buried deep inside me. "When I went to visit Row at the hospital, I thought about who could do such a thing. Only someone with high stakes. And who is going to suffer the most if he sells the lot? You, as the mayor. All anger would be directed at you. Plus, I knew you had the guts to go the extra mile to make a statement. So far, so circumstantial. But I decided to do a little digging myself." Specifically, I had asked Taylor to give me access to the restaurant's security cameras that showed the edge of the car the attackers had disappeared into.

I reached for my coat, pulling out the footage I'd printed out and a paper I had scribbled at home before I came here. "This is the part where I should tell you that, unfortunately, you messed with a true crime junkie. One with a passion for unearthing and solving mysteries. I'm a long-standing member of an amateur crime-solving forum and posted the picture, asking if there were experts who could help me figure out the make of the car. Turned out that it was an Acura RLX, which is widely unpopular in our part of the woods. Only eighty-three Acura RLXs are currently registered in Maine, and out of them, only seven are in our area. Since I could clearly tell the car was dark—navy or black—I found the license plate and the man it belonged to in no time.

"Niall Burks is the husband of your assistant, Lucinda, and the owner of the car. The person who normally drives it is his stepson, who lives all the way down in Massachusetts—which I guess was why you thought he wouldn't be recognized—but that's some interesting connection." I offered her the papers I was holding. She tore them into shreds without looking at them. Staring at her pitifully, I let out a sigh. "That's okay. I have extras."

Allison knew she was caught. Her mouth screwed into a grimace; her eyes were five times their normal size. Her sins had finally caught up with her, and not a moment too soon.

"Lucinda and Niall have their own reservations about this deal Row decided to go for. I have nothing to do with it."

"He already signed the contract." I smiled, putting the final nail in her coffin. Her body wilted with dread. "And if that's the case, then I'm going to have Sheriff Menchin go directly to them. Hope they have good legal representation. How lucky are you?" I stepped forward, wiping invisible dust off her shoulder. She flinched. "So many wrongdoings around you, and yet you are totally innocent. I'm sure your track teammates, Tucker, Lucinda, Niall, and Sanders are going to be totally on board with your version of things."

I made a move to open the door. Her hand came clamping down on my wrist. Desperation clung to her face as she tried to tug me back to her. "No, wait."

I popped an eyebrow. "Yes?"

"How do I make all of this…go away?" Her nose twitched. "Give me a number."

A number? She thought I could be bought? "Nine one one." I laughed.

"Oh, come on." She rolled her eyes. "Be serious."

"I am serious. It's not about money."

"Everything is about money."

I turned to walk away again. She slid between me and the door, blocking my way.

"I want you to know," I said slowly, "that I will not be intimidated again. If you try to hurt me like you did when we were teenagers, I'm going to break every bone in your body in self-defense."

Having these words come out of my mouth had a healing effect on me. They made me feel powerful and strong, a woman who didn't need a Prince Charming—who was her own savior.

Allison licked her lips nervously, raising her palms in the air. "I'm not going to hurt you. I just want to talk. How do I make this disappear? Obviously, I'm not going to jail."

Why was it so obvious? Her rich white woman privilege was through the freaking roof.

"You can't make this go away." I shook my head. "This is not an uncomfortable headline. This is about people's *lives*. Your entire existence, you've been running people over to get your way. Well, I'm not letting you off the hook. Your best shot is to come clean to everyone in town, tell them what you did to Row, and then to back off, face the consequences."

She looked disgusted, like I had just suggested she bathe in dog vomit on national television. "Why would I fess up if you are not offering me anything in exchange?"

"I *am* offering you something in exchange," I said. "If you confess to what you did to Row and me, I will spare you the humiliation of outing you and Tucker in public. You'll be known as a thug, not a hussy. That's the best and only offer I will give you."

"You're crazy if you think I'll go for it."

I shrugged, making my third attempt to reach the door. She sighed, knocking the back of her head repeatedly against the wood. "I could be thrown into prison."

"You'll fit in there better than you think."

"You don't understand." She pushed a hand into her hair, raking her fingers through her luscious locks. "You really don't. I couldn't…I couldn't let Row's deal go forward."

"The deal wasn't your fault as a mayor." Why was I comforting her? She was Satan's formidable adversary. "Yet you had people put a dead coyote on his property, send him hate mail, slash his tires. He thought the entire town was against him. Did you do all of those things yourself?"

"No!" she said desperately. "I…I… Lucinda's stepson…"

It hadn't been Lyle. Or Randy. Or any of Row's suspects. It had been an out-of-towner. All this time, he had been tormented by a man hired by Allison.

"It's a good deal," I continued, trying to wrap my head around what had made her do something so stupid and dangerous. "You're evil, but you aren't stupid. Surely, you knew once the dust settled on this thing, people would see there were benefits to the mall and the hotel too."

"It wasn't just about the backlash." She shook her head, her tears falling freely now. "I could've handled that. My dad wanted the deal to fall through so that GS Properties would buy *his* lots." She sniffled, wiping her nose with the sleeve of her dress. "He's in a dire financial situation. Some of the investments he made were… not smart, to say the least. I wanted to back Row off from selling so my dad could get a shot at saving his own skin. He'd been in contact with this Blackthorn guy, trying to sway him to buy his lots. Part of the reason he went bankrupt is because he spent so much on my election campaign. He bled money to make it happen."

I took a jagged breath and closed my eyes. I was definitely *not* feeling sympathetic toward her. "Row has his own business to take care of."

Allison waved a hand, growling tiredly. "Row is TV gold. His name precedes him. He'd have made the money back in six months if he passed on the deal. He's on the fast track to becoming a billionaire, and nothing can stop him, least of all me." She couldn't keep the bitterness from her voice. "That's why I tried so damn hard with him. He was another option out of the financial mess I put my family in when I ran for mayor. The man wouldn't budge. Just as well. He's…not nice."

"No, he isn't," I agreed. "He is something better than nice—he is kind. He won't tell you what you want to hear. Actually, he'd rarely do that. But he'd always do right by you. And what about Tucker?"

"Tucker isn't nice either," she snorted.

Christ with this woman. "I mean, what's your relationship like?" I asked slowly.

"Tucker and I are in *love*." She tossed her hands in the air. "It's just the timing that messed everything up. He wanted to break things off with Dylan the week she told him she was pregnant. There's no love lost between those two. I think they're both equally miserable together."

I couldn't argue with that one, especially considering Dylan's reaction to the news Tucker was cheating on her.

"But you still tried to be with Row." My eyebrows slammed together.

She looked at me blankly, like she didn't understand why this was peculiar to me. "What does love have to do with marriage? The two don't have to coexist."

"You've always been evil," I said, to myself more than to her. "What you did to me in high school scarred me for life."

"About that…" She stared at her feet pensively, licking her lips. "Calla, I—"

Another knock on the door snapped us out of our trance. Allison's father, this time. "Al, need any help?"

Tears clung onto her eyelids as she stared at me. She shook her head silently, as if he could see her. "No," she croaked, barely audible. "I'm fine, Daddy."

We both took a breath before she continued. "Franco. He…"

She gulped, shaking her head. "We were together when you started hooking up. I..." She closed her eyes, one tear escaping past her lashes. "I...I was pregnant."

The whole room began spinning, rapidly spiraling downward, toward a black, bottomless abyss. He had been two-timing us?

"That day...in the woods...i-it was the day after I found out. I was rabid. I was so mad. At him. At myself. At you. You were the other woman, the one standing in my way to a happily ever after. In my mind, we stood a shot. Only I guess you didn't know that."

"And the baby?" I choked out. I still thought she was a horrible person. It was her choice to take the worst road possible when faced with a problem. But I no longer felt she was carelessly malicious.

She pressed her head against the door, sliding along the wooden surface all the way to the floor. "My father forced me to have an abortion."

"I...I'm sorry." And I was. For the girl she had been. And for the woman she'd become as a result of everything that had happened.

"Yeah. So am I. Most days, anyway."

I bit my lower lip, trying hard not to cry myself. "You could've communicated this to me."

"I really couldn't, though." She looked up, trying to control the tears. "I had to take this secret with me to the grave. Before you dug it out, that is. Yeah, I took my anger out on you. Yeah, it was... horrific. But no one knows what it's like to be me, okay? The expectations. The arm-bending. Being at your entire family's beck and call. *You* didn't have that. You walked around school *proud* that your dad was the kooky, fanny-packed physics teacher with the reading glasses that were taped together with Scotch tape."

"Why wouldn't I be?" I blinked, surprised. This time it wasn't a tic—it was pure confusion. "He was the coolest thing a person could be—unapologetically himself."

She gave me the sad smile of a woman who knew she had lost the battle—and the war. "See? That was why I was jealous of you.

Because of silly things like that. And here I was…with all these rules to follow. I needed to be the best. And I just got…*tired*." She let her head drop between her hands. "So I decided to be ruthless."

"Well, you are going to have to be something you haven't tried so far. *Honest*. And tomorrow seems like the perfect time." I stepped around her, nudging her to open the door. "If you won't tell people, I will. *Kul kalb biji yomo*."

"What does it mean?" She glanced up, wiping her nose.

"Every dog shall have his day."

CHAPTER SEVENTY-THREE
CAL

"I Try"—Macy Gray

Everyone stared at me.

That included pets, small children, and out-of-towners who had come to support the 10K for Kiddies charity run.

"What're y'all staring at?" Dylan stomped along the police barriers that bracketed the road, Grav strapped to her chest, bundled in her BabyBjörn. Posters for small businesses that sponsored the event were plastered along the barricades, and the Christmas crowd was thick and festive, nursing hot cocoa with extra marshmallows. "Never seen a woman running before?"

It wasn't that I was running that made people do a double take, though. It was that I was doing it wearing a neon-yellow windbreaker, neon-purple leggings, rainbow sneakers, and my mom's technicolor mittens. I looked like I'd been vomited up by a unicorn. Glass half-full: if I veered off course and got lost, they could probably detect me from space.

"How do I look?" I asked Dylan, running in place by the barricades.

"Like my firstborn's godmother." She winked, grinning.

My breath hitched. "Really?"

"Totally." She adjusted Grav's beanie on her tiny head. "Hey, it's only fair you get more responsibilities, now that I dumped Tuck."

"How are you feeling, Callichka?" Mom yelled from across the fence.

I nodded to her. "Perfect, Mamushka."

"Focus on your breath," Zeta instructed seriously, standing next to Dylan. We were going to run a circle around the town and come back to the exact point we'd started from. There were maybe a thousand runners from all across the state. I looked around, trying to spot Row, but couldn't find him. Instead, I saw Allison, huddled in a corner with her dad and her former BFFs from the track team. They were all whispering and pointing at me. Allison looked cheerful, all perky and festive, like our conversation had never happened. To make matters worse—because they were always worse where I was involved—the number plastered on my back—you guessed it—was sixty-nine.

You can do it.

For Dad.

No, not just for Dad. For yourself too.

"Five minutes to go!" someone announced into a megaphone.

"Break a leg, Dot!" Dylan two-thumbs-upped me.

"Knowing me, I think you can count on it." I stretched and twisted, ignoring my bullies, my trauma, my past, which was right there beside me.

"Don't you dare!" Dylan wiggled a finger in my direction. "You're Cal Litvin and you are as tough as a diamond, baby! Show these girls what you're made of!"

The horn tooted noisily, ringing between my ears, and before I knew what was happening, my feet carried me forward, fast and wobbly. It took me a few minutes to gain my balance. To realize what was happening.

Then, I became steadier. More confident. I soared, hovering over the ground, feeling invincible. The air rolled into my lungs, clean and fresh, and I took it in greedily. I was alert but not scared. And I realized that without even trying, I was passing people left and right, until there was no one beside me and I was leading the race.

Once I let go of my fear, I shed it like snakeskin, letting it drop to the side of the road as I plowed through.

It took me less than an hour to return to the starting point, leaving everyone else far behind me. I almost wanted to stall when I spotted the barricades, cheering people, and hot cocoa stands. I didn't want the run to end. But as I inched closer, the pitter-pattering of my heart had nothing to do with the run and everything to do with the man standing behind the barricades, holding a glittery, totally nineties-inspired sign that said:

McMonster: oBITCHuary, I like your stamina. CALL ME!

It was in the same chat format we were used to, nestled inside a blue bubble.

I nearly stumbled over my feet, laughing hysterically, wiping the sweat off my eyes so I could see him better. Row waved the sign high, holding it above his head with that panty-melting, opaque smirk of his. There was a cigarette tucked in the corner of his mouth, and if that wasn't the most Row thing I'd ever seen, I didn't know what was.

I sliced through the red ribbon that was stretched across the road, pumping my fist in the air.

"You did it!" Mom squealed from the sidelines.

"I won!" Dylan did a little dance beside her, blowing a raspberry at my old track team members. "I did it. Victory is mine. Pay up, suckers!"

"Row!" Somehow, I found myself running straight toward him. I didn't even care about people watching. He discarded the sign and ran toward me. We met halfway. I jumped on top of him, lacing my legs around his waist and hugging him close. He smelled of cigarettes and winter and pure masculinity. I never wanted to let go.

"I'm so fucking proud of you," he murmured into my sticky, sweaty hair.

"I'm so proud of me too." *Maybe* I was a little tingly in places I didn't have the right to be tingly in. "And not just because I did Dad proud in heaven."

He withdrew his face from my hair, pushing my wet hair out of my face. "Why else?"

"Because I stood up to Allison."

He pulled back, frowning. "When did you have the time?"

"Christmas dinner."

"Dot, you *savage*." He squeezed my waist. God, I hated that we were going to be friends now. Platonic. Cordial. I wanted his all.

"Row?" I asked. He lowered me down to my feet. Adrenaline still coursed through my veins when our eyes met. "She was the one who sent those people after you. She did...*everything*."

"I know."

"You do?" I cocked my head sideways, surprised.

He nodded. "She came over to my house late last night, probably after you paid her a visit. Looked like a wreck. Came clean. Begged me not to press charges."

"And?" I held my breath, my eyes unwavering, studying his face.

"And I'm fucking thrilled you stood up for yourself because now I can finally get my pound of flesh."

With perfect timing, Sheriff Menchin breezed past us, escorted by his cronies. He sailed straight to the corner where Allison and her mother stood.

"Allison Murray, you are under arrest for conspiracy, aggravated assault, and election fraud. You have the right to remain silent. Anything you say can and will be used against you in a court of law..."

CHAPTER SEVENTY-FOUR
ROW

oBITCHuary: Thank you for being there for me.

McMonster: I will always be there for you, regardless of what we are.

McMonster: How did it feel?

oBITCHuary: Like coming full circle.

McMonster: Well, if you want to come in any other way, you know where to find me...

oBITCHuary: Very mature.

McMonster: I never claimed to be mature.

oBITCHuary: What do you claim to be, then?

McMonster: Unfortunately, yours.

CHAPTER SEVENTY-FIVE
ROW

I oftentimes thought of my life as a string of unfortunate events, sparsely punctuated by orgasmic food, pompous TV executives, and my mother asking me if I was wearing a sweater. The shittery that was my luck could not be further highlighted than on January first, when I found myself sharing a cab with Cal, which took us straight to the airport.

Friends, my ass. I still wanted to feast on her pussy and fill her everywhere with my fingers, cock, and tongue.

Naturally, our flights were only an hour apart, so our families had urged us to ride there together. "That way, Cal won't have to pay for a cab. You are very poor, aren't you, *bambina*?" My mother possessed a lot of positive traits, but a filter wasn't one of them.

"They do make a point." Cal had winced, glancing at me. "I mean, we can eliminate some of our carbon footprint?"

I didn't have the heart to tell her I regularly rented private planes to run errands, or that I had owned seven cars simultaneously while living in Paris. Instead, I had nodded stoically. Now here we were, twenty-four hours later, crammed in the backseat of a yellow Ford Galaxy, buried in duffel bags and backpacks, with Cal using an enthusiastic voice while the driver told her earnestly about how a week ago, some dudebro had tried to short him ten bucks for a ride, so the driver had pulled out his gun and told the dudebro to give him everything in his wallet. *Including* some credit cards, a picture of his mom, and a condom. I didn't know if Cal was aware we were listening to a tale of a man who'd robbed his customer and was too frightened to point it out or if it flew right over her head. Either way, I scooted close to her in case she needed me to take a bullet for her. Forever the knight in chef jacket's armor.

"Anyway. So. Thanks for the super fun conversation," she muttered, plastering her shoulder to mine. Yup. Her creep-o-meter was definitely dinging. "I'm getting sleepy. Are you getting sleepy, Row?"

"No," I said aloofly. "Wide-awake and as alert as a fucking dog who heard a can opening."

"I think I'll take a little silent nap." She ignored me, squeezing her eyes shut like a child to stop the conversation. Unfortunately, with Cal being Cal, she really did fall asleep on my shoulder for the remainder of the journey to the airport, which meant I had to deal both with an impending heartbreak and an erection from hell.

An hour later, we were dropped at the airport. Cal checked her watch. A pink Casio with pastel-colored numbers and no frills. "We still have time for a coffee together." Her gaze was hopeful.

We did. But I didn't want to prolong the inevitable. Didn't want to spend another second with the woman I knew was going to walk away with a piece of my heart.

I slung my duffel bag over my shoulder, shaking my head. "I think I'm going to catch up on emails in the first-class lounge."

Her face fell. I knew she liked spending time together. She liked the banter, the talks into the night, the running, the orgasms—she just didn't want to put her heart at risk. I accepted that. Respected that, even. But I didn't have to fucking like it.

"I understand." She swallowed. We stopped in front of TSA. Three feet apart. The bustling of people running in all directions to make it to their flights drowned us in noise. "Seriously, you've been nothing but amazing to me. With the employment…and the running...and the sex. And I didn't reciprocate." There was a beat. "Other than the sex part—I was a goddamn nymph and we both know it." She held up her chin.

She thought she hadn't done shit for me? That was ridiculous. I stepped forward, driving the point home one more time.

"Let me make something very clear here—I love cooking. I love traveling. I love money." I took a breath. "But I love you more than all of those things combined. That won't change tomorrow, next month, or next year. You've given me in eight weeks what I haven't had in twenty-six years. You've given me smiles, laughs, warmth, and hope. But I have to protect my own heart too, and right now, spending time with you is killing me. If, one day, be it near or far, you change your mind, you know where to find me. Until then, it's all or nothing. And I'll take nothing over something."

"I understand." Her voice was strained, and she raked her fingers over her hair. "Jesus, I hate myself for not throwing caution to the wind and just going for it. What's wrong with me?"

Someone bumped their shoulder against mine on their run to catch a flight. I smirked. "Nothing's wrong with you. You're perfect just the way you are. Hey, I got you a goodbye gift." I slid the duffel bag from my shoulder and unzipped it, rummaging to find a box the size of a cigarette pack. I tossed it into her hands. She caught it midair, about to pry it open.

"No." I snapped it shut before she could take a peek. "Open it when you get back home."

She arched an eyebrow. "I'm flattered that you think I possess that kind of self-control, but have you ever seen me next to a Cinnabon box?"

"If the time in Staindrop has taught me anything, Dot, it's that you possess a lot of things you don't know you do. That's why I didn't spear Allison's head after you told me what happened between you two. Because I knew it was your fight to fight. And you did it. You stood up to your bully and you annihilated her. You showed yourself that you can. That you always could. You broke the cycle and didn't let the cycle break *you*. You are a fucking rock star, and I want you to remember that every time you doubt yourself. That there's a guy out there in the world who worships the ground you walk upon. That you marked him so thoroughly, he'll never forget you." I grabbed her hand and laced our fingers together. We both looked down, and she noticed the new tattoo on my inner forearm. Of a perfect, round dot. She closed her eyes, fighting tears.

"I want you to know, Ambrose Casablancas, that if I could ever be with anyone, it would be with you."

I smiled, letting go of her fingers, drifting away, apart. "I know, Dot. I know."

CHAPTER SEVENTY-SIX
CAL

oBITCHuary: Hey.
<The user McMonster is no longer active>

CHAPTER SEVENTY-SEVEN
CAL

"Everybody Hurts"—R.E.M.

I spent the flight from Maine to New York crying hysterically in my seat, smearing saliva, snot, and other bodily fluids onto the window. The person sitting next to me was so alarmed and uncomfortable, he took four stretch-your-limbs walks on an hour-and-a-half flight.

I should have been elated Allison had finally gotten hers. Karma had delivered a knockout blow. My childhood enemy had to pay $50K in bail as she awaited trial for what she'd done to me and Row.

Speaking of Row—his good reputation in Staindrop had been restored. Mom texted me that everybody now realized that the deal had always been good for the town. It was all Mayor Murray's manipulative spin that had gotten people reeling. Word had gotten out and spread like fire in a desert field. The fact that Allison had done the walk of shame into jail helped. But what also helped was that awful Tate guy, who'd decided to send his lovely assistant to one of the town hall meetings and explain what they should expect. She had brought blueprints, renderings, and even did an entire presentation. It turned out that when you were transparent and open with people, they really did come to the table with open hearts and minds.

Glass half-full? I was relieved to leave an encouraged and strong Mom behind. Before I'd left, I'd opened her an Etsy seller account and had even taken super cute pictures of her mittens from all angles. Her first order had come through half an hour after the store was up and running. We'd both jumped up and down and screamed in each other's faces for five minutes straight.

I'd never told her it had come from a friend in New York who I'd specifically asked to purchase the mittens. I had Venmoed her beforehand to show her I was good for the money.

Glass half-empty? I was devastated to say goodbye to Row. But, I reminded myself, the last eight weeks had been nothing but a weird, roller-coaster experience. The job, the affair, the running... I was just confused. On sensory overload. Yup. That must have been it. I would go back to New York and return to my normal, curated life. Where boys were unwelcome and I was safe to procrastinate in the comfort of my own home.

And by *home*, I meant *apartment*.

Okay, *shoebox*.

All I needed was to slide back into my routine. To my job as a waitress. To good tips. To writing, then deleting, then giving myself excuses for why I didn't record my first podcast episode. I'd lived my entire adult life without Row Casablancas and survived just fine. He wasn't going to turn everything upside down on me because of a few orgasms, a heartfelt love declaration, and two tattoos of me. I wasn't so easily swayed.

I stumbled out of the plane straight into the arms of a snowstorm. It took me three hours to get to my apartment, which greeted me with a stench more fitting an assortment of rotten bodies jammed inside a sewer. I didn't have a pet, did I? No, I was sure I'd have remembered adopting one. Who had died, then, and more importantly—what had made them think it was okay to do so at my place?

The answer to that question presented itself in my kitchen, when I realized I had taken out my milk with every intention of throwing it away before leaving but had ended up just leaving it on the counter. The red carton had molded at the edges, its mouth adorned with green crusty milk, a halo of flies flying around it. *Back to my glamorous life, it is.*

"You're fine. It's just bad luck," I singsonged to myself as I wrapped the carton in a garbage bag, triple-tied it, and threw it in the trash can. I then cracked a window to let the air circulate, took a quick shower, slipped into super warm and comfy clothes, and made my way downstairs to the bodega to stock up on necessities. In necessities I also included a two-buck, discounted wine I polished off in front of *Love Is Blind*. This wasn't a cry for help. This was a wail that could probably have been heard in parallel universes.

Was love blind? I didn't think so. If it hadn't been for Row's and my mutual attraction, I would have never found out that beneath the grumpiness and dry one-liners hid my favorite person.

Truth was, love was the best or worst thing that could ever happen to you. It all depended on whether you had the courage to accept it. I turned off the TV and tossed my head against the back of the couch, letting out a groan. Maybe everything felt off because I still hadn't slid back into my old routine. I took my phone out and texted my previous boss at the eatery I'd worked for.

> Cal: Hey, Steven! It's Cal. I'm back in town. Any work available for me? Looking for full-time. Thanks

He answered after less than a minute.

> Steven: Hey, Cal. Yes. We need someone full-time who is willing to pull some double shifts sometimes. Should I put you on next week's schedule?
> Cal: Yes, please.
> Steven: How about that date I've been vying for, for the past three years?
> Cal: No, thank you.
> Steven: Hey, doesn't hurt to ask! LOL

Unless you've asked that every day since we met while I was still in college. Then it's just creepy.

See? All good. Great, even.

I made myself ramen with an egg in it, snapping a picture of the culinary miracle and sending it to Taylor, who'd always tried talking me into giving my food a facelift. He answered almost immediately.

> Taylor: Does that mean you're going to start using garlic and scallions like an actual grown-up?
> Cal: Let's not get ahead of ourselves. I'm still drinking Kool-Aid with this meal.

I put on my favorite true crime podcast. I waited for the pesky feeling of hollowness to leave me. It didn't, so I called Mamushka. Talked to her for twenty minutes. She was working on a new mitten collection, eating orange cake, and sipping tea. She sounded normal. *Happy.* I hung up, pulling my lips into a smile and convincing myself that it was real.

Nope. I was still feeling hollow.

You're probably just exhausted from the last two months. Better call it an early night and try again tomorrow, a voice inside me soothed. Another voice, that sounded uncannily like Dylan, snorted out, *It's only six o'clock in the evening, and you know exactly why you're like that, bitch.*

I rubbed at my forehead, sitting in my tiny kitchen, convincing myself that I hadn't made the biggest mistake of my life.

"You're still you," I told myself aloud. "Scared of men. Scared of relationships. Scared of life."

I washed my bowl of ramen, crawled into bed, and forced myself to sleep, hoping tomorrow would never come.

CHAPTER SEVENTY-EIGHT
CAL

"Closing Time"—Semisonic

I woke up in a pool of my own tears. They soaked through my oversized Columbia sweatshirt, dampening the pillow beneath me until it flattened.

The first thing I did, before even opening my eyes, was shoot a hand to my nightstand and pat it for my phone. Once found, I unhooked it from the charger and blinked at the screen, checking to see if Row had sent me any texts. He hadn't. Instead, I got his half-civilized sister:

> Dylan: OMG I think she just smiled at me!!! For the very first time. What do you think?
> <Dylan Casablancas sent an attachment>
> Dylan: NVM. She was just passing gas. According to Google she has a couple more months before she starts doing that.
> Dylan: Smiling, not passing gas. She passes gas ALL the time. I cannot stress this enough, we need to keep an eye on this girl or she'll NEVER find a date.
> Dylan: In other news, I just mustered the courage to look at my C-section scar in the mirror. It looks like

my stomach is smiling. Like, straight-up laughing. The
belly button is the nose and my tits are the eyes.
Dylan: But you know who isn't smiling? ME. No one's
ever going to date me. Should we start a women-only
commune? I can create an interest form.

I tossed a hand over my eyes and groaned in frustration. I
didn't know why I was so surprised Row hadn't reached out. He'd
said he wouldn't. Even deactivated his account on Androphobes
Anonymous. *All or nothing.* And the "all" option scared me to death.
I couldn't even commit to making a damn podcast, and true crime
was pretty much my entire being.

Row, Row, Row. Beautiful, raw Row.

What was he doing? What was he thinking? His new restaurant
was due to open really soon. That reminded me...hadn't he given me
a box to open when I got home? I was home now. Even though this
place felt like anything but.

Before brushing my teeth, I ran to my backpack, discarded by
the door, and retrieved the small box. My fingers shook when I slid
it open. What could he possibly have given me? Money? A family
heirloom? A *ring*?

*Sure. He didn't want to have coffee with you yesterday, but he got you
a ring. Order that Vera Wang catalog right away, honey.*

But when I opened the box, all I saw was a...key? An insignificant, small silver thing. The type to fit the cheapest door lock. I
reached to finger it, and felt a bump underneath the red velvet it was
swimming in. There was something else under the key. I set it down
and uncurled the rich fabric, pushing it aside.

117 York Avenue, Lenox Hill
Don't google the address, just go.

—*Row*

I choked on the orb of emotions jamming my throat.

This man challenged me every step of the way. What would life with him be like? Full of surprises. And sex. And laughs. *Happy.* Did I deserve happiness? Or had I turned my back on him because I never believed I could have it in the first place?

Even though I was the nosiest human recorded on earth, I didn't have it in me not to follow his instructions. What if he was there, wherever it was? Waiting for me on one knee, ready to ask for my hand in marriage?

Then he'll have to make himself comfortable and wait a little longer. I had to fix myself to minimize the chances of him getting fined for littering for standing next to me.

I immediately proceeded to glam up. I washed, dried, and curled my hair to perfection. Contoured my face to its last inch. I wore my most flattering pair of jeans, pairing them with trendy, non-neon boots. Put on an elegant jacket that did not offend entire continents.

The whole time I got ready, I had no doubt in my mind that Row would be waiting for me. That this was all an elaborate way to win my heart.

But as I settled into my seat on the subway, my Body Shop perfume mixing with the greasy takeout the person next to me was scarfing down, I began second-guessing myself.

First of all, I *knew* he had gotten on a plane to London yesterday. He'd mentioned an early morning meeting with Tate, and Row wasn't the type to screw people over.

Second, he hadn't seemed on the verge of trying to win me over yesterday. On the contrary, he'd put the ball firmly in my empty, stupid, dead-grassed court.

Third, it just wasn't Row's speed—begging for affection. We all made peace with the treatment we believed we deserved. Ambrose Casablancas knew his worth. And he was worth more than a flaky woman who was scared to have feelings.

He loved me, I knew. Was crazy about me, even, and would

always, *always* be there for me if I needed him. But he wasn't going to chase me around like a puppy.

Then what was the key in my hand supposed to symbolize? Where was I going?

I got off the train and walked the rest of the way to the address on the mangled piece of paper. The crisp winter air slapped my face, and my fingers were frozen to the point of numbness. Manhattan felt extra lonely, if only because I knew we didn't share a city.

The journey took forever, and yet in no time at all, I stood in front of a low redbrick building. My eyes stung, the ice-cold air scorching a path down to my lungs.

Soundbound Recording Studio: Recording, Mixing, Mastering. Make Your Dream Your Reality!

I knew Row wasn't waiting for me on the other side of the door. He didn't have to. He was doing the most chivalrous thing of all—chasing my dream for me.

I sank to my knees and began sobbing.

CHAPTER SEVENTY-NINE
CAL

"Doo Wop"—Lauryn Hill

Ten minutes later, I was standing in front of a bored-looking receptionist, eyes puffy, cheeks storm-struck. God, was I going to cry all day, every day like a *This Is Us* character?

I waved the key in my hand. "I, uhm, got this?"

I was blinking and twitching like crazy. Strangely enough, I didn't care anymore. It was like once I'd experienced being truly and thoroughly loved by a man whose love I valued, I had genuinely started believing my own hype.

So what if I had tics? I also had great boobs and a quirky sense of humor. And I could pickle *anything*. I was a damn good catch. Case in point—I had gotten the hottest man in the world hooked.

"Wow. A key." Her eyes assessed me coolly behind thick-rimmed reading glasses, voice dripping sarcasm. "Good for you. Now all you need is a door." She was in her late twenties, completely tattooed, with bright red lipstick and super short bangs. *Tough audience.*

"I think it's a key to one of the rooms here. I…er, a friend got me this to encourage me to record…" I was about to say *something* before Row's voice in my head demanded I own it. "My true crime podcast."

"*Oh*. It's you!" She perked up, looking up from her phone and gulping me in, sizing me up. "Chef Casablancas told us all about you. Calla, right? Oh my God, he said you are a true crime expert. My cousin was murdered when she was sixteen!"

Oh. 'Kay. "Great." I plastered on a smile. "I mean, not great. Awful. Terrible. So sorry for your loss."

"Don't worry." She waved a hand. "I didn't even know her. He said you were the most beautiful girl in the world. That's how I was supposed to recognize you."

Don't you dare cry again, Cal. Pull yourself together.

"I'm…glad he spoke fondly about me."

"He booked you an entire room for a month. Said not to let you out before you finish recording and editing a podcast." She stood up, brushing cracker crumbs from her black dress.

I stared at her, dumbfounded.

She laughed. "Look at your face! Don't worry, we'll let you out. But seriously, he is so awesome. Also paid for five editing sessions with our producer, Tom. That should have you covered. He'll show you the ropes. You need to book him in advance, though."

My first thought was that I couldn't do one-on-one sessions with a man and that I should find a girlfriend to bring over to those appointments. But my second thought was…why not? In the past eight weeks, I'd been kissed by Kieran, devoured by Row, and had found myself in close quarters with men all the time. Without even realizing it, I had faced my fear. What's more, I had *braved* it.

"Wait, so…when can I come in?" I was waiting for the panic to settle in my stomach, but it didn't happen. All I felt was excitement to start working on this. I was going to record my own episode about the Towpath Murders. A little English twist as a homage to Row, who was in London now.

"Anytime." She shrugged, rounding the reception area and hooking her finger, motioning for me to follow her. "As I said before, he booked you a room for an entire month. All hours of the day or night. We're open twenty-four hours, by the way." She guided me through a long, dark corridor full of doors, stopping in front of one. She turned to face me, opening her palm expectedly. I deposited the key in her hand. She twisted it inside the keyhole. "We have a contract I'm going to email you that you need to sign. Terms and conditions. Basically, don't eat here, get drunk or high, trash the place, or have sex in it. How does that sound?"

"Ridiculously doable." I snorted, getting extremely giddy about the entire thing.

"You'd be surprised." She pushed the door open. "He had the room made for you. Hope you like it."

I gingerly took a step inside and flicked the light on. Put a hand to my heart. Then collapsed against the wall with a gasp. "No. He didn't."

"Did too. Took him all night long." The receptionist propped a shoulder on the doorframe. "You must give great head. Do you have, like, tutorials or something? All I got for my five-year anniversary with my boyfriend was a Starbucks gift card."

Laughter bubbled out of my throat. The walls were completely covered in genuine articles about murders, mysteries, and crime scenes. *All* from the nineties. All yellow and worn-out. There were dozens of them. A skull-shaped mug rested by the screen, next to a brand-new coffee machine and a scented candle that looked like a skeleton in a milk bath, chilling.

"By the way, you totally can't light that." She pointed at the candle. "Fire isn't allowed, no matter how small and controlled."

The corners of my eyes burned with unshed tears, and I was laughing and crying at the same time, because apparently, I was no longer in control of my own emotions.

"How did he manage this?" I whispered. "He wasn't even in New York this week."

"Yeah, he was." She frowned, giving me a strange look. "Christmas Eve."

Christmas Eve? The last night of Descartes? The most important evening for his former restaurant, and he had chosen to be away and do…this?

"It was so cool. Came in with all of these newspapers and nineties horror movie posters and two handsome friends." Taylor and Rhy, I bet. "Charmed everyone's pants off and worked all night." A dreamy sigh escaped her lips before she cleared her throat and straightened her back. "As a figure of speech. No pants were dropped. He is clearly obsessed with you."

"Yeah." I looked around us. "Clearly, he is."

"You're so lucky. True love is hard to come by."

Even harder to keep, I thought, *especially when you are me.*

CHAPTER EIGHTY
CAL

Cal: Hey! How are the preparations for the restaurant going?

Cal: Hi. Just checking in. Miss you.

Cal: Hello. I just wanted to thank you for the studio you rented out for me. Very unexpected. I've been recording and editing like crazy. I'll send you the first episode when it's ready.

Cal: Hi. Saw you on TV today! So cool. You're doing another season of *Chef's Kiss*! Just don't go around kissing anyone for real, HAHAHAHHAA.

Cal: Not that you can't, obviously.

Cal: You don't owe me anything.

Cal: Not that I have been doing any kissing or otherwise any...mouth things with people.

Cal: Speaking of mouth, excuse me while I shove a foot into mine. I'll stop bothering you now. Hope you are having the best start of the year <3.

CHAPTER EIGHTY-ONE
CAL

"You Get What You Give"—New Radicals

If you ever wondered how long it takes to produce a one-hour-and-fifteen-minute podcast, the (unlikely) answer is seven and a half hours.

Yup. Four days later, I finally did it. I recorded and edited a full true crime episode of *Hot Girl Bummer*. It had a beginning, a middle, and an end. I made jokes, I got serious when needed, and I dished out some not-so-known facts. During the production, there were tears, screaming, and a lot of breaking points. Tom the producer's, mostly, but that still counted. He called me an anal-retentive perfectionist.

It was done, and it was great. Not to toot my own horn here, but I would listen the heck out of it. I was proud of myself. Proud of my achievement.

"Listen, I don't want you to get bigheaded or anything, but I've edited and produced a lot of podcasts." Tom sat back in his chair, stretching lazily. He had the whole gamer vibe down to a T. Bearded, with glasses, a baseball cap tugged on backward, and a *Zelda* shirt. "Yours takes the cake."

"Really?" I clapped my hands together. "Why?"

Was I fishing? Yes. Was I in the right to? Also yes. I'd never received any kind of feedback about my podcasting skills. Never had a chance to hone them. And I was celebrating two victories—not only had I finished a podcast, but I'd also worked on it with a man in the room. Just me and him. Zero freak-outs. No meltdowns. It wasn't that I was trusting men more. It was that I trusted myself now. I felt safe because I knew I was with *me*. And I would never let myself down. Not anymore. I had my back.

"You're a natural." He hitched a shoulder up, laughing. "You manage to make it interesting and serious, but also know when to lighten things up. I mean, I had no idea the Scotland Yard was such badasses. The way they hunted the murderer down..." He shook his head. "Crazy."

I darted up, licking my lips and looking around me. I had grown to love the solace of the soundproof recording room. The cool of the air-conditioning, that tangible smell of expensive equipment. "So... what now?"

"Now, I'm going to email you the finished episode, and you can post it whenever you're ready." He grinned. "Oh, and obviously, you need to implement everything I taught you about producing your own show, unless you wanna hire me. I charge two hundred and fifty dollars an hour."

"Hmm. Thanks, I'll remember that for when I can afford anything beyond ramen and tap water." I gave him a thumbs-up.

He laughed. "Now go share the link to your episode with your loved ones! You killed it, Cal."

I slipped out of the studio, waving goodbye to Kathy at the reception on my way out. "Bye, Kath!"

"Bye, girl-who-is-sleeping-with-the-hottest-man-alive!"

We still had to work on her nickname for me. I didn't have the heart to tell her Row and I were no longer an item.

As I poured myself out onto the streets of Manhattan and made my way to the subway, my phone pinged with a new email.

Subject: Hot Girl Bummer, Ep1 (file attached).

My heart missed a beat. I thought about Tom's words, about sending the podcast to the people I loved the most. Dylan, *obviously*. And Mom too, even though murder talk wasn't exactly her love language. Then there were some friends. Colleagues. The neighbor down the hallway who always gave me sugar cookies. And they were all great. They were. But...

They weren't Row.

The one person whose opinion I wanted about this was *Row's*.

In fact, he was the only one whose opinion I cared about in the first place.

I stopped dead in my tracks. Not a smart thing to do when you lived in New York and the pedestrian traffic was insane. Two people immediately bumped into me, groaned, and muttered, "Tourist." I tipped my head upward and closed my eyes, anguished.

It was Row.

I was in love with Row.

I had *always* been in love with Row.

From the moment I'd first met him on the edge of the community pool, and he was a scrawny thing of a kid, and I was an awkward thing of a girl.

He was the reason why I was still feeling hollow even though I had overcome my biggest fears—Allison and starting the podcast. This was why I'd had sex with him when I was a teenager, before I had gone to college. Not because I'd wanted to get rid of my virginity but because I was desperately, pathetically in love with him.

And my love for him was bigger than any fear I struggled with.

I had fed myself lies. Wicked little lies to protect myself from disappointment and heartbreak.

Loneliness is safe.

You're not in love with Row Casablancas.

This was just a winter affair.

You can totally pull off low-waisted jeans like it's still the early 2000s.

Lying to yourself was like indulging in an entire bottle of wine.

It felt great in the short term but was totally destructive in the long term. I'd told myself I couldn't catch feelings, couldn't fall in love, when all this time, I was already in love. An all-consuming, radical kind of love.

Oh shit. I needed to tell him. No, I needed to *woo* him. To show him how much he meant to me. A simple love declaration wouldn't do. I needed a nineties movie–inspired homage to show him I was serious. As it was, Row had made it clear he didn't want to hear from me—or read from me—unless I was all in.

And then—*eureka!*—it came to me. My grand gesture.

"Yes!" I threw my arms in the air, tilting my chin up at the sky. "Yes, I now know what to do!"

"Lily, honey, step away from the…*special* lady." Two obvious out-of-towners sidestepped me, throwing an assessing glance my way. But I didn't care.

I knew what to do.

My first step was where it all had started, in Staindrop.

Where I had given my heart to a boy who had given me his all.

And had forgotten to tell him that he was the one.

CHAPTER EIGHTY-TWO
CAL

"Emotions"—Mariah Carey

I managed to spend the duration of my flight to Maine not crying on anyone's shoulder or exhibiting any mentally unstable behavior.

I found Mamushka and Dylan eating pickles in my parents' kitchen. Gravity was glued to Dylan's boob like a magnet, suckling greedily on what appeared to be a full family-sized-pizza nipple. Dylan looked gorgeous—like she hadn't popped out a giant baby a month ago—glossy hair, flawless complexion, and a body that would make Elle Macpherson weep with envy. I was panting from running the short way from my rental car to the kitchen, catching my breath as I slouched onto an empty chair in my dining room. "I screwed up," I declared.

"You're going to have to be much more specific than that." Dylan unlatched a sleepy Gravity from her nipple and handed her over to my mom, who immediately put her on her shoulder for a burp. They seemed to have a system going. I was glad Mom had Dylan and Gravity to keep her company after Dad's passing. I also made a mental note to ask for a Tucker update. I'd been avoiding the subject in recent days, knowing Dylan found the subject uncomfortable.

"Row." I grabbed the edges of the dining table, catching my breath. "I screwed it all up with Row. He's the one."

"Is this a love declaration?" Dylan picked up her half-eaten pickle, leisurely munching on the tip.

"Yes, Dylan, it is the mother of all love declarations." I snapped my fingers. "Pay attention."

My confession was met with a loud, earnest burp from Gravity. "There you are, sweetie!" Mamushka laughed, cooing at Grav, who didn't even bother to wake up for the eructation of stomach air. "That's a good girl."

"Mom, did you hear what I said?" I eyeballed her through angry slits. I was spilling my darkest secret on the kitchen floor and these two—well, technically, *three*—didn't seem to give two shits.

"I did," Mamushka confirmed, placing Gravity inside her car seat on the table for her nap. "Good for you, Callichka."

I whipped my head to my best friend. Maybe she'd understand the weight of this situation. "I figured it out. *This* was why I slept with Row all those years ago behind your back. Not because I was a shitty friend. But because I was in love with him. *Am* in love with him. I never stopped being in love with him. He was always the one. I just didn't want to admit it to myself."

Dylan stared at me wordlessly, a small smile on her lips.

"Oh. Sorry for the TMI confession, Mom." I cringed.

"It's okay, sweetie." She patted my arm. "I figured out the cause of your rift long ago."

"Well?" I probed Dylan. "Isn't that shocking?"

"Hmm." Dylan nodded obediently, plucking a heart of palm from her plate and taking a crunchy bite. "Riveting. The local news is on their way."

What was happening? I'd thought Dylan would be thrilled to hear Row's love for me was reciprocated.

"Wait a minute…" My face fell. "Oh, shit."

"There's a baby in the room," Mom chided with a scandalized gasp.

"Shit, shit, shit."

"Yup." Dylan rolled her eyes, giving my mother an exasperated look. "Baby's still here, but go ahead, please ruin my child's delicate ears."

"You knew all along, didn't you?" My stare ping-ponged between them. "About me being in love with Row. You're not impressed because it was all clear to you."

"Bingo." Mom saluted me with her cup of tea in the air.

"Why didn't you tell me?" I shifted my gaze between them accusingly.

"Would you have listened?" Dylan asked.

"Yes!" I flung my arms in the air. "Of course I would've."

All Dylan needed to do was elevate one carefully plucked brow.

"Fine, I would have fought you until my last breath and denied it through my teeth. But oh my God, this sucks so bad. I'm in love with a man who was in love with me and tried to make it work, and all I did was stand in our way like an idiot!" I buried my face in my hands, placing my elbows on the table.

"*Is.*" Dylan washed down her pickled meal with a Liquid IV drink.

"What?" I moaned into my palms.

"A man who *is* in love with you. Present tense. It's not too late."

"He's in London now." I sulked, looking up to glance between them. "That is so, so far away."

Now that I wasn't high on my own supply with finishing the podcast, I was afraid he'd forgotten all about me. He hadn't answered me back, had he? And I'd texted him plenty.

"There's this thing…" Mamushka frowned, stroking her chin. "I heard about it the other day in the news…can move really fast in the air."

"I know which one you mean." Dylan turned to look at her, putting a hand on Mom's shoulder. "That big metal thing? Long wings? Gross preprepared meals? Very crowded."

"Yes. I think it's called a helicopter…no, an eagle…" Mamushka looked deep in thought.

"A plane!" Dylan exclaimed. They high-fived each other.

"Way ahead of you. Already bought a ticket," I announced. Because even if he would reject me, it would still be worth it.

Row was worth it.

Worth getting my heart broken.

Worth trying and failing.

Worth breaking my bank account *and* my savings for a ticket to a foreign land I'd never been to.

Worth sitting in a metal tube for half a day, basking in the unknown, headed to a love declaration that was one hundred percent going to be awkward and klutzy, like my entire being.

"So what do you need from us, exactly?" Dylan frowned.

"Some help finding a few things in the clutter that is my room." I pushed up my sleeves. "I'm going to win him back if it's the last thing I do."

Mom grinned. "Your father would be so proud. Go get him, Callichka."

CHAPTER EIGHTY-THREE
ROW

Another restaurant opening night. Another reason to want to shoot myself in the face.

The only thing stopping me at this point was the fact the floor was pure amethyst crystal. I'd dropped $50K a slab on that shit.

"Full house tonight." Tate turned to his assistant, Gia. "Too bad it's full of fucking nobodies. Didn't I tell you to invite actual celebrities?"

"The entire cast of *Wicked* and *The Lion King* RSVP'd. Three MPs and a duke too." She was frantically brushing her thumb over her iPad, the blue screen lighting up her face.

I wanted to turn around and walk out of here. Nothing felt worth doing since I'd parted ways with Cal. And the worst part was, she kept on texting me, and every time she did, it took all my fucking mental strength to ignore her.

I couldn't settle for half-assed. No matter how lovely said ass was.

"You're giving me politicians and West End actors? Do you want to lose your job? Are you allergic to money?" Tate snapped. We were sitting at the bar. The kitchen was running smoothly, thanks to Taylor, whom I'd brought with me. Sure, in my own asshat fashion, I'd had to be all the way in London before I had given him a call and offered him a position, an apartment, and a one-way business-class ticket. But it was the right thing to do. My head wasn't in the game. I needed someone with an eagle eye to watch over people.

"I'm allergic to assholes," Gia muttered to her iPad.

"What was that?" Tate scowled.

"If you're going to ruin everyone's evening, kindly get the fuck out," I growled at Tate. My mood was shitty without the added bonus of his unpalatable personality. Glitzy people roamed the place, taking selfies, cooing at the décor, at the designer plates in front of them, and at the delicious food on them. Wineglasses clinked. Black caviar mafaldine and aromatic pork buns floated on pink brass trays across the room. I should have been on top of the world, but I felt six feet under.

"Didn't that friend of yours, Ronald, say he was going to be here?" Tate scowled, glancing around.

"Huh?" I checked my phone for the millionth time this evening. If she was going to text now, I was going to break and answer her. "Said he would. Guess he's late."

The truth of the matter was, I didn't care one iota about Rhyland not being here. I only cared about one person. A person who had sent me her podcast two days ago. I'd listened to it three hundred times since. It was funny, adorable, smart, interesting, enchanting, *her*. It was her.

"Well." Tate grabbed his whiskey—neat—and knocked it back. "I am exceptionally bored. Excuse me while I go find someone to bury my dick in." He stalked off.

"Please, God, make that someone be a great white shark." Gia pressed her palms together in a silent prayer, looking heavenward before continuing to work on her iPad.

"You don't have to stand up, you know." I patted the stool next to mine.

She shot me a polite smile, taking a seat. "Tate calls people who sit down at the office slackers. He bought everyone treadmills for their laptop stations."

"Why are you working for this douche canoe?" I parked my elbow on the bar. I was genuinely interested to know. And it wasn't like I was needed in my own fucking kitchen for my debut night. Taylor was doing a fantastic job.

Gia considered my question with a small frown. "While as a person and as a boss, he is a complete disaster, he actually pays a lot and is generous with my bonuses too." She glanced down, a little embarrassed. "I tried to find another job several times. But each time I get an offer, it's like he senses it. He calls me into his office and gives me a twenty percent increase or something ridiculous like that. I am making mid–six figures for an admin job while all my mates make a fraction of that and work the same hours in banking and HR. I'd be mental to leave."

I opened my mouth, about to tell her that it seemed to me as though Tate Blackthorn had a crush he couldn't articulate properly, when something caught my eye beyond the floor-to-ceiling windows of the restaurant. A flash of light. *Neon* light. My neck snapped up, and I looked over Gia's slender shoulder.

She kept droning on, obviously thankful to have someone to listen to her. "…quite compelling bonuses, such as healthcare both in America and the UK, which is practically unheard of, and a share structure in some of his companies. Admittedly, it isn't fun to work during Christmas, federal holidays, and from the hospital when I had my tonsils removed, however…"

I saw it again. The flash of color. This time nestled between two bulky doormen outside. Whatever this thing was, it stood behind the golden barriers with the burgundy ropes.

Wait a minute. A head full of messy, wavy brown hair.

Pink bomber jacket.

High-waisted Levi's.

Bright red Doc Martens.

Dot.

She was here. In London. At La Vie en Rogue. I spotted her

arguing heatedly with the doormen, using wild hand gestures and mimicking a…sleeping baby?

Her tics were out of control. She was blinking hard and fast. I was about to stand up and let her in—and fire the two doormen on the spot while I was at it—when she spotted me through the glass window.

I immediately knew what it looked like. Me. Sitting next to a beautiful woman who had her back to her. To make shit worse, Gia seemed animated and completely engrossed in our one-sided conversation.

"…thought about leaving so many times, but at this point, my entire bloody family is on *my* payroll. I told Mum she could retire early, she loathed her job so much…"

My eyes snapped back to Cal. She stared at the scene, wide-eyed. I knew how her mind worked. She thought I'd moved on. That it was game over. It had probably taken everything she'd had in her to even get here. I stood up, about to run over there and chase her…

When she did the unthinkable.

The improbable.

She reversed on her heel, turned her back, and walked away…

Only to turn back around and face me. She took a deep breath, gained momentum, and literally *barreled* through the doormen, bypassing both of them like an NFL player and running straight into the restaurant. They ran after her. I stood up, but she managed to get to me before I could come to her rescue.

"Row!" She slammed headfirst into my chest. Instead of moving back, she clutched my shirt, looking up and blinking at me with wonder. "Sorry to crash your, er, big day…te? Day or date? Or should I say evenin—"

"This is not a date." I all but shoved Gia into a commercial oven to bring the point home. "Gia works for Tate, one of my business partners."

"Oh. Sweet. Hi. I'm Cal!" Cal offered her a hand with a smile.

The doormen reached her, about to wrangle her from my arms.

I turned my chilly look their way. "Lay a hand on my girlfriend, and she will be the last thing you touch, since I'll chop your fingers off with a cleaver."

"Sorry, boss." They both retreated with their palms up, scurrying back outside.

"I'm Gia." Gia offered Cal her hand with a sweet smile. "Lovely to meet you. Love the pink hair tips."

Pink hair tips. Pink only symbolized two things—love and vaginas. I was fond of both.

"I love your dress!" Cal exhibited more of that Lab energy of hers. "It's gorgeous. Where did you g—"

"Dot, baby? Focus."

"Oh, right." She returned her attention to me, clearing her throat, her freckled face turning serious. "I...uhm, came here because I have something to tell you."

This was so fucking wild. "Yeah?"

"But..." She rubbed the back of her neck, gulping. "I'd really rather...*demonstrate* it to you."

"I'd strongly prefer to receive any demonstration somewhere private, but I'm not going to stand here and pretend I'll reject a public display of...eh, *demonstration.*"

Cal snickered. People began stopping what they were doing to turn their attention to us. I knew Cal absolutely despised audiences, so the fact that she was doing this, in front of the entire world, told me every word that still hadn't left her mouth.

"Rhy?" She peered behind her shoulder. Rhyland materialized from one of the back tables of the room. He had been here all along? Fucker hadn't even come to say hi. He wrestled his way past the masses, holding a cardboard box and looking none too happy about it.

"This is why I stick to paid romance gigs." He shoved the box into Cal's hands, piercing me with a look. "Get ready to be wood."

"*Wooed*," Cal corrected with a frown.

"Same difference." Rhy shrugged. "There's always wood involved for him when you're around."

I punched his shoulder. Hard. "You are ruining my big moment, fucker."

He made a face and rubbed the spot.

Cal took a deep breath, focusing hard on my face to drown out the curious glances and recording phones around us. "I thought about recreating the *10 Things I Hate About You* moment when Heath Ledger sings to her on the bleachers, but I really didn't want to get on top of your new tables. It's totally unsanitary."

"I sincerely appreciate that."

"So instead, here are ten examples that will prove I have always, from day one, loved you. That all I've done all these years is fed myself lies and excuses for the way you made me feel every time you were around. I know I don't make my own chocolate bars from scratch, and I didn't tattoo you on my skin, but you were always there. The best part of my day. The man to dominate my dreams at night. My anchor."

She loved me?

She loved me.

"Proof number one." She reached for the box and pulled out an old Christmas card. "The first holiday card you ever gave me. I kept it."

"It's…blank?" I frowned.

She grinned winningly. "Your mom made you give me one, and you scribbled on it to pretend like you were writing something. I still kept it because it was from *you*. And that made me extremely giddy. Even when I was ten. Moving on. Proof number two."

She dipped her hand inside the box again, this time pulling out a picture. She held it in front of me, her face bright red. She didn't like doing anything publicly. She was way out of her comfort zone. For me.

"This is a picture of me and Dylan doing cartwheels in your backyard. If you look closely, you'll see a hint of your arm on the right side. For years I wondered why I'm so attached to this picture, why I keep it in my wallet at all times—we both look horrible in it. It was because of you. Because a piece of you was there, and the reminder of you put me in a good mood every time I looked at it. Proof number three."

She took out a ticket stub. "This is from when you went to a Weezer concert. I'm not even a fan—although the *Blue Album* was kinda good, in a totally ironic way. Anyway, *not* the point. The point is you kissed the ticket when you managed to buy one because they sold out so quickly. I picked it up and saved it, because you had your lips on it once, and I liked the feeling of owning something like that."

I pressed my lips together, suppressing a laugh.

"What?" She frowned.

"I was looking for that stub all over. I used to collect them. Thought I was losing my mind."

"Nope. You were just gaining my heart. *Four.*"

She pulled out a black wristband I recognized as my own. "Hey." I frowned. "That was my favorite wristband. I gave Rhy a shiner in junior high because I thought he stole it from me."

"Well, you obviously cannot have it back because I'm obsessed with you—and now the entire world knows it." She gestured wildly to everyone around us. "Proof number five I'm so unbelievably, insanely in love with you…" She took out an Oh Henry! wrapper. "Need I explain?"

I laughed. "Nope." She had been keeping the wrappers too. *Note to self: check if my girl has a hoarding problem.*

"Proof number six—by the way, I only stopped at ten because Rhy said he couldn't fit all my garbage in his suitcase, and I couldn't afford to pay for a suitcase here myself."

"True story," Rhyland groaned behind her back.

She had come here using her last pennies to tell me she loved me. I was so going to marry the fuck out of this girl.

"Number six is the hard soap you used your entire adolescence. I bought one so I could get a sniff of you whenever I wanted. I, uhm, may or may not have dried my hands to the point of peeling due to washing them so often. I just wanted to smell you."

She pulled something else out of the box. "Number seven is a cigarette butt. Not just any cigarette, though. This was from the first time you let me try smoking."

"You hated it," I pointed out, ignoring the traffic jam of servers with trays waiting for Cal to move out of their way. And the entire universe staring at us, for that matter.

"Yeah. But I loved you."

"So you did it to impress me?"

"Why else would anyone try smoking?" she snorted. Good point. "Ready for number eight?"

"Never been more ready for something in my entire life." Other than the make-up sex we were about to have in my upstairs office in about five minutes.

"Number eight." She took out something brown and small, biting down on her lip. "Okay, *don't* judge me. But this is…"

"Baby, no." I screwed my fingers into my eye sockets.

"Yes."

"Cal, that's unsanitary."

"So is having sex on your chef station." The entire room gasped in unison. "*Kidding*," she choked out.

Fuck. I was about to be closed down an hour into my restaurant launch, and I didn't even give a shit. "Why did you save a…? How old is this taco?" I grimaced.

"Seven years old," she confirmed with a nod, "…and a half. Fine, closer to eight. But it was the first handmade taco you created from scratch, and you gave it to *me*."

"To taste, not keep."

"Semantics." She waved her hand with an eye roll. "You wanted me to have your first taco. That's like handing over your V-card. Number nine is more orthodox."

Thank God.

She hunted for something in the box, fishing it out with flourish. "Your favorite hoodie."

Motherfucker. I had looked for that hoodie for months. Came with the territory of being too poor to afford a replacement. It was an tattered old black thing but seemed in pristine condition.

"Did you wear it?"

"What? Of course not." She looked abhorred. "It would've erased your perfect smell with my overbearing Victoria's Secret body mist."

"What's number ten?" I crossed my arms over my chest, smirking. I didn't care that everyone was looking. Didn't care that this was unprofessional, uncomfortably public, and would probably leave an internet trail forever.

Cal pressed her lips together, looking at me unsurely. She blinked five times in a row. I softened, reaching to squeeze her shoulders. "You don't have to show me here if it's too private. You've already gone beyo—"

"It's not a keepsake."

"Baby, it could literally be my nuts and I'll say thank you."

She took a deep breath, nodded, and pulled out a square, black box. Slowly, she put the tiny box down on the floor. But she didn't stand back up. No. She stayed down, on one knee, her shaking fingers about to open the box.

Calla Litvin was about to propose. To *me*.

Fuck my life sideways.

"Row, may I—"

I couldn't let her do it. No matter how good this felt for my ego, I wasn't going to deprive her of her princess moment. She deserved all the good moments after what that garbage human Franco had put her through.

"No," I blurted out. Her face paled, eyes flaring. "You can't ask me to marry you."

Her brows furrowed. "I...can't?"

"No." I lowered myself to one knee. "Because I get to ask you that first."

Now we were both on one knee on the floor in front of the entire fucking restaurant.

Rhyland groaned from somewhere behind my shoulder, "This is the most cringe thing I've ever seen. And I was there when Paris Hilton tried to launch a music career."

"Row." Cal's eyes were glittering with tears. "You don't even have a ring."

I rummaged in the front pocket of my cargo pants, producing a Tiffany box.

Her jaw dropped. "How?"

I shrugged. "You never know when the love of your life decides it's a good day to take her head out of her ass and come say hi."

"How long have you been...on standby?" She dropped her own ring box, covering her mouth as I popped mine open. It had a diamond so big, it could barely fit in the box. It was a solitaire cut—the nineties' popular design.

"I prefer not to say," I drawled.

"I didn't ask for your preferences."

"In that case, since our first kiss after you came back."

"That night on the swings?" She looked puzzled. We hadn't even been together. "Wow, you've got it hard, dude." She grinned.

"Not the only hard thing about him right now, I can bet." Rhyland cupped his mouth, hollering from the sidelines.

"I asked you a question," I reminded her, ignoring my best friend. He got a pass for helping her put this together. "I don't want to look back anymore, Dot. I want to look *forward*. So do you have an answer for me? Preferably this decade. This moment is probably streaming live on YouTube."

"Oh. Yeah. Sure. I'll marry you." She flung her arms over my shoulders and gave me the best kiss of my life.

As a chef, my future wife ticked all the boxes.

She tasted delicious, just the right balance between sweet and biting.

Most important of all...

She tasted like forever.

CHAPTER EIGHTY-FOUR
CAL

ONE YEAR LATER

oBITCHuary: Hey.

McMonster: Hi.

oBITCHuary: You're back.

McMonster: Only momentarily. I needed to sign in so I can keep all the conversation records before they're gone forever.

oBITCHuary: Are you ready to celebrate Christmas?

McMonster: Celebrate is a big word. I'm ready to tolerate it.

oBITCHuary: Oh shush. You'll have fun.

McMonster: I will, but only for one reason.

oBITCHuary: Red reminds you of blood?

McMonster: I will be spending it with the love of my life.

EPILOGUE
CAL

"Back for Good"—Take That

"Doesn't she look so much better now that her face caught up with the size of her nose?" Dylan cooed, nuzzling her nose against Grav's cheeks. Grav gave her a *bitch, you ain't no Gisele either* look, spinning on her chubby heel and stumbling her way to the open arms of my husband.

Let me say that again for emphasis—my *husband*. Whom I'd woken up next to every day for the past year, in our gorgeous London apartment. The first thing he'd done when he carried me back to his place after my love-declaration-turned-engagement was give me a tour around our flat. Everything was so classy and decadent. I had turned to face Row and asked, "Can we please christen the floor?" He'd dutifully obliged. Since then, we'd christened the carpets, each bedroom, the laundry machine, countertops, cupboard, library, and drawing room. We were faithful like that.

I never ended up returning to the U.S., let alone Staindrop. There was nothing left for me in the States. A week after I'd come to London, I had found myself a recording studio for my podcast, which was now taking off and already had ten thousand subscribers across all platforms. Maybe it wasn't huge for other people. But for me, it was a win.

Mamushka visited us often. She loved traveling and the plane time was a great excuse to knit more mittens. Her Etsy shop was thriving. She made a great living and enjoyed helping Dylan with Gravity.

As for Dylan, she'd tried encouraging Tucker to get involved with Grav, but he'd seemed grossly disinterested. He was still with Allison, who was awaiting trial for her Staindrop shenanigans while on house arrest. Her reputation was in the same place her personality was—the shitter. Frankly, they deserved each other.

"Don't listen to your mother." Row snatched Grav after she tumbled into his arms, tossing her in the air like pizza dough. She almost hit the ceiling. He always gave me so much anxiety when he did that to her, but it made her produce that never-ending toddler giggle that danced across my skin every time I heard it. "You are the most beautiful girl in the world. Only second to Auntie Dot."

"Grav was always going to be beautiful," Kieran, who was now good friends with Row, pointed out. We were all sitting at a Christmas table, Zeta, Mom, and Taylor included. "With a mother like Dylan."

Dylan smiled charitably, taking a slow sip of her wine. She'd been dodging Kieran's efforts ever since she'd come here three days ago, and it didn't look like she had any romantic interest in him whatsoever. Guess once the raging hormones had subsided, the idea of entering a passionate affair with one of the most famous soccer players in the world hadn't held the same shine.

"I do know how to make them." Zeta beamed proudly.

"That, you do." Mamushka patted her knee from the seat next to her.

"This is very wholesome." Taylor drained the dregs of his beer, surveying the place nonchalantly, one hand tucked into his front pocket. "I'm wondering when Row's forehead vein is going to pop from sugar overload."

"Soon. Let's go to the living room to start the gift-opening portion of the night." Row stood up with Grav tucked under his arm, like she was a football. "I'm ready to give my wife her present."

What more could he give me that he hadn't already? I loved our life.

Rhyland made a face. "Please don't give it to her in front of a full audience. There's a child here."

"Shut up," Row said flatly. "Let's go."

"Okay, eager much?" Dylan looked around but slowly rose to her feet. We all ambled to the living room, ignoring our plates and half-full wineglasses in the dining area. The Christmas tree stood tall in front of the window overlooking King's Road.

"Mine first." Zeta shoved a gift in Row's hands as soon as he put Grav down on the carpet. He opened it.

"Nicotine patches? How...*useful*."

Row had quit smoking four months ago out of the blue. We had walked hand in hand along the Thames on a lazy Saturday stroll and he had seen a couple pushing a stroller and smiling down at the baby. Wordlessly, he'd tossed his pack of smokes into a bin and never bought another one again. He didn't say a word about it to people, though. He hated it when people fussed over him.

Mamushka made everyone kick-ass mittens.

Dylan got everyone thrift-shop finds that were wonderfully and uniquely suited to their individual personalities.

Kieran got Dylan a whole-ass diamond necklace that looked like it had cost the same as a luxury car. Dylan stared at it for an entire minute before smiling at him. "Thank you, it'll look great with my finest Walmart frocks."

Kieran chortled, undeterred. "It's a statement piece, darling. No need to wear anything but the necklace."

"*Tsk.*" Row shook his head. "I see you're not too attached to your teeth, Carmichael. Dot?" He turned to me.

"Hubs?" I batted my eyelashes at him. I couldn't wait to give him my gift.

"Follow me for your gift."

"Thank you." Rhyland pretended to wipe invisible sweat off his forehead. "From the bottom of my heart. Nobody needs to see that."

Even though I had just gotten comfortable in the recliner by the fire, I followed Row's broad back as he waltzed through the corridor of our apartment. How big was it that he'd had to hide it in his office?

He stopped by the door to said office and turned to look at me sheepishly. "I'm going to be honest with you…"

My face fell, and I immediately went on guard. "There's not a dead body in there, is there, Row? *Shit.* I mean, you know I'm your girl for making it disappear, but you could've waited until everyone went back to their hotel."

He stared at me blankly. "How much of a shitbag do you think I am?"

"What is it?" I conveniently changed the subject. Row was definitely not a shitbag to me. But I couldn't say everyone had the same experience.

"I was going to say—I'm going to be honest with you, no gift you can give me is going to top mine." He arched an eyebrow, one hand slung on the door handle behind him as he blocked the way to his office.

"Don't be so cocksure, Mr. Casablancas."

To my surprise, he didn't offer a sexual innuendo. Just drew a quick, nervous breath and said, "*Hot Girl Bummer* is the best thing to happen to people's ears since Pearl Jam. I'm totally not biased either, because I'm screwing the host. I don't even need an office. My office is the kitchen. So…"

He slowly opened the door. I peered inside owlishly. My breath hitched.

It was a recording room. All four walls thickly padded. A gorgeously curved desk took over the center of the room. State-of-the-art equipment adorned it. Microphones, keyboards, huge

Mac screens, and a lit tripod were erected in front of it. The wall was covered in graffiti art that said *Hot Girl Bummer*. It had a total nineties feel to it. I was going to cry. A big cry. Not like the small one I'd had this morning when I'd woken up and felt happy because everyone was here and Christmas was my favorite holiday. Or the teeny tiny one at breakfast when Row had made me smiley pancakes with raspberries. Or in the afternoon, when Mamushka and I had gone for tea at the Savoy and they'd accidentally poured me the wrong flavor.

Man, I was a mess.

"Row...this is...insane."

"Good insane, I hope." He stood next to me, scanning the place like it was the first time he'd seen it too. "It was a bitch to work on, by the way," Row admitted. "I had to wait for when you were out recording your podcast."

I was so overwhelmed with emotions, I threw my arms around his neck and began sobbing into his ugly Christmas sweater. "I love you so much." I hiccupped into his chest, not so demurely, I suspected. "I'm just... I can't even explain it." Another bout of tears emerged.

"Is everything okay?" Mom called out from the living room.

"Row, are you breaking up with her?" Dylan sounded pissed. "Or, let's be honest, is she breaking up with you? Because I can totally yell at her for you."

"She's fine," Row growled to our guests, gathering me in his arms, holding me tight. "You *are* fine, right, Dot? I didn't mean to upset you. I just thought it would be nice to make it official. And figured that this way, you wouldn't have to book time in advance. But you don't look happy at all." He disconnected from me, frowning deeply into my face. "Look, we can forget about the entire thing. It's not a problem. I'll have someone remove it—"

"Don't you dare." I pressed my finger to his lips to stop the profanity. "I love it. It's perfect. I'm just...a little overwhelmed."

"By how my gift is so much better than yours?" He gave me a cocky once-over.

"Honey, you are not even in the race. Which brings me to my gift to you…" I pulled out an envelope from the back pocket of my mom jeans, handing it to him. "It's not a gift card, so be careful when you rip it open."

He eyed me suspiciously as he meticulously and gently peeled the top part of the envelope, slowly tugging out the unmistakable black-and-white printout of ultrasound film. His eyes flared, and the rest of him turned into a pillar of salt. Oh no. Was he going to burst into tears now too?

"I know we haven't discussed it," I hurried to say, licking my lips. "And I know that it is way too early, with both of us so focused on our careers. I don't know how it happened. I guess…I guess I forgot to take a few pills. Are you mad?" I bit my lower lip.

It was hard to tell, since Row's usual expression was *IDGAF*. He wore it so well, he'd never bothered to develop any other faces. It was as eternal as a little black dress. Which, I bet, he'd look good in too. God, my husband was infuriating.

"Mad?" he repeated wryly.

"You know, that it wasn't planned."

"Dot, baby." He took the long ultrasound film that showed a very blurry little dot—Dot Junior—wrapping it along the back of my neck and tugging me closer with it so our lips touched. "You'll never be able to top this Christmas present in a million years, so don't even try."

"I won, didn't I?" I winked.

"The Christmas gift competition? But, Dot, you're my biggest win."

He kissed me long and deep, in a way every girl deserved to be kissed. Many times. By the boy she loved.

And the next morning, we woke up for our joint morning run. With our feet pounding the pavement, the winter sun warming our faces, I tipped my head up and smiled at Dad, who was somewhere up there beyond the clouds.

"My hair tips are orange today, Dadushka," I whispered. "Because I'm finally happy."

AUTHOR'S NOTE:

Thank you so much for reading this book. If you have made it this far, please consider writing a brief, honest review so that future readers can decide whether they want to read this book or not.

If you want more of Row and Cal, make sure to subscribe to my newsletter to receive an instant bonus scene of the book:

bit.ly/3LhsIrb

ACKNOWLEDGMENTS

There are many perks to being an author, but spending six months with (in my opinion) thoroughly charming humans and then having to say goodbye to them is not one of them. To say I had a blast writing this book would be the understatement of this century. I wanted something light, something fun, something to put a smile on my readers' faces. But I still wanted that same gut-wrenching angst that tugs at your heartstrings until they're completely tattered and torn.

Truly, Madly, Deeply was written to remind people everywhere that you can be damaged, imperfect, indecisive, insecure, and still worthy of a great, all-consuming love.

All books take a village to write, but this book took a whole town—and not even a small one. In absolutely no particular order, I would like to thank my Bloom Books editor, Christa Desir, as well as Letty Mundt and Gretchen Stelter.

To my editor, Erica Russikoff, and to my proofreader, Paisley McNab, thank you for helping this book reach its full potential.

I would also like to thank Tijuana Turner, Vanessa Villegas, Beth Wojiski, and Ava Harrison for beta-reading this book. (Yes, when I said I was writing "all the words," I literally meant it.)

To my agent, Kimberly Brower, who convinced me not to title this book *Chef's Kiss*—you were right. I would have never been able to come up with a title for book two.

To my cover designer, Letitia Hasser, for always knowing what I want, even—and especially—when I have no clue what it is.

To the readers who always go the extra mile to shout out my books <takes a deep breath>: Ratula Roy, Steph Ratavicius, Mata Bor, Liah Reads, Yamina Kirky, Sarah Plocher (who also proofread this book!), Lena Lange, Amelie Broune, and to my work wife, Parker S. Huntington.

I am also forever grateful for my Facebook group, the Sassy Sparrows (join us—we have snacks!), and the readers active on my Instagram and TikTok. Thank you for always being kind and gracious.

Finally, I would like to thank my husband, three sons, and cat. They have done absolutely nothing to help with this book. The sons, in truth, hindered all efforts to finish it early. But I still love you all to death. (Okay, maybe not the cat. I just love my cat very, very much. She also turns seventeen this September. Happy birthday, Murphy. You don't look a day over ten months!)

Hope to see you again for the second book in the series (which, by the way, is super delicious).

All my love, always,

L.J. Shen xo

ABOUT THE AUTHOR

L.J. Shen is a *USA Today*, *Wall Street Journal*, *Washington Post* and #1 Amazon Kindle Store bestselling author of contemporary romance books. She writes angsty books, unredeemable antiheroes who are in Elon Musk's tax bracket, and sassy heroines who bring them to their knees (for more reasons than one). HEAs and groveling are guaranteed. She lives in Florida with her husband, three sons, and a disturbingly active imagination.

Website: authorljshen.com
Facebook: authorljshen
Instagram: @authorljshen
Twitter: @lj_shen
TikTok: @authorljshen
Pinterest: @authorljshen